# RADIANT SKY

# RADIANT SKY

### ALAN SMALE

CAEZIK
SF & FANTASY
ARC MANOR
ROCKVILLE, MARYLAND
❋
SHAHID MAHMUD
PUBLISHER

www.caeziksf.com

This is a work of fiction.

Cover art by Christina P. Myrvold; artstation.com/christinapm

Interior illustrations by Udimamedova Leylya; facebook.com/lkiudlkiud

ISBN: 978-1-64710-115-2

First Edition. First Printing November 2024.
1 2 3 4 5 6 7 8 9 10

An imprint of Arc Manor LLC

www.CaezikSF.com

# CONTENTS

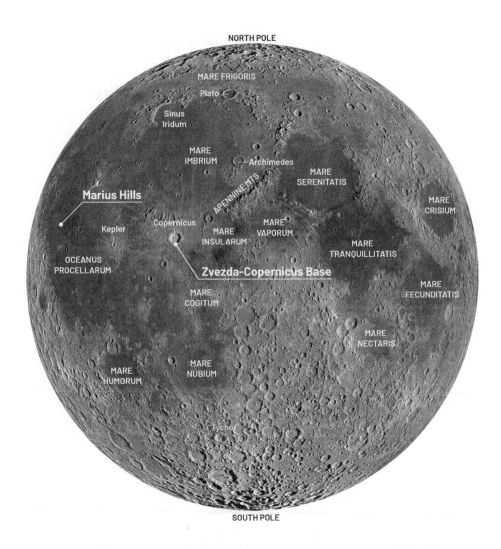

NORTH POLE

MARE FRIGORIS

Plato

Sinus
Iridum

MARE
IMBRIUM

Archimedes

MARE
SERENITATIS

MARE
CRISIUM

APENNINE MTS

**Marius Hills**

Kepler

Copernicus

MARE
INSULARUM

MARE
VAPORUM

MARE
TRANQUILLITATIS

OCEANUS
PROCELLARUM

**Zvezda-Copernicus Base**

MARE
FECUNDITATIS

MARE
COGITUM

MARE
NECTARIS

MARE
HUMORUM

MARE
NUBIUM

Tycho

SOUTH POLE

LUNAR NEAR SIDE

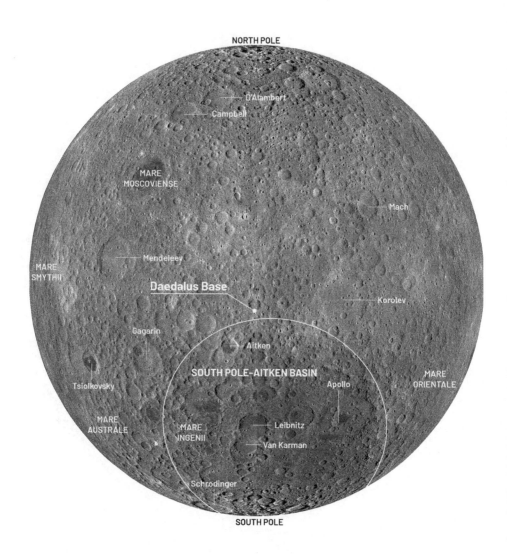

NORTH POLE

D'Alambert

Campbell

MARE
MOSCOVIENSE

Mach

Mendeleev

MARE
SMYTHII

**Daedalus Base**

Korolev

Gagarin

Aitken

SOUTH POLE–AITKEN BASIN

Tsiolkovsky

Apollo

MARE
ORIENTALE

MARE
AUSTRALE

MARE
INGENII

Leibnitz

Van Karman

Schrodinger

SOUTH POLE

**LUNAR FAR SIDE**

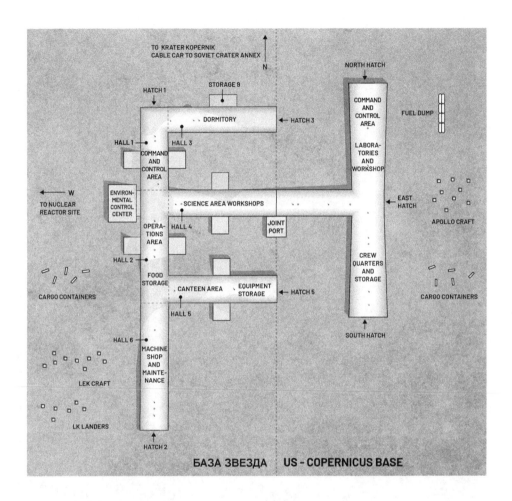

TO KRATER KOPERNIK
CABLE CAR TO SOVIET CRATER ANNEX

N

HATCH 1

STORAGE 9

NORTH HATCH

COMMAND
AND
CONTROL
AREA

FUEL DUMP

DORMITORY

HATCH 3

HALL 1

HALL 3

COMMAND
AND
CONTROL
AREA

LABORA-
TORIES
AND
WORKSHOP

W

TO NUCLEAR
REACTOR SITE

ENVIRON-
MENTAL
CONTROL
CENTER

SCIENCE AREA WORKSHOPS

EAST
HATCH

OPERA-
TIONS
AREA

HALL 4

JOINT
PORT

APOLLO CRAFT

HALL 2

FOOD
STORAGE

CREW
QUARTERS
AND
STORAGE

CARGO CONTAINERS

CANTEEN AREA

EQUIPMENT
STORAGE

HATCH 5

CARGO CONTAINERS

HALL 5

HALL 6

MACHINE
SHOP
AND
MAINTE-
NANCE

SOUTH HATCH

LEK CRAFT

LK LANDERS

HATCH 2

БАЗА ЗВЕЗДА     US - COPERNICUS BASE

ZVEZDA-COPERNICUS BASE

Copernicus Crater
Кратер Коперник

Central Peaks

■ ANNEX

● Downstation

● Upstation

■ ZVEZDA–COPERNICUS BASE

COPERNICUS CRATER

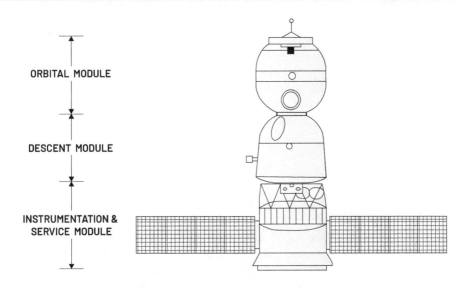

ORBITAL MODULE

DESCENT MODULE

INSTRUMENTATION &
SERVICE MODULE

LK LANDER          LEK LANDER

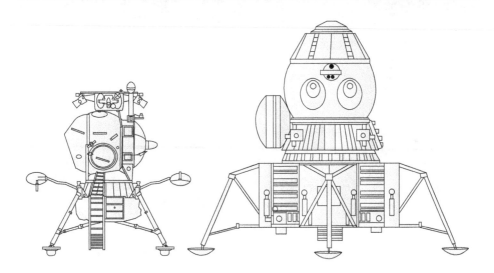

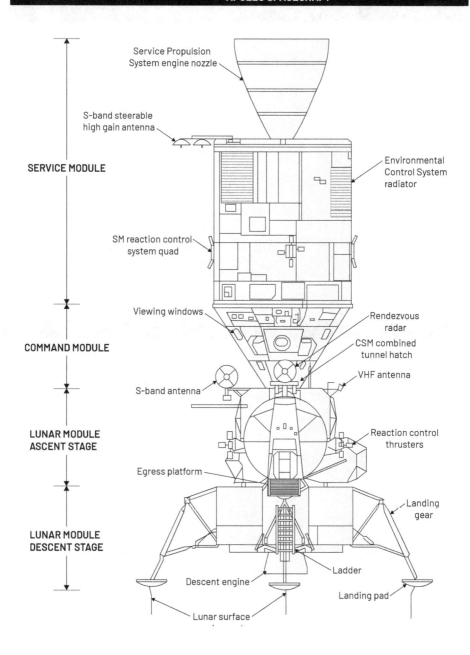

Service Propulsion System engine nozzle

SERVICE MODULE

S-band steerable high gain antenna

Environmental Control System radiator

SM reaction control system quad

COMMAND MODULE

Viewing windows

Rendezvous radar

CSM combined tunnel hatch

VHF antenna

S-band antenna

LUNAR MODULE ASCENT STAGE

Reaction control thrusters

Egress platform

LUNAR MODULE DESCENT STAGE

Landing gear

Ladder

Descent engine

Landing pad

Lunar surface

# PART ONE: TRANSPOLAR

November 1982–February 1983

# CHAPTER 1

## Lunar South Pole: Vivian Carter
## January 22, 1983

FREEDOM was a dirt bike on the Moon.

Vivian Carter bounced down into a small, deep crater, and bumped up the other side. As she crested the rim her front wheel lifted off the regolith, and she gunned her engine and pulled the bike higher into an impromptu wheelie before guiding it back to level motion, or what passed for level on the uneven lunar surface. Dust flew. *Cool. Eat your heart out, Evel Knievel.*

A low rocky ridge extended out to her right, stark against the sky. That ridge currently separated Vivian from her crew and she was out of their sight, which wasn't supposed to happen: against safety protocols, and all that. Which was ironic, since Vivian herself had written the stringent protocols for this mission. But what was the point of commanding the first transpolar lunar expedition if she couldn't have any fun?

Besides, on her first extended stay on the Moon three years ago, she'd been isolated from the rest of humanity for *weeks*. If anyone was overqualified to bend the rules, it was Vivian. Even her CAPCOMs back at Mission Control had given up chiding her about it.

It wasn't like she could get lost for long. Since Vivian's last mission, lunar navigation and comms had improved immensely. Just last year, four NAVSTAR satellites had been placed in lunar orbit for tracking and data relay. Those orbits were well separated and of varying inclinations, so the satellites regularly swept the higher latitudes as well as the equator. Between the NAVSTARs, Eagle Station in its equatorial orbit, and any other Apollo Command and Service Modules that might also be up there, these assets greatly improved communications between the various US contingents in space and on the surface, as well as enabling coarse location-finding. At the equator, radio coverage was almost constant. This close to the South Pole, though, Vivian's LGS-1 mission experienced irregular dead spots in coverage that could last a couple of hours or more.

They were in one of those comms holes now, so it was all quiet in Vivian's headset. Which was nice because it allowed her to both relax and concentrate.

She needed that concentration because the sunlight was coming at a really weird angle. At these extreme southern latitudes, the Sun was constantly less than five degrees from the horizon, and that grazing incidence affected *everything*. Even relatively meager hills nearby could block the Sun's rays altogether, casting knife-edged shadow pools of deep darkness. The long, jagged shadows emphasized the sizes of boulders and the heights of crater rims. To avoid pocks and furrows that might throw her, Vivian had to weave erratically across the surface.

Plus, it was almost impossible to drive directly toward the Sun when it was that low because of the difficulty in gauging the true height or depth of any obstacles ahead. Due to an effect the scientists called "zero-phase lighting," the same tended to happen when they traveled directly *away* from grazing-incidence sunlight: its scattered reflections off the soil and boulders were almost as bright, while their own shadows would also obscure the path immediately in front of them. So right now, Vivian's team was taking a somewhat circuitous route, keeping the Sun behind them and to the left—effectively following the terminator around the pole.

Occasionally the blue orb of the Earth would peep over the horizon, and then appear to dip below it again due to the local terrain. Vivian found it a cheering sight. The sky had been lonely for all these weeks without it. And once Earth came reliably above the horizon again, LGS-1 would be back in direct S-band contact with Mission Control in Houston.

"Time for a break," she said, to no one. Took her gloved hand off the throttle lever. Let the bike bump to a halt, stuck out her legs to keep herself upright, and drank in the solitude.

Magnificent desolation. The craggy line of the ridge above her. No one else visible. No Earth in the sky. Out of contact. Completely alone.

Once, any one of those things had ranged from unsettling to terrifying. Now, this solitude was a rare joy.

Sunlight sparkled off moondust. She heard only her own breathing and the fans in her helmet. It sure was a beautiful day.

In just a few hours, she and her team would pass as close to the South Pole as it was possible to get on a journey like theirs. The true ninety-degree-south point was just inside Shackleton Crater, which was thirteen miles across and two and a half miles deep. The peaks around its rim were in almost constant sunshine, but the crater floor within suffered permanent cryogenic-temperature darkness.

Vivian would have loved to go down into Shackleton, just for the joy of some really gnarly exploration and to plant the US flag at the true pole, but that wasn't on the cards: it was too dangerous and would take too long. The geologists hypothesized that the crater, or others like it in the far north and south, might contain water in the form of permanent ice from accumulated comet volatiles, but testing for that was beyond Vivian's mission parameters, and even if they discovered it, extracting it in any useful quantities would be quite the feat.

Still. Just six weeks ago, Vivian had been exactly at the Lunar North Pole, and now she was about to check the farthest-south off her bucket list as well. That didn't suck.

She drank in the landscape for a couple more minutes, and then got started again. No sense in spooking her crew with her absence.

It *was* easy enough to get lost, or at least badly confused, on the Moon. Its surface was far from featureless, especially to a trained observer and field geologist like Vivian, but one crater or escarpment, outcropping or ridge tended to look similar to a hundred others, and the additional gentle undulations in the lunar surface made it all even less intuitive.

On one of their EVAs at Fra Mauro, Al Shepard and Ed Mitchell of Apollo 14 had hiked out to sample a young, deep impact crater called Cone. The landmarks they'd memorized looked different than they were expecting, and they hadn't gauged the distance they'd traversed accurately enough, and they'd turned back only about sixty feet from the edge of Cone Crater. Vivian now had thousands of times more experience navigating her ass around the Moon than Al and Ed could have dreamed of, but even she wasn't immune from getting herself … temporarily mislaid, on occasion.

But not this time. She completed her circuit of the ridge and, sure enough, there was her MOLAB a quarter mile distant and trundling away from her, with Feye Gisemba presumably still at the wheel. And there was the Earth again.

Two telltales lit up on her chest pack: she'd reestablished VHF contact with her MOLAB, and the piggybacked S-band with Houston. Vivian's precious moments of isolation were over.

"Breaker one-niner, LGS-1, this here's Viv. You got a copy on me, come on?"

Over her headset she heard Ellis's time-delayed sigh from all the way back in Mission Control in Houston—Vivian would recognize an Ellis Mayer sigh anywhere—and then Gisemba's deep voice cut through it. "Ah yeah, fer shure, fer shure. Come on and join our convoy."

"Ten-four. About to put the hammer down."

"Jeez, you guys," said Ellis. "Give it a rest, maybe? For just one single day?"

"Back off, good buddy," Vivian responded, just to tweak him some more, and Gisemba laughed.

By now no one remembered who had been the first to use Citizen Band radio trucker slang on the mission, but once the Astronaut Corps had started referring to LGS-1—Lunar Geological Survey 1—as "Carter's Convoy" it had only been a matter of time. It had gotten old for Ellis real fast, though. Vivian felt half-sorry for him, having to put up with them, but a stupid and belabored sense of humor had always helped to keep astronauts sane.

The MOLAB—Mobile Laboratory—was a shiny silver truck with a six-wheeled articulated chassis. It could easily mount and conquer crater rims and the larger boulders, but it was hardly graceful. Even as Vivian watched, the vehicle lurched up and then down again as Gisemba went straight over a rocky outcropping rather than skirting it. It had likely tossed him and everyone else aboard sideways. Gisemba had probably laughed. Better suspension: that would be Vivian's number one recommendation in her mission debrief.

6

The chunky MOLAB towed two trailers behind it, both similarly articulated. The first carried a small radiation-hardened emergency shelter known as the Pod, along with three stacked containers of supplies and extra storage. Outside of solar flare contingencies, the crew took turns to go through the narrow connecting tunnel from the MOLAB and sleep in the Pod. It was hardly luxurious—an interior space seven feet by four feet, and six feet high, with a fold-down bed, a fold-up chair, a bathroom facility so small it almost guaranteed accidents, plus its own rear airlock to the outside world—but for sixteen hours at a time they each got it to themselves, their own private space to decompress from the incessant closeness of their traveling experience.

That was okay for a while, but being outside on a freaking *lunar dirt bike* was way cooler.

Behind the Pod, the second trailer was a flatbed to carry their rover and bike when they weren't being driven—when Vivian and her crew were all exhausted, or when they were traveling across one of the safer and geologically more boring mares, and really needed to crank out the miles to get themselves back on schedule. The rear flatbed also held their RTG, the radioactive thermal generator which provided most of their power. The rest came from the hinged solar panels that studded the roofs of the MOLAB and Pod. Because, ideally, they'd never be out of sight of the Sun.

This MOLAB had several advantages over the USAF version that had arrived with Apollo Rescue 1 during Vivian's Hadley days. That one had been hammered and battered and darn near wrecked by Sandoval's journey from Hadley to Daedalus Base and was still there. Partly refurbished, good enough for short-haul work, but nowhere near reliable enough for a road trip of this magnitude. Vivian's MOLAB was luxurious by comparison, with eight bunks in the main cabin, plus the driving cab and the personal hygiene cubicle, and a crew of only six. Even at that, it still felt snug.

Three years ago, Vivian would have given her eyeteeth to just do Palus Trek with Ellis Mayer in a vehicle like that, three hundred miles in all, across Palus Putredinis to Archimedes and Autolycus craters and back. At the time that had seemed like a scary long way, a prohibitively distant trip. Her current Polar Trek completely blew that away.

Over the past couple of weeks, they'd been traveling through the South Pole-Aitken Basin, the Moon's largest and deepest impact crater, located on its far side. The SPA Basin was sixteen hundred miles across and generally four to five miles deep. However, once they were actually in it, the smaller craters and other features superimposed upon the basin were much more obvious than the fact they were inside the biggest geological feature on the lunar surface. And to be honest, the terrain was so bad around the South Pole that Vivian had no idea whether she was technically still within the SPA or had just left it.

Given the basin's depth, the Houston geology backroom had predicted that the Moon's crust would be thinner there, and its geology significantly different. That it might even be mostly lunar mantle material, which would be quite the scientific coup.

That now looked unlikely. Vivian had hoped for big things from the SPA Basin, but all they'd really learned so far was that its rocks held a slightly higher proportion of iron oxide and titanium dioxide. Maybe also a bit more thorium—perhaps twice the concentration in most other places—but not enough to be really interesting.

Drawing closer to the MOLAB, she could now glimpse Bill Dobbs and Andrei Lakontsev scouting out some two hundred yards ahead of it in the Lunar Rover, a white pilot fish guiding the silver shark of the MOLAB. Looking for the best route through the unpredictable terrain, checking for rilles and gullies they'd need to avoid. This far south, the Moon was not as well mapped, and every day brought a new surprise.

They rotated the duties, of course. Vivian's favorites were skidding around on the dirt bike and driving the MOLAB. Ponderous though the big rig was, it had a grandeur all its own. At the wheel she could wear a T-shirt and shorts instead of a spacesuit, and even better: she didn't have to take core samples. Two months into the LGS-1 expedition, and after all her varied experiences with them, Vivian hated core drills with a passion. First, because she'd killed a man with one on her first trip to the Moon three years before and sometimes still had nightmares about it. That man had been a Soviet soldier bent on killing her, but still. Vivian had *felt* his faceplate fracture, through the handle of the drill. Macabre.

And second, because the drill was a pain even when it was used in its more benign and customary role. She had to wrestle it into place and then fling all her weight onto it. The rotary percussion sent shocks up through her shoulders and down her back. And then there was the fun problem of not breaking the core as she extracted it from the Moon's crust, then bagging it.

But she could hardly complain. She'd found anorthosites and green glasses, all kinds of breccia from all ages of the Moon. She had personally taken most of the samples and thus undoubtedly done the most complete and wide-ranging job of any lunar geologist so far. It would take scientists on Earth years to comb through it all.

Her final two crew members on LGS-1, Katya Okhotina and Christian Vasquez, would be sleeping, or trying to. It was Okhotina's turn for the Pod, and since Super-Kat could fall asleep anywhere and anytime, she was undoubtedly sacked out despite the bumpy ride. Vasquez, on the other hand, six hours into his rest shift in the main body of the MOLAB and a poor sleeper at the best of times, would have given up trying by now and be reading a book. You got to know people pretty well after riding around the Moon with them in a confined space for this long.

For both Katya and Andrei, it was their first time on-surface, and their excitement stayed high even when the all-veteran American crew of Vivian, Feye, Bill, and Christian flagged. Andrei in particular was hell-bent on enjoying every moment of it. By far the youngest team member, his enthusiasm was infectious. He practically danced across the surface on every EVA. And to Vivian, anyone who loved the Moon was a cut above the rest of humanity. Lakontsev and Okhotina were good people, for Soviets.

The ultimate lunar road trip had been designed by Vivian herself, with lots of help from Ellis Mayer and Feye Gisemba, and ample contributions and support from Bill Dobbs and Christian Vasquez from Apollo 26, geologist-astronaut Harrison Schmidt from Apollo 17, and the entire Houston geology backroom. Thank God it had eventually paid off because the stack of documentation, feasibility studies, budget tables, logistical analyses, signature chains, and other documentation Vivian had assembled for this gig stood a whole lot taller than she did.

Once back in Earth's gravity well after her Marius mission three years ago, LGS-1 had quickly become Vivian's obsession. First, because obsessing about the Moon was entirely Vivian's style. And second, because she hated being back on Earth. *Hated* it.

9

Just being back in one full gravity threw her into a major depression.

But once her proposal had finally been accepted by the astronaut office and worked its way up through all the necessary channels, she'd been back on the Moon in six months. That was the new NASA: fast and adaptive. That part, Vivian liked a whole lot.

Vivian's very first ten-page draft of the proposal, scribbled in thick 2B pencil on yellow legal pads and accompanied by amateurish freehand drawings, had been titled *The Luna Nova Project*. Luna Nova, for New Moon. She'd planned to head around the equator, sometimes diverting above it and sometimes below, following the Sun just as Sandoval and his crew had, but prioritizing key geological sites along the way. Learning to see the entire Moon through new geological eyes, as you might say. Doing a complete survey of mares, highlands, craters, rilles, and a whole bunch of other different terrains in between. It had made sense to her at the time, but as soon as she pitched it to Ellis, he'd burst out laughing. "Might have yourself a branding issue there, Vivian."

"What? Why?"

"Echoes of the Terra Nova Expedition? Robert Falcon Scott's last expedition to Antarctica?"

*Earth* exploration wasn't Vivian's thing. "It didn't go well?"

"You might say that. In 1910 or thereabouts, Scott made it all the way across the ice to the South Pole, only to find that a Norwegian team led by Amundsen had beaten him by over a month. And there was no prize for coming in second. No glory. Scott was crushed. And then he and a bunch of his men died on the journey back out."

"Well, crap." Vivian whistled. "That would sure add injury to insult."

"Oh, and as a sidenote, Apsley Cherry-Garrard's book about the expedition was called *The Worst Journey in the World*. You should read it. For inspiration."

Even while Ellis was still laughing, Vivian had snapped her fingers. "That's it! You're a genius."

"I am?"

"I'm not going around the equator," she said. "Screw the equator. I'm going around the *poles*."

Ellis stopped laughing, and looked at her as if she was insane.

"The early Apollos sampled quite a few areas along the equator anyway. But the poles? *No one* has done the poles. Has anyone even been much above the fortieth parallel? We can cross mares no one has even stepped on before, cross the Aitken Basin from top to bottom, and …. Wow. Why didn't I think of that sooner?"

"Because you're not a genius like me?"

"The poles. Holy crap, what an adventure."

Ellis looked dubious. "I doubt it can be done. Logistics? Risks? Sunlight?"

Vivian brandished a pencil. "Sure, let's talk about those."

In fact, the details quickly fell into place. Starting at lunar dawn from the combined Soviet-US base at Zvezda-Copernicus, LGS-1 could take the entire fourteen-plus days of daylight to head up to the North Pole, creep around it following the Sun, then wend their way south for the next two weeks, sampling Farside, to arrive at the near-equatorial Daedalus Base just as the Sun was setting there. They could "overnight" at Daedalus for the next two weeks of lunar dark and set off again at dawn with a similar pattern: another two weeks to the South Pole through the Aitken Basin, and around the horn at lunar day's end to stay with the Sun, and at last find the Earth once again in their sky. Another two weeks on the last leg, heading north through the next lunar day, would take them back to their starting point at Zvezda.

They'd be on a tight schedule. The Sun would be their friend, and also their enemy. Solar power could provide much of the energy they needed, although they could survive a while with just the RTG. But the Sun would also roast them. It would take a large chunk of power just to cool themselves against it.

The Sun obviously also lighted their way. Navigating by lunar night could be slow, painful, and potentially dangerous. If their progress fell too far behind the terminator, LGS-1 might eventually find itself in big trouble.

"So. Traveling a circumpolar route like that would take a grand total of seventy-five Earth days, including that two-week night period in the middle at Daedalus where you rest up, recover, and reprovision." Ellis scribbled a few more numbers on his pad. "But you should make moonfall at Zvezda-Copernicus a few days early to do your final prep and expedition kit-out, so LGS-1 can get on the road promptly at dawn. Maybe even slightly before dawn. Why not; you can snatch a few extra hours by getting a head start on well-mapped terrain before sun-up and recharge the batteries right away once you're in full solar irradiance. And at the other end, once you arrive back at Zvezda with a full complement of samples and cores, it'll take a couple more days to unpack and catalog everything and get ready to launch back to Earth."

Vivian was already grinning. "Around the Moon in Eighty Days."

"Great." Ellis sat back in satisfaction and took a chug of his beer. "That's a *much* better vibe than 'Luna Nova.'"

"Yeah. All that Jules Verne energy. It'd be a good omen."

"Not that we believe in omens."

"Not officially."

"Ha."

They put their heads together again and got back to work.

"Total distance, ten thousand nine hundred and sixteen kilometers. Almost six thousand eight hundred miles, as the lunar crow flies."

"We won't be crows. We'll be zigging and zagging all the way, hitting all the cool sites." Vivian paused. "Ellis. Man. You're *sure* you don't want to be on my crew for this? It would be a *ton* more fun with you."

He shook his head. "Maybe in a different lifetime. One where I haven't already used up all my Moon-energy fighting Soviets. And then running away from them."

"Ellis. That wasn't running away. That was strategic withdrawal."

"It sure felt like I was abandoning you."

"So maybe don't abandon me this time? And come along?"

Ellis sighed. "Vivian. Manipulative."

"Sorry."

"Sure. Anyway, thanks, but no thanks. Been there, done that."

Vivian hadn't given up yet. "Dude. You only went *halfway* around. In a ridiculously overcrowded MOLAB, under massive stress. You didn't even stop to take pictures."

"And thank God for that. Vivian, jeez. I saw more of the Moon than any sane person ever needs to see, and I'm not signing up for a do-over. But by all means, knock yourself out."

"Sure will. But if you change your mind?"

"Not going to."

"And you'll help me write it? You do words so much better than I do."

"Oh, I don't know. You word pretty good. But, sure, Commander— absolutely. And while you're slogging across boring mares, I'll sit comfy in Mission Control as your lead CAPCOM and go home to my wife and daughters and a home-cooked meal every night. And breathe fresh Earth air." He took a deep breath, exhaled theatrically, and grinned.

"Each to his own. And you're really not going to let me retitle this, 'The Worst Journey on Another World?'" Her eyes glinted.

Ellis pursed his lips, pretended to consider it. "With all due respect ... I think not."


This wasn't merely a lunar boondoggle. It would be yet another neat US first, but Vivian's mission also possessed a rock-solid scientific, and even economic, rationale.

Ellis had laughed again at that. "You're seriously going to put 'rock-solid scientific rationale' into the proposal Executive Summary?"

"I totally am."

The LGS-1 crew would dig, bag, and tag their way around the Moon. Obtain cores and rock samples both typical and unusual, from basins and craters young and old, mares and mountains, lowlands and highlands. Map and analyze the lunar surface as best they could, along the line of the journey. Determine how quickly or slowly the regolith composition, and other significant markers, changed with distance and terrain. The resulting geological analyses would transform mankind's knowledge of the Moon and refine their theories of its formation and evolution.

LGS-1 would take many other measurements along the way, on science topics Vivian knew much less about. Surface magnetometer readings. Soil electrical potentials. Cold cathode ion gage measurements of the super-sparse lunar atmosphere. Charged particles from the solar wind. Lunar surface gravimetric data. Sure. Whatever. Just as long as they were all *in situ* measurements that vocal groups of scientists cared about and were willing to argue for getting. People who'd throw their weight behind Vivian's cause.

But Vivian was in it for the adventure, and the glory, as much as her complicated science justification. They'd be the first people to orbit the Moon ... at ground level. A grand circumnavigation, from pole to pole.


"You do realize that for this harebrained scheme to have any chance of acceptance you'll need to take Soviets along for the ride?"

Vivian had looked sideways at John Young, head of the Astronaut Office, whom she was briefing on the mission concept. "Take along who, now?"

"Soviets. This'll have to be another US-Soviet collaboration, or it'll fall at the first hurdle, at NASA HQ. Sure, the US will lead it—*you'll* lead it—but you'll have to take a couple of our Red brothers along for the ride. Politics, Vivian."

Vivian thought quickly. "How about a Red sister?"

"Creep." Katya Okhotina had looked uncertain. "I think that is not a good word?"

"KREEP," Bill Dobbs corrected her, patiently. "K-R-E-E-P. The K is the chemical symbol of potassium. The REE in the middle stands for Rare Earth Elements. And the P is phosphorous."

"Rare Earth." Beside Katya, Andrei Lakontsev nodded, but Vivian had no idea whether he really understood.

"Bunch of elements with hard names," Dobbs said. "The lanthanides?"

"What do they teach you Soviet astronauts at Star City, anyway?" Gisemba grinned as if he were making a friendly joke and not a jibe.

Katya ignored him, still looking at Dobbs. "Lanthanides are what?"

Dobbs paused, then began to rattle them off. "Scandium, yttrium, lanthanum, cerium …"

"Praseodymium," Vasquez added helpfully.

"… Neodymium." Dobbs stopped. "Crap. I knew them all, once."

"I was ready to be impressed. Now, not so much." Vivian turned to Okhotina. "There are seventeen of them, mostly all silvery metals. They have extensive uses in electronics and lasers, and other cutting-edge tech, and they're going to get even more important in the future."

"And they're rare?"

"Not all of them," Vasquez said. "There's more cerium than copper on the Earth, as it happens."

"Problem is, many of the important rare earth elements are most abundant in Red China, and the People's Republic isn't keen to give them to the decadent West. Or to their Asian adversaries in the Soviet Union, for that matter. Which obviously puts both the United States and the USSR at a big disadvantage."

"Hmm," said Andrei.

"And they have been found on the Moon?" Okhotina stayed on-topic. Her persistence and focus were two of the things Vivian liked about her. Plus, the memory of her essential help against Yashin

14

and his thugs, back on that terrible day that might well have ended with them all smeared into atoms, riding Columbia Station as it plummeted down onto the lunar surface.

Vivian pushed that memory away. "Yes, here and there. Apollo 12 found some in the Ocean of Storms. Apollo 14 tracked a whole lot more in the Fra Mauro highlands; 15 identified some in the Hadley basalts. Some of the later missions turned up REE, others didn't. On Apollo 32, Ellis and I isolated a few small deposits at the Marius Hills. So far, the rare earths seem very patchy. But that doesn't rule out major deposits below the surface, in the crust, or even *on* the surface in other places on the Moon."

Dobbs took over. "Part of our job is to learn just how patchy such deposits might be. Plus, if we were to strike a particularly rich vein, that would be a honking great big deal."

"Probably pay off the cost of this mission right then and there," Vasquez added.

"NASA HQ liked that part," said Vivian. "So did Congress."

Okhotina met Vivian's eye. "And all of this you would share with my country, of course."

"Of course," Vivian said readily. "That's why you're here. That's why we're having this conversation."

Vasquez grinned. Most of their geological survey results wouldn't be fully analyzed and published until long after the mission was over. And since the US was paying the lion's share of the costs, they'd get first crack at the mineralogical analysis at NASA's Lunar Sample Laboratory Facility in Building 31N of the Johnson Space Center in Houston, Texas. The results would be shared with the Soviets, for sure—hell, eventually they'd all appear in *Nature*, the *Journal of Geophysical Research*, and various other public documents and monographs. But the US would inevitably get a head start in exploiting any mineralogical trove they discovered. If they identified a KREEP mother lode, they'd be off and running as a matter of urgency.

Seeing Vasquez's grin, Lakontsev shook his head. "You jokers." One of his favorite English phrases.

"Hey, it's *my* superpower that's footing the bill for this jaunt."

"Please, do not rub it out," Okhotina said.

"In," said Vivian. "Don't rub it *in*."

Katya shrugged. "Very well."

"Better still, don't rub it at all," Feye murmured, and the Soviets looked puzzled while the rest of them laughed.

Vivian had nodded. For once, her people instincts were good. This crew was going to work out just fine. Dobbs and Vasquez had been a solid team at Hadley, and even back on Earth were basically inseparable. Once Vivian had broached the idea to them of returning to the Moon, they'd immediately signed on and pitched in, doing invaluable work helping to scope out the most scientifically useful route around the lunar globe.

Katya and Andrei? Russians both, obviously. Even good Soviets. But Vivian and Katya had gotten on as well as could have been expected during those long post-Yashin days in lunar orbit, waiting for rescue. The two of them, plus Terri Brock, had bonded well. Andrei was a newcomer, and none of the Americans had known him beforehand, but he was one of Nikolai Makarov's protégés and came vouched for by Okhotina. And Vivian could already tell he was going to be great.


It had been obvious from the start that they'd need a *lot* of supplies. Vivian's original idea had involved dead drops, seeding the path ahead of them with Cargo Containers with caches of food they could pick up, and leaving rock samples in their place for later retrieval. Then Gisemba did the math on the costs that would add to the mission, and they gulped and shook their heads and went back to the drawing board.

The money was getting tight. Gone were the days when NASA could throw cash at lunar exploration. It was the 1980s now, and every dollar was scrutinized. As far as the American public was concerned, the Space Race was over. US-Soviet collaboration on the Moon was much less interesting. By and large, lunar exploration was no longer a national priority.

Plus, due to a new Earthly focus on environmental issues, triggered ironically enough by the Apollo views of the Earth as a fragile jewel in space, polluting their path around the Moon with wrecked Cargo Containers was no longer a viable option. Vivian actually agreed with that. She liked her lunar surface pristine.

So, they had to carry everything they needed: four weeks of food supplies, replacing them as they went with four weeks-worth of rocks. They recycled as much of their water as they could and packed out their trash.

16

Naturally, they screwed up sometimes. In the final week before they'd arrived at Daedalus Base the Pod had become almost unusable due to the bags of rocks and sealed personal waste they'd had to move into it. But everyone had been good-natured about it. The mission was going well, and Daedalus and a two-week break had been right ahead of them, at a facility none of them but Vivian had visited before. They'd known that once they arrived, they could all shuck their suits, get away from one another for a while, and sleep somewhere that wasn't almost constantly *moving*. And despite the obvious daily perils of vacuum, heat, and dust, nobody was actively trying to kill them.

At least, not that they knew of yet.

# CHAPTER 2

Lunar South Pole: Vivian Carter
January 22, 1983

**THE** assault came just a few hours after LGS-1 turned the corner.

They had crawled around the South Pole now, the difficult light angle and the poorly mapped terrain combining against them. They'd approached it as close as possible, following the rim of Shackleton Crater to the thirty-degrees-west line. At that point they were within a mile of the geographic pole, so to the resolution of the maps they had, LGS-1 was at that moment basically *there*, with the absolutely true Pole just over the crater rim in permanent shadow.

"Farthest South," Vivian said. "Ninety degrees, within a sneeze. We did it. Both poles in the bag, done and done."

"Congratulations, Commander," said Gisemba.

"Me? Nope. It was all of us. Go team."

"Go team!" Lakontsev agreed, wholeheartedly.

And that was that, and they kept moving along. They had many more miles to cover that day.

From Shackleton, they headed north—but wasn't every direction north, now?—passing the much larger Shoemaker Crater to their right, and approaching the craggy, rugged, irregular, and equally broad Haworth Crater on their left. The lighting was terrible. They tried to keep the MOLAB, rover, and bike in the oblique sunlight as far as possible but still occasionally had to navigate precariously through pools of deep darkness, following the path they'd laid out months before, using several painstaking physical models of the landscape. And, of course, the modeled terrain wasn't exactly true to reality.

The Poles were *hard*, and everyone had known they were going to be.

But the worst would be behind them soon. Shoemaker and Haworth butted up against each other, their boundary forming another broad ridge. Follow that around Shoemaker, pass beneath a higher ridge illuminated by bright sunshine, and they'd be through the roughest ground and truly back on Nearside. Earth would soon be consistently above their horizon again, the oblique Sun would be a steadily decreasing pain in their asses, and they'd be able to drive on more straightforward terrain for four or five hours before stopping for a rest period and a few hours of blessed stillness, with nothing tilting and jerking and rumbling around them. And then they'd truly be able to celebrate their latest milestone in lunar exploration history.

They had earned it, and Vivian would smile with her crew. But the South Pole was the last great challenge. Everything ahead of them should be easy. And Vivian wasn't a big fan of easy. When had *easy* ever gotten her juices flowing?

Vivian was dreading their journey's end. Once safely back at Zvezda-Copernicus, her team would spend three days conducting their preliminary debriefing, unpacking the MOLAB, and classifying and repackaging the samples and other science data for transport back to Earth. And then Vivian would launch up into lunar orbit for what would likely be her final time. She and Gisemba would rendezvous with Eagle Station, and transfer into a Command and Service Module for the ride home.

And then what?

If this really was Vivian's last trip to the Moon, she'd have to find some other passion for the rest of her life. And she had no idea what that might be.

Ah, well. Her dirt-bike shift was almost over. Time to get herself back aboard the MOLAB and take what passed for a shower.

19

Earth could wait. It was back below their local horizon right now, and comms were quiet once more. Out of sight, out of mind, right? *Sufficient unto the day is the evil thereof.*

And just as Vivian thought the word "evil," it began.

In a sharp motion, Andrei slewed the rover to the left and shouted "Danger, danger!" which made Vivian think briefly, stupidly, of the robot in *Lost in Space.*

Then came the explosion.

Vivian's split-second reaction was *Volcano!* The Moon hadn't been actively volcanic for a billion years, but it sure *looked* like some kind of small eruption had gone off right in front of the Lunar Rover, almost between its front wheels, flipping it into the air like a toy.

The rover sailed fifteen feet off the ground, rose almost vertically, and then dropped back down in lunar-gravity slow motion to spike into the ground on its right rear. Dobbs and Lakontsev, both wearing their lap straps, stayed roughly held in their seats as their ride crashed down on its back. She saw their arms flailing, their bodies twisting.

The latest Lunar Rovers were equipped with roll bars, to protect the crew from the more ambitious terrain they were required to navigate. The roll bar on the LGS-1 rover had just saved her guys' lives, but it hadn't been able to prevent them from being pummeled by all the rocks and gear that been thrown at them when the vehicle went over.

And the rover was still moving. It bounced a second time, and under that stress the roll bar twisted and bent into scrap and the chassis broke in the middle, folding around Vivian's crewmen and obscuring them from her view.

All happened in that eerie lunar silence. Vivian stared in disbelief and then screamed aloud: "Bill! Andrei!"

And then, both at once, Dobbs and Lakontsev started bellowing in pain.

"What the hell! What the hell!" Vasquez, from the passenger seat of the MOLAB, shouted almost as loudly, freaking out about what he'd just seen happen to his partner.

Vivian skidded the bike to a halt, looked around her, saw nothing. Nothing except Moon.

Gisemba jerked the wheel of the MOLAB left, heading toward the wrecked rover. Vivian tried to cut through the din of everyone shouting at once. "Break! What just happened? A mine, a shell, a rocket, what? Christian, quiet! Feye, talk to me!"

Whatever it was, Vivian hadn't seen it coming.

*So I might not see the next one, either.*

Still a babble of voices on her main loop. "Break! Break! Switch to secure radio." She took a deep breath. "Are we under *attack*?"

Here? So far away from anywhere?

And why attack LGS-1?

Gisemba's voice: "Vivian, shooter on the ridgetop. See him?"

"No, where?—*Shit!*"

It came fast from the ridge ahead, almost out of the Sun and almost too swift for the eye to track, and then it exploded just to the left of the MOLAB. This one was definitely a rocket or an explosive shell. The MOLAB lurched right as Gisemba yanked the wheel again. Rocks rained down, not quite reaching Vivian as she came roaring in on the bike from behind.

It had come from a distance, though, that rocket. The top of that ridge was a ways away—a good four hundred yards. The accuracy of a shoulder-mounted rocket wasn't terrific, and infrared homing devices never worked worth a damn on the Moon in daytime because *everything* was hot.

But that first explosion hadn't been a rocket. Meaning there could be more mines. *Crap.*

The hostiles had chosen the perfect time and place for an ambush. The MOLAB—and Vivian—were constrained to the channel they were in. Canyon to the left of them and that rocky scarp to the right. A narrow throughway in between. Her convoy could go forward or back, and that was that.

And the enemy had timed their attack for when LGS-1 was out of contact with Earth, blocked by the ridge. They weren't stupid.

*Stop thinking. Move.*

Vivian twisted the accelerator on the dirt bike to maximum and it *leaped*, coming adrift from the ground as the wheels spat gravel and eventually made proper purchase and propelled her forward.

Ahead of her, the MOLAB was still on the move. "Feye, you're driving *toward* the shooter."

"Yeah, what, you want me to *stop*?"

"Can you turn around?" She eyed the terrain. "Uh. Doesn't look likely."

"Not in one go. I'd need a three-pointer."

A three-point turn, making them an obvious sitting duck for the next rocket? Bad idea. But there were no good ideas Vivian could see. "Okay, but don't take the easy road. Drive a route that looks like shit, like no one could ever get a MOLAB through it. It's less likely to be mined. Go over rocky ground, use the slopes, keep eyes peeled for another mine."

"What about Bill and Andrei?" Vasquez cut in, shouting, clearly ragged.

"What about not dying?" Vivian snapped back. At the same time, Gisemba said, "Chill, man. We'll get to 'em, never fear."

Vivian had already cut off Dobbs and Lakontsev's channel so she could talk around their cries of pain. She couldn't even think about them right now. Maybe she'd have reacted like Vasquez if it was Ellis who had just been bombed and was now pinned beneath a rover, but …. She swallowed, breathed, kept going. "They're alive and conscious. They'll keep. Priorities. We need to take these guys out first."

"Take *out*?" Vasquez again.

She ignored him. "Feye, put a distress call on repeat on the Houston loop."

"Ten-four," said Gisemba.

How long did it take to reload a rocket launcher? Longer than this, apparently. Or maybe their attackers knew the MOLAB was just about to drive over a mine anyway? Cold fear flooded Vivian's spine.

Vasquez wasn't done yet. "Take out how, exactly?"

Gisemba, at the wheel: "God's sake, Christian, hush up and patch me onto S-band, emergency channel, and start a recording. And while you're at it, start cameras and voice tapes on all channels."

At last, discipline took over. "Patched. Recording. Video and audio start. Go."

"Mayday, Mayday, break-break. LGS-1 is under Soviet attack. Houston and all US forces at Zvezda-Copernicus and Daedalus, ears on me. Mayday. LGS-1 is under attack."

No response, of course. They were still in the dead zone.

Soviet attack? Vivian's mind whirled. Were the Soviets really firing on LGS-1, with two of their own people aboard? "What the hell?" she said aloud.

22

Hopefully their suits had protected Bill and Andrei from the worst of the impacts. From a quick glance Vivian could see them still moving, maybe trying to squirm into a position where they could get the leverage to shift the rover off themselves. In the Moon's gravity it would weigh less than a hundred pounds, but pinned as they were, that would be a challenge.

Fortunately, the rest of Vivian's crew was inside the MOLAB, and its radiation shielding *might* help a bit as armor against explosive shells.

Vivian, on the other hand, was out in the open.

But not defenseless. At least, in principle.

She swung the bike around, put the hammer down, and headed for the Pod. Her wheels skidded—too much torque, too little care—and as she slid left, she jammed her leg out to keep herself upright. Her boot bumped painfully across regolith, sending shocks through her ankle and calf. She wrestled the bike back under control and opened it up. "Feye, I'm coming alongside. Warn me on swerves."

"Need me to slow down?" Gisemba asked anxiously. He knew what she was up to.

"Negative. Keep her straight and sure for a moment." The last thing Vivian needed was for the MOLAB to brake or swing around into her path.

Tracer rounds swept the terrain in front of her from right to left—bullets, shells? She couldn't tell—but she was through and past them before she even had a chance to react. She'd seen the sparks as they ricocheted off the MOLAB, though. "Hey, you guys suited up?"

She could already guess the answer: nope.

"Negative," said Gisemba.

"Then seal all the bulkheads in the truck, stat."

Vasquez objected immediately. "Wait, no, Vivian. If we do that then we can't get back into the—"

*Main cabin.* "Break, yeah, I know. Just do it."

"But Katya is—"

"I know, *I know. Seal them now*, that's an order."

"Sealing," said Gisemba, and at the same time Vasquez said, "On it, Commander."

Well, good: Vasquez was calling her *Commander* again. About fricking time.

So, yeah. Now Katya was stranded in the Pod, unable to regain access to the concertina-tunnel back into the MOLAB. But the Pod was the safest place for her anyway, and now if the MOLAB was breached, the boys in the cab up front should survive it.

*Hmm.* How handy was it that their attackers had picked a time when Okhotina was safe and sound in the Pod, the most armored space they had? *If anyone survives, it'll be Katya.* There were very few coincidences where Soviet attacks were concerned.

Lakontsev had been easily identifiable by his orange Soviet suit, so different from the white NASA suits. The hostiles had taken out the rover, sure. But they weren't shooting at it now.

And if that first blast had been a mine, they had to have planted it long before LGS-1 came over their horizon. Maybe before Andrei went out to relieve Christian riding shotgun. They might not have known that one of their own would be first in the firing line.

Maybe they wouldn't care even if they'd known. Yashin and his other Bad Soviets hadn't been squeamish about Good Soviet lives, last time around the block.

The dirt bike had a wide, deep basket mounted in front of its handlebars. Some days it held Vivian's core drill and other equipment. Right now, it just held her most recent rock samples from Shackleton's rim, neatly bagged, plus her rock-hound equipment clipped to a rack: her geologist's hammer, scoop, rake, tongs, spring scale. Plenty of space. No need to unlatch the basket and tilt it sideways to empty it out.

She came alongside the storage racks on the trailer. This was the tricky bit. Still at speed, still bumping along on the uneven surface, Vivian had to choose her moment to take her right hand off the handlebar.

She reached up, banged on the side panel to flip it open, and reached in to grab her M132 and the associated munitions pack.

Into the basket they went. And off went Vivian, punching the gas again on her electric-powered bike.

The M132 Viper was a small shoulder-mounted rocket launcher, designed by General Dynamics for use in vacuum. Made of fiberglass, with an extensible tube and pop-up sights. On her previous side-tracked lunar mission, hostile Soviets had shot at Vivian on at least two occasions with their equivalent of one of these. It was long past time Vivian returned the favor.

The launcher came preloaded. The munitions pack held four more rocket-powered high explosive grenades, plus a large Night Corps machine pistol, also thermally designed for in-vacuum use.

Gone were the days when US astronauts traveled unarmed on the lunar surface, at least this far from a base. The NASA high-ups hadn't even attempted to persuade Vivian to save weight by not carrying ordnance, and John Young would likely have given her grief if she *hadn't* included some self-protection in her mission manifest.

Now Vivian was armed and—with luck—dangerous to people other than herself. All she had to do was to kill her attackers before they killed her.

Not that she'd ever fired either one of these weapons in space. Only on Earth a year ago, during the week of weapons instruction that was now included in NASA astronauts' continuing training.

The launcher was nearly three feet long and stuck out of the basket, but it was heavy enough that Vivian had no fear of it bouncing out. She could fire either weapon one-handed, though with no great accuracy. The M132 would be better stabilized on her shoulder—but reloading it would take both hands and a good fifteen seconds with the bike at rest.

Vasquez's voice cut in again, all business now. "Guys, check behind. More hostiles on our six."

"Seriously?" Vivian was driving so fast that looking back over her shoulder was a risk, and she hardly wanted to stop. Instead, she kicked the bike left, swung it around in a three-sixty, a tight loop that brought her close to the canyon rim.

Sure enough. Far back, several hundred yards away, shiny and moving fast and difficult to see: a rover of some kind.

This damned slant-Sun lighting was a pain. Bad enough during normal operations, hopeless in an emergency.

"Confirm. Hostiles on our tail."

Gisemba swore. "Looks like a Lunokhod."

"Like it would be anything else," Vasquez muttered venomously.

"I'm gonna have to turn anyway." Gisemba again. "Gets even narrower ahead. What are the odds it's mined? And even if not, I'll have to slow up and become an easy target for the goddamned shooter. I go in there, we're dead. Turning now."

"Wait, shit …" Vivian scanned the terrain again. "You don't have the room for that."

"Says you."

"Feye …"

25

"Gotta keep moving. And we've got to be head-on by the time that Lunokhod gets here."

"Head-on?"

"So here goes."

The MOLAB lurched to the right, heading toward a wall of rock. "Holy cow," Vivian said.

"Turn, for God's sake," Vasquez shouted. "Turn!"

"Quiet, dipshits." Gisemba threw the MOLAB into a hard left at the last second. And naturally, it skidded.

"Damn everything, Feye," said Vivian.

The MOLAB made it partway around, but its hard-and-fast turn forced its trailers out wider than the path the main vehicle had taken. Vivian heard the screech through her radio as the Pod scraped against almost vertical rock, and then the bang as the flatbed trailer hit and bounced away, almost jackknifing. Then the MOLAB was off and running, continuing its arc … toward the drop-off.

"Your curve's too wide," Vivian said, as calmly as she could. "You won't make it."

"Crap. Buy me time." Gisemba slammed on the brakes, and the MOLAB skidded to a messy halt.

"Oh, sure."

Vivian jammed on her own brakes, yanked the M132 out, swung to aim up at the crest where her best guess was for the Soviet rocket launcher, and squeezed the trigger gently.

The Vipers were designed to have no recoil, but this one sure as hell did. The thing had a kick like a mule, and in one-sixth G Vivian wasn't as stable as she'd be on Earth. The punch of the strip powder charge shoved her back into the cloud of gray smoke that the ignition had caused. And once the grenade was a dozen meters out of the tube its rocket motor fired, hurling it even faster. "Holy *damn*."

In the blink of an eye, it had powered all the way to the ridge. A spout of rock plumed into the air, and in seconds she felt a corresponding vibration through the ground. Even with all Vivian's Moon experience, it still felt weird that something that spectacular and deadly made no sound.

The MOLAB was now scooting in reverse at half speed, Gisemba turning to gain space. The trailers didn't want to go that way. The Pod wheels were scraping across the ground at an angle, the whole trailer swaying alarmingly. "Yikes," Vivian said. "Pod's gonna roll. Feye?"

"Enough, Vivian? Am I far enough back?"

"Yes. Yes! Stop! Take her forward again."

She caught another glint of sunlight off metal, up high, and twisted her head to look.

*Oh, come on. Really?*

Vasquez, from the cab: "Wait, what the hell is *that*? Vivian, look up!"

She already had. The damn thing was hard to miss.

"Holy shit," she said. "They even have a bear in the air."

It was still up high, above the ridge where the sniper was, but easy enough to make out in the full glare of the Sun. It looked like a pair of tubular rover seats strung up on a frame over a small, gimballed rocket engine. Four spindly landing legs stuck out, defining corners.

About as simple as it could be, but it was an honest-to-God lunar flyer with two men crewing it, side by side. And what could easily be some kind of gun mounted in between them.

"Aw, for crying out loud," said Gisemba.

"No kidding."

It resembled nothing so much as the notorious "flying bedstead" the Apollo commanders had been forced to train on at Johnson Space Center. The Lunar Landing Training Vehicle, LLTV, that had nearly killed Neil Armstrong and, later, Vivian Carter, long before their respective first trips to the Moon. The LLTV had a single engine, gimbal-mounted vertically, augmented with two hydrogen peroxide lift rockets and a bunch of thrusters. And, fortunately, in the JSC case, an ejector seat.

This one was much smaller, obviously. It only had to function in one-sixth gravity. And the LLTV hadn't been armed.

So. Triple threat. Bears on the ridge, shooting at them. Bears from behind. Plus that ridiculous flying bedstead, floating above them.

*Crap. This isn't good.*

The flyer was already dropping, much lower now. Vivian could see the two crewmen piloting it more clearly. One wore a chunky suit, dark as space. The other suit was white-gray and eerily familiar. "Christ …. Is that an *Apollo* suit?"

*Can't be. Can't be.*

As it dipped toward her, Vivian remembered how a Lunar Module engine had taken out a Soviet biker during the first battle for Hadley. She'd need to watch out. That rocket engine could be just as deadly to her as the cannon.

But they'd have to catch her first.

Vivian gunned it again. Took the bike up the rim of a crater, and for a few moments she was off the ground, in midair. Mid-space. Then she was steering right and heading up the scarp, just as fast as she could, to gain height and get herself up closer to their level.

This was a good bike. American technology, not Soviet, and they'd poured a lot of money into improving them in the last couple years. But even Vivian was impressed at the short work the bike made of the height. Careening uphill like a crazy person wasn't her usual driving mode.

She kept pushing and pushing, swerving to throw off their aim. Driving so hard it almost felt like she was vertical. She was gaining on them, height-wise, that was for sure. And then the bike scooted out from beneath her, skating on scree. Vivian tumbled painfully onto the rocks and slid, and her M132 fell out of the basket and bounced along beside her.

*Well, okay then. Guess that's as high as I'm getting.*

She rolled onto her side and boosted herself up the slope until she could reach her weapons. Pulled them close and sat up.

Ideally Vivian would be on one knee, the M132 lined up neatly on her shoulder, but she was on a steep grade and the flyer was now across from her and only slightly higher.

She reloaded, set the range fuse this time on a wild guess, lay back and plonked the tube onto her shoulder, and drew a bead on the flyer.

*Steady, Vivian. You're down to four grenades now and counting. Don't be wasting any.*

The flyer swooped down toward the MOLAB. Vivian forced herself to wait. They couldn't fire on her while moving at that speed. The pilot would need to stabilize it to let the gunner aim, or they'd just be wasting their own shot.

"There—there, you swine!" The flyer went into a hover, and just as it came to its momentary standstill, Vivian squeezed the trigger.

Again, that punch to her shoulder, and another terrifying *whoosh*—the vibration transmitted through the grenade launcher into her suit—and then she saw the flare as the grenade took powered flight and went off like a rocket. Well, it *was* a rocket. A grenade with a rocket attached.

Damned thing was *fast*. The grenade shot past the flyer and detonated just beyond it, hurling shrapnel everywhere.

She'd set the range fuse for three hundred meters, and that was the distance the grenade had exploded at, not having hit anything by then. But she'd guessed long—hard to estimate distance on the Moon at the best of times, and especially when the target was off the ground—and aimed wide, too. The bear was still in the air, swaying but apparently undamaged. It swerved to the left, away from the explosion, and looped away from her.

Vivian reached down for the next grenade, blinking away the afterimage of that rocket exhaust.

At last, the MOLAB was off and running again, bouncing and lurching back the way it had come, which meant it would pass Vivian again from the right in just a few moments. On an unwavering path directly back toward the Lunokhod, which was still bumping onto the scene from her left. Now that Vivian could see it more closely it didn't look quite like a Lunokhod, but it was certainly more similar to one than to a NASA LRV. And it was clearly armed with two long rifles set up on tripods .... What were the damned things called? SPG-9s? Something like that. They fired rocket-assisted projectiles with high-explosive rounds, anyway.

They weren't firing yet, though. Likely waiting to be in range.

Suddenly, a booming voice came in on their principal frequency, nearly deafening her in a perfect Midwest American accent. "LGS-1, please halt, and no harm will come to you."

"*What?*"

"LGS-1, please stand down."

Gisemba cursed, fluently. Vivian cut in. "*You* stand the hell down, you bastards. Stop your attack, maybe we'll stop ours."

"LGS-1, please halt, and no harm will come to you."

"It's a recording," said Vasquez. "Same intonation."

"LGS-1, please stand down."

Vivian grimaced. "Whatever. Switch frequencies. I don't need to hear these jerks."

She finished loading her next grenade, but swapped in the machine pistol instead and fired it at the flyer. Every fifth bullet was a tracer, and she watched them sparkle as they flew, trying to use them to gauge range.

The lunar flyer was swaying even more, shoved back and forth by its engine as its pilot tried to avoid Vivian's fire, and the gunner sitting

29

next to him had lurched, sending his own shells harmlessly off toward the scarp. Three explosions in a line showed that he'd switched to live ammo. She hoped he didn't have a lot of it.

Of course, all those shells flying out of the enemy cannon were also having an equal and opposite reaction on the flyer, which was light and inherently unstable at the best of times. At least that was working in their favor.

"Man, that thing is batshit," said Gisemba, and Vivian couldn't fault his description.

Batshit, dangerous as hell to fly, but quite likely deadly to them down here on the ground, once the pilot and gunner got their acts together.

Vasquez again: "Hey, guys: is this *Night Corps?*"

The elite USAF dark-ops team. It made even less sense for Night Corps to be attacking LGS-1 … but for a demented moment Vivian had wondered the same thing. "Pretty sure not."

"Only pretty sure?"

"Jeez, get a grip," Gisemba said. "It's not Night Corps. It's *got* to be Soviets."

"*Svolochi!*" came Katya's snarl over the loop from the Pod, and Vivian grinned tautly, almost a twitch. She'd learned enough Russian swears by now to know what that meant.

Vivian blinked, squinted again at the enemy rover coming in from her left. Not Night Corps, but she could see why Vasquez might say that. Four guys aboard, all in the same gray chunky suit as one of the flyer guys. They weren't quite like Night Corps exosuits, but they did resemble the smooth gray Moon suits that most of the USAF contingent at Daedalus wore, that Vivian had noted as standard when she'd first arrived there three years before.

White suits reflected the most sunlight, obviously. Dark suits might be fine for those Night Corps heroes with lots of power to play with, but when you were operating in a marginal energy-conserving environment, you really wanted your suits to be white. Right?

The MOLAB was up to full speed now, and Vivian didn't need to ask. *Head-on*, Feye Gisemba had just said. She knew he wouldn't blink, wouldn't swerve. This would be the first ever game of lunar chicken.

Their closing speed would be something like fifty miles an hour. The MOLAB likely outweighed the Lunokhod and was sturdier. Her guys *should* survive the impact, even if their vehicle was totaled.

Might not, though.

The MOLAB looked like a tank, but it wasn't. Damned thing was made of aluminum. Not the thin aluminum of the Lunar Modules—it was structurally sound, with radiation shielding besides—but it certainly wasn't actual armor. But Gisemba's gamble was smart: the front of the MOLAB was more built-up than its sides and rear, to protect the driver cab against collisions.

Not collisions like this one, of course.

"Feye, you're insane."

"Love you too."

Then another missile came arrowing in from the ridge, slamming home. Dust flew up, obscuring the MOLAB completely. "Feye!"

She heard nothing in return, but the dust dropped quickly, in that uncanny lunar way.

The Soviet missile had exploded in the dirt just a few meters to the right of the MOLAB. The detonation had blown a brand-new crater in the lunar surface but hadn't slowed her truck down an iota.

Then the flyer lifted away from pursuing the MOLAB … and came directly for Vivian. *Gah. Guess I got their attention.*

Tracer, shells. A line of silent explosions strafed the regolith, passing within ten feet of Vivian. The flyer rocked sideways again in reaction, and the gunner swung the cannon to compensate. Tracer flew over her head now.

That cannon was nowhere as large as the Richter on the orbiting Almaz she'd seen three years ago in lunar orbit, but it could be just as lethal. The shells from that Richter could blow a spacesuited astronaut apart, but it wouldn't take that level of force to kill her. Carving a big hole on the torso or limb of her suit would work just fine.

Vivian dropped the pistol, grabbed up the Viper again. Fired. Off went her third rocket, and it looked good, but at the same time she saw muzzle flashes from the Soviet cannon. Lunar soil erupted as the line of shells exploded into the ground, sweeping toward her.

*Move, Vivian.* Stopping to reload now would be her last mistake.

She jumped to her feet and pushed off, taking high leaps down the slope. The cannon's tracer was bright in her vision, *damn it, too bright.*

Her right boot came down, twisted. She tried to kick with her left but mistimed it and went ass over teakettle. Great. *Graceless to the end,*

*Commander Vivian Carter died during a lunar pratfall.* She landed on her back, skidding on rock, the Viper flying out of her grip.

The enemy flyer exploded above her as her grenade struck home. Hot metal cascaded down all around her. "Whoa!" The uncanny silence of what must have been a gigantic explosion was surreal.

*Hands up. Gotta keep that shit away from my helmet. Better still ….* She shoved against the ground with her left hand and leg and flipped herself over. Face down to the ground, her arms awkwardly covered her helmet to the best of her ability. Her visor was the weakest part of her suit, especially with a rain of destruction falling out of the sky. Again.

"Vivian! Vivian!" Katya cried out through the comlink. *"Kak vi?" Are you all right?*

"Okay, I think." She raised her wrist in front of her helmet to check her suit pressure. Holding steady at 4.5 psi. She twisted, looked across at the two vehicles.

Just a couple of hundred feet separated them now: the MOLAB and Lunokhod were both pedal to the metal, still on a collision course. And one of the SPG-9s on the Lunokhod was spitting flame.

# CHAPTER 3

Lunar South Pole: Vivian Carter
January 22, 1983

**SUDDENLY,** all she could hear in her headset was Ellis Mayer's voice. "Vivian! LGS-1, Houston, what's happening? Report!"

One of the NAVSTARs must have appeared back above the local horizon. And Mission Control had checked their emergency voice channel to find Gisemba's tape-looped Mayday.

"Hang on, man," Vivian said. "Super busy."

"Ambush," Vasquez cut in. "Shooter, rocket launcher and assault weapons. Hostile rover, plus a two-man flyer."

"Now toast," Vivian added. "The flyer, I mean. I killed it."

"Really?" said Vasquez. Well, maybe it wasn't surprising he hadn't noticed. His gaze was likely locked on the Lunokhod. "Good."

"Wait … *what?*" Ellis said, almost at the same time. He sounded stupefied. Which was fair.

"MOLAB is engaging the Lunokhod," she said.

"Engaging? How?"

She swallowed. "You don't wanna know."

Both cosmonaut gunners were firing their SPG-9s now. Vivian could see the muzzle flash. But the way their rover was jumping and bouncing across the surface, getting a good aim would be a trick. The MOLAB still sprinted across the lunar surface toward it, but now

Vivian caught an odd glint, a movement upon a movement. Something appeared to have sprouted out of the top of the Pod.

Not something. Someone.

Super-Kat must have suited up and egressed from the Pod's rear hatch, reached around to climb the ladder, and ascended to the Pod roof. Because there she was, clinging to the top of the goddamned Pod. With something slung over her shoulder, bouncing against her life support backpack.

"Katya, jeez …"

Vivian looked up at the ridge again, then across at the flyer wreckage, and saw no movement from either. When she glanced back at the MOLAB, Okhotina had clipped herself to the solar panels on the Pod roof with a short tether and was unfolding something shiny, stubby, with a hinged stock. Clearly a weapon because she now dropped forward, prone onto the Pod roof, resting it in front of her and aiming at the enemy rover barreling toward them.

Where the hell had Okhotina gotten that? Vivian's Soviets weren't supposed to be armed. That was a mission rule that the Soviets themselves had agreed to.

*Well. At least she's using it to fire at other Soviets.* Okhotina's life was on the line too. And she must have moved fast, getting herself up and out, with the Pod thrashing all around her.

Damn, Katya was hardcore. *Whip it, girl.*

Okhotina fired. Vivian couldn't see the bullets, but the jerking reaction against Katya's suit was unmistakable.

*… Whip it good.*

The gray-suited cosmonauts jerked and shook visibly as Okhotina's bullets hit home. The gunner on the left twisted, letting go of his rifle. Sparks flew along the Lunokhod, and it skidded to the right. Its shells flew out at random, well away from the MOLAB, but Feye pulled the truck left to maintain the collision course. Katya pushed herself upright and continued to fire, strafing the entire vehicle.

Something in the rear of the Lunokhod exploded, just a heartbeat before the MOLAB plowed into it.

The US truck rode higher off the ground than the Lunokhod. Its prow powered across the front left of the other rover with a scream of twisted metal that transmitted through the MOLAB's hull and was audible through the radio link. Then the Lunokhod reared up, but not

34

cleanly. It broke, almost tore under the impact, fatally weakened by the explosion from its rear. The cosmonauts aboard flipped out like rag dolls, their suits burning red, flailing.

"Oh, wow." It was hideous. Vivian had to look away.

But as she did, a figure flew over the wreckage, thrown through space by the impact.

Katya Okhotina. The impact had dislodged her from her precarious position on the Pod roof, perhaps torn the clip from her tether. She'd been flung forward, bounced off the MOLAB solar panels and just kept going, straight over the disaster that the Lunokhod had become, to tumble in slow motion toward the lunar surface beyond.

"Katya!"

*God. Damn. It.*

"Vivian! Report!" Ellis again.

"I'm still here. Hostile rover decommissioned. Stand by."

Which left … the shooter on the hill. Was he still a threat? Vivian twisted to scan the ridge. Saw nothing, no one. And no one was firing at her, or at any of her people.

But still. She stood, limped over to the M132. Picked it up, dusted it off, grabbed another grenade, and reloaded. Turned, surveyed the area again.

The enemy flyer and rover must have been transported here somehow. Even on the Moon, that hostile flyer must be short-range, tens of miles at the absolute max. So, some other craft had flown or driven it here. Which meant the hostiles must have another vehicle nearby. Behind the ridge? Should they go try to find it, or just get the hell away from here?

Vivian was beginning to get the shakes. That wasn't rare after she'd been in action, in a situation that could have gotten her killed. She hated the danger, but … almost liked the shakes? Their immediacy, and the feeling of being completely in the moment, super-aware of herself and her surroundings, it helped convince her she was still alive.

*Come on, Vivian. Do something.*

She tuned back in to all the shouting on her comms. Gisemba was calling out to Katya, Vasquez was arguing with him, Ellis was still trying to cut through the din, and in the background, Vivian thought she could hear Dobbs. All male voices, anyway. Nothing from Okhotina.

"Guys. *Guys!* GUYS! BREAK! Give me the channel! Houston, stand by. Katya, report. You okay?"

35

Okhotina was lying on her back. Now, Vivian saw her raise a hand, and in the sudden silence on the loop, heard her voice. "*Da.* Yes, I am mostly uninjured."

"Mostly?"

"Just bruises and other hurts, I think. Suit is not compromised. I am … a little out of breath."

"Roger that. Feye, report."

"Bruises and hurts, likewise," Gisemba said. "Nothing serious."

"The MOLAB?"

"We got hit at least twice, maybe three times or more. But cab and main body still have integrity. Pressure is nominal. The Pod, too. We still have power. We'll need to run full checks, but right now, we're … okay? I guess?"

"Sure." The MOLAB had already started backing up, easing away from the Lunokhod wreckage. "Go easy."

"Roger."

Vivian looked back past the MOLAB to the crumpled mess that their Lunar Rover had become and unmuted their comms. "Bill, Andrei. Report."

Dobbs's voice. "I'm here. Andrei's out cold now. His suit's intact, not breached. Based on what he was screaming at me, and where he was reaching before he faded out, his leg is broken at the thigh."

"Oh, God. He's still breathing? You're sure?"

"That's a roger. I'm looking in at him right now. Can see his face clearly. Breathing looks steady and calm. Lots of sweat. No blood."

"And you? You're really okay?"

A long pause. "What?"

"Bill?" He still wasn't answering her. "Bill! Are you all right?"

"I … sure. Sorry. Banged around like hell. Little woozy. I'll be fine."

It was a weird moment, but Dobbs sounded stronger again now. Trapped under an LRV, he might be excused for being in a bit of a funk.

"I only have the one eye working well, though."

"Christ, what? What happened to the other one?"

"Oh. Blood in it. Leaked down from the cut on my head. I didn't tell you that already?"

"No!"

"Huh. Okay. Anyway, no big deal. That's why we have two eyes, right? Helmet's a mess inside."

"Least of our worries."

"Andrei has likely broken his leg. He was screaming and holding it, and now he's lost consciousness, maybe from the pain. But he's still breathing steadily and there's no blood in *his* eye, lucky dog."

Vivian frowned. Did Dobbs know he was repeating himself? Anyway, he was lucid enough, and they'd get him inside soon. Without her needing to tell him, Gisemba was already driving slowly over toward the rover. "Okay, hang tight. We're coming."

Adrenaline still surged through her system. But they were all still alive. She hadn't lost a single one of her crew.

Mostly due to rapid action by Lakontsev, Okhotina, Gisemba, and Vivian herself, and a healthy dollop of luck.

Luck? Well. Maybe Gisemba and Okhotina had made their own luck.

She stared up at the ridge again. Still nothing. If only she knew for sure … "Great job, everyone."

Gisemba grunted. "We punched back like champs."

"I'm guessing they weren't expecting us to be armed, and to react so quickly. Assumed we'd be a soft target."

"We are not soft," said Katya. She was standing up now, walking slowly toward the wreckage of the Lunokhod, her gun up in front of her.

"We sure aren't." *Especially not you, you badass.* "Okay, everyone, listen up. Here's how this goes. Kat and I will head across to the rover boys, pull them out of there. Feye and Christian, stay inside but suit up, in case of surprises." Sudden explosive decompression, for example, due to a structural issue. That would be a surprise.

"Copy that," said Gisemba. "Everything looks sound. But we'll wrap. Then I'll check the MOLAB drive and electrical systems from soup to nuts, while Christian goes back to put eyes on whatever chaos has happened in the main cabin. We'll give you a full report."

"What?" Vasquez said. "No way. I'm going out for Bill."

Vivian swore. "Damn it, Christian, do as you're told. Katya and I will bring Bill and Andrei in. Well, we'll carry them back and stuff them in the airlock, anyway. Your job right now is to check everything out and tidy up. Clear some space, get the med kit out, and scrub down in case we need to do surgery." *God, I hope we don't need to half-ass an actual surgical procedure out here.*

"But …"

37

"No buts. That's the best thing you can do for him right now, and that's an order. Copy?"

"But I .... Ow! Jeez, man."

"The doofus copies," Gisemba said.

Vivian grinned tightly. Gisemba had likely lost patience and bopped Vasquez on the arm. *Well, whatever gets the job done.* "Thanks. Roger that."

"They are all dead here," Katya said, peering down at the wreckage of the Lunokhod. "Dead and burned."

"Good," Vivian said, a little brutally.

Still, she saw nothing from the ridge. Had there been any response after her last grenade in that direction? She couldn't remember now; it had all happened so fast. She saw no glints in the sunlight, though. Maybe she'd taken him out, after all?

No way of knowing. He might have gone quiet because he was re-positioning for a better shot. He might be approaching her right now, working his way down.

Or: he might already have disengaged. Given what the hostiles had already suffered, it might best for any survivors to cut their losses and get out of Dodge.

Either way, Vivian needed to move. Once she was off and running, she'd be a much tougher target than she was right now anyway.

Even as the thoughts passed through her mind, Vivian was up and bounding up the hillside in the bright Sun, back to the bike. She almost overshot it but got her hand down to grab the frame and anchor herself. Jumped astride it, slung the rocket launcher and her other ordnance into the basket. Started it up and twisted the throttle.

The bike jumped forward, spitting regolith. She pointed its nose down the steepest part of the slope, opened it up, and held her legs out left and right.

*I'm going too fast.*

*Nah. There's no too fast in this situation, babe.*

The bike bumped up and over a rock, skipped to the left, kept going.

And then the Moon throbbed beneath her, as if by seismic activity, and something slammed into Vivian's back like God's sledgehammer, seeming to vibrate, and sent her hurtling over her handlebars. She flipped over and banged into the ground in a tumble. She rolled twice, three times, and then skated to a painful halt, looking up at the sky, all the wind knocked out of her. *Whoa. Shit. Damn.*

Suddenly, it was very quiet. Very quiet indeed.

*Oh, that's not good.*

Then her ears filled with shouting. Three voices: Gisemba, Vasquez, and Ellis Mayer from Mission Control, all yelling at once: *Vivian! Are you okay? Report!* Plus various curses, their words all tumbling over one another just like Vivian's limbs had, a moment before.

"Jeez, hush," she said, and reached up to turn off her radio, just briefly, so she could listen.

*Yep. Sure enough.*

The noise of the fan in her helmet had ceased, and it clearly wasn't temporary deafness. "Well, shit." She switched her radio back on. "Uh, guys? I'm in big trouble."

"Report," Gisemba said, alarmed at her tone, and a time-delayed Ellis spat out the same word immediately afterward.

"I'm not getting air. Or water." At least there was no doubt about where she'd suffered the critical damage. Right in the life support system. *I'm surprised at my own calm.*

No need to worry about suffocating. Without the cooling water flowing through her LCGs, she'd boil to death in seconds.

"Vivian, your telemetry is all zeroes," Ellis said. "What's your—"

"Dead suit," she said flatly.

"Stay where you are!" Katya shouted, and at almost the same moment Gisemba said, "We're coming. Hold on, Viv."

*Hold on? To what?* The temperature in her suit was already rocketing.

The bastard up the hill had just been biding his time. He'd shot at her, raked her with automatic fire. She'd felt the staccato punches of dozens of rounds. Her PLSS backpack, already likely damaged from the falling flyer debris, had been shot to hell and was no longer functional. No fresh oxygen, no more chilled water, no more $CO_2$ purges.

Her oxygen purge system contained thirty minutes of emergency life support. It should have switched in automatically on the failure of her primary supply but had not. She cycled the switch manually. Nothing happened.

A similar system had kept Ellis Mayer alive after he'd been shot by Soviets near Bridge Crater three years ago. But Vivian's wouldn't be saving her today.

She had no life support whatever. All that was powered by a single, large, replaceable battery pack. Her radio, though, had its own separate battery—the Apollo radios were one-piece sealed units. So, radio was all she had.

But she couldn't breathe radio, and it certainly wouldn't keep her cool.

"OPS?" came Ellis's voice from Mission Control, now relaxed into that supernatural calm that always came across him in tense moments.

"Nope," she said. "Already checked."

*Great. Ellis tuned in just in time to hear me die.*

The heat being transferred though the many layers of Vivian's suit was already scalding her wherever it touched the fabric of her undergarments. Her remaining oxygen seared her nose and throat as she sucked it in. Her hands and feet already felt as if they were roasting. "Ah, crap."

Sweat poured down her face as she squinted down at the plain.

Her guys weren't waiting. The MOLAB was on its way; it skidded on regolith and lurched toward her at full speed. Alongside it, Katya Okhotina leaned forward into a loping, high-kicking sprint, damn near keeping up with it.

"Lead-foot Gisemba." It would still take them thirty seconds or more to reach her. Too long. She struggled to her feet.

"Stop *talking*, Vivian," Katya said, in some irritation.

*Yeah, talking takes more breath, but I have to wisecrack my way into hell, right? Military tradition.*

*I'm boiling alive. Dying like a crab. Shit.*

Vivian ran, though it was more of a stagger, gasping and panting. Fear and sweat drenched her.

"Vivian! Stay put!" Gisemba bellowed. "Save your breath!"

"Nope." They didn't get it. Right now, Vivian needed shade more than air.

She staggered into the lee of the cresting ridge, tripped, and fell headlong into the dirt. In a shockingly abrupt transition, she was now in almost complete darkness, lying on rock that hadn't been heated above the boiling point of water by the Sun, might even have been deep-frozen for eternity. Almost immediately the temperature in her suit pivoted and began to drop.

Vivian was panting uncontrollably. It wasn't from the heat, or the coming cold. Carbon dioxide was building inside her helmet from her exertion. She flexed her arms and legs, trying to waft, to circulate whatever oxygen might be left in the rest of her suit. *This is goddamned hopeless.*

40

Her sweat chilled. She felt her skin cooling, could almost feel the spikes of frost drilling into her. She tried to move, found she couldn't. *For God's sake.*

The jitters started. They were different from the shivers, Vivian wasn't shivering at all, had already shot straight past that. Her brain fogged. Nausea rose in her throat.

*I'm going into shock. And next up I'll freeze to death.*

*God* damn *it.*

A figure loomed over Vivian, almost tripping over her legs. Katya grabbed Vivian's boot and yanked, throwing all her body weight into it. Vivian skated painfully on her front across the lunar soil. She was briefly back in direct sunlight. *Oh, hell's bells.* "Hot …" she tried to say, or thought of saying, but there was nothing in her lungs. And then Katya pulled her into the shade from the Pod again anyway.

*Aw, sweet Jesus, this is never going to work.*

Katya flipped her over, and now Vivian was staring up into the sky. "Sit up," Katya said.

*Oh, sure.* Vivian couldn't move, certainly couldn't reply. She was soaking wet all over. Freezing cold. And shaking uncontrollably.

*Yeah. This is shock, all right.*

Katya leaned over, grabbed her helmet with one glove and her shoulder with the other, and yanked. Vivian came into a sitting position, but her icy sweat was pouring into her eyes, and she couldn't see anything, couldn't breathe, couldn't move.

A jarring impact almost awoke her from her fatal grogginess. The Soviet woman had somehow managed to haul Vivian into the Pod airlock and jammed her in there.

"Activate!" Kat screamed. "Now! Now!"

*You talking to me?* Vivian's mind was swimming. *Girlfriend expects me to operate an airlock in my state?*

"Roger that," said Gisemba, and with the last moments of conscious thought, Vivian realized the air pressure around her was rising, her suit getting less stiff, as Gisemba powered up the airlock remotely from the MOLAB main console.

*Too late. I'm about to die. Sure of it.*

*So cold.*

Vivian blacked out.

# CHAPTER 4

## Lunar South Pole: Vivian Carter
## January 23, 1983

**SHE** awoke groggily to find herself clamped in a strong grip. Out of her suit, and with another body wrapped around hers. *What?*

Vivian had no idea where she was, couldn't remember what had just happened, but this wasn't unpleasant. She was alive and breathing, and that seemed somehow significant. But she was still freezing, despite the warm embrace. And wet, as if she'd been plunged into ice water, held under, and then yanked out. Or was she burning?

Sometimes freezing felt like burning. If it was particularly bad. Right?

She remembered Ellis's tale of Robert Falcon Scott, dying out on the polar ice. *Worst journey in the world.* Was she dying, too?

But ... someone was holding her. "Peter?"

"Not Peter."

Vivian's eyes snapped open to find Katya Okhotina's face less than a foot from her own. "Eh?"

"Vivian, you are safe."

"Where?"

"We are in the Pod."

Vivian licked her lips. Her tongue felt like an eel. *So cold.* "What ... hap?" *Is happening?*

"You were freezing. I had to warm you up. Raise your core temperature. This was the way."

It was *Okhotina*, holding her so tightly. *Well, shit.* "Maybe ... just turn ... the heat up?"

"It is up, or really the cooling is down, the Pod is in sunlight. It is an oven in here. And still, you are cold."

"I ...?" She wasn't shivering. Was that good or bad? She had no idea.

But she sure knew she was almost naked, and so was Katya Okhotina. Skin against skin. Direct body heat. Mountain rescue technique. *God, how embarrassing.* "Uh. Just us ... in here. Right?"

"Of course."

In the Pod, and they weren't moving. Memories were returning. "How ... was I out?"

"How long, unconscious? Fifteen minutes, only."

Fifteen? Panic surged through her. "What's happening? Is everyone all right?" She struggled against Okhotina's grip, and Katya released her, but now Vivian felt that cold again, that fearful cold crawling back into her bones. Didn't matter. "Have to get back out there."

"Vivian, Vivian, lie still. It is all under control."

"Oh, sure." How likely was that? "The shooter!"

"No further missiles, no bullets. We think they are gone. Those we did not already kill have retreated, we think."

Yeah, Vivian had thought that last time too. "The boys?"

"Your people have got this, Vivian. Breathe. You are still so very cold. We are disconnected from the MOLAB, Feye has driven it back to Andrei and Bill. Christian is egressing. He will get the rover off them, do what he can."

"They're all right?"

"Nothing has changed. Andrei is unconscious. Bill is talking, but some things he says are strange. They should not be moved until we have medical advice, in any case—this is what Mission Control told us before we lost them. We regain NAVSTAR contact once again in twenty minutes. Spend ten of those, at least, in here recovering. You are still very weak."

That was for sure. Vivian could never have forced herself free of Katya's grip if the woman hadn't willingly released her. Her teeth started chattering. "Okay. All right. If you're ... okay with it?" She leaned back toward Katya, and without another word, the Soviet enveloped her again.

"Keep talking to me. Don't let me pass out again." Was that important? Vivian felt like it was. "So. You brought a *machine gun* on my mission? Without my …" Permission? Knowledge? "My anything?"

"Sub," Okhotina said.

"What?"

"It is a mini Uzi, a submachine gun. It folds up very small. It has a folding stock."

"Yeah, so I saw. But … Uzis aren't Soviet."

"No. The Israelis make more reliable submachine guns than we do. More reliable in vacuum, anyway. Kalashnikov, Stechkin: those Russian guns are too big, or too small, or jam too easily. The Tula, like Yashin used—those do not easily penetrate a spacesuit. The Uzi has a punch. A nice gun for space."

"A nice gun for space. Good to know."

Okhotina hugged her closer. Peered into her eyes, perhaps assessing her pupils. At least, Vivian hoped that was what she was doing. "It can fire nine hundred fifty rounds per minute, although the magazines I could bring hold only fifty rounds. A range of one hundred meters. Easy to remove the trigger guard, for a cosmonaut glove. Weighs just six pounds. Seven-inch barrel."

By now, Vivian was feeling woozy. "I love it when you talk dirty."

"What?"

"Nothing."

"In fact, its rate of fire is greater than the usual Uzi. Because it has a shorter bolt. Vivian, are you hearing me? Focus."

"I'm focused. Sort of." Vivian took a deep breath. Her lungs still hurt.

"What is the range? What did I just say?"

"A hundred feet?"

"Meters!"

"Jeez, give me a break, I'm American." She forced herself to take a deep breath. All the way in. All the way out. "Katya, I'm fine. I'm Vivian Carter, the President of the United States is Ronald Wilson Reagan, actor, Californian ex-governor, and now in his second term. The Pod is off-level, leaning to the left, likely still on the same slope as when you rescued me. Your … nice gun fires nine hundred fifty rounds a minute, if only you had magazines that size, and my *actual point* remains that you smuggled a *fricking submachine gun* aboard my transpolar geological survey and didn't tell me."

Katya raised her hand. "How many fingers?"

"Three, goddamn it. Stop trying to change the subject."

Okhotina nodded, satisfied. "You pick a strange time to complain."

*While being cuddled by an almost-naked cosmonaut after a battle. Yeah, I get that, Super-Kat.*

Katya reached around and grabbed something. "Drink some coffee. And, here. Pills for the pain."

"… Okay." Vivian took the bulb and squeezed it. Space coffee was still awful, but at least it was warm. She could feel it going all the way down her throat. She glanced up at the TV screen, which showed a spacesuited Feye in the MOLAB driver's seat. "Wait, shit, the camera's not on in *here*, right?"

The ghost of a smile visited Katya's lips. "Correct. No one can see us, right now. Or hear."

"Phew. Good to know." Vivian swallowed some more coffee. Brandy would be better. "Okay, fine. I guess I'm glad you had it. The gun."

"Andrei and I: we did not know you had brought a, uh, fricking grenade launcher, either."

"Well, it's my damned mission."

"Turn over. Your back is still freezing."

"Yeah, I know." Time to regain some dignity. "We really do need to get back out there."

"Listen to your own teeth," Okhotina said, simply.

Vivian hesitated. "Listen, Katya. We never tell the boys about this, right?"

"Right. We do not tell the boys."

"Then, sure. Please warm up my back."

She turned over, and Okhotina enveloped her again. Despite being exposed to Vivian's freezing body, Katya's skin was somehow still very warm.

*Wow.* "It's been a long time."

"What has?"

*Since I've been spooned.* "Uh. Nothing. So. You shot back at your own people."

"My own people? To me, that is not so clear. But whoever they were, I could not let that happen." She squeezed Vivian. "I saw the

45

Apollo suit worn by one of the men on the flyer. And other suits dark, like Night Corps."

"And yet not really like Night Corps suits."

"It was hard to see well. The MOLAB was bumping around."

"Katya, you of all people know that not all Soviet suits are orange. Your new Krechet-94 suits are white."

"And there are few of them yet on the Moon, and those were not Krechets." Katya began to rub Vivian's arms. "And so, Vivian, if you had known for a fact that our attackers were Night Corps, you would have stopped fighting and let them kill us all?"

"No. I guess not."

"Well, then."

Vivian glanced at the clock and forced herself to relax. Just for a moment. "Thanks, Kat."


They hit the ten-minute mark. Yet again, Vivian checked all the comms were off. "Well, fun though this is, I guess we should get dressed."

"I suppose so." Okhotina disengaged. "I will find you clothes."

"What about my …. Oh." Vivian's jumpsuit was lying on the floor, tossed on top of her dead spacesuit. It was soaking wet with her sweat, and it looked as if Katya had ripped it down the back getting it off her. "Huh. Okay, thanks."

As Okhotina rummaged, Vivian looked her over. Bright bruises were flowering on the Soviet's arms and legs, but she seemed to be moving fine, basically unhurt. Her arm and leg muscles bulged. Were all female cosmonauts cut? "Guess you bounce well."

Vivian herself wasn't looking anywhere near that good. Large areas of her skin looked either pasty-white or abraded red, and there were burn marks around her shoulders, elbows, knees, and wrists. Her hands were a shade of white she'd never seen before on her own body. But her fingers moved fine, apparently not frostbitten.

Well. The sooner she covered all this mess up, the better.

Katya handed her a jumpsuit, and Vivian swung her legs off the bed. "So, that wasn't awkward at all, right?"

"What?"

"That whole Warming Vivian activity. With us stripped down to our underoos."

Katya did not blink. "We are crew."

"Well, sure."

"And we needed you to live," Katya said.

"Okay. But anyway, thank you so goddamn much for saving my life."

"You say, 'No problem,' I think?"

"No problem. Sure."

Okhotina looked at her. "Earlier you said, Peter."

"Peter who?"

"When you were coming awake, and we were ... on the bed, you said 'Peter.'"

"Did I?" *Out loud? Crap.*

Okhotina nodded. "Peter Sandoval, I think. Interesting."

"And a topic for another day. Since we get comms back in five and I'm still, well, undressed."

Katya grinned. "Very well."


"LGS-1, Copernicus, do you copy?"

Ryan "Starman" Jones, one of the founders of Hadley Base and now the commander of the US side of Zvezda-Copernicus. Vivian ran her fingers through her hair, flipped the comms on. "Starman, Viv. Hey, you missed all the fun."

"I'm here if you need me," Gisemba said. "But busy." She could hear him setting switches, muttering something on the other loop to Vasquez.

From Mission Control, Ellis Mayer overrode them all. "LGS-1, Houston. Report."

"Well, I'm alive," she said. "And okay. Mostly."

"Oh, thank God ..." Vivian heard a soft thump. Ellis had likely just banged his fist against the console in Mission Control in tension relief. "And the others?"

"The attack is over," she said. "No deaths on our side, just the two seriously injured: Dobbs and Lakontsev. The rest of us just have bruises, bangs, and burns, but are still mobile. At least six hostiles dead. Situation is stable."

"And your transport?" Starman asked.

"The MOLAB crashed into a burning Lunokhod and got bounced around pretty good aside from that. We're still checking, but as yet we see no signs that it was compromised. Those things are built tough. Right, Feye?"

"Right," said Gisemba. "Looks sound as a bell, pressure hasn't wavered. Everything reads nominal so far, but we haven't run all the checks yet. Had my hands full."

"Your rover?"

Gisemba said: "Got flipped over and rolled. Looks like a wreck. And the two men who were underneath it are still out on surface. Only one is conscious."

"Okay, got it," Ellis said. Even over the loop, Vivian could hear him scribbling notes. "Let's divide and conquer. From here in Houston, we'll bring the medics onto the B loop with Gisemba and Vasquez, work with the injured, and deal with the rover situation. Starman, Viv: you guys talk medevac, security, whatever, next steps here on A loop. All right?"

"Sure, roger that," said Starman, and Ellis and Feye clicked out.

*Security, hmm.* "Starman, still there?"

"Here."

"We told our Air Force friends in orbit about the attack right away, yes?"

"Yes, that's a roger." Starman at Zvezda-Copernicus, or Mission Control in Houston, would have done so immediately, of course. LGS-1's ordnance notwithstanding, NASA was still nominally a non-military enterprise.

"Any intel back from them yet?"

"Not as yet. It would be pretty fluky if they'd been right in position, especially at your latitude."

And even flukier if they could have got and processed the data and communicated it back to NASA, all in the last half hour. "Worth a try."

The USAF now had two Manned Orbiting Laboratories in lunar orbit. Vivian knew that Lunar MOL-A was in a 30-degree inclination orbit, and that MOL-B's inclination was much higher. But she didn't know what altitude they flew at, and so what their orbital periods might be, and how often they could scrutinize any particular part of the surface. None of them did. The MOLs ran quiet; they weren't part of the NAVSTAR network and rarely communicated with the NASA teams directly. That was kind of the point. And anyway, they likely had powerful boosters attached so that they could tweak those orbits at will and make them even less predictable.

With no atmosphere to contend with, and even if they were in higher orbits than they were around Earth, their DORIAN optics would be almost overkill. And they surely took data at such high rates that it was impossible to telemeter it all back to Earth on S-band even if they'd broadcasted around the clock. They had to be ferrying film back to Earth regularly, which meant that if one of the USAF operators didn't see it with their own eyes in real time, it might be days or weeks before they got hard intel on a particular area. And their current deep-southerly location would make that even worse, of course.

"And you never intercepted any radio chatter from the hostiles the whole time?"

"No. Vivian, listen: you have medevacs coming."

Okhotina had brought Vivian her spare suit. Vivian set about donning it. It was a good job that she had plenty of practice by now with Soviet suits. "Grand. How long?"

"Still working that. Your rover is scrap metal, confirm?"

"Chassis broken like a twig. I'd be stunned if it could be saved."

"Okay. We'll manifest you another. The bike?"

"That's fine. Undamaged, as far as I know. Though I did bash it around a bit." Vivian paused. "Starman. You're saying we're going on, after *that*?"

"Sure. You thought you were scrubbed?"

"I'm down two men."

"You'll make it work." Starman's turn to pause. "Do you want to terminate?"

"Well, no." She swallowed. "But Starman, if the Soviets are trying to kill me and my crew … again, then maybe that was just the first attempt. There might be more coming. The Soviets don't tend to give up after getting bloody noses. They just come back harder and stronger. And I can't put my crew at risk again like that."

"I hear you. And we're working on that. But even if you did want to terminate, it would take more resources than we have available to pull you out anyway."

Vivian thought about that a moment. "Huh. Okay."

"It'll take two craft just to reprovision you and take your wounded out. It would take several more to ferry you and all your stuff out of there. And you'd have to leave the MOLAB behind. Abandoning it

49

in place? Maybe that's exactly what your attackers wanted. And that would be a loss in matériel that we can't afford. Also, your mission. Your circumnavigation of the Moon is another US first."

"Mostly US."

"US-led. US glory. An achievement we're not ready to give up on just yet. But the main reason is the same as always: the US doesn't get chased off the lunar surface, or out of cislunar space, by its enemies. Ever. Right?"

"Except when its enemies have nukes."

Long silence. Eventually, Starman said, "Well, okay, yeah."

Hadley Base. *Vivian, you moron.* Abandoning Hadley had to have hurt Starman, hurt him really bad. "Sorry. That time was different. Please disregard."

"Right, and since I'm not seeing any nukes around here ..."

"Sorry."

He took a breath. "Anyway, even if we went ahead with a mission abort it would take us days to work an extraction plan. And unless we destroy it, which would be dumb, someone would have to drive your MOLAB back here to US-Copernicus anyway. So that someone might as well be you, right?"

"Uh, sure."

"The folks on the ground—NASA and the Department of Defense—are keen for you to continue." She heard paper rustling. "For what it's worth, they're thinking your attackers wanted you to surrender rather than die. Like they didn't really want *you* at all. They wanted your gear. The MOLAB, in particular."

It really did look that way. Otherwise, they'd already be dead. And also, that had been what the hostiles' recorded message had said.

Then again, one of them had shot Vivian in the back .... But then *again*, Vivian had blown away two of his—or her—people, and they'd just seen four of the others die. The shooter's priorities might well have changed at short notice.

"Okay," Vivian said. "Okay. So, we killed six of them. Plus, they had the sniper we never laid eyes on, who likely survived. Maybe they had other surviving crew. Not enough to carry on the attack, but enough to get back to their main vehicle and bug out with it. Or at least hide it somewhere we're not going to find it in a hurry."

"Sure," he said a little impatiently. "Where are you going with this?"

"Well, if they'd had double the number of people they'd likely have continued their attack. And as we know, it's hard to get more than six people anywhere on the Moon without quite a bit of support and expense. I'm basically trying to talk myself into believing we won't get attacked again, or at least not soon." She glanced up at Okhotina, who was now fully dressed in her own suit and handing her a helmet. Vivian gave her a quick nod and smile. "Starman, it's going to really piss me off if the Soviets were attacking their own cosmonauts."

"If? We've been here before, Viv. The Soviets are very willing to off their own people if they're seen to be helping the US, sympathizing with the US, fraternizing, whatever …. And even without that, they'll accept quite a bit of collateral damage. We saw lots of incidences of Soviets dying by Soviet so-called-friendly fire in 'Nam. Casualties are acceptable if the mission succeeds."

Vivian thought of Okhotina's skin against hers. *Fraternizing.* "Except that this is a joint venture. We have an agreement with the Soviets. Cooperating with us is their *job.*"

He sighed. "Viv, I don't get this any more than you do. And I've got to go."

"Sure. We're almost suited up anyway. We need to get out there."

"Roger that. I'll get back to you with medevac details for your crew in our next contact, in a half hour or so. We're moving, but still working the flight math. Yeah?"

"Roger. And, thanks, man. I'll buy you a drink real soon."

"Okay, cool. Copernicus out."

Vivian and Katya looked at each other.

"Phew," Vivian said. "Uh, gloves, I guess?"

Okhotina studied her face. "Perhaps sit for just one more moment?"

"… All right." Even that conversation had taken a lot out of Vivian. And now she had to go outside and do real work again?

She sat and focused on evening out her breathing. She wasn't shivering any more, not with warm water already flowing through the LCG under her suit. And she wasn't exactly shaking any more, either.

But she still wasn't quite on top of her game. Which was hardly surprising.

For two of her crew, this voyage would soon be over. But at least they were still alive.

Okhotina was holding her hand. Vivian hadn't even noticed.

Fraternizing. *Maybe time to nip this in the bud. Whatever this is, and even if there is a "this."*

Vivian took her hand back. "Okay. I'm fine now. Glove me."

As Vivian stepped down from the Pod, back onto the lunar surface, she had to work even harder to control her breathing. She glanced instinctively at her air pressure and oxygen supply, but they were all nominal. It was her problem, not the suit's.

Now, the Moon felt more dangerous.

Of course, she'd always known intellectually that it was dangerous. That a moment of carelessness could kill her. But, right now, Vivian Carter was distinctly leery about even being outside the Pod.

*Maybe I've outstayed my welcome on this rock.*

*Focus, damn it.*

Two hundred yards away, the MOLAB was parked next to the canyon edge, next to two supine astronaut forms. Vasquez had hauled the rover off them and away; it was right-side-up now but bent out of all shape, one of its wheels stuck up into the air. That rover wasn't going anywhere ever again—at least, not under its own power.

She tuned into B Loop. "Hey, guys. Bill? How are you doing?"

"Oh, I'm fine," said Dobbs. "Rattled, though. Took a big blow to the old noggin."

Vivian frowned. She knew about the cut over his eye, but …. "How big a blow, exactly?"

"Hard enough to see stars during daytime. That's how I cut myself. But I'm okay. Didn't lose consciousness. I don't think I'm concussed. Do I sound concussed?"

"You sound like you always do. So, y'know …"

"Yeah, so either I'm always concussed, or I'm fine."

"You can feel everything? All your limbs, your fingers and toes?"

"Yes, of course."

"Just checking. And you told the Houston medics all this?"

"I did. They were very thorough. Oh my God, were they thorough."

"Did they seem concerned?"

"They're doctors. It's their job to be concerned."

Vasquez broke in. "They think he might have hypoxia. I'm checking into it."

"Except my oxygen flow is just fine." Dobbs sounded a bit ticked off. Apparently this wasn't the first time he'd been around this conversational cycle. At least he was remembering *that* part.

"They also said maybe it was hypoglycemia, low blood sugar." That was Gisemba, from inside the MOLAB.

None of this sounded fabulous. "What is *it*?" she demanded. "What's the cause for concern?"

"As I'm sure you've noticed … he's repeating himself a lot," Vasquez said, the worry clear in his voice. "Occasionally confused. He swings in and out."

"Oh, for the love of God," Dobbs said. "You fuss worse than Mission Control. I just got banged around a bit, is all. The worst part is my eye. Blood's starting to dry now, and it feels like crap. Can we go in?"

Vivian looked at Vasquez. "Well, can he?"

"Yes. Now they've talked to him, Houston wants us to get him into the MOLAB and stripped out of the suit ready for the medic."

"And Andrei?"

"He's still unconscious, but his vital signs look okay. As long as he remains stable, he's to stay out here until help arrives."

"You're kidding."

"The Soviet medics don't want to risk us damaging him any more than he is already. But yes, let's get Bill in."

"Hang on. Gisemba, report. How's the MOLAB checking out?"

"Good. Everything's coming up either green and good to go, or orange and tweakable. No showstoppers. Stand by one." As they watched, the MOLAB wheels engaged and their prime vehicle trundled forward ten feet, weaving left and right, and then braked hard. "Traction nominal. Steering is responsive. Brakes work. All motor systems look green. ECS is fine, airlock is fine. But the galley is a hot mess."

"That's not unusual."

"Roger that. Whee." He exhaled loudly. "So, yeah. It's safe to bring Dobbs in."

"Okay, on our way."

After what felt like forever, Starman came back onto Loop A. "Be informed that a Soviet lander will be arriving at your location in ten minutes or less. It's a friendly, one of Zvezda's. Cleared with us. It's the first part of your rescue medevac. So, uh, don't shoot it down, you hear?"

"The *Soviets* are coming to rescue us?"

"Vivian, one of your Soviets got badly injured. You think they trust us to look after him? The incoming LEK will airlift Lakontsev to Zvezda. A LM from Daedalus Base will arrive five minutes later for Dobbs."

"Uh, okay, sure. No, wait, come back: that means the Soviets are blaming *us* for the attack?" Okhotina looked over at her, impassively.

"Vivian, the Zvezda Soviets and Moscow Mission Control are both swearing up and down and sideways that your attackers weren't their people. That they know nothing about it. And frankly, they're goddamned prickly about it."

"They think *we* attacked *ourselves*? That US forces attacked a US-led geological survey? What are they smoking?"

"And we think Soviets attacked a mission with a Soviet component. Sauce for the gander?"

"No, not sauce for the gander, not any sauce. Insanity is what *that* is."

"Unfortunately, on the mission recordings we were sent, one of your guys said on open channel that they looked like Night Corps. The Soviets have heard those recordings too. And you yourself said 'Is that an Apollo suit?' loud and clear."

"God's sake, Starman …. Vasquez just asked a *question*. And they *weren't* like Night Corps suits. Vasquez just said that because some of their suits looked armored like Peter's people, and …" Vivian took a deep breath. "If the Soviets are seriously alleging that this was a false flag operation, they're full of crap."

She turned to Okhotina, intending to say "No offense" or something, but Katya was now deep in conversation on a different loop.

"Vivian, take a breath. Feelings are running high. Leave all that for later. For now, focus on medevacing the wounded out. And listen: a couple of soldiers from each ship will be staying with you. Two US, two Soviet, to guard you the rest of the way back to Zvezda."

"What? Absolutely not. No freaking way."

Starman ignored her. "And before y'all get on the road again, that combined squad will scour the area to make sure there's no residual threat and collect up some of the wreckage from the hostiles you shot down for forensics. Maybe the bodies, if they can handle the weight. If they get it all done in time, the contingency LMs will airlift as much of that material out as they can. If not, you'll need to make room for it in your sample chest."

"Good job I blew their crazy flyer into teeny tiny pieces, then."

"Vivian, the Soviets are treating this as just as big an emergency as we are."

"And you believe them?"

"I don't know." He paused. "It's not my job to believe them, or not believe them. It's my job to cooperate with them."

"Cooperate. Shit."

"Vivian. I myself do have sufficient reason *not* to trust Soviets, if you recall?"

"… Yeah. I do recall that."

"So it was a hard sell. But, yes, I believe *maybe* these particular Soviets are sincere? But either way, that doesn't matter for now. I have my orders."

How long would they still have comms? Vivian didn't know and hurried back to the main point. "Starman, even if the incoming folks are all boy scouts, we can't support four new people, replacing two. We may have the berths, technically, but not the food and water, and likely not the air."

"No worries. They'll bring their own supplies. Bikes for patrolling. Both teams will bring their own inflatable habs. You'll need to carry their habs when they're not in use, but they weigh almost nothing. They'll need a power cable when you're stopped, and you'll need to let them in to shower and restock occasionally. Might even be good politics to eat a meal or two with them. You'll be one team for the next two weeks, after all. Okay?"

"But still …." She looked at Katya, the one Soviet she knew she could trust. But even then …

"Vivian. This is the deal. I don't have veto power over it. Neither do you."

"Shit." Vivian took a breath, aware that she was likely overreacting to just about everything at this point. Wasn't it better to have more firepower on their side? Better protection? Of course it was. But … Soviets? "Copy that. But I'm not happy about it."

"You don't need to be."

Well, that was blunt.

"Cool," she said. "Roger that, US-Copernicus, good buddy."

"Vivian …"

"Work to do. Mission clock's a-ticking. Talk more later." Vivian cut the link.

# CHAPTER 5

## Lunar South Pole: Vivian Carter
## January 23, 1983

**BESIDE** her, Katya had been holding her own conversation, and from her gesturing she seemed to be arguing just as hard as Vivian was. Now she raised a hand to the instrument panel on her chest and switched back to the LGS-1 loop. "A Soviet lander will arrive in minutes. Friendly."

"Yeah, I just got that memo too."

They scanned the sky, and soon caught sight of the harsh red glow of its rocket motor.

"Sure, glad they gave us the good old heads-up," Vivian muttered.

Katya's smile was a thin line, with little humor. "You would have shot at it, had they not?"

*Tempting.* "Maybe not straight away. But I'd certainly have made sure I had a weapon handy."

"As would I." Okhotina patted her own right side, and it was only now that Vivian saw the Soviet had her Uzi looped over her shoulder again.

Down came the LEK, at quite a rate. Soviet pilots came into final approach and crunched down onto the regolith much faster than the more cautious and measured NASA approach of hovering and assessment. When the LEK's pads hit surface, its landing gear flexed to a scary degree.

Its final landing point was only sixty feet away from the MOLAB, which seemed a bit close to Vivian. But Katya did not flinch, so Vivian held her position too.

Soviet LEKs were just plain ugly. The froglike bulbous cabins of both the LEK Lander and the Soyuz just struck Vivian wrong. Lunar spacecraft should be angular, not curvy, and to her eye the Soviet landers were otherwise bad copies of the US Lunar Module. The LEK, *Lunniy Exspeditionniy Korabl*, "lunar expeditionary craft," was a strange, bastardized ship.

Then again, some people claimed that the Apollo LMs were unsightly. They were, of course, wrong. LMs were beautiful.

"There are your Americans." Katya was pointing back over her shoulder, and Vivian dutifully turned to look at the LM plume in the high distance. "I will tell my people to stay aboard their craft until after your Americans land."

"Likely a good idea. Safety is our number one priority."

Katya's brow crinkled. "It is?"

"On good days."

Katya just shook her head. Vivian grinned. "Okay, fine, that's aspirational rather than realistic. At least in our case."

The second incoming ship was already recognizable as a LM. Odd not to know who was piloting it. But it made a textbook and slightly flashy landing, curtseying onto the surface twenty feet from the LEK and fifty from the MOLAB. Someone had a point to make about precision flying, emergency medevac notwithstanding.

Vivian had never before seen a Soviet lander on the lunar surface right next to a US Lunar Module. Likely, no one had. At both Zvezda-Copernicus and Daedalus, the American and Soviet craft parked well apart, on opposite sides of the bases. At any other time, this might have been a Kodak moment.

Now both ships were opening up hatches, their crews disembarking. As they did so, Vivian studied the two craft with professional interest. The NASA machine was one of the newer heavy-lift LMs. These came in two flavors: the crewed LM, of which this was one, and an uncrewed orbit-to-surface-to-orbit cargo vessel.

Additionally, this one was rigged up as a "Contingency LM." Part ambulance, part medevac, with a maximum crew of four. Without the availability of this type of LM as an emergency response vehicle,

Vivian's proposed LGS-1 route across the lunar poles would likely have been deemed too risky.

When an Apollo LM landed fully loaded from orbit, it generally needed to be refueled on the ground before it could take off again using its descent stage. If you didn't get a tank refill, your only option was to leave that bottom half behind and take off in the ascent stage. But the Contingency LM wasn't fully loaded, and its payload was stripped to the bare minimum, even more brutally than for normal LMs. Lots of mass margin. In addition, they had a drain valve so that the ascent stage fuel could be decanted downward into the descent stage tanks as needed. This had its own risks: emptying your ascent stage tanks meant that you'd given up your backup if the descent-stage rocket motor failed. No dump-and-fly option. But hey, contingencies were contingencies.

Naturally the Soviets had then developed their own version, although it was neither as high-powered nor as heavy-lift. Their contingency LEKs could still carry only three crew.

The Apollo LM was to leave two Night Corps soldiers and their bikes, supplies, and inflatables, plus a new rover for LGS-1, and take the injured Dobbs back to Daedalus for treatment. The Soviet rescue LEK would also leave two soldiers and their gear. Then, the lone Soviet pilot would take off, bearing their injured cosmonaut, Lakontsev, to safety.

The US soldiers wore the full Night Corps exosuits. The Soviet cosmonaut guards, evidently a man and a woman, were not so heavily armored, though they were packing some serious heat: the now-ubiquitous grenade launchers, plus an Uzi each.

Just seeing Soviets so close by, idly toting semiautomatic rifles, made Vivian's skin itch. Guarded by Soviets, after having been presumably attacked by Soviets, and also … having been defended, and her life saved, by a Soviet.

The Moon was getting a lot more complicated, and Vivian didn't like it.

The four soldiers convened, clearly talking on their own loop—a frequency no one had bothered to tell Vivian. Then one American and one Soviet mounted their bikes and headed out in opposite directions to secure the perimeter, while the other pair joined up to scale the scree up to the ridge.

Like they'd been working together all their lives. Vivian was both impressed and a tiny bit intimidated.

By now the next two had descended the ladders. Neither wore armored suits or bore weapons, and they moved less like military and more like a regular astronaut and cosmonaut. Each carried a metal box, presumably a medkit. They came over to Vivian and Katya.

"Hi," she said to the NASA astro. "Vivian Carter. Despite the Soviet suit."

"Hi. Doug Greenberg. Sometimes called Doctor Doug. Dobbs is inside the MOLAB?"

"Sure is. Right this way."

He held up a hand. "No worries, Captain. I've got this. I'm familiar with MOLABs. You should stay here and liaise with the tactical force."

"Okay, will do."

Doctor Doug nodded and loped toward the MOLAB airlock.

The last man out of the Contingency LM again wore the sinister hulking black suit of Night Corps, its weight giving him more of a stride than a lope. He'd been scanning the horizon, watching his people, waiting for her to talk to the medic.

God help her, the guy saluted her. "Good afternoon, ma'am."

"Good afternoon. Captain Vivian Carter, Navy and NASA."

"Yes, ma'am." No names, no pack drill. Definitely Night Corps. "Understand you've had yourself a little difficulty hereabouts."

His tone bugged her. "Nothing we couldn't handle, as it happens."

Even through his suit, his demeanor read *Uh-huh.* He turned away, scanned the skies, glanced up the ridge, scanned the horizon again.

"And you are?" she prompted.

He turned to look at her. "You can call me Alpha."

Vivian's eyebrows raised. "Seriously? You're the alpha male?"

"Just my code name, ma'am." He pointed to the US soldier biking the perimeter. "Bravo." Up to the ridge. "Charlie. And Delta is the call sign for Doug the medic."

"Understood." This was going great. "I was told the US and USSR were providing just two guards each."

"That's correct. Charlie is the pilot. He'll return with Delta and your man-down. Myself and Bravo will provide your escort."

*Man-down. Nice.* "Very well, Mr. Alpha. Carry on."

Silence for a few moments. "Roger that, ma'am."

His pause had lasted long enough to convey his meaning. *Ma'am, I do not take my orders from you.* Without him needing to actually say it out loud.

"Oh." He turned back briefly. "And we've brought you a new suit. So you don't need to keep that Russkie unit on for a moment longer than you need to."

His tone was clearly disapproving. "Wasn't exactly my choice. Did no one brief you?"

"I was fully briefed, ma'am." He turned away again.

"Okay. Thanks. And the suit is where?"

He indicated the Contingency LM. "Bay Two. That's external, numbering around from the ladder."

"Yes, Mr. Alpha, I do know where to find Bay Two on a LM."

"Of course, ma'am. Then you'll have no trouble finding your new rover in Bay One."

"Indeed. And you're staying with us for the rest of the trip? Swell."

"Affirmative, ma'am," said the suit of black space armor.

This was ridiculous. "Hey, Night Corps, I'm standing right here in front of you. You can just talk to me like we're people, if you want."

Alpha paused, nodded, and lifted his visor. It was too dark in his helmet for her to see much of his face, but at least she could see he *had* a face. "Sorry, ma'am. Just keeping this professional. But me and Bravo and our Soviet partners, we'll need to be out there on terrain just as much as we can be. Watching out for y'all. And my suit allows for efficient and comfortable cycling of waste. I won't need to recharge as often as the rest of y'all. I can sleep outside, come in to purge and recharge maybe one hour out of twenty-four."

"Dang. Tough guy. No wonder they call you Alpha."

"Yes, ma'am." He glanced over to where the Soviet medic and Ok-hotina were bending over Lakontsev. "Now if you'll forgive me, I'll assist our Commie friends with their wounded."

"Sure," she said. "Dismissed."

Alpha gave her a look that might have been amused and might not. Flipped his visor closed again and stepped away.

Vivian found herself standing alone on the lunar surface, the only one who wasn't actively doing something. And by now she was ready to sit down again.

She might as well go grab her new suit, then climb aboard the MOLAB and see how it was going with Dobbs.

"Their spacesuits maintained integrity but couldn't save them from injuries due to crushing or blunt force trauma. And their bodies got tossed around inside those suits, and then crunched into the ground."

"Indeed." Vivian had been tossed around inside her own suit too, and also crunched into the ground. "I doubt any of us would be here right now if our suits weren't damned tough."

"Right. Dobbs has an acute subdural hematoma caused by a rapid acceleration and then deceleration of his head inside the helmet." Greenberg, aka Doctor Doug, peered at her to see if she understood. Vivian just nodded as if she did. "Such a shock can cause the veins to tear, in between his skull and the dura mater—that's the tissue covering the brain. As blood starts to accumulate, the neurological symptoms begin, which are just what we're seeing—a gradually worsening headache, slurring, nausea, confusion."

"He seemed better earlier," Vivian objected. "At least for a while. He was the lucid one, talking to us, helping Andrei ..."

"Yes, that happens. Most subdural hematomas don't progress rapidly. They can develop over minutes to hours. But they can be fatal if untreated. We'll likely need to surgically evacuate the blood. But unless he dramatically worsens while we're prepping him for flight, that can wait till we get him back to Daedalus."

Vasquez paled. "You're going to *trepan* him?"

"Not exactly. It's a little more sophisticated than that. But, yes, we'll likely be cutting into his skull in what's called a burr hole procedure."

"Shit." Vasquez turned away. "I thought he was going to be okay."

"And he probably will be. We'll work on it. Take it easy, man, we've done this before."

"On the Moon?"

"Well, no. But that doesn't make much difference. Being in zero G would complicate this, but blood still drains downward on the Moon."

Vivian swallowed. "Okay. Got it. What about Andrei Lakontsev?"

"I haven't looked at him myself, but from what I'm hearing from my Soviet colleague, it seems clear he has a distal femur fracture.

Everything is consistent with that. Severe pain, but likely only slow blood loss. Getting him out of the suit will be rough, especially in a space as small as that LEK, but after that it should be straightforward for them to splint his leg, airlift him back to Zvezda, and keep him under observation in case there's something else going on that we haven't seen yet. He was likely knocked up and bruised quite a bit as well."

"Yeah."

"Can't rule out other problems, though. Not without seeing him. But I'm sure the Soviets will keep you informed."

"Understood. Thanks."

Greenberg looked at his watch. "Okay, we'd better get this guy boxed up and out of here."

Vivian shook her head. "Oh boy."


The PTM, Patient Transfer Module, was a box eight feet by three feet by three feet. Despite the sleek aluminum sheen of its exterior and its tastefully rounded corners, it still looked alarmingly like a coffin. If coffins had a window at face-level.

The NASA astronauts had all trained with them on the ground. They'd each been packed away into one for a half-hour period during that training, to familiarize themselves with the instrument layout inside, and to get accustomed to the feeling of being almost totally immobilized.

When Vivian had done that training, she'd volunteered for the full experience, so they'd even connected up all the hoses, fired up the rudimentary life support systems, and loaded her into a vacuum chamber for an hour.

It had been daunting. For most men, and some women, the PTM interior was too cramped to bend their knees or reach to scratch much of their bodies. Turning over was out of the question. You could slide your hand up to your face, which was useful so that you could drink water, wipe your eyes or nose or mouth. At neck level was a small instrument panel you could use to toggle the radio, adjust the heater settings and fan strength inside the PTM, and that was it for your personal autonomy. If you were conscious at the time, of course. On the two previous occasions a PTM had been used in a real emergency, its occupants had been sedated and unconscious.

Dobbs watched in bemusement as Doctor Doug adjusted the headrest, connected his catheter to the bags, and set dials and switches on a console Dobbs couldn't reach, in order to keep him alive while they ported him to the LM. "Guys, you do know I could have just gotten back into a suit and walked myself over there?"

"I'm afraid not." Doug grinned. "Sorry, man. You know the drill."

"Sadly, yeah." Dobbs seemed fine right now, but that could change in a literal heartbeat.

"Besides that," the medic added, patting the top of the PTM, "this way you make a great bench."

"Nice bedside manner." Vivian peered into the box. Even for a woman who'd spent a couple of weeks in an emergency inflatable pup tent in complete isolation, the PTM was very snug. "You don't get claustrophobic, Bill, right?"

"Ask me again in ten minutes."

Greenberg turned serious. "Hey, listen. If you do get wigged out, just say the word. Don't try to be a tough guy, that's not going to help. I can knock you out in two ways, remotely, by injection or gas. Simple anesthesia. And I won't even tell the medical officer back on Earth we did it. Won't end up on your record."

"A likely story."

"For real, man. These things are a rough ride."

"Well, okay. Thanks. But I'll probably be fine. I get to look out the window, after all. And I've never launched *outside* a LM."

"That sounds like fun to you?" Vivian shook her head. The PTM was too big to fit through the Lunar Module hatch. Bill would indeed be flying all the way to Daedalus strapped to the outside of the LM.

She put her hand over his. "Hey, Bill, I'm really sorry the mission ended this way for you. You did great, all around. Couldn't have asked for better."

Dobbs patted her hand, awkwardly. "Uh. Thanks."

"See you on the flip side. Take care."

"You know it."

A sudden lump appeared in her throat. She backed away, and let Doctor Doug seal Dobbs into the box.

"Sure does look a lot like a coffin," Vasquez said hollowly.

"Only in the way a gurney looks like a bier," Vivian said absently, thinking her own thoughts.

"Not helping, Commander."

Vivian pulled herself together. "Sorry. But it's not a coffin, Christian. It's looking after him." Feeling callous even as she said it, she added, "Now, we've got to focus. I need everyone's attention back to a hundred percent. Kinda right now."

Vasquez took an additional moment, then raised his head and nodded. His eyes were clear. "Sure thing. Understood, Commander."

Vivian turned to Gisemba. "So. Logistics for mission continuation and completion?"

"What?"

She couldn't help noticing that Feye looked a little shell-shocked by all this as well. Tired, worn around the eyes. Gisemba may not have been blown up, boiled, frozen, and then snuggled by a Soviet, but he was clearly showing signs of stress and fatigue.

She empathized. But they had no time. "Talk to me. We need to decide. Houston says we're going on, but it's *our* mission, our call. So how are we going to call it? Are we all okay with that? Because if not, I need to start a conversation with Houston about it, real soon."

Gisemba blinked. "We go on. I guess. If we can."

"Yeah, on that last part? Convince me. Tell me how."

"Ah." Those were the magic words. Already Vivian could see Gisemba scraping up his energy and sliding back into his logistics groove. "Okay. With two fewer people in here most of the time, we could dial back our energy usage a bit, which will provide extra for our, uh, new friends. But with only four of us on-mission we might need to go to longer shifts. And we won't be able to have two people in the cab at all times. We'll need to trust Okhotina to drive the bus solo." He cocked an eye at Vivian. "You okay with that?"

Visions of Katya strapped to the solar panels atop the Pod, firing her illicit Uzi at what was almost certainly her own people. "Uh, yeah. I think Kat may have earned our trust."

"Will we need to run that past NASA?"

Vivian waved it away. "All that stuff about never leaving the Soviets unmonitored was just to keep HQ happy during the planning. I don't think we're worried about tech transfer at this point, at least not MOLAB tech. Or Kat's loyalty to the mission."

"Okay. You're the boss. I just don't want us to get in trouble over that."

Vivian thought about it a little longer. "You know, if we're moving to solo driving shifts, we should set up the camera in the cab anyway, so Mission Control can keep an eye on us, monitor us for anomalies so no one falls asleep at the wheel, or screws up in any of twenty other ways. And that means *all* of us. Kat will know she's being watched, but we all will be. But, yeah, we'll need all four of us to drive to get this shit done."

"Okay." Gisemba had already moved on. "Supplies won't be a problem. We'll have more than enough. But we'll still have too much work to do between the four of us. We'll need to cut back on rock sampling and the other science stops."

*Over my dead body.* Vivian shivered. *Yeah, that's right—it might well have been.* "Maybe. We'll see as we go."

"They brought us a new rover, but whether we even need it or not now, I'm not sure. We still have the bike."

"Probably good to have both. The rover is more stable on bad terrain. And … well, I don't really want to see that bike again any time soon."

Gisemba studied her for a few moments, then went on. "I'll need to think more about how the shifts work and all. Give me a few hours. But I don't see any showstoppers. I'm okay to continue."

"Christian?"

He grunted, then said, "Also okay to continue."

Vivian tried to read his expression. "You're sure about that?"

"I am. Well … okay, sure, I'm worried about Bill, but I don't want to go back to Daedalus with him and then fly out. I want to finish this. I want to stay."

"Okay. Thanks."

"How about Katya?" Gisemba said.

Okhotina was still helping with Andrei Lakontsev, over at the Soviet LEK. "She'll want to go on," Vivian said. "Guaranteed."

"Will her bosses let her?"

Vivian blinked. That hadn't occurred to her. "I guess we'll need to confirm that. But if they were to pull her out … that would suck."

"They'd hardly be giving us two Soviet soldiers if they were planning on yanking out their remaining Soviet crew member," Vasquez said.

"Oh," Vivian said, blinking. "Right."

Gisemba nodded. "Then we can do this. It's only another two weeks. We have what we need. It'll be hard, but nothing we can't handle."

Vivian nodded. "That's all I needed to hear. So what should we be doing first?"

"I've been focused on the MOLAB engines and physical integrity, but there's lots of systems I haven't got to yet. We should doublecheck everything for damage: from the crash, from shrapnel, from my crazy stunt driving, anything. And soon as we can, we should drive over and hitch the Pod back on, and check that out too. I did bang it into a cliff face."

"Okay," Vivian said. "And we need to unload our new rover. Oh, and check the old LRV, I guess. Pull everything worth keeping off it. Cameras, tools, load them onto the new rover, or the trailer. Wow."

*Wow* was right. That was a lot. Vivian rubbed her temples, gave a big sigh. "Well, I guess we'd better get on with it then."

"No rest for the wicked," Vasquez said.

Vivian could only muster half a grin for that.

# 6

## South Pole to Zvezda: Vivian Carter
## January 23–24, 1983

"**OKAY.** Our new LRV is deployed and loaded onto the flatbed." Vivian pulled off her helmet and sagged backward onto the small bench by the airlock to breathe for a moment. "Our guard force will be leading the way for the first hundred miles or so, till we're sure we're not going to discover any more mines."

Behind Vivian, Vasquez cycled himself through the airlock, walked in, and started getting out of his suit. Vivian didn't have the energy for that just yet.

Gisemba poked his head out from the MOLAB cab. "Cool. Rather them than me. So what did they find?"

"Boot tracks going up and down the far side of the ridge."

"And down?" Okhotina shook her head. "A pity." Because that meant that at least one person, presumably the shooter, had survived and gotten away.

"Tire tracks, or wheel tracks, also in two directions. Fairly large rover, by the looks. The tracks go a couple hundred feet, then ... poof."

"Poof, what?"

"They disappear," said Vasquez.

"Yeah." Vivian had her gloves off now, began unzipping. "No sign of a landing or takeoff. Major Alpha doesn't believe they were taken

67

off-surface by LEK, or whatever. They'd be too heavy. He thinks all this indicates they have a large ground transport with some mechanism for covering its own tracks. And we sure never saw anything take off, afterward. Other than that, the Night Corps guys have collected up a couple large bags of metal shards, bits of electronics and burnt fabric, and they're pretty much done." She looked up at Gisemba. "Did you get any chance to think more about logistics?"

"I did." Gisemba came all the way into the main cabin, took a seat at the small table in the tiny galley area. "I'm assuming we still only have the four of us to drive this bus?"

"Right," Vivian said. "I did ask whether our new soldier friends might be interested in taking a turn occasionally. A respite indoors, out of suits, during calm areas like mares. No dice. All they'll do is scout and guard. I even offered them the Pod for occasional sleep breaks. They turned that down too. I think they're having some kind of weird competition among themselves about how little time they can spend in here showering or refreshing or being human."

It hadn't surprised her. The soldiers' orders were to keep a steady guarding presence outside for the rest of the trip, and Major Alpha, for one, wasn't a guy to go easy on his orders.

Gisemba grimaced. "Okay, in that case, I'll suggest we switch down to two shifts, twelve hours on, twelve off. Stagger them for over-laps. It'll mean fewer meals all together, but we can't have everything. A twelve-hour cycle gives each of us a better chance of eight hours sleep during our 'down' shift. And we'll need our sleep because this endgame is going to be intense."

He sighed. "Ideally no one would drive alone, but with one or more of us sleeping or eating or doing maintenance, one or two outside for guiding and sampling …" He tailed off. They could all do that math.

"As for the sampling, we can likely still do some, just so long as we can stay on schedule. If we fall behind, we'll need to start skipping sites."

Gisemba looked at Vivian and Vasquez, who could be relied upon to complain about any compromises to their science mission, and they both started speaking at once.

Vivian deferred to Christian, since he was the actual PhD geolo-gist. He said: "We'll rank the remaining sites, overall and day by day. Maximize our bases covered. If time gets short, we'll skip the lower priority areas. But we need to hit the prime sites and keep a good cadence on the routine sampling if we're to do a good job of mapping mineral distribution and rates of change of ..."

Gisemba raised a hand. "Okay, sure, I get it. That's your area, to figure out how to juggle it. Knock yourselves out. But our top-level requirement is to stay on a schedule that gets us to Zvezda with six hours to spare before nightfall." He paused, looking surprised Vivian hadn't objected. "Maybe when we're closer we can cut that margin, whatever. You're the boss. These are just my recommendations. But I'd certainly advise we allow contingency time for breakdowns, injuries ... well, you know: contingencies."

"Fair enough," Vivian said. "We should finish this in style and not cause anyone any headaches. But there won't be many key sites in the final few days anyway because, that close to Zvezda, they'll already have been studied. Once we finish up at Tycho Crater and get off the highlands onto Mare Nubium we can crank out the miles and sprint for home. A couple representative basalts from Nubium and Mare Cogitum and we're done. Apollo 14 did the Fra Mauro highlands well enough, and Apollo 12 got the ..." Vivian realized they were all waiting patiently for her to shut up. "You get the idea."

"I do." Gisemba jotted down notes.

Vivian looked at Vasquez. "Anyway, guess we're taking another look at the sampling schedule, figuring out how to make it work with less outside coverage."

"Copy. Want me to make the first pass at that, then run it by you?"

"That would be great." Vivian was happy to have the calm, logical Vasquez back. It had been tough for her to watch him unraveling when his buddy was down, but now Dobbs was safely at Daedalus and under expert medical care, Vasquez had stepped right back up to the plate as if he'd never been gone. "As for the risks of future incursions, I'm inclined to think they're small. We're now on high alert, we're in constant contact with home, and we have four extremely well-armed troops watching over us. However: when we come up on any constrictions, tight spots, obvious choke points, those hard-ass soldiers will go in first to check for traps, ambushes, mines. Which might slow us down a bit, and means we'll need to do less scouting ahead ourselves in those difficult terrains. Unfortunately."

They all nodded. Everyone knew Vivian wanted herself and her crew to be the first to tread the new ground, the first into any new area.

Vasquez looked unhappy too. "They've been briefed about contamination protocols?"

"Yes. They promise not to vent anything, anywhere other than behind LGS-1 once we've already passed through. And we'll tell them what formations to steer clear of on a case-by-case basis."

"That's the price we pay for protection, I guess," Gisemba said.

"Okay." Vivian had finally struggled out of her suit. She hung it on its hook, looked at each of them in turn. "We okay to move on? If so, I'll alert our escort that we're ready to roll. They're all set on their end."

"Roger that," said Gisemba, and the rest of them nodded. "But all this means one of us needs to hit the sack right away, to be fresh twelve hours from now. That person gets the Pod. And another needs to begin a sleep period in six hours, sleeping here in the main cabin. So, who does what?" He cocked an eye at Vivian. "I have to point out that our glorious leader is the one who's been awake the longest right now."

"And ..." Okhotina's voice trailed off. "Well, you know."

"Yeah, I know," Vivian said. *I'm the dead-suit chick who boiled and then froze and went into shock. Whatever.* It already seemed like a long time ago. But to be honest, at this point it was likely only adrenaline that was keeping her upright. She wasn't sure she could safely handle even a few hours driving the MOLAB on top of that, and she certainly wouldn't risk going outside again until she'd rested. Meanwhile, Vasquez and Okhotina had been most of the way through their own downtimes when the battle had begun, and Gisemba had only done half a driving shift.

Plus, she was already visualizing the map and doing math. Sleeping immediately then staying on that schedule meant Vivian would be the one taking samples among the irregular highland peaks at Malapert, plus the southern reaches of the Newton crater region, expected to be a complex mixed terrain.

Her enthusiasm for her mission was starting to return.

"Sold," she said. "Pod's mine this time. Thanks."

"I will take the first suit sleep?" said Katya Okhotina. That would maximize her driving time and sampling overlap with Vivian. *Hmm.* "Four hours, then I will awaken for a shift outside. If that is all right?"

"Fine with me," said Vasquez. "I'm way too keyed up to sleep anyway."

"You got that right," said Gisemba.

Vivian studied them, noting the tiredness around their eyes. None of them were exactly fresh at this point. "Uh, wait up. Sanity check. Guys, are you really game to get back on the road right away? We could take a couple hours break, even four to eight, and just stay right here. Go nowhere and rest up, everyone just relax and take a time-out. Recharge our batteries. We've been through some crazy shit today."

"We sure have. But, nah." Gisemba shook his head. "I'd really prefer to put some miles under the wheels and get us the hell away from here. Hard part's over. And Christian and I can trade the wheel more often than usual, go easy on ourselves." His eyes twinkled. "Maybe sing some party songs to keep ourselves awake."

"Oh my God," Katya said.

"I'm kidding, princess."

Vivian nodded. "Okay, fine. Sounds good. But if you need to rest, you just stop the damn bus and rest. That's an order. Your health and our safety trump the schedule. No one needs my permission to rest when they need to. If we get too tired, we make mistakes, and we can't afford mistakes. So we rest, and then we adjust the schedule however we need to. Clear?"

"Clear as a bell, Commander."

"Okay. Then let's get to it, people. Places to go, rocks to collect, naps to take."

"Food to eat," said Vasquez.

Gisemba looked at him with a mixture of respect and frustration. "Man, you are just *always* hungry."

Vivian was too—in fact, by now she was starving—but she could heat up a tray in the Pod. She headed for the rear tunnel. "Guess that's my cue. Goodnight, all. Get on the horn if anything breaks. Otherwise, I'll see you in eight hours."

"Take ten," Gisemba said. "Twelve-hour shift clock, recall?"

"Roger that," she said. "Vivian out."


Fourteen hours later, Vivian Carter was at the wheel of the MOLAB with Katya dozing by her side. Out on surface two hundred yards ahead of them and off to the right, Vasquez was kneeling on regolith next to their new rover, drilling a core sample. Gisemba was asleep in the Pod.

Just another day on the road for Carter's Convoy. If, of course, she could ignore the soldiers. Well ahead of Vasquez, she could see Major Alpha out to the left, scouting craters, presumably to make sure nothing dangerous was about to pop out of one. An equal distance to her right the female Soviet guard, Nina, had just reappeared from behind a low rise, weaving on her bike to avoid boulders. They were a little distracting, and Vivian always enjoyed it when both of them were so far ahead or off to the side that they were no longer visible.

In the way-back, about a mile behind, Major Bravo and the other Soviet, Konstantin, would be bringing up the rear and making sure no one was speeding up behind them. Vivian wasn't sure when the guards planned to sleep, but she wasn't the boss of them. They had their own chain of command.

Speaking of command chains … she glanced at the chronometer, toggled the comms button to VOX. "Houston, LGS-1. Five o'clock and all's well."

"Copy that, LGS-1," came Ellis's voice. "Your telemetry is mostly nominal. Consistent with the anomalies previously logged, anyway. Seeing no trends."

To Vivian, the MOLAB seemed to drive just fine but perhaps needed a little more effort on cornering. Maybe dust in the wheels. Some of the status numbers were a little off true, but nothing too concerning. And best of all the ECS, Environmental Control System, numbers were steady, meaning they were maintaining usual pressure. No holes in Vivian's truck, at least none that hadn't been there the whole time.

"You're showing a higher than usual temperature in your brake-wells, but it's likely that dust thing, plus solar irradiance. And your $O_2$ is running a little rich."

"Yeah, I was leaving it like that to help keep us awake." She glanced down at Katya, who was still breathing regularly, eyes closed. "Well, me, anyway. But I'll tweak it. And we'll do a routine wheel and axle check-and-clean at our next scheduled meal stop, unless you advise it sooner."

"No, that's fine. By the way, our last location fix puts you back on schedule after your polar misadventures."

"Roger that." Vivian had already done that math for herself, based on sextant sightings she'd taken just before starting her driving shift, as well as Katya's most recent NAVSTAR fix. If there was a way of doing math twice, Vivian would always do it twice. By now her slide rule was looking distinctly well-worn.

"I need an update on my injured crew. Dobbs and Lakontsev. What's their status?"

"Hang on," Ellis said. "Let me patch Copernicus in."

A long pause, and then a third voice. "LGS-1 and Houston, here's Copernicus, come in?"

"Hi, Starman. How's tricks?"

"Tricks are good," said Starman. "And your crew news is good as well, or about as good as can be expected. Dobbs had to undergo a second medical procedure to relieve the blood pressure on his brain, or something, but he's through it and out the other side. He's stable and resting, and Doctor Doug says he should make a full recovery."

"Excellent."

"But he won't be heading home any time soon. There's no way he could endure the five or six G's of deceleration needed for a splashdown, and it's better that he stays in gravity, so they won't be shipping him off the Moon just yet."

It was a shame they'd taken Dobbs to Daedalus, on the wrong side of the Moon. It might be a long time before Vivian saw him again. "Okay. At least he's all right. How about Andrei?"

"Lakontsev is even better. I talked to him myself just a couple hours ago: his leg is in plaster, or something that passes for plaster. A cast, anyway. The Reds are already working on a couch refit for one of the LEKs so that they can get him up into orbit, and figuring out how to rejigger the Soyuz reentry module to support the leg for Earth return. He's in good spirits overall but bummed that he couldn't finish the grand tour."

"I'm sad he couldn't, too," Vivian said. "He can really reenter with a broken leg?"

"If it's supported. Our US docs agree with the Reds on that."

"Don't Soyuzes smack into the ground kind of hard when they land?"

"I guess. I'll ask."

"Okay. Hopefully they won't be too eager to get rid of him and he'll still be there when I get to Zvezda. I'd like to see him again before, well, the end."

Starman was amused. "Vivian, you're not about to die."

"From your mouth to God's ear. I meant the end of the mission. Obviously."

"Obviously."

"Any more intel on our mystery attackers?"

"LGS, Houston: not a thing," Ellis said. "The Air Force has nothing. They've confirmed that none of their orbiting assets were in place for a clear view during the excitement. They'll do a thorough scan at their next pass, to look for any residual evidence. Meanwhile, the Soviets down here continue to deny any involvement. Bit of a hornet's nest buzzing, so hey, guess it must be Tuesday. No big deal. And that's that."

"War hasn't broken out at Zvezda, then."

"Not exactly, just the usual seething discontent."

"Cool." Vivian sighed. "Okay, then. Guess we'll continue on our merry way. Thanks, guys."

"LGS, Houston. Uh, Vivian?"

After all this time, Vivian knew that tone. Ellis was bracing himself. "Hit me with it."

"NASA wants to schedule a public broadcast, real soon."

"What? Really? About …?"

"The Lunar South Pole?" he prompted.

"Oh yeah. That." Vivian put one hand up to her head, rubbed her eyes. Steered around a boulder. "That was only yesterday, wasn't it?"

"*That* was a big deal, and they want to milk it a bit. And also, it'll be a very visible poke in the eye to the folks who attacked you, to see you calm and fit and well and chatting away on TV like nothing's happened, with not a hair out of place."

"Frankly, the hair might need work." She paused. "Keeping the soldiers and all their bristling weaponry out of frame, am I right?"

"Riiiiight."

"Oooookay."

Okhotina, half-forgotten at this point in the conversation, rubbed her eyes and smiled, straightening herself in her seat.

Vivian considered Ellis's words. It was fair enough. Part of Vivian's duties, even. NASA was struggling to maintain the public appetite for lunar exploration. If the public lost interest, then so did Congress. NASA's funding was already on shaky ground: the high spending levels through the Space Race to the foundation of Hadley Base and now the Zvezda and Daedalus efforts were suffering close scrutiny.

The cool things NASA did would always resonate with some fraction of the US. But others were increasingly concerned about the state of America's inner cities, social unrest, and spiraling welfare problems, and wanted NASA's many billions to ameliorate social issues on Earth rather than supporting high jinks in space. The effects of inflation and the oil and gas shortages affected everyone. PR had been a critical part of Vivian's LGS-1 proposal, and the same number of people had helped her develop that aspect as had worked on the science plan.

So, Vivian's lunar circumnavigation was being covered by news organizations around the world. The daily broadcasts at the beginning had slackened off, mercifully, and they'd done relatively few stories from Farside for logistical reasons, but mankind's first visit to the lunar South Pole—a key milestone in their journey of discovery—did need to be marked.

"You want Katya involved as well?" Okhotina was young and photogenic, with her long dark hair, and the more people Vivian could split the chore with, the better.

Okhotina's eyes widened, and she shook her head vigorously. Vivian stuck out her tongue, then said, "Emphasizing the superpower cooperation? Might be in everyone's interests, and perhaps now even more than usual."

"Great idea," Ellis said, and Okhotina slumped back in mock despair. "Let's include Feye again too. He got good numbers last time, and he's, well …"

"Black, yes, Houston, I'm aware. Sure. But he's asleep for the next four hours."

"No problem. Maybe at the end of shift, after your meal break? That'll give us some extra time at our end to work up some of the visuals."

"Okay, can do," Vivian said. "Anything else? If not, signing off now."

"Roger that."

"Okay, good buddies. Be seein' ya both soon. LGS-1 out." She flipped the comms switch.

"Gah," Okhotina said. "Cameras again."

Vivian grinned. Katya had picked up *Gah* from her. It sounded funny with a Russian inflection. "And a good morning to you, sunshine."

Katya studied her. "How are you?"

"I'm fine. Still sore in some places, still popping the pain meds, but basically good to go. You?" This was the first time they'd been

75

alone together since the Pod, and Vivian was determined not to make it awkward.

Katya shrugged. "I am also good to go. But I hope that nobody shoots at us today."

"Well, that would be nice. But I like to keep my expectations low." Vivian glanced at her. "So, Katya, there's a military squad on the Moon that we know nothing about, that attacked us."

"Yes. Apparently."

"And, in all likelihood, well, they were your people."

Okhotina stared out of the window at the lunar landscape. "Yes."

"Well … how do you feel about that?"

"I would apologize to you, for my country but … it is not my fault. Not my idea. Not really *my* people."

"Not your fault. Agreed." Vivian paused. "But let's make sure we're on the same page here."

"Page?"

"Do you intend to honestly report what happened to your superiors?"

"Yes, of course."

"Even though you actively defended LGS-1 against the attack?" *Call a spade a spade, Vivian.* "Katya, you shot and killed some of them. That could put you into a heap of hot water."

Okhotina stretched. "A heap of hot water sounds very good to me, around now."

"Katya."

"I was on a team. My team came under attack. I do not know what else to say, other than the truth. And *my* people say the attack was by *your* people, and so that means I was shooting at your people, no?" Okhotina thought a little longer. "Vivian, you would have been ready to lie for me? To cover up the part I played in defending us?"

"I need to be straight with my chain of command. I'll tell it the way it happened to NASA or the CIA, or whoever else needs to know. But if I'm asked about it by other Soviets? I'd back up your version of the story. Sure I would."

Katya nodded. "Thank you. And is there anything you would like me to lie about, if asked by your people?"

"Not a damned thing. Um, maybe gloss over that girls' warm-up time in the Pod, if you could. That feels … private. Just say you provided medical assistance. But Katya: if you need anything, if you ever need any help, now or later, just let me know. Okay?"

"Thank you," said Okhotina. "I will. But I do not expect to need to."

"And I hope you don't."

"It is very strange, to me, the attack," Okhotina said.

"How so?"

"Because those men were not well-trained. They did not seem experienced." Okhotina glanced at Vivian, then turned her attention back to the terrain. "Even from how they held their weapons. Vivian, I have been through Army training. And I have watched men even more trained than me, the Spetsnaz men, our elite. Our attackers yesterday were certainly not Spetsnaz, far from it. They were not even good Army."

"Good to know, babe." That matched Vivian's own impressions. She thought about it a little more. "So, then: our attackers were doing something new for them? First time they'd been in a conflict? So why send them, and not the best of the best?"

"Because they were trained for something else entirely? Scientists, prospectors. Not even soldiers at all?"

"Damn. Or because they thought we'd be such a pushover that they didn't need experience to take us?"

"They had weapons and believed that we did not. And perhaps were trying to stop us, rather than destroy us, at least to start." Katya shrugged. "I do not know. But even if they had been experienced, the first time doing something is always new. A new situation, with new weapons. Especially if someone is shooting back at you. Might explain why they seemed less … experienced."

"Yeah," Vivian said. "Always something new. Or maybe they were there to make a point? Cause trouble? Not even necessarily to win?" Vivian shook her head. "Not seeing the logic behind that either, to be honest."

"Either way, they just kept coming. Even after the sniper had not been successful, and the flyer had been shot. The rover just kept coming. It was …" Katya just shook her head.

Vivian sighed. "Just hope we get some forensic evidence that's worth something, that could shed some light on it all."

"Forensic?"

"Analysis of the wreckage." *And the corpses*, Vivian thought, but didn't say out loud.

"Ah."

Silence fell. Vivian checked her course against a photograph lying on the seat on her other side, did a quick round-robin radio check-in with Vasquez and her four guards, glanced back at Katya again. "Well. Maybe time to change the subject."

Okhotina nodded and appeared to be considering. Finally, she said: "So, you are not married?"

*And with that, Super-Kat finally joins the long list of people fascinated by my marital status.* "You haven't read my file? Nope, not married. No husband."

"And yet the Americans permit you to fly to the Moon?"

"So it seems."

"Interesting. In the Rodina, all cosmonauts must be married. It is … safer that way."

Again, Vivian glanced at her in amusement. "Safer for whom?"

"Is it not?"

"So, you're married, then? What does your husband do?"

Okhotina looked surprised to have the question turned back on her. "Mine? He is also in the Army of the Soviet Union. He is a mechanical engineer."

"Nice. Not a cosmonaut, then."

"No. Two cosmonauts, married … that is not healthy, I think." She smirked. "So, then, what about Peter Sandoval?"

Vivian sighed. "Katya, all I did was say his name when I was confused, coming out of shock."

"No. I learned about you and him from some of your NASA astronauts. They like to gossip."

"Seriously?" Vivian shook her head. "Swine."

"No self-discipline." Katya grinned. "Like so many corrupt Americans. At least, that is the story I am told before I join LGS-1. Now, I think perhaps it is not so simple."

"I think it is not so simple, too. The NASA astros I know are among the most self-disciplined people I've ever met, at least when they're on a mission. Ellis Mayer? Dave Horn? Rick Norton, God rest him. Josh Rawlings. Terri Brock. Feye and Bill and Christian. Everyone.

And they're just the ones I've served with. Don't get me started on the earlier astronauts."

"And Peter Sandoval?"

*Dang, there's no distracting Katya when she's on a roll.* "Yep, he's self-disciplined as well. He's a pretty buttoned-up guy."

Katya raised her eyebrows. "Buttoned up?"

Vivian was negotiating the MOLAB around a crater rim, avoiding the edge. Now, she slowed down a bit so that she could spare more time to look sideways at Okhotina. "Listen, Kat. You're terrific, and you've been a great crewman. But I'm not really one to chat about my personal life. And even if I was, after this mission is over, your people are going to debrief you. Your KGB will want to know anything and everything you can tell them about me and the other Americans you've met—anything they might be able to use. So … maybe I won't be saying anything more about Peter Sandoval."

Katya nodded, unoffended. "Your family, then?"

"Sure." That was much safer ground. Vivian's family relationships had already been publicly analyzed in exhaustive detail by *Life* magazine. "Military parents, now divorced and living in different places. No siblings. A couple of aunts, one uncle, a niece or two. But we're spread out all over, not really close; we don't do the whole Thanksgiving-and-Christmas family thing. Too awkward. The one I'm really closest to is my Gran." She looked at Katya and forced a cheerful grin. "Fair warning, don't ever mess with my Gran. If she'd been here with us during that battle, she'd have stormed the heights and taken out the guy firing the rockets with a single blow from her rolling pin."

Okhotina's eyes widened. "And a rolling pin is, what?"

"Kitchen tool. For pastry deployment prior to baking." Even having deflected the Sandoval topic, Vivian wasn't keen to get into the details of her rather distant and tortuous relationship with her parents. "Okay, maybe it's time to talk about you a bit more."

"Me?"

"Sure. The Columbia trip was your first spaceflight?"

"Perhaps you mean Salyut-Lunik-A?"

Katya's eyes were twinkling. Vivian could tell she was being tweaked. She bumped the other woman lightly on the arm with her fist. "Exactly, the Soviet Union's historic first space station in lunar orbit. Sheesh."

"Yes, that one was my first flight into space. And now this is my third because I was in Earth orbit at a Salyut for two weeks in between."

"Salyut or Almaz?"

"Salyut. Really. Although they are mostly the same except for the equipment they carry." Okhotina shook her head. "Being in space is much easier than training for space."

"It is? How so?"

"My training was hard. Very long days. Dangerous, too. Often, I wondered whether it would all be worth it and whether I would ever fly. I almost ran away from the program, resigned out of it, more than once. I thought perhaps I might die on Earth before I ever made it into space. But then, once I finally launched, flying in space was so much better and easier than the training."

"I hear you." Vivian herself had had two extremely close calls in training, once while flying a helicopter over rugged terrain in the rain, and then soon after, trying to get the knack of that damned LLTV.

"Really, some days I only stayed in the program for the parachuting. If I had left, they would not have let me jump anymore."

Vivian raised her eyebrows. "Parachuting? You *like* that?"

"Of course. Training in parachute jumping is very important in our space program. It is a good test for controlling the emotions and good practice to prepare your mind for danger. All cosmonauts must jump. Also, if something was to go wrong with the Soyuz capsule on reentry, perhaps you would have to jump."

"Jump from a capsule, on its way down through the atmosphere? Is that likely?"

"It used to be required. Gagarin and others of the first cosmonauts in space who flew the Vostok, they left the capsules four or five miles in the air, before the ground. It was considered safer, I think. And other times, perhaps a cosmonaut *should* have leaped instead of crashing hard in the spacecraft and trusting to his luck."

"Wow. That's nuts."

"That is why so many of the early cosmonauts were expert parachutists, even before they were selected to be cosmonauts, and all of the first women, the five chosen in 1962. Tatyana Kuznetsova and Irina Solovyova had both set world records as parachutists, even though they were so young, only twenty years old or a little older. Valentina Tereshkova was an amateur skydiver first, too."

"But Belyakova was a pilot."

"Yes. Svetlana was in the second group of women cosmonauts chosen, along with only one other woman, Marina Popovich, in a group who were all needed to be jet pilots, test pilots. She was a colonel at the time, and had flown MiG-15, MiG-17, MiG-21 fighter aircraft, all difficult airplanes." The pride in Katya's voice at her friend's accomplishments was evident. "I do not think they would have put a woman who was just a parachutist or a glider pilot onto the Moon first. Svetlana immediately leaped ahead in priority, over all of the other women in the program because of her flying skill, and because Aleksei Arkhipovich, and Nikolai, and other men with voices supported her utterly. As did Yuri Alekseyevich before he died, and also Valentina herself."

Leonov and Makarov, who ended up the first two men on the Moon. And Yuri Gagarin, first man in space. Odd to hear Leonov and Gagarin referred to by first name and patronymic, as if they were family.

Perhaps to Katya, they were. All these big names would have been ten to fifteen years older than her. Katya might well look up to them the same way Vivian looked up to Neil, Buzz, Mike Collins, Frank Borman, Jim Lovell … "I can imagine they would have quite loud voices."

"In this they would be heard, yes."

"I've never done a parachute jump," Vivian said. "Don't ever want to, either."

"No?" Okhotina was clearly startled.

"Why jump out of a perfectly good aircraft? Anyway, it's not part of Naval Aviator training. Hardly worth training for something that's never going to happen in real life. There's enough else to focus on."

"Never?"

"Babe, if you're in a jet, you're never just going to climb out of it and jump. Doesn't work that way. In the worst case you'll be ejecting, in an ejector seat. And ejecting is brutal. You'll likely get your spine compressed and some bones broken. The seat has its own parachute, but if you survive ejection, landing is the least of your worries. Most of us would opt to go down with the plane and risk trying to crash-land the sucker."

Okhotina shook her head. "Scary."

"Yes, indeed. Sometimes."

Katya studied her. "Why do you call me 'babe'?"

"Oh." Vivian flushed. "That's just an astronaut thing. Straight male astronauts in the early Gemini and Apollos used to call each other 'babe' all the time. Still do. The women call one another that, too. It's a bit weird between the sexes, though, I'm not about to be okay with Gisemba calling me 'babe.' Or the other way around. Just doesn't work, somehow."

"Okay," Katya said. "Ten-four, babe." And smiled at her.

Vivian just nodded, and they fell back into that companionable silence.

Okhotina had always been guarded with Vivian, until now. She'd been an exemplary team member: competent, well organized, and rarely complained, and they'd had a good working relationship, but Vivian wouldn't ever have described her as a *friend*, exactly. But now Katya's demeanor with Vivian was much more relaxed, and the reason for that wasn't tough to decode.

*Don't overanalyze it, Vivian. You can always use a friend.*

*I mean, you always* need *friends. That's it. That's what you meant. You don't use your friends.*

And at least Katya didn't make her skin crawl the way Svetlana Belyakova did. Being hugged by Belyakova, like she'd needed in the Pod to get warm? Vivian would have needed to shower for a year afterward.

Katya yawned, teeth showing, like a cat, and then said: "I am still sleepy. Tell me about Apollo 32."

"Which version?"

"The real one. Tell me about the Marius Hills."

"Well, lava tubes are really cool. And big." She glanced at Okhotina. "Be careful what you wish for. I can blather on about Marius for hours."

Katya gestured. "Then, start. I will tell you when I need you to stop. Or just fall asleep."

"Fair enough." Vivian marshalled her thoughts. "And some of this, I have difficulty telling the other NASA astronauts anyway."

"Why?"

"Okay …. Earlier we were talking about how tough the training is. But, yes, all that stress just dissolved once I was assigned to command Apollo 32 and its destination was finalized. I was *so happy* to be sent to Marius. It was like I'd hit the jackpot, and all the way up to launch I was convinced they'd yank it away from me before I got to go.

"Which is what happened, of course. At least for a while. When I lost the mission due to *your* people attacking Columbia, Marius was taken from me, and I was devastated." She paused. "It's not considered cool by the other astros to be quite so emotionally invested in your mission."

"What made Marius so important?"

"It was always important. Right from the start, even before we landed on the Moon, it was right up there as a high-priority science area because it includes so many sites important to understanding its volcanic history."

"Ah." Katya nodded.

"One of the many ironies of all this? Apollo 15—Scott, Irwin, and Worden. Commander Dave Scott had his choice of Hadley or Marius, and he chose Hadley. Which, to be fair, is more scenically spectacular, and more of a challenge on the descent." Vivian mock gulped. "Trust me. Mountains underneath, mountains on either side? It *is* a challenge. So obviously, red-blooded Dave S. really wanted that one. Which is fine because it left Marius for me. So, it was kind of ironic that I ended up at Hadley anyway.

"In betweentimes, Marius was also under consideration for Apollo 17. But the reason it kept getting put off is that it had so *many* key geological sites, and they were so far apart. The first in-depth astrogeology plans in 1968 and 1969 were all saying, 'To get the most out of this site, the astronauts really need to haul ass, travel around quite a bit.' So it ended up on hold until 1979, when we had the capability to do ten EVAs for ten days straight, and good rovers to help us cover the ground. Even a rover that could be telerobotically steered."

She glanced at Katya. "You know I love a good rover ride as much as the next astro, but by Day Five or Six at Marius Base I was like 'For the love of God, someone else drive this beast.' So they did. Ellis and I just sat aboard and played passenger, while the geeks at Eagle Base and back at Houston steered us around the lunar surface. Took us where we needed to go, without us having to lift a finger. It was pretty cool to be able to take a break for a while. Plus, it was a good workout for the equipment. That was always one of the technology goals of Apollo 32.

"We attained *all* our mission goals. We didn't screw anything up—even if it got off to a late start. We did it right. So right that they trusted me when I came up with *this* nutty LGS scheme. Marius was a peach of an assignment."

Katya nodded. "And so, they gave it to a peach." She looked at Vivian sideways.

"Uh. Thanks?" She elbowed Okhotina. "Okay, that's it. Stop flirting with me, Soviet Mata Hari, or I'll put you off my ship."

"No, you won't." Okhotina glanced across the boards, checked power loads and temperatures, like the copilot was supposed to do from time to time, and made a couple of adjustments. Checked their position, scribbled notes into the log, and sat back.

"No, I guess not. You have your uses. I suppose."

Katya just smiled again. "Ellis Mayer. You and him—you must have been very close."

Another familiar topic. "Best crewman ever. And a great guy, but—*just* crew. If that's what you're asking."

"Well, because ten days you spent at Marius in only a Lunar Module? It sounds very close."

"Sure it was. But we managed just fine. We were used to sharing the space by that time. And, honestly, doing ten long exploratory EVAs back-to-back-to-back?" Vivian shook her head. "Exhausting. Once we got back inside after each EVA, we weren't exactly about to do jumping jacks or pace around. Mostly we ate and cleaned up and then slumped into puddles. And, of course, spent goddamn hours scrubbing the lunar dust off our suits so we wouldn't end up sucking that crap into our lungs. Also, hammocks are really comfortable. More than once, I've wished that we'd brought hammocks along on this trip."

Katya looked behind them, appraisingly.

"Yes, I know they wouldn't be space-efficient for a MOLAB, not with six people moving around, or even four. While we're on the move they'd just swing around and bang into everything. But in a stationary LM with just two people, it's honestly about as good as it gets."

Katya looked at Vivian thoughtfully, and then away.

"Katya? What? Spit it out."

"Can I ask about—afterwards?"

"After Apollo 32?" She considered. "Maybe. Not sure. Why?"

"Because, for me, after this ... I do not know what happens."

"Sounds familiar."

"After this mission is over, once I am flown back to the Rodina?" Okhotina shook her head. "I am not a pilot. I have this, all of this experience of walking on the Moon. I have had three missions. But I have no plan. What happens to me? Do I ever return to the Moon?"

*Oh, you haven't felt anything yet.* "Might Zvezda need you?"

"I have no training in Zvezda systems."

"But you have friends with voices, right? Makarov, Leonov?"

"Yes, but there are limits to what I am willing to ask of them."

Vivian nodded. "Fair."

"And so, I want to know what it was like for you, after Marius, and before this." Vivian said nothing, and Katya looked away. "Never mind. I am sorry. It is not my business. It does not matter."

And because Katya had let her off the hook, Vivian started talking and couldn't stop. "Well, I'm sorry to tell you this, but if you're anything like me, going home after this is going to *suck.* After Apollo 32 I felt empty, like I had nothing left. Like everything good in my life was behind me. You know about Buzz Aldrin, right?"

"Yes."

Both women fell silent. Buzz Aldrin had been very public, very candid about his clinical depression and alcoholism once he got back to Earth after Apollo 11. And Buzz wasn't the only one. Other astronauts had ruthlessly suppressed the information, and no one would blab to the media about it, but everyone knew. How do you follow the Moon?

Eventually, Katya said: "Such matters are sometimes known among the cosmonauts of my country, also."

"Well." Vivian cleared her throat. "I didn't think that was the way I was going. I mean, not diving all the way down to the bottom of a bottle, and beyond. Or off a bridge. But I didn't think I really had much to look forward to in the future, either.

"Earth just didn't *feel* right. The gravity, the fresh air. Trees. The beach. Everything I was supposed to love about the Earth, it all felt like it was behind glass. Not real."

Okhotina raised her eyebrows. "And this?" She gestured out the windshield of the MOLAB.

"Yes, this is real. Of course. So, I had some pretty bad days. Plus, my crew ..."

She missed Ellis and Dave Horn like crazy. *Boy, this is turning into a real pity party.* "Well, after Apollo 32, Ellis retired from active space duty, asked to not be considered for future crew assignments. And

Dave Horn moved on to the L5 project, as you know from Daedalus. Good for them. I want them to be happy."

"It is good for you that you had them. Me? I was not close to my other crews. Not like you were, and not like we are, here on LGS-1. It was not the same. Svetlana was my friend from training, but we were on Columbia together for only a day or two before she was injured. So I do not have the people—except the LGS-1 people—and once I go back to the Rodina, I lose you all."

*You could defect*, Vivian thought. But Katya was a smart woman. The possibility would have occurred to her. If she wanted to, she could bring it up herself. Vivian wasn't in the mood for that conversation right now.

Vivian felt *lighter* on the Moon. Not just physically in her body, but in her soul. The most important and vivid parts of her life had been spent on the Moon. And sure, some of them had been vivid for the wrong reasons: her torture by Yashin at Zvezda Base, her long walk from Vaporum to Hadley that the other astronauts had termed Vivian's Trek of Death—a joke, to be sure, but with an undercurrent of respect. But much more of her lunar life had been glorious. The flying: around the Moon, across the Moon. Exploring the area around Hadley Base with Ellis, particularly the rille, followed by their hugely successful trip to the Marius Hills. And now this: their around-the-Moon voyage. And all the friends she'd met along the way. What was there on Earth for Vivian that could compare with this?

And yet, she still couldn't avoid that quiet, calm voice in the back of her mind, telling her that perhaps enough was enough. That, at long last, it might be time to go home.

"Kat, there's another piece to all of this that you might want to think about."

"Yes?"

"After Apollo 32, once I got back to Houston, I was … well, for a while I wasn't exactly popular with some of the other astros." Respected, perhaps, for the long duration of her stay on the Moon and her resourcefulness, but not *liked*. "Some of them thought I'd worked against US interests in getting Dark Driver shit-canned, though in reality there wasn't much choice once your people discovered it." Some even seemed to think less of her, somehow, for getting captured by the Soviets at all. But that was a bit too much to reveal to Katya. "I'd worked closely with

Makarov and Belyakova there, at the end. And a lot of NASA astros couldn't handle that. Because to them, you're the enemy."

"Nonsense," Katya grinned. "We Russians are the heroes. You Americans are the dangerous imperialists. Everybody knows that."

"Exactly. That's what I'm saying. You might get some blowback from your comrades, for working so closely with the evil Americans. It might taint you, in their eyes."

"And for shooting back, when we were shot at."

"Yes. Maybe that, too."

"Perhaps. I suppose we shall see. You have given me much to think about. Thank you." Okhotina stretched. Looked at the map of the terrain ahead of them. "The next hour looks simple, no?"

Vivian glanced at the map herself, and around at the soldiers flanking the craft. "Yep. Duck soup."

"What?"

"Easy. But after that hour, I'll definitely need a break."

"All right. Then I may take another short nap, dangerous imperialist. Perhaps do not murder me in my sleep?"

"I'll do my best not to give in to my homicidal instincts," Vivian said gravely.

"And I thank you. After, we can switch seats, I will drive the rest of your shift, if you like."

"Well, *that's* an offer I can't refuse."

Katya smiled, curled up on the couch beside Vivian, and was asleep in moments.

Vivian glanced down at her thoughtfully. Sure, it was possible that Okhotina's new friendliness was an act, at least in part. That Katya was working her, trying to emotionally manipulate her. Be the good cop.

Vivian didn't really believe that and wasn't even sure whether she cared. But she had also been careful not to tell Okhotina anything that covert Soviet operatives back on Earth wouldn't be able to glean anyway.

So, either Katya was a friend, or they could both play this manipulation game.

Vivian experimentally patted Okhotina on the shoulder, rested her hand there for a moment, then focused her attention back on the road. Or, rather, the lack of any road whatsoever, as they continued their path across the southern highlands of the Moon.

One thing she knew for sure: she wouldn't be telling Katya anything else about Peter Sandoval.

Where was Peter now? Vivian had no clue. She wasn't in contact with him, and she didn't have need-to-know. He was either on Earth, or in Earth orbit. Which, frankly, didn't narrow it down much.

Peter's determination to quit space had lasted just a few weeks. The weeks it took him to realize that Vivian Carter had no intention of settling down back on Earth and that there was little chance of the two of them getting together as a permanent item, at least not right away.

Vivian had given it an honest try. Gone out for the dinner she'd promised him, and several dinners afterward. She'd tried to be half of a couple. She really did care for him. But it hadn't quite gelled. It just wasn't where Vivian brain was.

She'd been hard to deal with during those first weeks back on Earth. She knew that for a fact. Peter had been a saint to put up with her as long as he had.

And Earth geography hadn't exactly aided them. Vivian was based in Houston, Texas. Peter divided his time between Colorado Springs, near USAF Mission Control in Cheyenne Mountain, and their launch facilities in Vandenberg, California, meaning that they were generally separated by either a thousand miles or eighteen hundred miles. So several of their dinners had been at the halfway point between them, in Amarillo or Lubbock, Texas, or Las Cruces in New Mexico. That hadn't helped, to say the least.

And when their final night together came, neither had known it ahead of time.

"You can't spend the rest of your life looking back," he'd said. "You need to be looking forward. You can still make great contributions to NASA. What about L5?"

"God, no. I'm not an engineer, and not qualified to manage them. And I have a low boredom threshold for just hanging around at a geometrical point in the middle of nowhere."

"Okay, well, even if you never leave surface again, you could move up in the organization. Wield some power. Get shit done."

Vivian had grimaced. "Become a manager? Or a politician?"

"I've seen solid evidence that you'd be good at whichever of those you chose."

"Oh."

"Maybe even put your hat in the ring to be Chief Astronaut once John Young retires. He's hung on *way* longer than anyone expected. Just couldn't quit Apollo, I guess."

"Yeah, I get how that works."

"He's been saying he's going to retire since 1974 but somehow still hasn't done it."

"Well, sure, but either Dan Brandenstein or Hoot Gibson *has* to be next in line for that job."

"Okay, then, so something else. Training. Mentoring. Or you could leave NASA, travel the world."

She'd shaken her head. "And go where?"

Sandoval's exasperation was growing. "Or, you know, even start a family. Do whatever you want."

"Wow, you really went there." Vivian shook her head. "I'm too old."

"Vivian. You're thirty-seven. Women do still manage to procreate at your 'advanced' age."

"And I'm too irradiated. Getting pregnant is probably not the best idea ever." She shivered involuntarily. "Stuff might happen that no one would like."

A long silence. "Then, hey. We could just hang out together. Have fun. Go on trips. Be normal human beings."

She put her hand on his. "I hear you, Peter. I do. And … maybe, one day. I'm not ready yet. I know you are. But I'm just not. I'm sorry."

"That's okay." His tone said otherwise. But he was really being very patient with her, under the circumstances.

"There's something here I just can't let go of. I don't know how. But when I figure it out … I'll let you know."

Peter looked at her for a long time.

Eventually, he said: "Sure. Well. I'm just gonna …" he gestured, *let myself out.*

*Perhaps in more than one sense*, she thought. "Okay."

As he moved away, she suddenly said: "You're not committed, you know. To me."

"Sure I am."

"No, what I mean is, you shouldn't feel an obligation. If you need to be with someone who's less of a giant pain in your ass, I would absolutely understand that."

"So noted," he said. "But you might find me harder to shake off than that."

She had nothing to say to that. "Okay."

He hesitated. "Vivian. Try not to get too depressed."

Vivian resisted the urge to snap at him. Resolving not to get depressed about no longer being on the Moon, about feeling rudderless now, didn't prevent it from happening. She'd already tried that experiment. "Peter. It's not like there's a switch I can throw. But copy that. I'll try."

"Good. I'll be in touch." And with that, he finally left.

And once he was gone, Vivian had put her head on one side and thought about it.

*Really* thought about it.

"Travel," she'd said to the closed door. "Hmm."

And that was the night that the seed of the LGS-1 mission had been sown in Vivian's mind.

A mission that, now, today, still had two weeks left to run. A quarter of the Moon's circumference still lay ahead. Time enough at Zvezda and later to analyze what had just happened to them all, and what might be in store for Vivian next.

*Enjoy the now. The rest of the mission. Your people. Sufficient unto the day …*

This time, Vivian didn't allow herself to complete the sentence. Just in case.

# 7

**CHAPTER**

## Daedalus Base: Vivian Carter
## December 22, 1982–January 6, 1983

*"WHAT about L5?"*

Dave Horn had asked Vivian a similar question a month earlier, during LGS-1's sojourn at Daedalus Base on Farside, and her answer had been much the same.

By the time the crew of Carter's Convoy reached the halfway point of their grand tour, they had been more than ready for a break from being on the road, and from executing their grueling schedule, day in and day out. The long lunar night at Daedalus gave them the opportunity to stretch, spend much more time alone, read books, and even stare into space and think about nothing for a while, in addition, of course, to slogging through all the necessary cataloguing and packaging of the samples and data they'd collected thus far, plus the sorely needed and time-consuming maintenance and deep cleaning of their vehicles, suits, and other equipment for the next leg of their journey.

The new Daedalus still had the strong ambience of a military base, even though half of its US community were now civilian scientists, and it was now staffed with an almost equal number of Soviet cosmonauts and scientists.

The original, emergency version of the Lunar Accord had been signed behind closed doors by Reagan and Andropov in early 1980

while Vivian, Dave Horn, and the other surviving astronauts and cosmonauts were still in their dangerous and eccentric emergency orbit
around the Moon. As a part of that agreement, Dark Driver was to be
dismantled by the USAF and never referred to again. Everyone would
just quietly agree that it had never existed.

However, after further high-level discussions involving top scientists from both the US and USSR and weeks of excruciating diplomacy, that decision had been rescinded. The Daedalus mass driver that
the American military had originally built in secret to enable them to
pepper the Soviet Union with nuclear warheads in the third wave of
a future global conflict, would have a much more inspirational future.
Instead of being decommissioned, it would form the basis of a joint
US-Soviet experiment into the feasibility of flinging raw materials off
the Moon in suitably small and well-shaped packages with the eventual goal of refining the metals and other content to construct a space
station at the Earth–Moon L5 point.

L5 was a location defined by celestial mechanics, one of five La-
grange points of gravitational equilibrium in the Earth–Moon system. The first point, L1, was located between the Earth and the Moon,
where their gravities were equal and canceled out. L2 was beyond the
Moon on the same line, and L3 was beyond the Earth in the opposite
direction. None of these was naturally stable, and any satellites placed
at one would require station-keeping burns to maintain their position.

L4 and L5, though, were points of stable equilibrium. An object
placed at one of these would largely stay put or, if given a gentle nudge,
orbit there. L4 lay on the path of the lunar orbit, sixty degrees ahead
of the Moon, so that the Earth–Moon–L4 system formed an equilateral triangle. L5 was the similar point on the other side, sixty degrees
behind the Moon.

So, L5 was actually a cool spot. From there, the Earth would look
the same size as it appeared from the Moon, and the Moon would
appear the same size as it appeared from the Earth, with both visible
in the sky at once.

The US—and the Soviet Union—had big plans for it.


Vivian hadn't seen Dave Horn in over a year, but even once they were
in the same base again, it was still another three days before they saw

each other. Vivian was keen to get as much of the grunt work as possible finished by Christmas, so that she and her crew could spend some time relaxing before they had to head out again on January 6. Plus, Horn had been on the opposite shift and was spending most of his time working at the small tech station at the far end of the mass driver, helping to fine-tune the math and the electronics for the First Throw.

When they met up at noon on December 25, typically neither of them wished the other a Merry Christmas. "I distinctly remember you telling me you didn't give two hoots about ever walking on the Moon," Vivian said by way of greeting, on entering his small cubicle.

They hugged briefly, and Horn waved her to the only seat while he perched on his bunk. "I still don't. Stupid, ungodly place … but the Air Force made me an offer I couldn't refuse."

"And you a good Army guy? Well, right now I'm glad you accepted."

"Seriously, you should consider joining us. Once you're done with your current joyride, of course."

"Ha." Vivian looked around the tiny space, which was even smaller than the Pod on LGS-1 and had a stark military feel to it besides. "I can sure see the appeal."

Horn eyed her curiously. "Okay, so what *do* you plan to do next?"

"Stick a flag at the South Pole for the US and science," she said promptly. "And after that? Just keep on rolling."

"You know what I mean. Once your grand tour is over. Vivian Carter is always thinking two steps ahead, right?"

"Is she? I barely have time to think about what I'm doing right now. And, once I've gone around the entire Moon, what else is there?"

"Well … again, what about L5?"

She squinted at him. "Not really much to explore out there."

"Well, I'm going," he said. "We don't have a date yet; the timeline's a bit fluid. Depends on whether the First Throw works, and how much effort it takes to refine the Driver's aim. Once we iron the wrinkles out, though—maybe even early next year—as soon as we can reliably send material out to L5, we'll need someone there to catch it."

"You're going to L5 to be shot at?"

He grinned. "In a way. We already have a Skylab prepped in lunar orbit to boost out there. We'll park it at L5 and set up a bucket to catch all the regolith pellets O'Neill will be chucking at us."

"A bucket? And then you'll build a space habitat?"

93

"Not right away. We're still cobbling together prototypes, figuring out what works. I'll be happy enough if we can get a small metallurgy lab going within a year to convert the regolith pellets into a ten-foot-wide square of material tough enough to not shatter if you kick it."

Vivian grinned. "Lofty goals."

"Baby steps. Proof of concept. But even that's a big deal, right? Building a piece of space-qualified hull, a quarter million miles from the Earth and Moon, entirely out of lunar material?"

"Sounds like fun," Vivian said politely.

He shook his head. "The way you say that it sounds like 'Gag me with a spoon.'"

"What?"

"It's something my nieces say. It's called Valley Girl speak, or something."

"Oh, right. Like 'Oh-ma-*Gawd*, awesome! Totally tubular!'" Vivian allowed her voice to lilt upward during each phrase, a girly tone she never used.

Horn shuddered. "Please don't ever do that again."

"Sorry."

"But … keep an open mind, okay? About L5. I might be giving you a call in a month or two."

"Well, a call would be nice," she said. "But don't get your hopes up."

L5 might be an entertaining, even spectacular spot to visit—for an hour or two. Beyond that Vivian would get bored because she'd basically just be floating at a stable point in space with nothing else to see and do, nowhere else to go, and no samples to take. Space for space's sake, and heavy-duty engineering projects: neither of those were Vivian's jam.

She looked at her watch. "Anyway. Don't we have some kind of shindig to go to?"

"We do." Horn stood up. "Oh, and hey, uh, I got you a Christmas surprise."

Vivian looked askance. She could tell by his sardonic tone that this wasn't for real. "You did?"

"Yup. We're assigned to the top table for dinner. With Gerard O'Neill himself. He really wants to meet you."

"Oh, crap," Vivian said, instantly deflated. "I mean, great. But not much chance of avoiding shop talk over Christmas dinner, then, am I right?"

"Not so much." Horn shrugged. "I'll make it up to you one day."

"So you say. Okay, fine. Lead on."

Gerard O'Neill hadn't invented the mass driver—the idea of a rail-gun or coil-gun powered by electromagnetic force predated him by decades—but it had been his vision that such a driver could be used to throw a steady stream of regolith pellets off the Moon to provide the raw materials for space colonies.

A vision then "corrupted," as he saw it, by the military. Which he'd told them to their faces. Although even O'Neill had been tickled pink when Al Shepard himself had shown up on O'Neill's doorstep to recruit him in late February 1980, shortly after the Accord had been rewritten and just before Dark Driver had turned Bright. Until that moment, he'd had no idea that the United States Air Force had been covertly cutting metal and building his mass driver on the Moon for the past several years.

And now they wanted to send him to the Moon to take control of the maturing mass-driver project as science lead. And all this had happened just a couple of weeks after his birthday. O'Neill called it "the best and latest fifty-third birthday present I got."

This was Vivian's second Christmas on the Moon. She'd been at Hadley Base over Christmas 1979, when Apollo Rescue 1 had been everyone's gift from Santa, dropping in unexpectedly from space on December 25.

Christmas 1982 was definitely more relaxing. At least, the day itself was: the 25 had been declared a stand-down for the US occupants of Daedalus Base, with a special and long-planned group dinner. The Soviet contingent was following suit with the time off and celebration, even though Christmas was not an official holiday under Communism, with some of its more secular traditions shifted over to New Year's Day. And even if it hadn't been, Russian Orthodox Christmas fell on January 7, not in late December.

And so, this afternoon the mess hall was decorated with actual Christmas decorations from home—tinsel and foil stars were light and took up almost no transport volume. No tree, of course, although there was a six-foot-tall color picture of one tacked to the wall, with real fairy lights stuck onto it, winking on and off. The Soviet side of the hall was also decorated, with pine branches and babushka and matryoshka doll ornaments. Their stars were five-pointed though, instead of eight.

Wonder of wonders, the spread was astonishingly good. Roast turkey, ham, mashed potatoes, stuffing, gravy, all mouthwatering-ly awesome compared to the routine space rations of LGS-1 and US-Copernicus. For their part, the Soviets had roasted pig, devilled eggs, piroshki, salmon pie, and meat dumplings, and each side was sharing their bounty with the other. Vivian had no doubt there was a competitive element at work here, with the two sides using the festive season to wage a more benign proxy war. This, however, was a superpower contest Vivian could totally get behind.

Against her expectations, Gerard O'Neill turned out to be engag-ing rather than stuffy, a warm and friendly man with a pageboy haircut and kind eyes. As soon as they were introduced, he showered her with so many questions about LGS-1 that she had difficulty finding time to put all this glorious food into her mouth.

Occasionally, she traded glances with Feye Gisemba, who was seated at the opposite end of the table. They also both grinned rue-fully at Bill Dobbs, who had really drawn the short straw and was deep in a very serious conversation with the US base commander, Johnston. Vivian was quite sure that her wide separation from the Major-General had been planned in advance. Vasquez, not really a party guy and still suffering from a substantial sleep deficit, had vol-unteered for the night shift.

As she babbled away about their crossing of the lunar North Pole and the challenges of navigation and core drilling, Vivian could see Lakontsev and Okhotina across the hall, celebrating with their own countrymen in a rapid-fire exchange of Russian and laughter. She suspected the Soviets had gotten into the bootleg vodka before the feast, and kind of wished she was over with them, whether she could have followed their conversation or not. Maybe she could pay them a visit later.

In the meantime …

"So," she said rather desperately, "tell me again how the US will have giant habitats in space, twenty years from now."

A good-natured groan arose from the diners around them, but O'Neill just grinned cheerfully and launched into his spiel, no doubt delighted to have a new audience for his breathtaking vision.

And it really was breathtaking. In Vivian's conversations with Horn, he'd been focused on the near-term goals. The sane next steps, the nuts-and-bolts achievable stuff.

O'Neill was much more of a big picture guy, and his canvas was very large. Because his ultimate goal was to build self-supporting space habitats, giant cylinders or spheres that would be pressurized and set spinning so that the people living on their inner surface would experience Earth-like gravity. Gerard O'Neill had absolutely no doubt that this could be done, and in his lifetime.

As Vivian knew as well as anyone, lunar regolith contained over 20 percent silicon, 12 percent aluminum, 4 percent iron, 3 percent magnesium, and in some places more than 6 percent titanium. And by weight, it was over 40 percent oxygen. Which meant that tons of very useful ingredients for life, rocket fuel, and construction could be thrown from Bright Driver to L5 at a much lower cost than hauling them up out of Earth's gravitational well. The trick would be in capturing the material once it arrived, refining it, and using it to build human habitats.

Sure. Vivian was on board for all that. But by the time O'Neill really got going, he wanted to be throwing *a million tons* of lunar soil into space every year. He claimed this could be done using only the existing Bright Driver facility, and his numbers were convincing ... provided the money and the will were there. They'd certainly need plenty of both because if they'd managed to construct his first two proof-of-concept space habitats, O'Neill's proposed Island Three was truly massive: a cylinder twenty miles long and four miles across. The total land area on the inside surface of that would be five hundred square miles, enough—in principle—to feed and support a population of several *million*.

Just like a small planet, but inside out.

Fortunately, his plan called for a (somewhat) smaller and more manageable start: Island One would be populated by "only" a few thousand people and have the minimum internal land area feasible for establishing an agricultural base. It would be a sphere, a mile in circumference. Set rotating twice per minute, its equatorial area would enjoy Earth-normal gravity. At a latitude of forty-five degrees within Island One, the gravity would be a third less. All told, the inner surface of the pressurized sphere would provide enough space for garden-apartment style housing, including rivers, fields, swimming pools, plus all the agriculture necessary to sustain it.

Even that was big thinking, of course. Massive thinking. Monumental thinking. And obviously a pipe dream.

"Perhaps later, we can even mine the asteroids," O'Neill continued. "Why not? Particularly the Trojan asteroids, the ones that tend to get trapped orbiting the Sun-Earth L4 and L5 points."

Vivian looked sideways at Dave. "You're sharing L5 with asteroids? Oh, wait. Sun-Earth."

"Right," Horn said. "Sun-Earth L5 is where the asteroids live. Earth-Moon L5 is where we're aiming right now. Gerry skipped a step, there."

She nodded. To her mind, O'Neill had skipped quite a few steps. She grinned at him anyway.

O'Neill was studying her. "You don't look convinced."

Vivian paused to swallow and chased the mouthful down with some fruit punch. "Oh, I'm convinced you know what you're doing on the technical side. Sounds good."

He grinned wryly. "Thanks."

She gestured at Dave. "Or, at least, I happen to think highly of this guy, and if you've convinced him, that's good enough for me. But … the thing is, I spend a whole lot of LGS-1 time on camera, filming TV segments for NASA Public Affairs and the evening news. Civilian interest in space is not exactly at an all-time high. Yours wouldn't be the first project to have a cashflow problem."

"You think the political will won't be there? I don't blame you. I'm not blind to all the protests, the folks who are saying we should fix Earth problems before we send a few thousand extremely lucky souls to live in space. Even though I disagree."

"Well, yes."

He leaned forward. "You know what everybody loves, though? And Congress will vote for every time, and even our Soviet partners love just as much? Free power."

Vivian blinked. "Uh. From where, exactly?"

O'Neill gestured at Dave Horn. "Your turn. My food's getting cold."

"Solar power satellites," Horn said promptly. "At Earth-Moon L5. Build a couple of satellites to transmit solar energy down to Earth as a tight microwave beam, and hey presto."

"Hey presto?"

He nodded and grinned. "We want to do it. And they're even more gung ho." Horn gestured toward the Soviet side of the mess hall with his fork. "The USSR has an energy problem. Huge empire, shaky infrastructure. This solves all that. The Soviets have the kickoff in their latest Five-Year Plan. They're talking about having their own solar satellite pilot project in operation by the mid-1990s, and substantial quantities of power flowing ten years later. And so, naturally, we're aiming to do that too. Like with everything, the first one is the hardest, right? After that, the second and third and twentieth of the satellites pay for themselves. And then we have cheap power, oxygen and metals, and it's off to the races."

"Even that startup must have quite the price tag," she said.

"Sure. But give us ten years, even at the current funding level, and just maybe we can process enough regolith at L5, combine it with whatever steel and electronics and other stuff from Earth that we can't get any other way, to convince the skeptics—even you. And then we, and the Soviets, and maybe the whole world can have free energy, essentially forever. Because the Sun isn't going away anytime soon."

"That does sound cool," Vivian said. "Can't deny it."

Far be it from her to cast doubt on anyone else's passion project, and she was hardly about to argue with the whole reason for Bright Driver's continued existence. But Vivian was pretty darned sure that none of this would be happening in *her* lifetime.


Vivian had worried the dinner would end with speechifying and toasts and all, but it seemed no one was in the mood for that. Johnston got up at the end, but merely to circulate, at which point Dobbs gratefully joined her. O'Neill shook hands with them both and went on his way as well, and Dave Horn stepped over to the next table to chat to the US engineers. Moments later, Gisemba slid into the seat he'd just vacated.

"Phew," Vivian said. "Schmoozing with this crowd is harder work than shlepping rock."

"True believers." Gisemba shook his head. "Well, more power to them, pun intended. Maybe I can put in for retirement in an honest-to-God space colony. Or at least not have to pay my electricity bill once I get home."

99

"Don't count on it." Dobbs stretched out his arm and shoulder, still working out the kinks from their last transfer of the heavy lunar sample bags. "Even putting all the technical roadblocks aside, the Soviets can't afford all this. Their economy is stretched to the limit already. Down there, and up here too. They're doing their best to keep pace, and talking a good game on L5, but it's all talk. It's all about national prestige for them. Until they crash and burn."

Vivian had heard this argument before. It was one of the reasons the US Congress continued to fund NASA at the level that it did, and the USAF in the dark Defense part of the budget, to expand their orbital and lunar presence, because then the Soviets would have to continue to match their spending. According to the theory, if the US could reliably outspend the Soviets for long enough, it could eventually wreck their economy and split the USSR apart. Bring it all tumbling down.

Vivian wasn't convinced about that, either. Sure, the Soviets were coming to the end of their recent oil boom, but who was to say they wouldn't discover oil somewhere else? Eastern Europe and Asia were huge, and the Soviets owned most of them.

Several folks on the US side seemed quietly optimistic about the eventual demise of the Soviet Union, but the Rodina looked solidly established from where Vivian was sitting. She saw little chance that the Berlin Wall would ever come down in her lifetime.

And if the USSR did fall apart, what then? Major turmoil across the world, for sure. Quite likely a bunch of wars. This might be a classic case of *Be careful what you wish for.*

Her crewmen were still shooting the breeze about geopolitics, but Vivian had had enough serious talk for one Christmas. "No offense, but I'm going to go hang with our Soviet friends for a while, now. Mix and match, right? Good for international relations."

She got to her feet and made her way across the mess hall.


O'Neill's science team had promised Congress that Bright Driver would be "operational" by the end of 1982, and so in true science and engineering fashion, right at the end of 1982 was when it would happen. It had thus been pure chance that had brought Vivian and her crew to Daedalus Base on the precise week Bright Driver was scheduled to throw its first payload, hopefully in the general direction of L5. Which the news media on Earth was inevitably billing as "The Shot in the Dark." It being nighttime on Farside, and all.

But when it finally happened on December 30, it wasn't all that spectacular because there was almost nothing to see. The payload went so damned fast and with so little fanfare that it was difficult to see that anything had happened. There were no flashing lights, or sparks, or really much of anything, and never would be unless something went wrong. It was all electromagnetism, plus lack of friction.

One moment the pellet was there, the next it wasn't. And, of course, its launch was silent. In space, no one could hear a rock screaming off the end of a mass driver at lunar escape velocity. Mostly what the bilateral science team did was look at instruments, write numbers down into notebooks, and—in O'Neill's case—jump up and down and swear a lot.

The launch was a success, and the launch of the other eleven slugs of glass-wrapped lunar rock after the first were successful as well, in that they soared far beyond the lunar gravitational field and out into a solar orbit.

It was *long*, though, the Driver. Spectacularly long. And, despite everyone's best efforts, the fine tuning at the station at its far end was *not* going well. Those dozen slugs wouldn't pass anywhere near L5 on the way. O'Neill's team still had work to do.

Even today, Vivian had learned something. She'd supposed that the mass driver shot its payload upward, at least on an upward incline away from the lunar surface. Now, she found out that this wasn't the case. In fact, Bright Driver hurled each chunk of glass-wrapped lunar materials at a slight downward angle so that it almost skimmed the regolith, to keep it low enough for long enough that the corrective way station a few kilometers beyond the rail endpoint didn't need to be mounted high on an immense tower.

Except that Bright Driver had been built with Earth in mind as the target, not L5. So the USAF hadn't located it and angled it to O'Neill's exacting standards, and once built it was hard to adjust and tune for a completely different trajectory.

O'Neill liked to complain about that. A lot. "Really, you guys should have brought me in sooner." But he was still having a ball, and so was Dave Horn, and the rest of the science team, American and Soviet alike. They were all living their best lives, and as a fellow obsessive, Vivian was hardly about to fault them on that.

It was a passably amusing way to spend a Christmas in space.

# 8

## Zvezda-Copernicus: Vivian Carter
## February 6, 1983

**THE** rest of their mission went off without a hitch. At least, nothing serious.

They had begun their lunar circumnavigation in darkness, departing from Zvezda-Copernicus just a few hours before lunar dawn, and they would end their epic journey in darkness as well. And so, Vivian would preserve her perfect record of never having seen Zvezda in daylight.

Vivian and her crew were all awake. They'd shared a last meal two hours ago and toasted each other with orange juice. No one would be in their bunk for the arrival.

Gisemba's meticulous plan had them scheduled to arrive back at Zvezda twelve hours ago. But his plan had not survived contact with Vivian Carter, and for better or worse, she was the boss. Vivian had insisted on staying longer than he'd planned at Tycho Crater, sampling the whole rim, and later on taking a detour to the Apollo 14 landing site at Fra Mauro to take the samples from Cone Crater that Al Shepard and Ed Mitchell had come just short of obtaining in 1971. And then, of course, they'd all wanted to see the landing site itself, and Mission Control had asked them to take some additional samples and pictures in the area, delaying them even further.

Vivian had thought that they could make up the time, but reality had worked against them, and so the Sun had set two hours ago, leaving them to drive the final leg by Earthlight.

In Vivian's heart of hearts, she'd known at the time that the odds were against them and simply didn't care. Call her contrary, impetuous, resistant to authority, or whatever, but the truth of it was that she couldn't bear to cut her last sample-taking EVA short. Didn't want to get off that bike for the last time, doff the suit, and know that their trip was almost over.

Gisemba was trying not to be grumpy with her for overruling his neat schedule. But Vasquez and Okhotina had picked up on that and kept ribbing him to make him laugh, and so the sting had gone out of it.

Vivian had driven the first fifty miles of their trip on their initial departure from Zvezda-Copernicus, and also driven their arrival and departure from Daedalus. With thirty miles to go, she once again took the MOLAB wheel for the final leg. Commander's privilege.

So here they were, on the home straight of their transpolar trek. Vivian wished she could enjoy it the way she had in the first few weeks when they'd gone up and over the North Pole and worked their way down the Moon's far side. When the expedition was still young and had seemed endless. Lunar exploration in the raw, with a crew she really liked. A physically tiring and mentally complicated challenge, surrounded by landscapes of amazing variation—at least by lunar standards. And always with the prospect of discovering something remarkable: identifying a vein of rare earth elements, say, or water ice. A cool mineral, or seeing a particular mountain, rille, or crater for the first time. Geologically speaking, breakthrough discoveries were almost certain to be made in the coming months and years, once all of their samples were analyzed rigorously and maps made of the elemental abundances in various regions. There must be tons of science buried in the ton of rock and stack of cores they'd taken on their circumnavigation. But the luster of their trip had been tarnished by violence, by the wounding and medevac of two of their crew, and by their even more demanding last two weeks with its ruthless, ever-tightening schedule. By the continuously visible presence of the armed Night Corps troops and their cosmonaut counterparts, flanking the MOLAB, arrowing out ahead or dropping back to check for threats. One or another of them clanked through the MOLAB's inner sanctum from time to time, an alien and not particularly friendly presence, to refresh their suit, take a shower, take a nap. Even though the LGS-1 crew's activities were much the same as they'd been since the beginning, it didn't feel like the same mission.

And now they were approaching Zvezda-Copernicus, back in known space. Even this far out, plenty of tracks crisscrossed the regolith: boots, rovers, bikes. This was no longer virgin territory.

Once the mission was over, Vivian would be goalless once again. Back into that state of limbo, where she had nothing to look forward to. No densely packed timeline to lead her to her next goal.

Vivian had once joked to Ellis, "Seriously, you never want to meet Unscheduled Vivian." Except that hadn't been a joke. Unscheduled Vivian felt empty inside. An emptiness she constantly had to keep moving to avoid.

"So, what d'you say we keep going? Do another loop?" Vivian forced a grin up at Katya, who was standing in the doorway of the cab, bracing herself against the door jamb. "A lap of honor, maybe around the equator this time, and really do this right?"

Seated on her other side, Gisemba mimed banging his head against the wall. Okhotina said, "That would be nice," at the same time Vasquez, back in the main cabin, said, "Uh, maybe next year," and they all laughed.

"No takers, really?" Vivian said. "Wusses."

"I believe they would not let us," Okhotina said, very seriously.

"I suppose not. This was good, though. Wasn't it?" Vivian smiled. "And I'm glad I got to do it with you all: Feye, Christian, Kat. And the others."

She'd expected ... what did she expect? But none of them responded right away.

And Katya just stared out the front window of the MOLAB and after a while said, simply: "It was the very best time of my life."

Vivian swallowed. "Wasn't it, though?"

Okhotina's brow creased. Vivian clarified. "In colloquial English, that just means 'Yes.'"

Silence descended. On they went. It felt somehow ... anticlimactic.

Those thirty miles sped by, and almost before Vivian was ready, the outline of Zvezda Base appeared over the local horizon ahead of them, connected to the habs of US-Copernicus.

Vivian's arrival at Zvezda to start this mission had been surreal. First, she hadn't landed her own craft—she and Gisemba had been ferried down from orbit in a three-person LM Taxi by an astronaut she'd never met, a younger guy from a different astronaut class. He'd been laconic and businesslike, experienced at lunar night landings. And Gisemba had called numbers for him. Having nothing to do during a lunar descent except sit strapped into the back bay of the LM, unable to even see through the small windows, had been a white-knuckle experience.

And then they'd been down. Vivian had seen Zvezda only once before from the outside, also in the gloom of lunar night, while fleeing in a stolen Soviet suit, convinced she would be dead in just a few hours. This time around, surrounded by a flurry of activity, the E-shape of the Soviet base had looked a little more benign.

Zvezda had grown in the past three years. Close by and connected to the middle tine of the E—Soviet Hall Four—was the American sector of the base, extending out to the east and then spreading north and south in a T-shape of Soviet-style halls, bookended by two US-style habs. The US sector now made up almost half the total volume of the combined base, though passage back and forth between the two nations' portions of Zvezda was strictly controlled and monitored.

As for the Soviets, they'd installed a new corridor extending the downstroke of the E, so that it now resembled an F with three tines. From above it really didn't look like letters anymore, so much as a Scrabble accident.

When Vivian and her team had kitted out the MOLAB at the start of LGS-1 they'd been working out east of US-Copernicus before dawn with a massive checklist and all kinds of work to do and had paid little attention to their surroundings. But now, approaching Zvezda from the south, Vivian experienced acid flashbacks.

The night she'd escaped, there had been a small row of Soviet LK Landers to the southeast of the base and another line of LEKs beyond. Vivian had been tired, disoriented, and frightened, but determined to keep going for as long as she had breath in her body and air in her suit. Now, two similar rows of LKs and LEKs were the first things that she saw. The Soviet landers were lit up from within, so that they looked

105

like Christmas baubles. She supposed their crews were still busy inside them, shrouding the instruments with thermal blankets, cycling the power down, completing the preparations for night.

"Nothing weird about this," she muttered.

And beyond those Soviet craft, the low profile of Zvezda Base. Not prominent, for much of it was buried, but its shape against the stars was too regular to be a natural formation, and she could see its periscopes and lighted windows.

The US habitats bore little resemblance to those at Hadley Base. At Hadley the cylinders had rested on their ends, squat and wide, reminiscent of the Skylab layout. Here the cylinders were on their sides, longer than they were tall, superficially more Soviet than American in style. The US base was darker, its windows better shielded against the deep chill of night. It showed few signs of life, and from here Vivian could not see the American LMs, presumably still spread out across the landscape to the east in the Hadley style rather than being arrayed in a line like the Soviet ships.

And so, from here, the visual impression was that US-Copernicus was deserted, and physically dominated by the submerged but larger spread of Zvezda.

It was all so silent and still, and it was so long since anyone had spoken in the MOLAB, that when Starman's voice came through the intercom Vivian and Gisemba both jumped.

"LGS-1, this is US-Copernicus. Welcome home. And congratulations on a job well done."

Vivian recovered. "Copernicus, LGS. Thanks. We had ourselves quite the time."

"That you did. Sorry we don't have a welcoming committee out on-surface to greet you. That was the original plan, but ... nightfall and all. You know how that is. Battening down the hatches."

"I do, and no worries. Happy to slink home."

"Slink? As if. Come in to park at Joint Port and we'll have a small ceremony for you."

"Ceremony?" For some reason, that hadn't occurred to her. She looked around at her crew: Vasquez rubbed his eyes and shook his head, clearly exhausted, and Katya and Feye didn't respond at all, blinking like owls. "That's really not necessary, Copernicus. The work was its own reward."

"For sure, but ... you know. Public Affairs. NASA's taking a hammering in Congress again, and we haven't had a lot of great news lately. We've been getting good press from your joint US-Soviet circumnavigation, at least, and we need to make some hay out of that."

Until today, Vivian had never realized what a strange saying that was. "Hay is just dead grass."

"Uh, roger that, LGS-1?"

"Sorry. That was random. I'm pretty darned tired right now."

Vivian struggled to concentrate. Starman's was the only voice she was hearing, but it would be naïve to assume they were alone on the loop. Especially if Public Affairs was involved. "Excuse my flippancy. We'll be happy to oblige. What's the drill? Cameras? Speeches?" *Please, not speeches.*

"Cameras, for sure. Live mics, for the happy babble of congratulations. I'll say a couple things, but we'll try to keep the speeches to a minimum. Mostly we just need footage of the weary travelers' return. Handshakes and a bit of conversation."

Vivian ran her fingers through her hair. In the doorway, Katya was doing the same. "Weary, we can do. I hope no one's counting on glamor. We're a bit short on that right now."

"No worries. You've come a long way; you're allowed to look suitably tired and grimy. Makes for a better story. And we're not putting this out live, anyway. Wrong time of day in the US for one thing. The PR people will massage the footage for a short news segment. But try to smile and look happy and satisfied with your magnificent achievement."

"Uh, sure thing."

Gisemba leaned over Vivian's shoulder to the mic. "We're returning with two fewer people than we left with. How do we address that?"

"Don't. They'll be named as full crew members and get their share of the glory. We just won't draw attention to the fact they're not on camera. Viewers will likely assume they're asleep, or still putting the truck to bed."

Vivian shrugged. "Copy that."

Feye was frowning. "So, to be clear: the public doesn't know about our South Pole event?"

"Correct. It's been agreed that it's in no one's interest for that to be widely known. Neither we nor the Russkies will say boo about it."

"No boo, affirmative," said Vivian.

"Oh, and your MOLAB is being filmed coming in right now, so park the bus neatly."

"And don't crash it into the base?"

"Uh … yeah, please don't do that. Vivian, are you all right?"

She took a deep breath. "Sorry, yes. I'm fine. Just punchy. But I'll be all smiley and competent once I'm on camera."

"I know you will."

Katya reached out, squeezed Vivian's arm, left her hand there. She felt Gisemba's hand drop down onto her other shoulder.

*My crew's got me.* She swallowed the lump in her throat. There didn't seem to be much more to say. "Okay, Starman, thanks. We'll park, suit up, give you a five-minute warning. Then we'll come in and say hi. Hit our chalk marks, grin and shake hands, and pretend to be returning heroes."

"Wearily," said Gisemba.

Vasquez called through from the main cabin. "You *do* have champagne and flowers ready for us, right?"

"Let me check around for flowers … just kidding. Also, no champagne, though you deserve it. They'll surely put some on ice for your return to Earth. As for right now, once the cameras are off, you're welcome to some of the rotgut crap from our strictly-off-the-record bilateral still."

Feye looked bemused. "Bilateral still?"

"Sure. We thought the Russians might be good at handcrafting bathtub vodka, but it turns out they suck at it as badly as we do."

"Yet another disappointment from our Commie cousins," Gisemba said. Katya leaned across Vivian and pretended to punch him, frowning mock-tough. Gisemba flinched dramatically and grinned at her.

"Or they keep the best stuff for themselves," said Vasquez.

"I think there's no 'best' here. It's all equally corrosive."

"Can't wait." Vivian yawned. "Okay, here we come. LGS-1 out, for now."


Joint Port was located in a larger rectangular hub at the junction of Soviet Hall Four and US Hall A, central to the Zvezda-Copernicus complex and marking the boundary between the US and Soviet sectors. It was the logical place for them to return: in the neutral territory unofficially referred to as the Demilitarized Zone.

Vivian parked neatly, and they all pulled on their grimy suits. For the greater part, no one spoke. It wasn't like they needed to talk; they were all suiting up for at least the five dozenth time. Grunts and nods for the suit checks. Everything by the book, but no one was reading aloud. They were all gloomy and deflated.

The one single human moment came just before Vivian was about to lower her helmet over her head, when Okhotina leaned in, brushed Vivian's hair away from the collar of her suit and touched her cheek with her fingertips. "Thank you, Vivian," she said quietly.

Vivian felt herself flush, and for a moment didn't know where to look. Fortunately, the men were suit-checking each other and not paying attention. "You're welcome."

Well. That was inadequate. She reached out, squeezed Okhotina's spacesuited arm. "Sure thing, Kat. You've been great. Thanks for everything." She moved her hand away, donned her helmet quickly.

"Seated," Okhotina said, all business again.

Vivian gave her the thumbs up and watched as her crewwoman put on her own helmet. And realized that might well have been her last one-on-one exchange with Katya Okhotina.

Maybe that was for the best.

"Go for egress?" Feye Gisemba, almost as careful as Ellis Mayer, was coming around checking their internal suit pressures.

Vivian looked at each of them in turn. "Hey, guys? All of you. Feye. Christian. Katya. Great job, everyone. You did the mission proud. We rocked it."

She held out her hand. All three of them reached out, too. Four gloved hands joined. They all nodded at one another, made eye contact individually in turn.

When Katya looked at her, eyes wide, Vivian bumped her shoulder. "Good job, USSR. Glad to have you along. Thanks for being Super."

"You as well, Vivian Carter. *Do vstrechi.*"

"*Do vstrechi.*" Vivian swallowed, and shook hands with Vasquez, and then Gisemba. The others all shook hands too. No one attempted a high five. "Well. That's it, then. I confirm: LGS-1 crew is Go to disembark."

"Roger that." Gisemba looked around the MOLAB for a long moment, then turned to the airlock. "Let's go."

They egressed two by two: first Vasquez and Okhotina, then Gisemba and Vivian. The captain would be the last to leave her ship. Along with her logistics guy, who'd performed sterling work as her deputy throughout.

Closing the airlock door with Feye Gisemba close beside her, then depressurizing and stepping down onto the lunar surface was bittersweet. They'd be back to load out the rock samples, tidy out their personal effects, and do some final cleaning and maintenance, but it wouldn't be the same. That would be housekeeping. The mission was over.

Katya and Christian had waited, and now the four of them trudged toward the Joint Port airlock. They all fit inside with room to spare, as the new shared Zvezda-Copernicus port was rated for eight astronauts or cosmonauts and their gear.

The inner door opened. "Helmets and gloves off, leave the rest of your suits on, okay?" came Starman's voice in their headsets. Of course. Playing to the crowd on Earth, she'd almost forgotten. If anyone tuned in, that was. "And Vivian, if you could enter in first? We're rolling."

"Roger that."

She walked into a strong glare: the lights were bright inside Zvezda and there were camera flashes going off besides. Her eyes watered, and she hoped that wouldn't show on the camera and make the viewers think she was being emotional. If she *was* emotional, that was no one else's business.

Naturally she turned to the right to face the American contingent first, and the lights were brighter that way anyway. Starman was saying something about historic achievements, great lunar adventures, and so on, but his voice was booming through the loudspeakers and drowned by applause, and Vivian found his words hard to latch on to.

She stepped up to him and shook his hand. Some of the noise dimmed.

His face opened up into that well-remembered mom-and-apple-pie smile. "Welcome home, Vivian Carter and the crew of Lunar Geological Survey 1! A fabulous voyage, and an amazing achievement!"

"Thanks very much," she said. "Wow, what a great reception—thank you all. Glad to be back around. And congratulations and thanks to every one of my crew. We did this together, as one team. Feye Gisemba, Katya Okhotina, Andrei Lakontsev, Bill Dobbs, Christian Vasquez. A *great* team. Best team ever."

Starman kept smiling, rather fixedly. She could feel his discomfort. This showbiz didn't really suit him, but he was carrying it off well enough. He looked like he was fishing for words, and she was just about to help him out when he said: "So, wherever could you go to top that?"

Vivian shrugged, making it large inside the suit, and made sure the cameras had her best side. "I'm sure I never will. I'll, uh, treasure the memories for the rest of my life. Plus, we've returned with an unparalleled array of geology samples from around the entire lunar sphere, plus complete sets of other data, from gravitational measurements through to cosmic rays and high energy particles. A scientific treasure trove that'll keep researchers busy for years, and transform our knowledge of the Moon, and its geology and evolution." Okay, that was only vaguely competent. Vivian had done better. She ran dry, shook his hand again, and waved at the astros standing behind him, only a few of whom she recognized.

"A truly international enterprise," Starman prompted.

"Absolutely. We couldn't have done it without our partners from the USSR. Well, y'know, *maybe* we could,"—laughter—*because let's keep this real, after all*—"but we wouldn't have done it anywhere near as well, and it wouldn't have been as much fun." *And maybe we'd all have died without Super-Kat and her smuggled Nice Gun for Space, but you folks in front of your TV sets on Earth don't need to know that.*

Vivian smiled, nodded to Starman again, and turned to greet the Soviet commander of Zvezda Base.

She was expecting Yelena Rudenko, who'd been in charge when she'd arrived two and a half months earlier. But that's not who she saw.

The tall blond woman waiting to greet her was Svetlana Belyakova.

"Holy *shit*," Vivian said.

# PART TWO: ZVEZDA-COPERNICUS

February 1983

# CHAPTER 9

## Zvezda-Copernicus: Vivian Carter
## February 6, 1983

CAMERAS still flashed in the sudden quiet. Starman cleared his throat. "Go again. They can edit that out."

"Uh, sorry," Vivian said. "Take two." She pivoted back to face the US contingent, smiled and nodded at Starman just as she had previously, and turned. "Major-General Belyakova! What a pleasant surprise! Great to see you again. You're looking fabulous."

"As are you, Captain Carter. One moment, please, for Mother Russia?"

"Sure. Any time."

Belyakova stepped up beside her, turned to her own cameras, began to speak in Russian. They were stock phrases, very formal, and Vivian understood around two-thirds of it, but then Belyakova paused, half-turned toward the LGS-1 crew, and repeated it in English: "Welcome home, brave pioneers! You have done great honor to both the Union of Soviet Socialist Republics, and to the United States of America. Truly, this could have been done by neither country by itself. An impressive feat."

Vivian smiled and bowed. *"Bolshoye spasibo."* Thank you very much.

Belyakova faced Vivian. "We welcome you and your crew back to Zvezda Base with bread and salt, in the Russian tradition." She leaned in. For a heart-stopping moment Vivian thought the Soviet was going to give her the friendship-kiss on both cheeks, but Svetlana merely grabbed her hand, pumped it in a firm handshake, and clapped Vivian on the shoulder with her other hand. And said quietly: "Good job, Vivian Carter. Thank you for safeguarding my people, and your own honor."

"Uh. Sure thing. Glad to …" Glad to what? Vivian looked into Belyakova's eyes, forced a smile.

"We need to talk," Belyakova said. "After you have rested. Come to Zvezda."

"Okay." Vivian backed up and waved at the cosmonauts as enthusiastically as she'd done with the US-Copernicus crew. Some of them came forward to shake her hand, apparently spontaneously.

Vivian suffered it all gamely for a while, then returned to her crew who were also shaking hands, and stepped back in line with them, smiling for the cameras.

*Svetlana Belyakova, first woman on the Moon, now commander of Zvezda Base. Hoo, boy. Suddenly, I'm even more exhausted.*

Soon enough, they turned off the giant light racks and the cameramen set about packing up their gear. All the fake bonhomie from the photoshoot evaporated about as quickly as dust fell back to the lunar surface. The Americans moved smartly back to the US side. The Soviets stepped away, too. Starman stared at Belyakova, who stared back, clearly daggers drawn.

"Whoa," Vivian said. "Jeez."

Starman turned and stalked away. "Vivian, with me."

Vivian looked at Belyakova, and then Okhotina. Belyakova raised her eyebrows sardonically and walked away. Katya raised a hand in wry farewell and hurried after her.

Vasquez and Gisemba stepped up behind Vivian as they walked out of Joint Port into the American sector, and that was that. In those final fleeting moments, LGS-1 had formally disbanded.

Behind them, two Soviet guards stepped into place on the Zvezda side, with two American MPs facing them from the US-Copernicus side.

The joint Soviet/US Zvezda Base had its own frigging Border Patrol these days?

*Jeez. Yep. Definitely time to go home.*

Vivian took a sip of the lunar-distilled hooch. Even leavened with fruit juice, it was still terrible. "You could have given me a bit more notice about the dog-and-pony show."

Across from her, Starman Jones rubbed his eyes, his earlier smiles gone. He looked as tired as Vivian felt. "Didn't want to jinx it. We'd been worried about you for weeks, and you weren't home yet. We never agreed on a script with the Soviets, by the way. That was all improv. Ad hoc."

"You don't say."

"And I didn't want you to overthink it. NASA PAO didn't want you all pat and polished. Wanted to show the magnitude of your achievement through your weariness, and all."

"Then, mission accomplished." It had gone well enough. Everyone had gotten the footage they needed. And, most important: it was over. "Belyakova, though. That was a shock."

"I guess I should have warned you. Sorry." Starman shook his head, made big eyes and blew out a long breath. "Yeah. That woman …. Wow. Wow."

Vivian looked at him sideways. "Personable, right?"

"What? Criminy, no. Ice cold. Terrifying."

"Good, that's a relief, it's not just me then. So how are you enjoying working with her?"

"I think you've already seen that for yourself." Starman drained his shot glass, poured himself another. "We can function together well enough on good days. On a nuts-and-bolts level and at arm's length. Despite everything, and there's a lot of *everything*. But we definitely rub each other the wrong way. And then afterward I swing back in here and drink strong coffee. Or, well …" He raised his shot glass and took a sip. "Something even stronger."

"Don't blame you."

"Things were bad enough even before you got attacked, what with all the pilfering. And since the South Pole thing, it's all gone even further down the tubes."

117

"Yeah, I got that vibe. Armed guards on each side of Joint Port? Really?"

"We call it Checkpoint Charlie now."

"That's not funny."

"It's not supposed to be. This used to be a single base, with adjoining corridors. And now the freaking Iron Curtain runs right down the middle of it. Another?" He pushed the flask across the table.

"Do I have to?" Vivian thought about it for a moment. *What the hell. You're only young once.* She filled her shot glass again. "Anything new on the attack on us?"

"The Soviets are continuing to deny responsibility and making the ludicrous claim that we somehow attacked ourselves. The bodies and debris that the medevac airlifted out are back on Earth, being analyzed by a US team with Soviet observers. All very diplomatic and very slow."

"Huh," Vivian said. "Great."

"Anyway. Other than that, Mrs. Lincoln, how did you enjoy the play?" He grinned at her. It was almost the first trace of the old, boyish Starman she'd seen so far.

Vivian leaned back and blew out a breath, trying to erase the memory of being under fire in an insane, broken landscape with the sunlight coming in at a sinister slant. And trying not to think about going home. "You know? Apart from the obvious, it was a really great trip. Very cool. Like I said out there under the lights, I'm going to be living off the *good* memories for a very long time."

Something in her voice got his attention. "End-of-mission letdown already? You're still a week from splashdown."

"Which I'll mostly spend counting rocks and doing housekeeping, and then being a passenger on someone else's ship."

"Half of being an astronaut is housekeeping and being a passenger," he said. "And, in my case, counting supplies. At least no one was stealing yours."

"True, yeah. How's *that* going?" she said, without much real interest.

She already knew about the thefts. Hard not to. It had been one of the main topics in the hallways of US-Copernicus at the start of LGS-1, and evidently still was, armed guards notwithstanding.

Over the past months, a *lot* of NASA equipment and supplies had gone missing. Oxygen tanks, food, water, tools, tech. And, predictably, just as soon as Starman had complained to Belyakova's predecessor, Yelena Rudenko, the Soviets had counter-claimed that *their* equipment and supplies were also inexplicably disappearing and pointed the finger at the Americans.

It was a source of friction they didn't need. Everyone was on edge, and it put a serious crimp in their joint scientific activities. Plus, it meant that Starman's people were going through supplies more quickly than planned, having trouble planning ahead, and—worse— sometimes not having the equipment at hand that they needed and having to improvise.

The Moon wasn't the best place to be forced into that kind of improvisation. Day-to-day living was hard enough when things were going *well*. And, in an obvious consequence, some of the US astros were beginning to hoard. They weren't quite as willing to lend each other their tools or help out. The usual cheerful constructive atmosphere was eroding, even in the US sector. "People are getting downright tetchy," Starman concluded.

"And it's not like you can search Zvezda, trying to track it all down."

"Right. Exactly. When Belyakova arrived, she started what she called an 'investigation.' Asked to search our storage areas. Said that they'd open their doors, show us their manifests and all, if we did the same. Of course, Houston wasn't about to agree to any such thing. And I'm sure Belyakova likely only made that offer once she'd made sure all the goodies they'd stolen were stashed away, places where we'd never find them."

"I guess." Covering up petty theft didn't sound like Belyakova's style. She frowned, something else occurring to her. "Or maybe it's all just going straight to our attackers."

"What?"

Vivian elucidated. "If someone at Zvezda is covertly supplying the group that attacked us, they'd need to find a way of covering that up."

"That doesn't make sense. Why draw attention to it by thieving from us? It's not like I'm going to know if the Soviets' inventory comes up short because they're supplying their own people. They could just provision their own hit squad and leave us none the wiser."

"Well, exactly. Which, you know, does support the idea that Belyakova and most of her Zvezda crew may not even know about the hostile group. I mean, once upon a time, Belyakova *did* shoot one of her own countrymen in the heart and stand up to a psychopath to do the right thing."

He looked at her sideways. "So you're sticking up for Belyakova, now?"

"Not really. Just saying. A few years ago, her actions helped save American lives. This whole petty theft thing just doesn't feel like something she'd want anything to do with." But none of this was Vivian's problem, and it seemed soluble to her anyway. "Maybe you should just guard everything better—lock all your shit up?"

"Easy for you to say. This isn't like a real military base where everything can be guarded easily. We don't have a lot of internal storage. We need to be oversupplied in case of flight problems, and we're used to leaving the excess out back in storage containers. You know that. That's hardly secure, and we don't have the time and energy to keep organizing and monitoring it. And until your South Pole Event, we still had a lot of back-and-forth between the two sectors of Zvezda."

"But not now."

"Of course not. I shut that down right away."

Was that a good idea? Vivian wasn't sure. She said nothing.

Starman sighed. "We're adjusting. Doing our best. And we have some more surveillance gear coming with our next supply run. It'll sort itself out."

"Okay." Vivian sipped her hooch. She had other worries, and very little time left here anyway. "She wants to talk with me, tomorrow."

"Belyakova does?"

"Presumably to talk about what happened at the South Pole."

Starman shook his head. "That's not a good idea. The way things are right now, we should be talking to the Reds as little as possible."

"You're kidding."

"You're the one who was attacked, and you're arguing with me on this? The Accord is going straight to hell, Vivian."

"And it'll go there a lot quicker if we don't even *talk*."

"Vivian. If they're stealing from us to supply a covert force that is now attacking us out in the field …. Whatever game the USSR is playing, at least some of the Zvezda Soviets have to be in on it. We can't trust any of them, from Belyakova on down." He frowned. "But if I forbid you to talk to her, you'll just go over my head, won't you?"

"Uh. I don't know." She'd hardly had time to think about it. "I mean, if you order me not to, I guess that gets me off the hook. Which might be nice, actually."

But then she would always wonder what Belyakova had wanted. And it kind of pissed her off that Starman was giving her orders about it. "Seriously, it might just be better all around if you didn't forbid me." And then, aware that had come out almost sounding like a threat, Vivian added: "She's invited me over to Zvezda. That means I'll be able to take a look around, right? And who knows, maybe she wants to tell me something useful."

"Or maybe she wants to play you. Pit you against me and the other NASA people."

"Uh, how?"

"You're saying you don't think Svetlana Belyakova is manipulative?"

"No, I'm not saying that at all. Jeez, Starman …"

He drummed his fingers on the table. Eventually, he said. "All right. Fine. If you want to talk to her, then talk to her. Maybe she'll be more reasonable with you than she is with me. Or more candid, given your last experiences with her. Or something."

"Blond Svet and I aren't exactly sisters under the skin, you know."

"Worth a try, anyway. I guess it could hardly make things worse. But keep your eyes open. And watch your back around those guys. Okay?"

"Will do," she said.


At least the astronauts all got their own sleeping quarters at Copernicus, their own private spaces, albeit small. Even smaller than the sleep spaces on Columbia Station. There were no Zvezda-style dormitories on the American side. Vivian had her own teeny-tiny cubicle, just long enough to stretch out in, with a door that closed and locked. After LGS-1, it felt almost stupidly luxurious.

And yet, as soon as she locked herself into it, she missed her crew. And Katya more than anyone else.

Maybe because she'd only just been getting to know the cosmonaut by mission's end? All her NASA guys had been open books to her for years. Plus, she'd see them again on Earth, in Houston or maybe Kennedy. Hell, they'd probably get together for a barbecue every year on the mission anniversary. Vivian might never see Katya again after this week.

She pushed it all away. *Time to sleep, Vivian. Time to let go of it all.*

But letting go was harder than she'd anticipated.

Her mission was done. Already in the record books. All that was left was for them to pack up and leave. In days, she'd launch off the lunar surface for the last time. The best times of her life were behind her.

They hadn't been uniformly great, of course. *It was the best of times; it was the worst of times.*

And, on the plus side, Vivian would have plenty of time to read Dickens after this.

*Great.*

# CHAPTER 10

Zvezda-Copernicus: Vivian Carter
February 7, 1983

**THE** Soviet side of the new joint Zvezda-Copernicus Base was more extensive now, and it had been cleaned up a lot since Vivian had been imprisoned there. They had extra space, but around the same number of crew, which likely helped. The high-powered American ECS, environmental control system, was also helping to keep the humidity down. Until recently the Soviets had been regularly invited to the American modules and vice versa. For all of Starman's usual cheerfulness he was almost as much of a martinet about organization and tidiness as Norton ever was at Hadley, and the US side was always kept spick-and-span. The Soviets likely didn't want to look scruffy by comparison and had adopted a higher level of tidiness in self-defense.

Vivian strode through the halls of Zvezda unaccompanied. No escort. The Soviet guards at Checkpoint Charlie had recognized her and waved her on through. Her blue jumpsuit labeled her as American, but none of the Soviets at their posts or eating at the food stations stopped her or said anything to her. No one even batted an eye when she halted, experimentally, to study one of the command and control consoles or read a noticeboard. They appeared to be talking freely in front of her, and as far as Vivian could tell, they weren't even talking about her.

So, she had the freedom of Zvezda, now? Was even welcome here, by implication? This kind of unfettered access was not the norm now. Svetlana Belyakova clearly had a point to make.

"Hello, Vivian."

Vivian turned. It was Belyakova herself, of course, walking up behind her. Vivian felt her expression closing down instinctively, her feeling of threat rising. "Hi. Nice base you've got yourself."

"Thank you. And once again, let me offer my congratulations on your journey. I confess, I am ...." Belyakova hesitated. Looking for the right English word, or trying to avoid it? "Part of me wishes that I could have done such a thing. Journeyed to the poles? An impressive achievement."

"Thanks. So, you're in command here now? When did you arrive?"

"Just after lunar dawn, one month after LGS-1 departed Zvezda."

Around the time Vivian's convoy had arrived at Daedalus Base. "And how long's your posting here?"

"That has yet to be determined. Or at least, I have not been informed. Many factors go into the lengths of our assignments."

"What happened to Rudenko?"

"She rotated home." Svetlana crinkled her forehead in a frown that Vivian might have found fetching on any other face. "Surely you cannot expect one person to be upon the Moon for always? Rudenko has spent several extended periods on Earth over the past years."

"Makes sense." An awkward silence fell. "So, how are you? How are ... your injuries from the last time? You're obviously much improved."

Svetlana glanced around. No one was near. "If I am honest, they still hurt me, often. I try not to let it show. It was hard to get the doctors to clear me to fly again. More than hard." She searched for the word. "Uzhas?"

"Um. A ... nightmare?"

"Yes, I think so."

"I'm sorry to hear that." Vivian meant it. Last time she'd seen Belyakova, in orbit around the Moon in the severely damaged remains of Columbia Station, the Soviet had been shot in her side, missing her lungs but breaking two ribs, and taken another bullet to the thigh. She was lucky to even be walking and talking, let alone flying. All pilots could agree that flight doctors were often not their friends.

"Thank you." Another pause. "How long until you leave? You have the filing and packing of the rocks, to be taken back to your laboratories in the United States, yes?"

"My mission timeline gives me two more full days here for that. And on the third day, I pack up and scoot. I'm pretty tired, and I don't want to work all that hard, but it should be doable in that time. Even though I'm short a couple of people, for some reason." She looked pointedly at Belyakova.

"Vivian, this is very important. I need you to know. We Soviets had nothing to do with the attack upon you, down at the South Pole. Me and my people here, none of us knew anything of it. We were shocked and alarmed when we heard."

Vivian studied her. "Trouble is, if you had known, you'd likely have just said exactly the same thing. Starman told me you were claiming this must be some kind of bizarre inside job by the US. That I was attacked by my own people. You know that's crazy, right?"

"And yet it is still a possibility." At Vivian's first sign of protest, she raised a hand to halt her. "I helped you defeat Yashin. Nikolai and I both did. And, before, Nikolai warned your people of the coming nuclear attack upon them, and we risked our lives to save your life and other lives, American as well as Soviet. Why do you think I would stand still for another Soviet attack on you, if I had known?"

"We're being absolutely honest, now? Woman to woman?"

"Of course."

"Then, in that case: because, Svetlana, you're utterly untrustworthy. You went along with Yashin when he was interrogating me because you were convinced I was a spy. You watched me be tortured. And next you went along with Nikolai Makarov because he has a kind soul and a sense of justice and believes in people from all countries exploring space together—believes it to the point of being naïve, perhaps, but he does. But you only accepted what he proposed because you were his … partner, his crew." Vivian's gaze hardened. "You were close, I get that. But if Nikolai had been less of a boy scout, you would never have thrown down against Yashin and his thugs. You'd have sided with him all the way, without even thinking about it. Because that's how you've made your way through life. That's likely how you were the first woman on the Moon. And that's how come you're here now. Because you're good at playing along with whoever is nearest to you at the time."

Belyakova was staring at her. "Have you finished?"

"I'm not sure. Let me think."

"For a tired woman, you talk a great deal."

"When I get amped up, I can't help it. And you amp me up."

"Amp?" Belyakova shook her head. "Vivian … that was long ago. A lot has changed in three years. Just look at the base around you. For now, if you would only give me the chance? I want to look into this. I want to find out who attacked your people and mine, and why they did it. And so, no: at the moment, I do not believe that it was Russians. That does not make sense to me—not here, not now. I do think perhaps it was Americans, playing their own game. A group among *you*, that you yourself do not yet know about. It is not possible? It has happened before. You did not know about the secret American military base on the Moon and the mass driver that your people would have used to bombard my country with nuclear weapons."

"Well, no, but—"

"And I do not want my country to be blamed before we have had a chance to investigate, before even the study of the wreckage of your attackers has been completed."

"Okay. Sure. But if we do prove that the Soviet Union is responsible, which is, to be honest, the most likely outcome, what then?"

"*Not* the Soviet Union. It would then be just some small number of people—a splinter group only. But if that is what we find out, then yes, I would find again myself opposing some actions by my countrymen. But if we find out *your* country is responsible, you will give me the same promise? That you will oppose it?"

"Damn it, Svetlana. Do you honestly believe that *Night Corps* attacked a geological survey crewed largely by NASA astronauts?"

"Yes. A fake flag operation, to spread doubt, to give your government its excuse to break up the Lunar Accord?"

"That's 'false flag operation.'"

"Fake, false—these things are the same. Vivian, do you follow the politics of your country?"

"As little as possible."

"Your President is no friend to the Soviet Union. He rattles his saber more and more every week. What better way for Ronald Reagan to advance his …" She waved her hands.

"Agenda?"

"… his agenda, than to make a false attack on LGS-1? An attack that killed, now let me think … none of you?"

"Only by blind luck and some *very* quick thinking on our part."

126

"Perhaps."

"And all of our attackers died. I doubt that a suicide mission is in Night Corps' repertoire. Or any other part of the US military. That's so *not* an American thing to do, Svetlana."

"But that is how I know your attackers were not Soviet," Belyakova said. "For if they had been, they would not have failed so badly."

"Oh, I don't know about that."

"Vivian, your attackers: I believe that it is their goal to divide us. I think perhaps they wanted some of you left alive. Able to report, angry. To destroy the Accord, remove the chance of us working together peacefully on the Moon, maybe even start fighting against each other. And perhaps they are succeeding."

"Or maybe they just wanted to steal our gear. Force us out of the MOLAB so they could take it for themselves. *I* was clearly expendable because I nearly died. And destroying the Pod would have killed Katya, a Soviet."

Belyakova shook her head and continued as if Vivian hadn't spoken. "So that is what we must avoid: that shattering, this division we have right now. Which means we need to work together. Already your Commander Jones will barely speak with me. We are on very thin ice, always."

"Maybe. But three days from now, I'm leaving."

"Perhaps."

"I don't think there's a 'perhaps' in there. NASA's going to want me home. And I think it's time."

"And three days can be a long time, up here. You know this."

"Good grief." Vivian rubbed her eyes, breathed, rocked back in her chair, and stared at the ceiling for a few moments. "Okay. So this theory of yours just leads into a bigger question: who gains if the Lunar Accord fails? Not the US. Even if the Accord collapses tomorrow, we're not about to reconvert Bright Driver back to a Cold War weapon. And our space collaborations have been a high point of superpower relations. Collaboration is in all our interests. Isn't it?"

Svetlana eyed her. "The Moon is expensive. There are some in your country who say that you want to keep that spending high, have the USSR spend more and more money, in the hope that eventually we will run out and will fail. I assure you, that will not happen."

"Is that logical? Don't we force you to spend just as much, or more, if we continue our collaboration, with the Accord still in place?"

"Or perhaps," Svetlana said softly, "the US, or at least NASA and the United States Air Force, do not in fact have everything they want. Your space program is growing less popular in your country, no? Your American people believe the race is won, and that it is not worth spending so much money on the Moon when so much is wrong in your broken cities, so much suffering among your beaten-down and exploited proletariat. And perhaps you should spend more of this money looking after your own people.

"And *that* is why it is perhaps in NASA's interests, and in your decadent President Ronald Reagan's interests, for the Accord to fail. For then, that supports his claim that the Soviet Union is an evil that must be fought, in space and on Earth. And then NASA, too, will receive more money to continue its lunar activities."

"Wow. So you're claiming Reagan would *gain* from this?"

The expression on Belyakova's face now was something like pity. "Really, Vivian? While we are up here on the Moon, collaborating? Do you even know what your President said when he addressed the British Parliament last month?" Belyakova riffled through some papers, found the one she wanted. "He said, exactly these words: 'The march of freedom and democracy will leave Marxism-Leninism on the ash heap of history.' Does that sound like a cooperative man?"

"Ouch. Sorry. But, well ... that's just how Reagan is. He's a showman, and he pulls no punches when it comes to putting on a show. In America, politicians have to say the words their voters want to hear." Not a life Vivian would like. "And what he's saying, that's just for America. *Some* Americans. The Moon is different. Space is different."

"Is it? But it is not just words. Perhaps you have heard of Project Excalibur?"

"No. What's that?"

Belyakova looked unconvinced. "It is an American X-ray laser project, developed at your secret Lawrence Livermore Laboratory, for missile defense."

"Shooting X-ray lasers ... at missiles? Uh, hypothetically taking out Soviet ICBMs with lasers?"

"Exactly."

"Are you sure? I'd be shocked if that was possible."

"It has already been tested, in 1980—the laser at least. By Edward Teller's group. You know of Teller? You will admit to having heard of the man who developed the H-Bomb?"

"Well, sure, I know who Teller is."

"It is not even classified, the X-ray laser. Or if it was, it was leaked. It was featured in your *Aviation Week and Space Technology* magazine in February 1981."

"1981." Vivian thought about it. "I was working LGS-1 documentation eighteen hours a day for most of the year. I wasn't exactly keeping up with my reading."

Belyakova was unstoppable now. "And Reagan is proceeding. As part of his so-called Strategic Defense Initiative."

"Really?" was all Vivian could find to say. *If this is true, Mr. President, you're not doing us any favors at the moment.*

"Ask your own people. Your newspapers are calling it 'Star Wars.'"

Vivian grinned.

"You believe this is a joke? Just words again, to win over the American people? Can you not see how much this brings danger to the entire world?"

Vivian canceled her smile. "Sorry. I do get that. But 'Star Wars?' That's kind of ridiculous."

"It is a film?"

"Yes, it was a movie. I didn't see it. And, Svetlana, I can agree from the bottom of my heart that we don't want any star wars. And especially here, where it might kill us and screw up everything."

"And yet. Your President Reagan's vision is of space as a battle station. With lasers that can shoot down dozens of missiles, all at once. Space lasers." Belyakova waved her hands again, struggling to find the words. "Weapons with particle beams. Directed energy weapons."

"I agree. I think. I'd need to know more about it." Vivian glimpsed a straw, clutched at it. "But, hey. Just maybe, if this all makes a nuclear war on Earth between our countries less likely, it might be better than mutually assured destruction."

Belyakova's tone was pure ice. "Vivian, please. This is an act of profound aggression. Do you not see that? Once again, your country must escalate, must provoke. How do you expect the Rodina to respond?"

"Maybe by attacking a US-led circumlunar scientific mission," Vivian said.

That knocked Belyakova back for a moment. She blinked. "No. That is absurd."

Vivian sighed. "Svetlana, why are we even talking about this? I'm not in charge of the President."

"Because if you have influence, I want you to use it."

"Influence with who?"

"With your country. Please. You have always had much more influence than you admit. More power than you claim."

"You're tragically misinformed."

"Am I?" Svetlana raised a hand, began to count on her fingers. "America's first woman Apollo commander. Likely also a US intelligence operative. Taking spy equipment to Columbia Station. Defeating Spetsnaz officers like Viktoria Isayeva and Yashin himself in fights, hand to hand. Most of all, Vivian, your recommendations for how our two countries could each save face after the Hadley nuclear affair were adopted immediately by your government, and then by ours."

"I'm not a spy. And that last one is a big 'maybe.' Maybe we all just had the same face-saving ideas at the same time."

"And you have just commanded a round-the-Moon mission that any of your colleagues would have killed for. During which you managed to fight off a surprise attack largely single-handed."

"I ..." Vivian stopped.

Svetlana waggled her hand. "See? Already, I ran out of fingers. Is it not interesting that everything you ask for, you get? What will you do next, Vivian Carter?"

*Likely, just fly back to Earth on schedule for once, and disappear into obscurity.*

Vivian bristled. "For God's sake. Commanding Apollo 32 and LGS-1? I worked my ass off for those assignments. For years. *Years.* This is all I do. I have nothing else. No other life. Being a spy as well—when the hell did I have the time? As for the Lunar Accord ... what other way could we have handled it, short of beginning a nuclear exchange and flattening each other's cities? The thing about mutually assured destruction is that, well, it's mutually assured. *Everything* gets destroyed. Every goddamned thing, and then we're all back in the stone age. No further escalation was possible."

"Hmm."

"And so, what happened in space had to stay in space."

Svetlana sighed. "Very well, Vivian Carter. So, you claim you have no influence that you can bring to bear on this?"

"No way to stop Reagan from being Reagan, no. Sorry."

"Then, at least with Commander Jones? He is so aggressive, so impossible to talk to. Convince him that we must cooperate, for everyone's benefit."

Vivian considered. "Well. I guess I could try. But, Svetlana, you have to realize: one of the reasons he's having difficulty with you is your theory that the US attacked LGS-1. Frankly, it's crazy. It's much simpler, and more credible, for the Soviets to be our South Pole attackers."

"That depends on where you sit."

Vivian looked at her watch and stood. "Major-General Belyakova, enjoyable though this is, I have a lot to do. My team is unpacking and organizing our lunar samples, and I should be with them."

Belyakova leaned forward. "All I want is the truth. Perhaps my people are doing this, yes. There, I admit it. Perhaps this is a covert Soviet military action, as you believe, and if that is what the evidence shows, I will accept it. But will you also admit that it is possible that this is a covert *American* military action intended to bolster up the dwindling support for space within your government and among your people?"

Vivian hesitated. "I guess it's possible. Or at least not completely impossible. But devastatingly unlikely."

"All right. Then perhaps that is all I can hope for. But I do believe we must fight together on this, to keep the Accord in place." Svetlana shook her head, half-grinned. "Nikolai and his ridiculous ideals must have finally got to me. That man can be infuriating."

Vivian grinned back. "Can't they all?"

"In this, perhaps we can agree."

Vivian decided. "Uh, Svetlana? Before I go, I have an odd request."

Belyakova raised a perfect eyebrow. Did she practice that in front of the mirror? "Name it."

"Would you permit me to take a look in Storage Nine? For old time's sake?"

Now, the Soviet looked perplexed. "You wish to visit the area where you were held?"

"Incarcerated, Svetlana. I was incarcerated there, and tortured. By you."

"I was not the one who tortured you. I was powerless in the matter." Belyakova blinked. "And why would you wish to pay such a visit? For I am sure that I would not, in your place."

"In America, we have this thing called 'getting back on the bike.' Like, if you're learning how to ride and you fall off and skin your knees, it's a great idea to get right back onto that bike as soon as possible. Ride it again, quickly, before you lose your nerve. I'm guessing there must be a similar idea in Russian?"

"*Popitka ne pitka* would be the closest, I think. 'An attempt is not a torture.'"

"Uh. Maybe?" Vivian took a deep breath. "The thing is: honestly, Svetlana, I don't want to be afraid of that room anymore."

"Afraid?"

"I want to stop seeing it in my dreams. My ... *uzhas*."

"Vivian ..." Svetlana held out her hand in a convincing show of sympathy. Vivian ignored it. "Vivian, you have nothing to fear here. Not today."

"Oh, I know."

Belyakova shook her head.

Vivian grimaced. "Well, let's see. I remember how this goes. What information would you like from me, in order for you to grant me this favor in return?"

Belyakova winced. "That was unnecessary." She held Vivian's gaze a little longer, then stood. "Of course. Let me show you the way."


She guided Vivian out of her office, and down through Halls One and Two to Hall Three. Other Soviets crewing the base eyed them curiously as they passed.

Outside Storage Nine, Belyakova glanced at her again, eyebrows raised. Vivian nodded, and the Soviet opened the door.

Storage Nine was ... a storage room.

Nothing remarkable. A metal table, likely the same one. But no steel chair in the middle of the room. No blood or sweat, or worse. No tears.

As Vivian walked in, she half expected the door to slam shut behind her. It didn't.

She turned around in the middle of the room and looked back toward the doorway. Yes, that had been her view, all right. For days at a time …. She grabbed the edge of the table, suddenly nauseous.

Belyakova took a couple of swift paces toward her. "You are all right?"

Was that genuine concern in her eyes? "I'm okay. I think." Vivian nodded toward the door. "Svetlana, humor me, just for a moment. I see a clock there, above the door. You see it too. Right?"

Belyakova glanced back at the lintel. "Yes, yes. Of course there is a clock."

"Good." For a terrible moment, Vivian had thought she was hallucinating. "But there wasn't one when you kept me prisoner in here. Yashin didn't want me to be able to keep track of time. Standard torture technique, I guess. But I *imagined* there was a clock right there, many times. And it looked just like that one."

"Interesting. All areas of Zvezda have clocks. I had not noticed that Comrade Yashin had removed it when you were here."

"Well, you wouldn't, would you?"

An American might have said *I'm sorry* or some other meaningless platitude to fill the silence, but Belyakova just looked back and forth between the clock and Vivian, and then down at the floor. She clearly had no idea how to react.

"Close the door for a moment?"

Belyakova did so and stood beside it.

Vivian took her time, looking carefully around the room again. Eventually, she nodded. "Okay. It's fine. Thank you, Commander. I've seen what I needed to see. Let's proceed."

Svetlana nodded, still clearly a little mystified. She opened the door and led the way back to the Zvezda control center.


Norton had told her that Starman didn't have the leadership gene. So Vivian was guessing that, along the way, Starman must have had some gene therapy—or, maybe, just some training. Because overall, he seemed to be doing … okay.

But he'd changed.

Back at Hadley Base, Starman had been the one guy who could raise Vivian's spirits effortlessly. Those days were long gone. Now he was frowning and broody, a man with the weight of a world or two on his shoulders.

133

He did have a tough job, but he was likely taking it a bit hard. He didn't even say "Gee willikers" or "Holy crapoli" anymore.

"How did your chat with Belyakova go?"

"Oh, about as well as could be expected. She still believes LGS-1 was attacked by Night Corps. But I asked if I could pay a visit to Storage Nine, where they held me, to exorcise my demons and all. I wasn't able to root through all the cupboards, but I didn't see anything that looked like contraband from the US sector."

Starman raised his eyebrows. "Ingenious. Good work."

"I had mixed motives in that one, to be honest."

"I can imagine. Anyway, guess what? News from Earth."

"Reagan has resigned?"

"Uh, no." He studied her face, obviously decided not to ask. "They've completed the first-cut forensic analysis of the material from the South Pole event."

"And?"

"The analysis was inconclusive."

"Oh, come on." Vivian stared, then shook her head. "Inconclusive? How is that possible?"

"It's possible because out of the debris and other artifacts analyzed, some were clearly Soviet in origin, and others were clearly American."

"Oh. Right."

Starman shook his head. "Perhaps it should have been obvious. The Soviets at Zvezda are taking US resources and equipment. If they then pass those on to the attacking group, then, guess what: US material is found in the debris, and it helps point the finger at the United States. Some of the material is Soviet, so equal fingers in each direction. It muddies the water usefully for them.

"Only three of the suits survived intact enough to analyze quickly. The two from the ground attack vehicle were of Soviet origin. And the one from the flyer was a US Apollo Moon suit."

Even though Vivian had seen that suit for herself, she was still shaken to have it confirmed. "An Apollo suit. Jesus. They managed to steal a whole *suit* from you?"

He looked at her in some frustration. "No, they did not. We keep meticulous track of suits, log them in and out, log the hours on each, just like we did at Hadley. Suits are kind of a big deal, and also kind of *big*. They're kept inside in high-traffic areas. It's difficult to just walk away with one. We're not missing one, and never have been."

"Except you must be."

"Except we aren't."

"If you say so." She let it go. "Okay, so *was* that ground attack vehicle a Lunokhod?"

"Superficially similar in design. But they found no Cyrillic markings, or markings of any kind, on the wreckage."

"Any identifying features on the bodies?"

"Apparently not. Heavy burns and other damage. No military dog tags or anything."

"Almost like whoever sent them wanted to preserve the mystery, huh?" Though Vivian wasn't that surprised. Neither US astros nor Soviet cosmonauts wore dog tags anyway. In space, they were just another piece of metal that could cause problems.

Starman got up, paced. "So, terrific. Here we are, over two weeks since you were attacked, and we're still no closer to understanding what it was all about. Why you were attacked. What the hostiles were really after. And we still can't even prove beyond reasonable doubt that they were Reds."

Vivian needed to ask him a hard question. One that she didn't really want to raise, but it stuck in her throat, so she asked another.

"Starman, did you want this job? As commander of US-Copernicus. Did you pitch for it, actually apply for it?"

"Want it? No," he said. "Who would? Apply for it, yes."

"How so?"

"Somebody had to do it. Someone with experience, who wouldn't screw it up. I heard the other candidate names being tossed around the Astronaut Office, and …" He shook his head, sat down again. "No. Not one of them was anywhere near Rick's caliber."

Rick Norton, deceased commander of Hadley Base. The guy who'd ultimately given his life for his base, for his dream that Hadley would one day become a lunar city.

Though giving up his life surely hadn't been his intent. Vivian bowed her head, briefly, in respect.

"So, I tossed my hat into the ring, and for some reason the higher-ups thought it was a good idea." He looked at her. "Why do you ask?"

135

"Because we're friends. Aren't we? To be honest, it just seems that a job like this isn't really your sort of thing."

"Is that so?" His expression didn't change.

Vivian hurried on. "Then again, being boss of Zvezda doesn't seem like Svetlana's, either."

"And yet, here we both are."

"Yep. Here you both are."

Starman Jones, assigned as boss of US-Copernicus, with the prime responsibility of maintaining a good working relationship with the Soviets.

The same Starman Jones who'd seen his friends and fellow crew die all around him in a Soviet attack on Hadley Station. Rick Norton, his commander. Jim Dunlap, his partner on Apollo 22. Klein and Ibarra from Apollo 27. Probably plenty of Peter's men had died nearby, too. Vivian had never gotten the full story of that terrible day and wasn't sure she ever wanted to hear it.

Starman was likely redefining survivor guilt all by himself, and the responsibility clearly weighed heavily upon him. He would never again be the cheerful, happy-go-lucky guy he'd been way back when; the guy Vivian had met on her first arrival at Hadley.

*Apple Pie boy is becoming a man. Poor bastard.*

And that man might legitimately have strong negative feelings about the Soviets.

Maybe it would have been better to bring someone in with a clean slate to command US-Copernicus. But experience counted for a lot on the Moon, and Starman Jones certainly had all the practical experience.

"Starman. How do you feel about the Lunar Accord? Really feel about it?"

"Like it's about to disappear in a puff of smoke."

She leaned forward. "It's important that we don't let that happen. That we do everything we reasonably can to maintain it. Despite the attack on LGS-1, the thefts, all of it."

He stared at her.

"Starman?"

"You've swallowed Belyakova's Kool-Aid. Damn it, I *knew* she'd get her hooks into you if I let you talk to her."

"Belyakova says she knows nothing of the attack on us. She also says she thinks the US was responsible. I don't believe that for a second, but I do believe that she knows nothing about the attack. And I think maybe she was assigned as Commander of Zvezda Base because of that, to try to stop the Accord from evaporating because some people on the Soviet side still believe in it." *And*, she thought, *I believe that maybe you were assigned as US commander for exactly the opposite reason.*

Starman was shaking his head. "Vivian. Nothing good is going to come of this."

"It might, if we fight for it."

"I don't think so. And I don't want you making waves here."

She broke his gaze. "Fine. Just wait a few days. I'll be gone."

"Okay," he said.

"And it was Flavor-Aid," she said. "Jim Jones, at the Jonestown massacre in 1978? Flavor-Aid. Not Kool-Aid."

"Vivian, for God's sake."

"I'm just saying. Facts are important. The truth matters. Details matter."

He shook his head. "Fine. Whatever you say."

Okay. Vivian had said her piece, done all she could, and really ought to go shift some bags of Moon rocks soon, before her remaining crew mutinied.

She sat back. "Sorry, Starman. I know I'm a royal pain. Always have been. Always will be. Can't help it."

To her surprise, he grinned. "Can't argue with that. How about we change the subject? Casey has been asking after you. I'm sure he'd be happy to see you again, before you leave."

"Casey Buchanan, wow." One of the founders of the ill-fated Hadley Station, and he hadn't left the Moon since. Which had to make him the record holder for continuous lunar occupation by now. Shame that record had come about as a result of—substantial health issues.

"Though he's sleeping now. That guy sleeps a lot."

Vivian wasn't surprised Buchanan needed a lot of rest. She *was* surprised he was still breathing. "Well, I'd be happy to see him too. Where's he at? He wasn't at our welcome-home shindig, and I haven't run into him in the hallways."

"He's down at the Soviet Annex. Inside Copernicus Crater. Doing some fieldwork with a couple US scientists and checking some things out for me."

"Just my luck. When we first got here for the beginning of LGS-1, he was at Daedalus Base. By the time I'd driven around to Daedalus,

Casey had been flown back here. And now I'm here, he's in the crater? It's like he's trying to avoid me." She paused. "Uh, he's not avoiding me, is he?"

"Not if he's asking after you." Starman glanced at his calendar. "This might work. Leave it with me, let me see what I can do."

"Okay," she said. "Thanks. I mean it. And, about the Accord ... just think about it, okay?"

He rocked his head forward in feigned exhaustion. Perhaps only lightly feigned. "All right. I'll think about it."

"Thanks." She stood. "Off I go."

# CHAPTER 11

## Zvezda-Copernicus: Vivian Carter
## February 8, 1983

YESTERDAY had been a long day of moving rock samples indoors, and today had been much the same. Rocks were still heavy, even in lunar gravity. Vivian could have left more of the brute force fetch-and-carry to her crew and their Copernicus helpers, but this had been Vivian's mission, and she wanted to pull as hard as anyone else. These were *her* rocks, and she wanted everything done right. Plus, she felt like she'd sloughed off a lot yesterday, with all the discussions with Starman and Belyakova.

They had to load out the samples in reverse order of course: last in was first out. So, first had been the rocks and cores they'd taken from the South Pole to Copernicus, many of which had been stuffed into various places in the MOLAB main cabin, since they'd once again run out of room in the trailer storage racks. Today had been for the samples from Daedalus to the South Pole. They had half of those out now and were taking a break to freshen up the MOLAB interior before they finished unpacking the trailer, which was still hitched to the MOLAB.

The radio crackled. "LGS-1, this is US-Copernicus."

Vivian pushed-to-talk. "Hey, Starman. So formal, all of a sudden."

"Well, you know. We're nothing without protocol. Thought you might like to hear that call sign just once more."

"Yeah. I was kinda missing it. What's up?"

"How's your schedule looking?"

She glanced around the cabin. "Great. Samples are out, all data is copied over and safe. We're mostly just doing system checks and cleaning up, ready to hand the MOLAB off to US-Copernicus. Then we'll finish unloading the trailer tomorrow. We'll have everything wrapped up in a couple hours and be back inside the base in time for dinner."

"Swell. In that case, could you spare some time for a spot of chaperoning?"

"Say what? Are we holding a debutante ball?"

Starman laughed. "Something like that. More of a gondola ride."

Vivian's heart skipped a beat. "The *Soviet* gondola?"

"Is there another one? Figured this was a duty you might like, and you're already out there with a charged-up suit. It turns out Casey Buchanan is scheduled for a bone marrow transfusion, so we need to get his ass back up here from the Annex. We give him a constant escort on-surface in case he gets weak or passes out or whatever. He's not as young and strong as he used to be."

"I'm sure." *And I bet that's an understatement.*

"And, since you're here, Casey specifically asked if you'd be available."

"Aw. Sweet."

"So, if you'd be okay with taking a ride down into Copernicus Crater? A US team will bring Casey from the Annex to the Downstation and hand him off to you. You'll take charge of him there and hang with him, like literally hang, for the ride back to the Upstation. Hold his hand into the airlock, and then we've got him."

A miles-long ride down into one of the Moon's biggest craters in an open cable car? "Sure. Sign me up."

"Thought you might say that. I should warn you that a lot of people find the ride, well, disconcerting. But they don't have your calm pluck and adventurous spirit."

"Sounds like a dare to me," she said.

"Disconcerting?" Gisemba said. "Terrifying sounds more like it."

She cocked an eye at him. "Not coming with me, then?"

"Nah. I've taken all my stupid risks for one trip. I'd rather stay here and swab moondust out of the electronics with a toothbrush."

"Weenie," she said. "Fine. US-Copernicus, LGS-1: Vivian accepts the assignment. I just wish I could be doing it in daylight."

Starman hadn't been kidding. *Disconcerting* was about right. And she hadn't even gotten into the gondola yet.

Not that there was any hurry. Way down below her in the dark of Kopernik, Casey was still suiting up in the Annex. It would be a while before he was ready for her.

The machinery of the Upstation was open to the "elements," with just a flat-roofed ramada on telescoping poles suspended over it to shade it from the Sun during lunar day. Technically it was an aerial tramway, not a cable car: two stationary steel track cables under tension supported the gondola, while a third loop cable provided the haulage, powered by an electric motor. Everything might only weigh one-sixth of what it would on Earth, but that electric motor was indeed—yes—disconcertingly small. At least the cables were thick. They had to be; the four miles of cable that would take her down and across were the heaviest part of the whole mechanism.

"Well, all aboard, Vivian," she said, and stepped into the gondola, which naturally swayed back and forth in slow motion as she moved to the control bench and sat.

Though the controls were marked only in Cyrillic, they were obvious: stop, three speeds of Go, an emergency brake, and a panic button. A mechanical readout of three numbered wheels presumably told her … something useful? Distance traveled along the cable, in metric? There was also a console light, which she switched off after her first scan of the board. Her helmet headlight would be sufficient to see what she was doing, and once she got herself settled, she powered that off too, wanting to be as dark-adapted as possible for the ride.

She was on the edge of shivering and tweaked up her suit heaters.

Hmm. The cables she was hanging from had been alternately heated to 250° F and cooled to –210° F every single lunar day for several years, now. Presumably someone had thought of what that might do to the steel, or whatever else they were made of. At least there were

141

two cables. If one gave, the other should still support the weight of the gondola and stop it from tumbling down to the crater floor. But Vivian couldn't help wishing this whole tramway had been constructed by the US rather than the Soviets.

No time for second thoughts. It had worked fine for this long, and she was committed now. She pushed-to-talk on her suit chest controls. "Here's Viv in the gondola, about to plunge into the abyss. Hopefully not literally."

"Enjoy the ride," said Gisemba in the MOLAB, and "Copy that," said whoever was on console in US-Copernicus. "We'll notify the Annex."

Vivian pushed the drive handle forward. And off she went, sinking into a deep shadow even darker than the usual lunar night.

Far below her, and a surprisingly long way into the crater, she could now glimpse the tiny L of dim blueish light that marked the Soviet Kopernik Annex. As her eyes adjusted, she became more aware of the craggy terraced rock walls just thirty or forty feet away, and the expanse of the crater rising around her.

A hundred kilometers across, this crater. Phew.

Her breathing sounded loud in her helmet, and she could hear her heartbeat as the blood pulsed in her ears. The night around her was a combination of eerie dark blues and grays, punctuated by utter blackness where the crater walls themselves occulted the sunlight reflected from the waning gibbous Earth in the sky above. And that Earthshine was nowhere bright enough to mask the light from a billion stars in the firmament above her.

"Thanks, Starman," she said, though she'd turned her microphone off and didn't have line of sight to US-Copernicus anymore. "This is cool. Makes up for a lot."

This was far from being a rigid system, of course. The wires above her had settled into a slow oscillation, maybe swaying back and forth in response to some lateral forces she'd applied right at the top, or maybe introduced by the haulage cable or the motor. "Sure glad I don't get seasick though."

At her current speed—the slowest, because Vivian didn't want or need to hurry—it would take about twenty-five minutes to get to the crater floor. "May as well get comfy." She turned her suit heating up another notch and watched the crater walls and uneven terracing go by at a stately pace, dimly illuminated by starlight.

No one was at Downstation yet when she arrived, so Vivian stepped out of the gondola to walk the crater floor and kick up the dirt a little. Far off in the distance she could see the shadowy spires in the crater center. "Sure would be nice to go exploring." In all her travels across its surface, she'd never had the opportunity to see central peaks like that up close.

No time for that, though. Not today because she had an old sick astronaut to escort back to US-Copernicus for medical treatment, and not tomorrow because she had a full final workday prior to being launched off the Moon for the last time. Back into lunar orbit, then once around before the trans-Earth injection burn, after which the Moon would shrink behind her forever.

For so long now, living and working on the Moon had almost settled into a kind of normality. But it wasn't normal at all. Her life was about to change again, this time irrevocably.

Some of the astronaut staff at US-Copernicus, and at Daedalus Base for that matter, were long-termers. Like Starman Jones, they might come to the Moon for repeated tours of duty at one or the other of the bases. But moonbase life required expertise that Vivian didn't possess, based on a substantially different training. Vivian had been trained as a pilot and explorer and part-time lunar geologist, and those were not skills that US-Copernicus needed. She might possibly worm her way into the chain of command, but then what? Then she would become Starman, constantly worried about logistics and duty rosters and thefts, and the shaky political balancing act he was playing with the Soviets. It would be a desk job, even if that desk was on the Moon and Vivian got to fly back and forth to Earth from time to time. Her career would trail off with a whimper, rather than a bang. It wouldn't be *fun*.

No, Vivian's glory days were over. Three missions, or four depending on how you counted them: her first Earth-orbital mission, Apollo 32 plus her Hadley Base "reassignment," and now LGS-1. That would be enough. She would be dead-ending here and going home.

And considering how many times she'd nearly died on or around the Moon—and the people she'd nearly taken with her some of those times—that was all for the best.

She put it out of her mind and knelt down. Kneeling was much easier in the newer suits than it had been back in the Apollo 32 days. She scoured the surface until her gloved fingers came up with a large pebble about the size and shape of her thumb. *One more for the mantel.* She tucked it into the calf pocket of her suit, stood, looked up and around again.

Three helmet headlights were bobbing toward her, still quite distant. She turned on her radio again. "Annex crew? Vivian."

"Vivian, Casey," came a voice she recognized well, though perhaps a little creakier than when last she'd heard it. "Long time no see. Not that I can really see you now. How's it hanging?"

"It's all hanging just fine, sir."

She tilted her head back again. Stars, stars everywhere, bounded by the hard cutoff of the crater wall. A type of view she'd never seen before because she'd rarely been out at night, and never been in the depths of a crater this large, with walls this sheer.

Relatively sheer. It was more like a giant's staircase. But those ridges, that irregular terracing, wasn't too evident from these depths.

All this time on the Moon, and still a new experience.

Maybe she should have come down a bit quicker, and spent longer walking down here on the surface? No, best not. Walking at night had its dangers, too. The further she went, the greater the chance she'd trip up and go ass over teakettle. Just because Vivian was used to being out alone on the lunar surface didn't reduce the ever-present risk. Especially at night, in the cold and the dark and far from safety.

Casey's honor guard arrived. The two NASA astronauts, loping slowly along to adjust their speed to Casey's, introduced themselves briefly and with a hint of awed deference. They were from an astronaut class long after Vivian's, and she vaguely remembered them as fresh-faced kids from one of the classes she'd taught on lunar survival. Casey, walking in between them, was obvious from his deliberate, fragile gait. He'd left his microphone on, and she could hear how heavily he was breathing. He was almost gasping, poor old dude. "Hey, Casey. Good to see you."

He nodded. "I'm not there yet, am I?"

"Nope. Downstation is about a hundred feet farther on. Thataway."

"Great. Carry me?"

"Not a chance. But take your time. I'm in no rush. It's great, out here."
He paused. "It's dark, Vivian. And cold."

"Yes, sir," she said. "Yes, it is. And deep."

"Well, each to her own."

They got him the rest of the way, his two astronaut minders each taking an arm to steady him as he stepped into the gondola. He sat, still breathing hard.

Once up at the crater rim, Casey would have another twenty-minute walk down to US-Copernicus, but at least that would be downhill. He likely wouldn't be in a hurry. They could enjoy their night out.

"Thanks, guys," she said. "I've got the crusty old coot from here on."

He grunted. "Nice bedside manner, Carter."

"Roger that," said the astronaut on the left—she could tell because his helmet bobbed in time with his words—but they both stood and watched as she fired up the motor. With a creaking that was transmitted through their suits, the gondola scraped on the ground and ponderously began its long progress back up and out of the crater. *So long, Copernicus, I hardly knew ya.*

"I hear you had a bit of trouble down at the South Pole."

"That? A breeze. We had it all under control."

Buchanan grunted again. "Hearing about it made me feel extremely safe down here, surrounded mostly by my Soviet friends."

"No one is going to mess with you," she said. "You're an institution. A monument."

"Oh, stop."

"Okay." She leaned forward, patted him on the leg. "But hey, I never said thanks. For the way it all turned out after Hadley. What you told me played a huge part in what happened after that."

"You're very welcome." He paused. "Uh, can I see you?"

"I don't know. Can you?"

"I mean, your face. It's been three years. So we can really talk." Casey turned on the telltale lights inside his helmet, illuminating his own craggy features.

"Sure, why not." Vivian flipped on her own interior helmet lights, blinked as the sudden illumination momentarily dazzled her.

"You look good," he said. "Haven't changed a bit."

145

"A likely story." She peered through his visor.

Buchanan looked terrible. Thin to the point of emaciation. Blotchy skin that looked like paper. It was at the same time shocking and not at all surprising.

She smiled cheerfully. "You too. Looking great."

He grimaced, touched his helmet self-consciously. "You're very kind to say so."

"No, really. Bald looks awesome on some men. So, uh. How are you?"

Buchanan looked at her thoughtfully. "Fine, how are you?"

"No, I really want to know."

He grinned. "Okay. Because some people really don't, and I don't want to inflict my sob story on anyone who doesn't want to hear it. And why would you?"

"I do," she said, and meant it. "I care. And I want to hear it. Tell me."

"Okay. You didn't expect to ever see me again, did you? At least, not alive."

"Frankly, no."

"You thought I'd shuffle off this mortal coil sometime over the past three years?"

"If I'm being honest—yes."

Casey grinned, not offended. "And in an equal spirit of honesty, I felt the same about you. From Soviet radio chatter and the disappearance of Gerry Lin's LM we were pretty sure you'd somehow made it out of Zvezda, but the chances that you'd survived augering in seemed remote, still less trudging all the way back to Hadley cross-country with no shelter or support. That day when Peter patched me through to Starman's LM so's I could drop my cryptic clue, I was fairly convinced I was just shouting into the void and that Captain Vivian Carter was already enjoying her well-deserved and eternal rest on the lunar surface."

"Enjoying." She tried not to shudder. "Yeesh. Anyway, why are we talking about me?"

"Because I'm old, sick, and boring, and you're young, cute, and accomplished."

"Uh, sure …. Anyway. Colonel Buchanan, I request a candid briefing on your health and prospects. For my own information, if nothing else, since I've taken quite the cumulative radiation load myself. Who the hell knows what's in my own medical future?"

"Roger that. I hope you have no pressing engagements." Buchanan paused. "But you're likely fine. Aside from the Hadley detonation, you've accumulated your total over a long time, and our ships and suits are much better at protecting us than they used to be. I got most of my exposure from a big solar storm event. Acute radiation syndrome."

"Must have been awful."

"It was. For the first three weeks after that, they didn't expect me to live out the month. Then, when I did: well, people with radiation sickness sometimes do appear to get better before they get worse again, so no one was giving me any long books to read.

"Anyway. Before you ever arrived at Hadley the first time around, Klein and the other NASA folks had done a lot for me by way of treating infections, maintaining my hydration. I was anemic and got injured easily. They gave me blood transfusions, and then platelet transfusions, and so many other transfusions that I lost track. Uh, are you sure you want to hear this?"

"Keep going."

"Okay. See, with radiation, a huge dose will just destroy your cardiovascular system in days. A bit less, and you'll still be dead in under two weeks from gastrointestinal collapse. Less again, and you have some chances of survival, and the thing that deals the killing blow is generally the destruction of bone marrow, causing infection and internal bleeding." He grunted. "Fun stuff, huh?"

"Yes, sir, sounds like … fun." She'd been about to say *a blast*.

"Not sure I like being 'sir' again. Anyway. It wasn't long before I started needing bone marrow transfusions."

"I'm impressed they can even do that on the Moon. Doesn't sound like an outpatient procedure to me."

"It's not as complicated as it sounds. It isn't a full-up operation, they're not exactly carving their way into my bones with a hacksaw. Let's just say that a really large needle is involved, and I feel like crap for a month afterward, every single time. But it sure beats the alternative." He peered over at her. "Want to hear my own personal half-baked, cockamamie fringe-science opinion?"

"Sure, why not?"

"I think that being on the Moon is what's kept me alive. Everyone I meet up here is fit and healthy, and was screened comprehensively before liftoff, which reduces the chance of any opportunistic infections that might take me out. And if my bones and joints are weaker than anyone else's—which they are—well, that matters less here, too. My spinal cord isn't what it was. It's basically twisted to shit, and aches like hell most of the time; it's aching right now. If they forced me to go back to Earth, the G's of reentry would kill me for sure, before I even made splashdown. I'd just snap in a whole bunch of places, while my internal organs raced to see which one could fail first. Even if I lived through it, I'd never walk again. But even if I was magicked back onto the Earth's surface without all that, I'd still be in poor shape, and likely wouldn't be walking anyway. One solitary G is probably way too much for ol' Casey right now. But as long as I stay here, I'm doing okay."

"So, your prognosis is actually … good?"

"Well, about that," Buchanan looked wry. "Hey, I survived long enough to get leukemia, so that's an achievement, right? It often shows up a couple years after a big radiation dose. So that's my current problem. That and the cataracts forming in my eyes. But I still might have another two years left, even three, and for all that time the space medicine people will be getting a ton of data on me. I'm my own one-man research project. Being tested to destruction."

Vivian winced. "Don't be like that."

"Well, it's true. I'm a radiation guinea pig."

She appraised him. "More like a lab rat. A hairless rat."

"Thanks." He grinned. "Just don't ask how many pills I'm on. If you shake me, I rattle."

She nodded, straight-faced. "So, all I need to do to stay here permanently is earn myself an even bigger dose of radiation than I've had already?"

He paused. "Wow, you're dark. I wouldn't wish this on anyone."

"Sorry. And, yes, you're right. Somewhere along the line, I did get dark. I'll try to lighten up sometime. Maybe in a month or two." *Sure.*

Vivian well knew how complicated radiation was. Every single one of them was suffering a steady influx of radiation, both from galactic cosmic rays—GCRs—and solar particle events. The GCRs were high-energy particles consisting of protons, helium nuclei, and other heavy nuclei. Produced in supernovae across the galaxy, there was no keeping them out. Solar particle events originated closer to home, when protons from the Sun were accelerated by solar flares and coronal mass ejections. It was an SPE that had originally irradiated Buchanan to that almost fatal level that still hadn't quite killed him.

On Earth, people were protected by the atmosphere. On the Moon, not so much. And when GCRs hit regolith, the collisions released neutrons and gamma rays, and God knew *that* didn't help. Which was why when the Zvezda people used regolith as a protection against radiation, they needed to ensure that it was approximately 80 centimeters thick. Paradoxically, any *more* than that, and the walls themselves would irradiate the dwellers within.

Staying alive on the Moon was complicated. Always.

Eventually, they crested the crater rim. "The journey back up seemed a lot quicker than the journey down," she said. "Guess that's because I had good company."

"Eh, flattery will get you nowhere."

"Oh, I don't know about that." Vivian looked around at the dark walls of Kopernik, across at its spires, and at the skies above. Drinking it all in, while she still could.

"Vivian?" A pause. "I'm very proud of you."

Suddenly, her throat closed up. "Uh, me? And why's that?"

He waved a hand. "Oh, I know, I know. I should only be *proud* if you're something I made, something I did. And I did nothing. But *you* did good work, Carter."

*Did.* "Thanks." The silence began to last uncomfortably long as the gondola rocked to stillness beneath them. "Well. I guess we should get out of this thing."

"Yeah. Seems like it's not going to carry me over to Zvezda."

" 'Fraid not. Stay put till I'm up and out, and I'll give you a hand."

"Sure thing, nurse."

"I know, I'm fussing … but see it from my point of view: Starman would be on my case for the rest of my life if I broke you."

"I'm already broken."

"Oh, stop."

She helped him out—he was actually pretty steady on his feet, now that he'd been able to rest—and they began the long trudge down to Zvezda Base. Casey was slow and careful, shining his headlight down at his feet to make sure he wasn't about to trip. Vivian walked beside him, adjusting to his pace, saying nothing and controlling the urge to hold onto his arm. At least he was walking under his own steam, which was something Bill and Andrei hadn't been able to achieve once they were injured. The Moon had damaged all of them, one way or another.

And through it all, Vivian was still fine. Still walking. She should really count her blessings more often than she did.

A sudden blow to the back of her legs threw her onto her knees, and the weight and momentum of her PLSS backpack kept her tumbling forward. Vivian raised her arms to block her fall, and then another hard thrust against her right hip robbed her of any chance of controlling it. She sprawled messily onto the lunar soil, trying to roll so that she might get her feet back under her again. "What the *hell*?"

A bellow of rage from Casey ripped her to the bone. She had no idea his wounded lungs could be capable of such a sound.

Vivian rolled onto her back. Three dark spacesuits loomed above her, and as one of them stepped forward, something came fluttering down to cover her. A heavy, wide-mesh net. "Damn it! Jesus H. Christ … Mayday, Mayday! Vivian under attack. *Again.* Zvezda—Svetlana! Starman!—we're being attacked out here. Three hostiles."

Even *in extremis*, Vivian's cold logical center noted that she'd called on Svetlana first. Odd.

Next, that cold center noted that the suits of her attackers once again looked similar to those of Night Corps. But they weren't. Gray, like many of their South Pole attackers. One of them had a red flash on his right bicep and right thigh. Maybe their commander? Vivian kicked at him, but still couldn't reach him. "Get the hell back, assholes. I'm armed."

She wasn't, though.

She scrambled, but the net hampered her; the more she moved, the more tangled up in it she became. Casey was on the ground to her right, also covered by a net, also flailing. But two of the hostile cosmonauts were focused on her, just one on Casey. Probably because she was younger and stronger, at least in theory. "I am *totally* going to kick your asses."

Hopeless bravado. They wrapped her in the net. The two of them started to drag her across the regolith.

"Who the hell *are* you shitheads, anyway? Spetsnaz? Night Corps? Santa's little helpers?"

Nothing back, of course. Vivian thrashed, and only got herself tangled up worse. "Mayday, Mayday, Vivian to NASA, Vivian to Zvezda, anyone: we're under attack by the crater's edge …"

Nothing. She hadn't heard a sound from Casey since they'd thrown the net over her. And no one would hear her now. The net was heavy, even on the Moon, so it was likely metal-cored. They'd wrapped her in a goddamn Faraday cage. No radio signals were getting in or out of it.

And they were dragging her uphill. The realization came like a sledgehammer.

*Oh, God. They're going to throw me into Copernicus Crater.*

*It's over two miles down.*

*I'm dead.*

She wasn't wrong. At least about being thrown into the crater.

Her attackers hauled her off the ground, still wrapped in the net, and swung her back and forth. Vivian shoved, trying to extend her arms and legs, but she was tightly cocooned. *Damn it.*

She ran numbers, almost reflexively. Weight of her spacesuit on Earth: two hundred and eighty pounds. Weight of Vivian plus suit: about four hundred and ten pounds. Divide by six and call it seventy pounds. *Even on the Moon they're not going to be able to whirl me around their heads and send me flying through space. It'll be a lob, not a pitch.*

But they were strong and getting the knack of this. They hefted her up higher.

Vertiginous swaying, and now their swing felt clean and steady rather than messy and uneven. Sky, rocks, attackers, all became a half-lit blur.

At the height of their swing, they let go of her.

Freefall. Vivian tumbled through the air. The net loosened as she thrashed, pushing outward with arms and legs. Her right arm felt freer, but she had nothing to grab.

Bright stars wheeled above her, broken by the stark blackness of the crater wall she was falling past.

*Shit …*

# CHAPTER 12

## Copernicus Crater: Vivian Carter
## February 8, 1983

*ONE, two, three, four, five, six, seven, eight ...*

Vivian hit on her left shoulder. Bad, agonizing, painful as all hell. She screamed, scrabbled, couldn't get a grip on anything because there was nothing there. She was flying through space some more. *I bounced, damn it.*

She hit again, this time on her ass, jarring her spine—felt herself turning over. Her right arm and helmet slammed down again, the impact sending another sword of pain through her left shoulder. "Gahhhhhh!"

Vivian skidded, spun. And then slammed into something that brought her to a sudden, shocking, merciful halt.

She lay still, face down, visor pressing against rock.

*Oh God. Oh God. Ow.* Her shoulder was killing her. And her ribs. *Oh God.*

Where was she?

On the staggered terracing of the inner rim, of course. Even two men couldn't throw her far enough out that she'd arc all the way down to the crater floor. She'd hit rock, then more rock. And that's what she was lying on now: rock.

Vivian lifted her head painfully and saw only darkness. Her headlight was smashed. Well, okay, but she still had the dim light from the telltales inside her helmet. She blinked, waited, breathed, and in a few moments brought the rock into dim focus, inches in front of her visor.

She looked the other way. Kopernik stretched out before her into the distance. But it was too dark to get a good sense of how much leeway she had before the ledge dropped off again.

She *really* didn't want to fall any deeper into Copernicus. The inner wall was extremely irregular. No particular reason to believe she would survive another big drop.

"Mayday, Vivian Carter down and inside Copernicus. I need help. I need it bad."

Radio silence. No line of sight to the bases, either above her or below, and she was still mostly inside the metal net.

She still had power, at least. The fan still whirred in her helmet. She couldn't get her wrist up high enough to see her pressure gauge, but her suit still seemed firm and well-pressurized. If it was compromised, the damage must be minimal.

She twisted again and craned her neck to look up. Sixty, seventy feet to the crater top rim? More? Hard to tell. Too dark.

She reached out as far as she could in each direction, tapping the rock beneath her. She shuffled closer to the rock wall and figured it out. She had at least a couple feet of horizontal space to work with between her and the edge of the ledge she had fetched up on.

So her next problem was the goddamned net.

Carefully, super carefully, she raised herself up onto her hands and knees—gritting her teeth against the sharp and insistent pain in her shoulder—and set about disentangling herself.

She had a clock on her helmet display, just above her eyeline, so she knew it took a full ten minutes to finally get herself free of the net. She was tempted to kick it over the edge, but maybe its materials or construction might provide a clue to who had made it.

Or perhaps she could use it to help herself climb back up?

No. That would be crazy. Climb a rock face in a spacesuit? Couldn't be done. At least, not by Vivian. If she was going to be rescued, someone was going to have to come and damn well rescue her.

*Casey …*

The attackers hadn't been after her. They'd been after Casey Buchanan. To kill him? Capture him? Why?

Well, that one was easy.

153

She swallowed bile, pushed the thought out of her mind. *Not now. That can wait. Unless I get out of here, nothing else will matter. At least, to me.*

She eased herself around and eventually, clumsily, pulled herself into a sitting position. Being very careful about scraping against the wall behind her, because her VHF aerial was sticking up out of her PLSS backpack. Not that she could see it, but she could feel it when she reached an arm behind her neck.

Okay, time to review. Suit pressure: okay. Oxygen: another four hours. Water: to drink, almost none, but Vivian could feel it still swishing around her LCGs, keeping her warm against the bitter cold of lunar night. Battery power: okay for now, but she would burn through it quite quickly. Two hours, maybe?

It would have been really handy if she'd had a flare gun. Or any kind of secondary lighting other than the low-level intrinsic lighting from her helmet and chest panels, which was … low-level indeed. Now that her eyes had adjusted, she could see glints of starlight off the rocky crater walls that seemed almost as bright.

Penlight. All suits had a penlight in the calf pocket. In all her time on the Moon, Vivian had rarely needed to use one.

She reached down, and there it was, and it even worked. She flicked it on and off.

Now she just needed someone to signal to, and that would be a matter of time. Eventually someone would come looking for her and Casey, but it likely wouldn't even occur to anyone to do so for another … half hour? Hour? Depended on how much Starman was paying attention. Or Gisemba. Or whichever doctor was waiting for Casey to show up.

"All by myself again," she said. "In trouble. In a spacesuit. Out on the fricking Moon. Again."

She looked up at the Earth, that blue jewel in the sky.

*Yeah. It's definitely time to go home. Past time. Enough of this shit.*

It actually felt like a weight off her mind, to not be dreading the return to Earth.

*Baby steps, Vivian. You're still partway down a very big cliff.*

"Mayday, Mayday. Vivian Carter. Been attacked and tossed into Copernicus. Currently sitting on a ledge all by myself. Casey has been taken. I need extraction, stat. Somehow."

*Damn, but I'm calling in a lot of Maydays these days.*

She made herself repeat the litany every five minutes. After the first hour, she didn't even sound like she was in peril. She just sounded extremely bored.

"Vivian Carter? Please respond."

Her head jerked up. "Yeah? Here. Here!"

"Where are you, Vivian?"

Was this the first time she'd ever felt relieved to hear Svetlana Belyakova's voice? "I'm down the cliff. Maybe a hundred feet down, on a ledge. I have a penlight. Or I did. Hang on." It wasn't in her hand. Where had she put it? Stupid.

"Status?"

"Suit seems okay. Air and water fine. Battery power is my limiting factor; I've got maybe another hour. But I've got a damaged left shoulder, hurt some ribs, and might even have broken some, can't tell. I'm pretty banged up."

"Have you coughed up blood, or anything else? Are you short of breath?"

*Wow, the ice queen even sounds concerned. Great acting job for the mission tapes, Commander.* "No, none of that. Just the pain. I'll live." *I guess.*

"All right. Is Colonel Buchanan with you?"

That was almost funny. Almost.

"No. I last saw him tangled in a net, up at the rim, before they tossed me over the side. I don't know what happened to him after that. If he's not up there, then he's … likely dead somewhere else, or he's been taken. Captured, kidnapped." *Probably by Soviets, Bel. Maybe check in with your own people?*

Or maybe also thrown into the abyss, but why kill a man who was at death's door anyway?

No. They'd taken him alive. That was the only answer that made sense.

"US-Copernicus, this is Belyakova. We have located Captain Carter with minor injuries. We will winch her out. Colonel Buchanan is still missing, status unknown."

"Belyakova, US-Copernicus. Roger that." Ah, that typical NASA lack of emotion in a crisis.

Vivian didn't recognize the voice. Not Starman, though he must be aware of what was going on. So, he was content to leave her in Belyakova's hands, right after another Soviet attack? Nice.

Vivian found the penlight back in her calf pocket where it was supposed to be and pulled it out. Flashed it on and off a few times, three shorts, three longs, three shorts. "Here I am. See me?"

"I see you, Vivian."

"Maybe tell Feye Gisemba what's up, get him over here? He's mostly suited up."

"Gisemba will be notified. But he is busy, and we have the winch. Stand by."

"Busy?" Helping to search for Buchanan and their attackers, maybe? It looked like Vivian was stuck with Belyakova's tender mercies. "Okay. Standing by."

And how convenient would it be if the Soviet winch 'broke,' while bringing her up?

No. Svetlana could have just left her right here on this ledge, pretend never to have found her, and Vivian would have been dead in an hour. Or maybe forty-five minutes. Deliberately killing her now would be a bad idea. "Accidentally," though?

"Hey, Svetlana, let's not cut this too fine, okay? If it's going to take you a while to get the winch secured, I'll need auxiliary battery power and a cable."

"Do not worry, Vivian. We will be swift."

Now Vivian saw a dark form against the sky, felt a vibration in the rock. The gondola was leaving the cliff top, much faster than when she'd ridden it herself. A searchlight beam played over the rocks around her.

"Vivian, tell me when my man in the car is level with your position. Also, shine your penlight at him."

"Ten more vertical feet." Horizontally, the gondola was maybe sixty feet distant, too far to be of any use in retrieving her. "Five. Three. Okay, he's there." Vivian flashed the light, and the next moment was blinded by the searchlight beam. "Ack, there goes my night vision. Tell him to point that at my feet."

Belyakova snapped out a command in Russian, and the bright light shifted downward.

"Thanks."

"Good. We have you triangled."

"Triangulated?"

"Yes. It will take us just a few more minutes to position the winch, and then I will come down."

"You do house calls, now?"

Belyakova didn't answer that. Vivian heard her giving terse instructions in Russian to her unseen comrades. She sipped the last of her water through her suit straw and waited.


Two lights now: one from the gondola, still trained on the ledge where Vivian sat, and the other from the crater rim, shining on Belyakova, guiding her as she rappelled down the cliff face. The rim seemed even farther up now that Vivian could see it illuminated, but Belyakova was making short work of kicking her way down it, bouncing off the rock face in long arcs.

"You've done this before," Vivian said.

"Yes. We have done drills, in case of emergency. I am the most experienced, which is why I am doing it now."

"Not just because you like me, then."

"Vivian, I must concentrate. Please just be quiet and wait to be rescued."

"Roger that, Commander," Vivian said meekly.

Minutes later the two searchlight beams converged, and a tall figure in an orange suit alighted precariously on the ledge right next to her. Through the faceplate Vivian could dimly see Belyakova's blond hair framing her face. "Here, Vivian. Take these clips; tether yourself to me so that you cannot fall farther. Do not try to stand up yet."

*Stand up? Here?* "Don't worry. That's not in my plan."

It took much longer to winch the two of them up than it had taken Belyakova to reppel down. Vivian did appreciate Belyakova's efforts to keep her from banging or scraping against the rock wall as they rose, but her concern was growing about her battery reserves by the time they crested the clifftop and the winch swung them around to the left, putting solid ground beneath her boots once again. "Uh, Svetlana? I only have fifteen minutes left."

"This is not a problem." Belyakova gestured beyond the winch vehicle, where three cosmonauts were busying themselves packing away the mechanisms. Beyond them, Vivian now saw a Lunokhod Rover waiting with a cosmonaut at the helm, vaguely sinister, dark against the regolith. "Get in."

"Stand by," she said. "US-Copernicus, this is Vivian. I'm back on the rim and headed down."

"Roger that, Captain Carter. The Commander has US-Copernicus under lockdown pending our rover sweeps of the vicinity. All emergency bulkheads are in place, hatches are sealed, and the power to Joint Port has been disabled. Please proceed to Zvezda Base with our friends." The "friends" was spoken with neutral clarity.

Vivian blinked. "Uh, sure. Wilco." She glanced at Belyakova, then at the Lunokhod.

"Good to see you again, Vivian," said the Lunokhod driver. It was Katya Okhotina.

"Still no sign of Casey?"

"None that we can tell. We see signs of a struggle, scrapes and scuffles in the dust. That is all."

The area around Zvezda-Copernicus was so crisscrossed with boot prints and wheel tracks, it was impressive if they'd even been able to discern that much. Maybe the scrapes and scuffles were off the usual Soviet beaten path?

Anyway. Time was ticking. "Copy," Vivian said, and stepped up onto the Lunokhod beside Katya.


"Understand that I requested an American doctor to come to Zvezda to treat you," Belyakova said. "I would not want any suspicion, any accusations of poor treatment that is alleged to be not up to your American mark. Nothing your country can use against mine. Commander Jones declined my request. I asked him twice."

Vivian nodded. "Understood."

They drove her to Zvezda and helped her into Hall Three, where Belyakova, Okhotina, and a Soviet medic maneuvered her out of her suit and put her onto a stretcher, carefully enough that Vivian only howled in pain a couple of times. They carried her to a small sick-bay area, which mercifully looked nothing like Storage Nine. There, the doctor checked her over thoroughly, assessed her rib fractures, then gave her a painkilling injection and swabbed her many abrasions. Okhotina stayed by her side throughout, while Belyakova stepped out to monitor developments from the Zvezda control center. Vivian lay quietly, breathing shallowly, asking no questions. Taking time to recover.

She still had faint scarring on her right shoulder from Yashin's bullets, three years ago, and now her left shoulder had gotten pummeled. *So now I've injured both shoulders in the line of duty. That's just great.*

The doctor turned to Okhotina, spoke rapid Russian.

Okhotina translated. "Your shoulder is sprained. A … ligament is torn. He does not believe that any of your ribs are broken—he cannot guarantee it—but you have very bad bruising."

That all made sense. Vivian would likely have felt even worse if the ribs were broken, but even if they were, they tended to heal themselves in a few weeks, right?

A few weeks? For the first time, Vivian wondered what that meant for her imminent departure. She said nothing, though. That would be up to the American doctors and NASA.

Belyakova walked back into the sickbay, looking grim. *Uh-oh.* "What's happened? Have we located Buchanan?"

Svetlana held up a hand and spoke briefly with the Soviet physician, so briefly that Vivian was able to follow even with her creaky Russian. "Yes, yes, I'm fine. Tell me," Vivian demanded.

"On Buchanan: Commander Jones has sent out armed search parties on rovers. He has refused my offer of Soviet assistance in the search. I believe that is a mistake. But there is more." She met Vivian's eye. "More bad news."

"Then spill it."

"Your MOLAB was also stolen."

Vivian's first reaction was to try to sit bolt upright, a major error that left her shrieking with pain again. Okhotina grabbed her arms, guided her back down, slipped her hand into Vivian's and squeezed.

Vivian gasped the breath back into her lungs and tried again. "Stole my freaking *MOLAB*?"

"Yes. And its trailer, the Pod."

"God damn it, Feye was in there!"

"Yes. He is safe, Vivian, unharmed. But yes, he was still in the MOLAB. Two intruders entered the airlock. Gisemba was not wary—he believed it was you returning. When he opened the airlock door, he was at gunpoint. They made him start up the MOLAB and begin driving it away. They watched how he did it and then directed him to

159

suit up and exit. He had to walk back five miles, but he is now safely back inside US-Copernicus."

"Good grief." Vivian breathed as deeply as she dared. No wonder Starman had sealed up the US sector. "This is major. Jeez."

"Yes."

They could just as easily have slit Gisemba's throat. For that matter, they could have shot through Vivian's visor or hacked open her suit. "Thank God they didn't want to rack up a body count. Okay, get your tame doctor to bind me up. I need to get back outside."

Okhotina put her other hand back on Vivian's arm. "Do not be foolish."

Vivian ignored her and addressed Belyakova. "I need a bike. A rover will never catch up with a MOLAB, if it ..." She winced as pain lanced through her chest. "If it has a head start. Do you have night-vision glasses on your base? I'm sure you must. I'll need to borrow those too."

"And then what? You fall off once, and what?" Okhotina shook her head.

"I've got more lunar dirt bike experience on more terrains than anyone else. Especially under crap light conditions. I never fall off."

Okhotina looked at her.

"Well, hardly ever."

Belyakova shook her head: "Vivian? You want to give chase alone? And then you plan to enter the vehicle and defeat two soldiers?"

Okhotina added: "Vivian, it is just a MOLAB. A truck."

"But it's *my* ..." Sanity returned. It wasn't even Vivian's MOLAB anymore. "You said they took the trailer as well? With the Pod ... and the rocks?"

"Yes."

Now Vivian was even madder. She and her crew hadn't completely unloaded the rocks. Many of the samples from Daedalus Base south through the entry into the South Pole-Aiken Basin had still been in the trailer. Plus, some of Vivian's personal effects, not that she gave a damn about those.

They'd probably just toss out all the rocks she'd spent a week collecting to save themselves the mass.

"The MOLAB will leave tracks. We can follow them."

"Commander Jones is already searching for them. His people are quartering the area beyond Zvezda, trying to pick up the MOLAB's trail. It may not be easy. There are many tracks around Zvezda."

As far as Vivian knew, the Soviets had nothing the size and power of a MOLAB. Or at least they hadn't until now. So, that "truck" would be extremely useful to an armed Soviet Spetsnaz group, or whoever the hell her attackers were. "What if they transferred Casey into the MOLAB? We *must* find it."

"They must have arrived in a different vehicle. Perhaps they took Buchanan away in that one."

"Belyakova ... Svetlana? You want to prove Soviets aren't behind this? Then help me, damn it. Cooperate with me. Help me catch them."

"I cannot. I am doing all I can."

"Look, if I do track the MOLAB down, I won't approach. I'll just call in for help, guide a strike force in."

Okhotina shook her head, though sympathetically. "They have a head start of ... what? Thirty minutes?"

Vivian's heart sank. "More."

"Too long."

"Maybe. Maybe not." Vivian almost spat in frustration. "*Damn* it, Svetlana. I need to talk to Starman!"

"I am not preventing that." Belyakova pointed behind her.

Vivian tried to turn her head. It was surprisingly painful, and again, Okhotina stopped her. "Vivian. Stop wriggling around. She is indicating a communications unit in the wall."

Belyakova nodded. "My people have been instructed to patch Commander Jones through whenever he calls. But he is likely still busy now."

*Well. Checkmate.*

Was that true? Did the folks in US-Copernicus even know she was here? Yes, of course. She'd heard the voice of an American radio operator. Hadn't she?

Yes. And there would be no sense in lying to her about something so simple, not after all this. Vivian's paranoia was rearing up again.

Which, perhaps, was not unreasonable, considering she was—once again—stuck in Zvezda Base and surrounded by Soviets, after an attack she had barely survived.

Vivian took a breath. "All right. Sorry. I'm just frazzled. I'll stand down and stop being an impatient patient."

Belyakova's brow furrowed. She looked at Okhotina, who said: "That just means that Vivian is regaining her sense of humor."

They'd taken Casey. *Casey.* Vivian swallowed, closed her eyes. "Well. Sort of."


The MOLAB tracks went due north for seven miles and then simply disappeared. Starman's rovers had driven around in ever-widening circles attempting to pick up the trail again and had found nothing. Other rovers had hunted in other directions, in case the attackers had split up and left the area in two groups. But, no.

"Nothing," Starman said tersely. "Nada. Zip."

"How can tracks just disappear?" Vivian shook her head. "Same way they did at the South Pole, I guess."

"If they airlifted the MOLAB and the Pod out, that would give them way more lunar lift capability than we have. Which seems unlikely."

"Concur," she said. "So, they have a way of covering their tracks."

Even now a second shift of astronauts were out there on freshly recharged rovers, scanning even larger areas, but nobody expected them to come up with anything. The hostiles had completed their mission. Succeeded.

After six hours, Starman had opened the bulkheads again, and Svetlana and Katya had brought Vivian back into US-Copernicus. Now, they were all—plus Gisemba and Daniel Grant, Starman's deputy commander—at US-Copernicus, crowded into Starman's office.

"The enemy cosmonauts …" Starman began.

"Not cosmonauts, please," Belyakova cut in immediately. "There is still no evidence to confirm that this was a Soviet action. I believe it was not. Already, I have said: it makes no sense."

"Pretty sure they weren't NASA astronauts, blondie," said Grant.

Vivian turned on him. "Hey, cut that out. Call her Commander, or by her name, or don't speak to her at all."

Grant glared. "Well, maybe that's a swell idea. Why are these two in the room with us anyway?"

"Because we might need their help," Vivian said.

Grant looked at Starman, who said, "Vivian is right on both issues. Show Commander Belyakova due respect. And she stays."

"Well then, I apologize," Grant said.

"To her," Vivian said.

Grant stared, then turned to Belyakova. "I apologize, Commander."

A curt nod. "Accepted."

"But how can you possibly believe it would make sense for Americans to kidnap another American, or to steal an American vehicle?"

"Because perhaps these are people from outside both of our organizations."

"Outside?" Grant laughed.

Belyakova ignored him, continued speaking to Vivian. "Likely, you were not the target. You were just *there*, and they had no orders either way about what to do with you. So they ..." She turned to Okhotina. *"Improvizirovali?"*

"Improvised," said Okhotina.

Belyakova rolled her eyes, grinned briefly. "Improvised."

"Right," Vivian said. "No way they could have known ahead of time that it would be me escorting Casey. Unless they could read Starman's mind." She shivered suddenly and tried to cover it up. "I was irrelevant. That's new."

"We have already held a head check," Belyakova said.

"Head count," said Vivian.

"All of my Zvezda cosmonauts are accounted for. Those who took Buchanan and the MOLAB—they were not from my people here."

"Including those at the Annex?" Grant asked.

"Of course."

"We have only your word for that."

Svetlana raised her eyes to the ceiling. "Commander Jones has a full list of Zvezda personnel, just as I have a full list of the Americans. You would like your pair of Americans still down at the Annex to review the list and confirm? Because we can do that."

"It might not hurt."

"Then we will do it."

To Starman, Vivian said: "Have we done that yet? A full roll call?"

Grant eyed her in exasperation. "For God's sake. You think men from this station kidnapped Casey Buchanan and made off with your MOLAB?"

"No, so let's rule it out for the record, and check that no one else is missing. That's an obvious next step, right?"

"It is literally the least you can do," Belyakova said.

"Sure, fine." Starman leaned away, pressed a comms button and gave the order.

"And one of my people may cross-check? So that there can be no doubt?"

"By all means. Send someone over."

Belyakova glanced at Okhotina, who immediately said: "Yes. I will do it."

Belyakova turned to Vivian. "One reason the Americans might kidnap their own man is to confuse the situation further. To point the finger at us, and create the accusations that Commander Jones and," she just gestured at Grant, "are making."

"All right," Vivian said. "But this is ridiculous. We have to call them something, the hostiles. Not cosmonauts. Not astronauts. Cryptonauts?"

Gisemba laughed, which at least cut the tension, and spoke for the first time. "Makes it sound like they're Bigfoot or something."

"Or like they're in code," Grant added.

Belyakova shook her head, irritated. "Vivian? Explain this, please."

"Sure thing. Cryptography is the study of codes, secret writing. Cryptids are animals that likely don't exist, like Bigfoot. 'Crypto' just means mysterious, or something."

"Bigfoot?"

"Is a ... Jeez. I don't know. A giant ape-man, a North American yeti? A prehistoric throwback? Probably just an urban legend."

Gisemba wasn't letting it go. "So Casey has been captured by Bigfoot?"

"Feye. You're not helping."

"For God's sake," Starman said. "Can we get back to the point, here?"

"Yes," Vivian said. "So what do we know? First: that the cryptonauts targeted Buchanan. He's on a more-or-less fixed medical schedule, right? His moves are no secret, predictable. Second: to take him, they had to wait until he came back up to the crater rim. Abducting him from the Annex, within the crater—it would be too challenging to make their escape."

"And that they were ready to go at short notice," Gisemba added, "means they were already in the area."

"Sure. Maybe the MOLAB was likely just a target of opportunity, too tempting to ignore? They came for Buchanan, and the timing just worked out right for them to snag the MOLAB too."

"Or vice versa," Gisemba said.

"Why would they take such risks to get the MOLAB?" Grant asked.

"It's a damned useful vehicle. And they tried to get it once before."

"Did they? Or did they just try to destroy it?"

Gisemba shrugged. "Either way, it deprives us of it. US-Copernicus now lacks a ground-based long-distance capability again. Which helpfully prevents us from searching for the cryptonauts, overland, over long distances. Right? At least for a while."

"Until we get another one sent up," Starman said. "Which we're going to need, to search the Moon for this group of terrorists, and wipe them out." He looked at Belyakova. "You're okay with that? You'll provide support? We go wipe them out, no matter which cryptic country they come from?"

"Of course. Unless I get orders to the contrary from Moscow Mission Control."

Everyone fell silent. Belyakova frowned. "Please. You will now pretend that if you were ordered by your superiors to stand down and abandon the hunt for the cryptonauts, you would disregard that order?"

"Might depend," Starman said darkly.

"That you would launch a killing attack on your own countrymen, if the attackers prove to be from the US? No. I do not think so."

"Who said they were my countrymen? They're Soviet. Have to be. So if I was ordered to stand down, it would be for some BS political reason. And the way I feel right now? I'm not at all sure I'd comply."

Vivian stepped in immediately. "No one here heard that, Starman, because you didn't say it."

"I at least admit the possibility that my people are at fault," Belyakova said. "Unlike you, Commander Jones."

"Break. Cut it out. Both of you." Vivian turned to Gisemba. "What else do we know? What did the attackers say to you?"

"Nothing. They pointed guns at me and gestured. I spoke to them, of course. Asked who the hell they were, what they wanted. I tried to goad them into speaking, so's I could hear their voices, but they gave me nothing. They shoved me into the driver's seat and pointed. That was pretty clear. Then, later, they pointed at my suit and then at the airlock. And that was the extent of our communication."

"What did they look like?"

"Like guys in spacesuits? They never raised their visors."

"They were definitely men?"

"Even that, I can't swear to. Moon suits de-sex everyone. I didn't really see them walk around a whole lot inside the MOLAB."

"And the suits themselves?"

"Gray. Looked more like our South Pole attackers than the usual US or Russian suits. They did look lightly armored. Not as much as those crazy-ass Night Corps suits, but more than our Apollo suits."

"The guns?"

He shrugged. "One had a rifle, the other a machine pistol. I don't really know guns, but I can try to sketch them, and you can make of them whatever you can."

"Okay."

Gisemba checked his watch, looked at Jones. "Anything else you need? Other questions? If not, maybe I can split. After all that, I could do with a snack and some rest."

"Go ahead. Maybe sketch guns before lights-out, while your memory's fresh."

"Okay, sure." Gisemba stood to go.

"We can show you pictures of Soviet guns," Belyakova said. "And of US, and Israeli. However we can help."

"So ..." Vivian's bound-up ribs gave her a sharp jabbing pain. She breathed, rubbed her eyes to cover, and carried on. "Long day, concur. But the important takeaway from this is that somewhere within overland driving distance of both the South Pole and Zvezda Base is another, secret base. Where our attackers came from and where they're going back to. And that's where Casey and the MOLAB will end up. We need to find it."

"And we will. Somehow." Starman looked around the room. "But not right now. Vivian, you should get some rest as well. Commander Belyakova, let's each go about our business, do what we need to do. Can we reconvene at sixteen hundred tomorrow and compare notes? By that time, US-Copernicus will likely be out of lockdown. Okay?"

Belyakova stood. "Very well. Until tomorrow, then."

Vivian half-raised her hand. "Permission to stick around for a few minutes, sir? I'd like to discuss a couple of quick personal issues with you."

Their eyes met. "Sure," Starman said neutrally. "Everyone else, thanks."

# CHAPTER 13

## Zvezda-Copernicus: Vivian Carter
## February 8, 1983

**AS** soon as they were alone, Vivian seized the initiative. "So, a bunch of things are bothering me about all this. First: we don't have radar looking out for incursions? You don't have cameras set up? You don't keep an eye on the Soviets at *all*?"

"Radar, yes. To keep tabs on landers coming and going. And those consoles are manned more or less constantly, and we keep recordings as well. We saw no evidence of an unscheduled flight coming in anywhere in the area. Or any flight at all, because we keep transport to a minimum during lunar night. So they came overland, at least for the final approach."

"Security cameras?"

"Only a couple. We do have two cameras on the external storage areas, but we only just installed them because we only just needed to, because of the pilfering. It's not like we have CCTV everywhere."

"That's crazy."

"What?" Starman shook his head. "Vivian. We've been cooperating pretty well here for the past three years, almost. The Soviets helped us construct US-Copernicus, with no funny business. They didn't even attempt to bug our living spaces like they might have on Earth. We've worked with them on science projects, *in situ* resource utilization experiments, and a bunch of tech stuff. That was the whole point, right? It hasn't always been plain sailing, we've had some fights—actual fist

168

fights, a couple times. A lot of squabbles over costs, ensuring credit was assigned where due, constant logistical headaches, all the usual stuff. But overall, a fair working relationship, about the best we could expect, till the thieving started.

"And we had no reason to believe Buchanan was at risk. Sure, there were a hundred times the Reds could have grabbed him, if they'd been going to. But it would have been obvious who'd done it. A clear act of aggression."

Vivian blew out a long breath. "Okay. Yeah." Daedalus Base had been the same. She had been impressed at how closely the USAF and Soviet teams had cooperated there. "But now with this new group in town, the Soviets can deny all knowledge."

"Can and are. So, we need to change our strategy, but I can't do it immediately. I just don't have the equipment."

"Okay, fair enough. But, about Casey?" Vivian took a deep breath. "Commander Jones, I have to tell you something, and it's really bad. Or maybe you know it already?"

Starman's eyes narrowed. "Go on."

"I think Casey's disappearance is my fault."

Now, his face turned into a mask. "Explain."

Vivian might have tried to make excuses. *I was being tortured. I was so tired. I was out of my mind at the time.* All were true, but did any of that matter?

No. It did not.

"At Zvezda, three years ago, I broke under Yashin's interrogation. Just once. And when I did, I gave them the name of someone who likely knew a lot more than he was saying. A senior NASA astronaut at Hadley who I was sure had full knowledge of the covert USAF side of the house. Who later on confirmed by his words and actions that he'd known about Dark Driver all along. That astronaut was Casey Buchanan. And that might be why he was just taken."

Starman nodded. "At last. I was wondering if you'd bring that up voluntarily."

"Oh." It was all she could find to say.

"I've read the full transcript of your statement to the CIA. Everything about your time at Zvezda, what happened to you here, your impressions of the place—all fifty pages of it. I was briefed fully before assuming my command here. Since I'd be so close to the Soviets, on the same turf, I needed access to any information that might be relevant."

Tears sprang into Vivian's eyes. She blinked them back. "Starman … it was literally the only thing I could tell them. They were asking for so much, but I had *zero* other information that could have been of any use to them. And I was so … fricking tired and beaten down." Okay, so she was going to make excuses after all. Oh well.

He nodded. "So who else knew?"

"Who else? Other than the Soviets?"

"Well, first: *which* Soviets? Did Belyakova know? Because according to your transcript you were alone with Yashin at the time."

Vivian thought about it. "Right. She wasn't there. And Yashin generally kept his cards close to his chest. Maybe he told her later? I have no idea. But he must have told his bosses in the Kremlin, right?"

"Presumably. And who else on our side knew?"

"Wait, you're taking seriously Svetlana's suggestion that someone on our side took him, after all?"

"No, but like you said: let's consider it so we can rule it out."

"Sure." Vivian reached back into her memories, marshalled her thoughts. "I was grilled about all this several times. First by the Air Force, by Major-General Johnston at Daedalus Base when I first arrived. There, I didn't mention Casey's hint because I didn't want to get him into any trouble. Protecting my sources, you might say. And *I* was already in trouble at the time. Second up was the CIA, who pulled me in literally a couple hours after splashdown. They were waiting for me on the aircraft carrier that pulled Minerva out of the Pacific. And like you saw, I told them every single thing I could remember. I'm not stupid enough to hold anything back from the CIA. And I *wanted* them to know, so they could take whatever measures they had to. I told them several times because they asked me several times. CIA guys go hard on their debriefs, let me tell you. It was like they were strip-mining my brain."

"I believe you."

"And then I had my big NASA mission debrief in Houston, but they didn't go deep into the Zvezda portion of my mission. Only the Hadley part up to my capture, then they picked it up again once I was on-surface about to be rescued by Gerry Lin. The details of my time in captivity were in the CIA's bailiwick. I think perhaps NASA had been told by the CIA not to go there, or that they didn't need to, though I honestly don't remember whether anyone said that out loud."

Starman thought about it. "So you didn't tell NASA, or Johnston either."

"Nope. But NASA told you."

"The CIA told me." He frowned. "So you didn't even tell Casey *himself* that you'd hung him out to dry?"

"No. I didn't. Dear God." Vivian closed her eyes. "Look. After Hadley—well, after we both ended up at Dark Driver—I didn't see Casey again until today. It was in the CIA's hands. If I thought about it at all, I figured they'd be the ones to decide. He was at Daedalus Base for the whole following year, right?"

"Sure."

A silence fell. Vivian thought some more, and gut-checked herself. "Okay."

"Okay, what?"

"Regardless of the details: yes. This is ultimately all my fault for giving Yashin Casey's name in the first place." Vivian drew herself up. "I have no defense. I shouldn't make excuses. This mess is my fault. It's my responsibility, and I own it."

Starman licked dry lips. "Look, I know Zvezda was really bad for you. Your transcript was harrowing. I'm not about to give you any grief for giving them Casey's name. Someone else might, but not me."

Relief, but still guilt. "Thanks."

"And to be fair, it didn't occur to me, either, that Casey would be at risk. I mean, I didn't have him under special guard or anything."

Vivian blinked. "And, you know what? There's no reason why you would."

He glanced up, surprised at the firm tone that had returned to her voice.

"Because this *still* doesn't add up. Why would Casey be more of a target than anyone *else* at, say, Daedalus Base? Or anyone here? Once the Soviets knew about the mass driver, Casey's value to them should have decreased, but it apparently hasn't."

"Well. Casey is presumably still as well-connected as he ever was."

"I guess so." She looked up at Starman. "But don't you think that's interesting? Casey is still a high-value target. So I can only guess that it was as obvious to the Soviets—I mean the cryptonauts—as it is to me right now, that Casey now knows something *else*, some *new* secret they think is worth stealing him to acquire."

Starman said nothing.

Vivian considered him. Light dawned. "And you know it too." She leaned forward. "Starman, jeez. What does Casey Buchanan know *right now* that's of so much use that it's worth kidnapping him from under our noses? Why would they take that risk, without some *big* reward?"

"I don't know."

"You do, though. You know something. I can feel it. Because you *still* have a terrible poker face."

Starman met her eye. "Vivian. I have no idea what you've been told and what you haven't. But if there's anything going on that you don't know, there's likely a reason for that."

Vivian stood so abruptly that her feet lifted from the floor. "Starman, *for the love of God*: if it's nukes again, I quit. I quit every goddamned thing. If we're militarizing the Moon, again … then we suck. As an Agency, as a country …" She ran out of words.

"We're not," he said.

Vivian took her time. "You're quite sure about that?"

"Very sure."

"And I can believe you?" She tried to breathe deeply without hurting herself. "Sorry. I mean: and yet, there's still something I don't know?"

"We can't have this conversation." Starman smiled thinly. "I'm sorry, too. I know how weird this is."

"Isn't it, though? You do realize that Svetlana Belyakova still believes the cryptonauts are US. Air Force, Night Corps, whatever. *Does* the US have a secret group on the Moon? You only denied the nukes."

"Of course I realize. She never shuts up about it." He paused. "She's wrong."

"Except that you shouldn't even have told me that either, right? You're really terrible at this."

He gave her a pained grin. "You know, maybe I am."

"Starman. I don't know what to believe and what not to believe, anymore."

He pulled himself together, clasped his hands in front of him, and leaned forward. "Then stick to what you *do* know. You were attacked. We need to find out who by. And Casey has been taken. We need to find out where. Vivian, I sincerely want those answers just as much as you do. And once we've proved it was the Soviets, beyond even their power to obfuscate the issue, we can bring all kinds of political and diplomatic pressures to bear. That's Job One. While they can still claim plausible deniability, we're hamstrung. And fighting among ourselves isn't doing any of us any good."

"Well, that I agree with, for sure." Vivian massaged her temples. This was an impossible conversation. "Listen, Starman: I want to believe you. I really do. But if the cryptonauts *do* somehow happen to be American, if all of this is like Svetlana says it is ... that means that I've killed Americans. A lot of Americans. And if I come across them again, I might kill more." She raised her head, looked him in the eye. "Are you telling me, right here and now, that you're okay with that?"

Starman met her gaze. "Yes, Vivian. I'm one hundred percent fine with you killing anyone who attacks you."

"Well, okay," she said. "Cool."

He looked at his watch, and grimaced.

"Nice hint. Got it." Vivian took a couple more deep breaths, holding her side against the twinges of pain, and stood up. "Guess I'll go crash for a while, try to sleep."

"Okay, but ... Vivian? Before you go?"

"Yes?"

"Last time you told me I had a terrible poker face? Right after that, I offered you a drink."

"You did."

Starman dug into a drawer. "Nightcap? Or call it medicinal."

"Seriously?"

"We're not enemies," he said simply. "And I don't want you to leave mad."

Vivian blew out a breath. "God damn this rock." Nonetheless, she sat again.

He stopped in mid-pour. "Wait, what? You *love* the Moon."

"Used to." Vivian accepted a shot glass from him, took a sip. "Ugh. Yikes ... Okay, I still do. But honestly, by now—*especially* now—I'm done with it."

"Say that again?"

"It's true. After all this, all the attacks and danger and kidnapping, and the blurred lines and lies and secrets, Captain Vivian Carter might absolutely be ready to quit the Moon."

"Well," he raised his own glass, and they chinked. "Cheers. Excellent. Because I'm pretty sure this is my last assignment up here, too. Once I get home again, there I stay."

"Doing what?"

"Who the hell even knows?"

"Same here. Then I guess we'll be figuring that out together."

"Maybe." He paused. "As friends. I hope."

Vivian bit off the response she'd been about to make. Because, despite all this: Starman *was* a good guy. He'd been one of her favorite people at Hadley. If his mood was darker now, he had good reason. And she shouldn't fault him for keeping secrets he'd been ordered to keep. Sandoval couldn't discuss large parts of his life with her either.

"I hope so too, Starman. Despite," she waved, "whatever the hell this conversation was."

He raised his glass again. "To a change of scenery. And soon."

Vivian chinked him again, and they both drank.

Starman studied her for a long moment. "So, one more thing."

"Oh, God. There's more?"

"Only a bit. And then you can sleep, I swear. You seem to have an in. For whatever reason, the Soviets trust you. Or Belyakova does, and she's the only Soviet here that matters."

The alcohol hit her, and Vivian couldn't help it: she giggled. "That's funny."

"What?"

"That you think Blond Svet trusts me. She *may* trust me just a *tiny* bit further than she trusts you. Like maybe a nanometer."

"I'll take that." Starman shuffled papers. "And I guess you're not flying home just yet, right?"

"Uh, my mission plan says I am. And I want to. But I have a shoulder sprain and maybe cracked ribs, so I guess it's TBD?"

"The doctors think you can still fly. At least back to lunar orbit, and back to Earth orbit. You could wait there until they decide you're Go for splashdown. But what sense does that make? I think maybe you get to stay here another week or so while you're recovering."

"A week or so. Jeez."

"Okay, let's just say a week. And during that time … like I said, you do have a bit of an 'in' with the Soviets. Belyakova trusts you more than she does me—or at least respects you. And, well … Okhotina can hardly take her eyes off you."

"Oh, please." Vivian blinked. "So now you *want* me to go back into Zvezda and play nice with Belyakova? Good grief. Make up your mind."

"I'm just saying, find out what you can, while you can. Help us figure out this mess."

She closed her eyes. "Starman, this mess is impossible. And I need to get off this rock. The Moon has nearly killed me too many times already. I'm not a politician, and hardly the person you want doing diplomacy for you."

"Then don't call it diplomacy. Just go and bug the hell out of them until they give something away, or till you figure something out on your own. That's just your normal style, right? Vivian being Vivian?"

"Wow," she said. "Pulling no punches tonight, I see."

"Just for a week. Then we'll check in with the doctors and talk again about possible crew manifests for Earth return. Okay?"

"I'll sleep on it. Starting in, like, three minutes."

"Sounds good. And don't be too surprised if I send Grant into Zvezda a time or two, as well."

Vivian made a face. "D'you really have to? He doesn't seem like the greatest choice."

"He's not. That's why I'm doing it. He's there to needle them. Which will make you look so much better, by contrast. Feel free to argue with him, to reinforce that."

"Should be easy enough … if I end up doing this at all. I guess the Soviets aren't the only ones who can play good cop, bad cop, huh?"

"Guess not."

"Okay. Fine. And now I'm really out of here." Vivian stood, saluted rather ironically, and walked a little unsteadily out of Starman's office.


All the Soviets were accounted for. Belyakova had allowed Grant to double-check the second Soviet roll call. And all the Americans were accounted for, as confirmed by Okhotina. No one from either sector of Zvezda-Copernicus, or from the Annex, was missing.

So, confirmed for the record, even though no one had really thought any different: the cryptonauts were an outside group.

But where they'd spirited Buchanan and the MOLAB away to was still a mystery. And likely to remain so.

# 14

## Earth Orbit: Peter Sandoval
## February 9, 1983

**PETER** Sandoval arced up out of the atmosphere. Five G's pushed him back into his seat. The Earth was far below him now. And he couldn't be happier.

*Home again.*

Even if he was riding a dinosaur. Sort of.

*Well, maybe I could be a* tiny *bit happier.*

Sandoval pushed that aside. *On a mission. Kids to teach. Let's do this.*

This was important. Not deadly important—well, Sandoval sure hoped not—but important enough.

The original Boeing X-20 Dyna-Soar—"Dynamic Soarer"—had been a single-seater military spaceplane, terminated by the USAF in 1963 after six years of investment. The far more sophisticated and highly classified Boeing X-22C spaceplane project that followed on from it, which had begun development in 1972 and only recently reached full operational status, bore only a superficial resemblance to the old Dyna-Soar project, but it pleased the Night Corps teams to refer to their superfast Earth-orbiting planes as dinosaurs, and no one was about to tell them they couldn't. Designed as an interceptor for space rescue, satellite maintenance, and the sabotage and destruction of foreign assets, the X-22C was a two-seater craft that could support EVAs and, if launched with the appropriate ordnance, could even perform very-high-level bombing runs over the Soviet Union. Though ICBMs could pack a far larger nuclear punch.

Since it was technically a direct descendant of the 1941 Nazi Silbervogel rocket-powered bomber concept, intended to rain nuclear weapons down onto New York City and other American population centers before reentering for rescue by the Japanese in the Pacific Ocean, Sandoval had a few uncomfortable feelings about the vehicle. But damn: it was still very cool to be riding an actual aircraft into orbit, atop a Titan booster, in the knowledge that after a few weeks he'd fly it back into Earth's atmosphere and eventually glide it down to land it like a real fighter jet.

Flying airliners for Pan Am might not have been *quite* this much fun. Or this dangerous.


In this current simulated scenario Sandoval's X-22C was the aggressor, and the defense crew would treat him accordingly. Which meant he'd come under concerted attack, real soon now.

But as he kept reminding himself: *This is only a drill.*

From behind him, a woman's voice: "Orbital stabilization burn expected in thirty seconds from my mark. Mark."

"Oh, hey, Brock," Sandoval said. "Forgot you were there."

"Yeah, I'm easy to ignore."

"I wouldn't go that far. I was just concentrating, here."

"On what? I'm doing all the work."

Sandoval had, by no means, forgotten Terri Brock was his copilot. She'd called numbers for him all the way through Max-Q and beyond, after they'd been launched in the usual hectic fashion from Vandenberg Air Force Base. And she wasn't really doing all the work, either. But by now it was just part of their schtick.

They were a great team. And Terri was having an outstanding time with Night Corps, thoroughly enjoying her new assignments and the fast pace of their training and war games.

"Time to target?" Sandoval knew the time full well. He just wanted to keep Brock on her toes.

"Three minutes thirty."

Their destination was already coming into view: MOL-11, the dark cylinder of a standard Manned Orbiting Laboratory. And close by it, in parallel orbit, the advanced twelve-person Blue Gemini that they called, somewhat predictably, Big G.

Big G was just like a standard Gemini, but longer. At launch the capsule would have held eight seats in three rows, with four more in a small mid-deck area immediately behind it; by now, in weightlessness, all those seats would be folded away when they weren't being used for sleep. Even without seats or gravity, the advanced Gemini was *cramped*. It was how the rookies they'd be training today had achieved orbit, and Sandoval knew from firsthand experience that launch must have been miserable for them, as only the two pilots were able to see outside. And even now they'd be breathing one another's air, banging into their colleagues left and right. No space, no privacy, no nothing. Over the last three days they'd have had familiarization exercises in MOL-11 and the two other standard-sized two-person Blue Geminis docked with it, but that would help only a little—the MOL living space was designed for four. The rookies' daily spacewalk training would have been literally the only times another human being wasn't within arm's reach, or even closer.

But that was life for off-world Night Corps crews. On the ground they'd all tested zero on the claustrophobia index and the maximum for sociability and discipline in confined areas, but being in orbit with hard vacuum just outside your living space made quite a difference. Sandoval knew for a fact that some of them wouldn't be able to hack it. Some might have washed out already for all he knew. Or be just about to.

They'd mostly be okay, though. This was a good group, and according to Rod and Pope, they were doing about as well as previous Night Corps astronaut classes had done.

"Okay, here we go. Time to put the fear of the living God into the squaddies. Ready?"

"I was born ready."

"I'm not getting my time checks, Captain."

"Jeez, we're twenty seconds out from the one-minute full-up. Which you know as well as I do."

Sure, Sandoval could read his own combat clock just fine, but Brock should have been giving him the readings anyway, and not sassing him. "Okay, Captain. Full battle protocol, starting now. Alert the MOL."

"Wilco." Brock's voice instantly switched up to the regulation clipped tone. She flipped the switch to activate the Instructor Loop, which only Rod and Pope, she and Sandoval, could access, and at the same time a red light lit up on both their consoles. "We've been detected."

Right on cue, they heard Pope's Southern accent on the loop. "Intruder, identify yourself."

"MOL-11, this is Aggressor 1, here to kick your asses."

"A likely story. Come and get it, Commie losers."

"Nice," Sandoval said. "You're really digging into the role."

"Just keeping it real, Aggressor 1."

On their private loop, where only he could hear it, Terri said: "Contact in sixty seconds."

"Arm cannon," he said, even though he could see from his readouts that she was already doing it.

"Armed."

"Double check ordnance."

He triple-checked it himself. Wouldn't do to shoot real explosive shells at his own people, even though he'd overseen the loading of the weaponry himself.

"Ordnance nominal."

Sandoval switched Full Loop to Receive, so he could hear everything that was going on at Pope's end as well. He was just in time to hear: "Eyes up, babies. NC Class Eleven is about to go into battle for the first time."

Sandoval grinned. He could imagine the scenes in the MOL and Big G at the moment, with half the rookies crashing into one another trying to get suited up while the other half pulled themselves onto consoles, powered up comms and weapons systems, and tried to figure out where the threat was coming from and how long they had to counter it. He was sure that the knowledge that this was only a drill had little bearing on the adrenaline flowing through their bodies right now.

"Ready to fire on your mark," said Brock.

"Fire at will."

Missiles streaked from the left and right of the X-22C, homing in on the MOL. Sandoval could already tell that both would be direct hits, unless the squaddies inside the target could quickly and accurately throw countermeasures. Which was unlikely. The fake missiles wouldn't damage the MOL, but they'd sure rock it around a bit.

"Ready to be up and out?" He checked the telemetry on his console from Brock's suit and glanced down at his own again, and a moment later Terri said: "Affirmative, we're both Go for EVA."

Another red light glowed on his board, indicating that the MOL's radar had just got a firm lock on them. "We're pinned."

"Thirty-six seconds. Not bad."

He snorted. "Not great."

"They've launched a missile. In the wrong direction."

"Pope will be skinning them alive right now. Let's lose the canopy."

On a spaceplane the transparent bubble that covered them was more than a mere canopy, but the term had a lot of military tradition behind it. It opened up as a solid piece, hinging out to port. "Egressing," he said. "Follow me in five."

"Five seconds, roger."

Sandoval pressed a button and let go of everything except his rifle as a tiny rocket underneath his chair nudged him gently out into space. The Dyna-Soar appeared to drop away beneath him, though both he and the craft were in stable orbits. They'd come back for it later.

A few seconds later, Terri Brock joined him in free fall, and they powered up their jetpacks and really got going.


On Earth, paintball had been a recreational sport for less than two years. In the space military, a very similar concept had been used in training for at least five. The guns and pellets Sandoval and Brock were armed with right now were more high-tech and sturdier, but the idea was the same: compressed-air tanks that fired thin-shelled pellets filled with a bright gelatin to mark their target as a "kill."

He keyed into the Instructor Loop. "MOL-11: DORIAN is shuttered and safed, confirm?"

"Shuttered, affirmative," said Rodriguez's voice in his headset.

"Good."

As Sandoval sped toward the MOL he took aim, corrected roughly for orbital motion, and fired. His first pellet went wide, and so did his second because this shit was nontrivial even for trained professionals. But his third shot smacked squarely into the crew compartment, marking it with a broad smear of luminescent red paint. "Gotcha, MOL."

"Sure, but say goodbye to your sweet ride because we just vaporized it. You're hitchhiking home."

"That fast? Must have been more luck than judgment," said Brock.

"Yeah, fluke shot, but it made Krantzen's day."

"Must have." In reality, of course, the Dyna-Soar was still all in one piece and coasting serenely in their wake.

The spacesuited rookies were egressing now, spilling from the Big G airlock in twos and separating to right and left. Very messily, and even as Sandoval watched, Brock nailed one of them in the helmet with a blob of green glycol that looked very much like mucus.

"Ouch," said Sandoval. "You might at least let them get out the door."

"Nuts to that," said Brock. "They're about to outnumber us."

She was flying fast and hard, Sandoval noted, her goal likely to get past the Big G and loop back around it. A bunch of rookies were about to get shot in the back, if they didn't look sharp.

Sandoval chose to drift out front and be a more visible target, and a distraction. No need to crush the newbies' spirit fresh out of the gate. He'd be hard enough to hit anyway, given the difficulty of figuring range and relative speed in orbit, and they all needed the practice.

He shot another couple of his students just for target practice and to boost their motivation, and smeared the Big G front window for good measure. By the end of this exercise, this rookie squad was going to have a *lot* of crud to clean off their suits and ships.

It was another four or five minutes before any of them got a hit on Sandoval, by which time everyone was thoroughly enjoying themselves. As was also traditional, the 'battle' went on long after everyone was officially dead. This was only an exercise, after all.


An hour later, a distinctly messy bunch of Night Corps recruits managed to regroup at least somewhere in the vicinity of the Big G. Coasting in freefall, Sandoval and Rodriguez ran lessons-learned, gave credit where due, and chewed out the less competent squad members. Terri brought the Dyna-Soar in to hang it off the MOL boom, and Sandoval took center stage again. "Okay, we'll be generous and chalk Part One up as a success. Those of you with homework and extra training know who you are. Get it done. Now, on to Part Two."

Their second exercise was more technical, and less like shooting fish in a barrel in a zero-G playground. In pairs, the squaddies would have to approach and collect intel on a hostile satellite and neutralize any threats that it might exhibit.

A fake hostile satellite, of course, but the DarkSat mockup was quite sophisticated. It was modeled on a Soviet communications satellite, and with a similar mass distribution because that mattered to the exercise. It was also tricked out with a complex set of customizable lights, rocket motors, and various threats, so that no two pairs of students would experience exactly the same configuration. They wouldn't know what was coming. And, since the sequence was randomized, neither would the instructors.

Someone had spent a lot of time designing DarkSat. Someone with a generous budget and a devious sense of humor.

No laughing matter for the rookies, of course. They had to take it deadly seriously. Soviet satellites could be booby-trapped in any one of ten ways, and so was DarkSat, in spades. Today, NC Class Eleven was about to put their classroom training to work in the field and try to neutralize those traps on the fly.

Literally on the fly, because their fake Soviet military satellite would begin the exercise in a slow three-axis tumble. Job One was to go and grab the damned thing—safely, by its rails or antennae, and not the body—and stabilize it with opposing thrust from their jetpacks, all while eyeballing the visible surface for threats and memorizing as much of the layout of the satellite features as possible. They'd be tasked with drawing it from memory once they got back inside.

This exercise was *hard* and required a lot of concentration, and Sandoval was truly glad he'd qualified as a Night Corps astronaut long before DarkSat had been completed and flown. The thing was a beast.

The first squaddies fared the worst, which always happened. Those who went later could learn a little by watching the mistakes of those who'd gone before them. But there were many failure modes, from fake gun barrels that could come swinging out from beneath retracting panels to the telltale signs of a "hot" surface, down to simple camera lenses to observe the infiltrating astronaut that needed to be blocked.

In real life, there were too many ways to die, tackling a potentially hostile satellite. Especially as it could just explode, right? But for the rookies, this was an exercise in maintaining their concentration, their powers of observation, and their attention to detail, all while performing an interesting feat of 3D ballet. You weren't expected to "survive." You earned a passing grade just by identifying the threat that was about to "kill" you and doing your best to avoid it before you "died."

And Class Eleven wasn't doing great at it, by any measure. Most pairs took way too long to stabilize the satellite, and that was just the beginning of the exercise. Then, airman after airman got "electrocuted," "shot," or just banged into a sensitive area. Afterward, very few of them could even verbally describe what had just happened with any fidelity.

Four hours in, the seventh pair of greenhorns dejectedly moved away from the DarkSat and Pope fired the jets to send it into a tumble again. Sandoval could almost see the eighth pair shaking as they awaited their turn, even inside their suits. "I thought you told me these guys were good?" he said, on the Instructor Loop.

"They *are* good," said Pope. "Better than Class Ten, anyway."

"They're getting tired," Brock said.

"Really? They're just standing around most of the time."

Rodriguez chuckled. "Standing."

"Looks like they're gonna need to stay up here an extra few days."

"It's too hard," Terri said. "It just is. For their first tour in orbit? Way too hard."

"I seem to remember *you* aced it this time last year," said Sandoval. "By yourself."

"Yeah, but it was my fourth mission, and I came in with months of space experience. Hardly a novice, right?"

"Fine. Who are these two again?"

"Newell and Scheer," said Rodriguez.

Pope completed the DarkSat spin-up, and waved the eighth pair in. They separated, jetting in arcs to opposite sides of the satellite. "You wanna know the truth? I sucked at it. Almost flunked out."

"You did not," said Rodriguez.

"Did so. And also? It gets harder every time. The brass can't resist the urge to add bells and whistles. Even I don't know everything this can do."

"Contact," said Brock. The squaddies had grabbed the slow-rolling satellite. Newell was clutching the base of its solar panel, while Scheer had lunged at the maneuvering bar, missed it, and instead snagged a grip on the base of the antenna. The satellite kept rolling, taking them along for the ride. They clung on, fired their zip guns, and managed to damp out the DarkSat's pitch and yaw in less than half a minute.

"Okay, fine," Sandoval said. "This pair doesn't completely suck."

A hatch-sized panel on the DarkSat flipped open, slamming into Newell and flipping him around, knocking him into the solar panel. A passable imitation of a Richter cannon slid forward out of the aperture.

"Jeez," said Terri. "Acid flashbacks."

Scheer's voice broke in on Full Loop. "Break, sirs! Mayday. Newell's out. Not responding."

Newell had released his grip and was now floating free, hands and legs starfished.

"Oh, swell," said Sandoval.

"Damn panel knocked him out." Scheer was scrambling around the satellite now, using every possible handhold he could to get to his partner.

Understandable, but dumb.

"Scheer, hold position. That's still a hostile satellite."

"Then turn the damned thing off ... sirs."

"On it," said Pope. "Takes a few seconds though."

On the surface of DarkSat, something moved very quickly, and the next second Scheer was flying through space, directly at Sandoval. A jack-in-the-box booby trap had flung him clear. Scheer fired his jet-pack, attempting to get control, but only increased his speed.

"Calm down," said Rodriguez. "Chill out. Turn it off. Get your bearings."

"Oh, for crying out loud," said Terri Brock.

Sandoval reached up and squeezed the throttle that should have fired up his jetpack engine and eased him out of Scheer's trajectory ... and nothing happened.

"Crap," he said, and grabbed his backup zip gun from his thigh.

Too late. Scheer banged into him and sent him flying. He lunged for the rookie but only succeeded in dropping the zip gun.

Belatedly, Scheer's jetpack sputtered out.

Turning lazily end over end, Sandoval found himself traveling away from the Big G and NC Class Eleven at quite the rate.

*Aw, that's just great. In front of the whole damned squad, too.*

"Nozzle fouled?" Pope said.

"Stupid paintball gunk," said Sandoval. It wasn't the first time this had happened after a combat session. That was what he got for setting himself up as target practice.

"Well, *this* is a cluster," said Terri.

"It's space," said Sandoval. "Shit happens. Okay, everyone, listen up. Priority one is Newell. Pope: lead a man-down emergency ingress into the MOL, that airlock's quicker and the medical kit there is better. Find out what's happening with him. Rod, make sure Scheer is okay, get him inside if necessary."

"I'm fine, sir. Sorry, sir."

"No worries. Except for not obeying orders. Which we'll discuss later. Terri …"

He heard the beep as she switched to the Instructor Loop. "Hang tight, boss. I'm coming for you. These noobs can sit in a holding pattern with Rod until we get back."

Pope and Rodriguez didn't dignify that with a response. Sandoval switched to the Instructor channel too. "Negative. I'm already too far clear. Stay put, wrap the DarkSat, get the rookies indoors. We don't put them at risk by leaving them on EVA with only one or two instructors … God's sakes, guys, look at them, they're already all over the sky. Get 'em under control. I'll keep. And it'll give them something to think about."

"Yes sir," Brock said reluctantly.

He was drifting farther and farther away. The MOL, the Blue Geminis and Big G, his guys and the rookies in their spacesuits: all looking kind of small now. It was by far the farthest that Sandoval had ever been from safety in vacuum, at least in zero-G.

He felt calm about it, but he did realize that he might feel a bit more agitated if he hadn't experienced far worse, and much farther from home.

But, hey. This was unusual, no question. Sandoval twisted to look down at the Earth and realized he'd be going into darkness soon. Not really a big deal, operationally. His people could home in on his signal just fine, dark or shine. But it would be weird.

*Just floating around up here, two hundred miles above the Earth. Like you do.*

Sure enough, the Sun soon went behind the Earth from Sandoval's perspective, but still glittered off his MOL and Big G. They were the only things he could see by now. He was already so far distant that his people were unresolved.

*No hurry, guys. I'll just hang out here.*

185

Below him, the continents floated serenely by. He was over Africa. Next would be the good old Union of Soviet Socialist Republics, God bless them. And then he'd sail across the mighty Pacific. That would take him half an hour or more, during which time he'd have flown alone over a third of the world.

As he watched the Earth rotate beneath him, idly picking out the countries and landmarks he was passing over that he knew so well from MOL photography, the Moon rose over the Earth's limb.

And without warning, a gut-crunching and sweating terror filled him. His heart pounded, and he began to pant out loud. He quickly flipped the switch on his chest that would mute his microphone. No need for anyone else to hear this.

*I'm not falling. I'm not falling. I'm not falling.*
*I'm not dying.*

He could tell himself this as often as he liked, but it took a while for the repetition to begin calming him. And some of that was just the evidence of his own eyes: he was still obviously in orbit. It took a *long* burn to break orbit. No way he could get knocked into reentry by anything that could happen to him on an EVA exercise, and he knew that as well as anyone. Sandoval was almost as safe as if he was at home in bed, as long as his people didn't just decide to leave him to die out here, and even his dumb hindbrain wasn't worried about that. It would never happen. Terri and Pope would come for him soon. That wasn't even an issue.

The issue was *falling*.

Slowly, slowly, the fear subsided. But he was wet with sweat from the crown of his head to the tips of his toes. And he was freaked out that he'd freaked out.

This type of panic attack had never happened to him before. Never. Not on Earth, and certainly not on any of his weeks-long assignments in orbit, with a cumulative total that was so far into the months that it would be a chore to do the math.

And it was seeing the Moon that had triggered it. Catching sight of the Moon unexpectedly, during his current isolation. He didn't need a shrink to help him figure *that* out.

*Well, crap. Going to the damned Moon really messed me up, didn't it?*

On the Moon, he'd been alone on the surface for quite the while after his Zvezda attack, running, climbing, then walking across

Copernicus Crater, followed by that long lone five-hundred-mile drive back to Hadley, all by his goddamned self.

At the time, that hadn't bothered him much more than being on the Moon at all had bothered him, but apparently it had left its mark on his psyche.

"Sandoval, this is Control. Report."

He flipped the switch without hesitation. "Still here, Control. Just floating around on my lonesome."

"We've been monitoring an anomalous heart rhythm here."

"Yeah, I know." Sandoval had to play it straight. He wouldn't tolerate hedging from anyone else, and he certainly wouldn't tolerate it from himself. "Frankly, I just startled myself and got … unsettled for a sec. I'm cool again now."

And he was. Talking to another person had helped to bring him the rest of the way down.

"Okay. If that happens again, you speak up directly. Don't wait for us to call on you."

"Yessir." *If I can actually speak, that is.*

A pause from Control. "This ever happened to you before, Colonel?"

It hadn't. Even on the Moon itself, Sandoval had never suffered anything like it. He started to feel stupid. "No sir. That was an honest life first for me, right then."

"Roger that. Proceed."

*Keep floating? Sure.* "Will do, Control."

Sandoval leaned back—or, anyway, tried to rest his head toward the back of his helmet, and looked away from the Earth. Deliberately focused on the Moon, waxing gibbous above him.

And it was fine. Looking deliberately at it was okay, apparently. Seeing it unexpectedly was not.

What a weird thing. Getting startled by the Moon?

*Hi, Vivian.*

She'd be in his line of sight right now. Back at Zvezda-Copernicus after her long haul.

Sandoval wanted Vivian Carter about as much as he'd ever wanted anything in his life. But he'd need to give her time to get the Moon out of her system first.

*After this, I'm done with vacuum,* he'd famously said back then, while they were still in lunar orbit together. Maybe it would have been better all around if he'd stuck to that and tried to move on. But he hadn't. It turned out that vacuum wasn't finished with him yet.

On a Pan Am flight across the country, traveling from Vandenberg back to DC, Sandoval had talked his way into the cockpit, which wasn't too hard for an Air Force astronaut with hundreds of military flying hours besides. He'd sat up there with them for three hours, chatting easily to the crew whenever they weren't too busy. Shooting the breeze, swapping tales. It beat sitting back in coach.

It had been a good time. Good enough. They were decent guys. But flying an airliner was a far, very distant cry from being in *space*.

By the time they touched down at Washington Dulles, Sandoval was bored to tears. Even the landing had looked straightforward. Routine, no challenge. The crew themselves were people Sandoval could get along with: fellow flyers, some with a military background themselves. It was the plane itself that was the problem. Being at the controls of a Boeing 747 might technically be piloting, but it wasn't really *flying*. It would be like a Formula One driver deciding to ride herd on semi-trucks for the rest of his life.

Vivian's initial skepticism had been justified. It just wasn't for him.

And right there on the other side of the coin was his Night Corps crew. Gerry Lin had augered in on the Moon, shot down by a Soviet surface-to-air missile while trying to fly Vivian Carter to safety, and that had left a painful hole in Sandoval's life as well as an empty slot on his roster. Lin had been a great guy, one of the best. But then Terri Brock had shifted gears and joined Night Corps. She wasn't the pilot Lin had been, but eventually she might be. And now they were a tight squad again: Sandoval, Brock, Pope, and Rodriguez. By the end of her first month on MOL-10 with the three of them, Brock was as solidly one of the crew as Lin had been. And Brock's husband, Toby, was cool as well. He might not be a pilot, but he was an aero engineer, which was the next best thing. He could talk the talk and he knew the life, even if most of the time he was on the outside looking in, and if most of the stuff that Terri did with Night Corps she couldn't tell him any details about.

It was good to have Brock in the mix. Better than good—great. No guy could have taken Gerry Lin's place, no way, no how. But Terri wasn't a guy.

When it came down to it, a job was about the people. And Sandoval's people were the best. He wasn't ready to let go of them yet. So to speak.

He looked down again at the Earth below—he was over the Pacific right now. Looked like there was a thunderstorm over the Hawaiian Islands, but Fiji looked like an array of jewels.

How had the ancient seafarers ever navigated themselves across something so immense? It beggared belief that they could deliberately travel from tiny island to tiny island in an ocean so vast. It had to be worse than getting orbital mechanics calculations correct, although Sandoval was fairly sure those seafarers hadn't done any of their wayfinding using calculus.

But with decent navigation equipment and the fear factor removed, what would it be like to sail across the Pacific, from island to island?

Might be nice. Blue sky, blue sea, white wavetops, wind in his hair. Maybe he should give that some thought …

Much to his surprise, and to everyone else's, Peter Sandoval fell asleep.


They could tell he was napping from his telemetry and didn't even bother to awaken him until they were two hundred feet away and closing. Then, all of a sudden, his helmet echoed with the Air Force song. "Off we go, into the wild blue yonder …!"

Sandoval thrashed awake, flailing but touching nothing because there was nothing around him to touch. Laughter accompanied the rather bombastic choir in the recording: "Climbing high into the Sun …"

Fortunately, he got his bearings quickly, before he could be embarrassed any further. A Blue Gemini craft was closing on him, a long tether stretched out behind it. And luckily, they stopped the song before it got to his least favorite line: "We live in fame or go down in flame."

"Nice job, guys. Never going to live this down, am I?"

"You certainly are not."

"No sir."

He'd expected Brock and Pope, but it was Rodriguez and Krantzen. Krantzen had already shown himself to be among the best of the new recruits, and this trip to pick up Peter Sandoval was a good enough excuse for some piloting practice. "So which of you is walking home?" A Blue Gemini had only two seats.

"Neither of us," said Rodriguez. "We figure we'll tow your sorry ass back."

Sandoval already knew that. He'd written the specs for the External Retrieve exercise himself, years ago.

He'd attach himself to the end of that tether and Krantzen and Rodriguez would then, indeed, be towing him back to MOL-11. A good bit of orbital maneuvering, with the additional challenge that they had to avoid burning through the tether or frying Sandoval with their thrusters.

Which was why it was more jocularly known as the Crispy Critter Retrieve.

Best to put a brave face on it. "Looking forward to it. Oh, and I'll be grading you both on this exercise, so don't screw it up."


Weary despite his nap, Sandoval entered the MOL and was only halfway through stripping off his suit when Brock shot through the hexagonal hatch, grabbing at its edge to brake herself right in front of him. "Whoa there, Captain. What is this, Scare Peter Day?"

"Apologies, sir. But guess what? While you were out enjoying yourself, we've been reassigned."

Somehow, he knew immediately. "You're joking."

She shook her head and held out a sheet of flimsy from the MOL teletype. Sandoval snatched it, scanned it briefly. "Oh, *hell* no."

Brock lowered her voice, glanced behind her, and said: "Sorry, Peter."

She put her hand briefly on Sandoval's arm, nodded sympathetically, and then turned to leave him alone with his thoughts.

# 15

## Zvezda-Copernicus: Vivian Carter
## February 21-27, 1983

**AGAIN** came the dawn, lancing across the lunar surface like an assault. Again, the crews of Zvezda and US-Copernicus raced against time to complete the rapid work of stripping thermal blankets from the outside hardware, disconnecting heaters, and adjusting instrument settings on every console before critical avionics and other materials baked or melted down.

Yet another dawn on the Moon that Vivian Carter had not expected to see.

By now, after a surprising amount of hands-on physical therapy, Vivian's shoulder had improved to the point where she could exercise, carefully. Which was good because losing muscle mass and general fitness was the last thing she needed, and besides that her forced inactivity and lack of purpose had been driving her nuts. The stabs of pain from her cracked ribs were much less frequent now, and less painful. The bruising all over her torso still showed, but looked worse than it was.

She'd tried to use the rest of her time wisely and stay busy. She had gotten to know the crews of both the US and Soviet sides of Zvezda-Copernicus a little better. The bases required less strenuous maintenance than Hadley had, and its crews had fallen naturally into a cycle where they worked their butts off for the two weeks of daylight, and then slept, researched, did paperwork, exercised, and generally enjoyed a little bit more time to either socialize or keep to themselves during the frigid two-week nights. Vivian had helped out wherever she could make herself useful, on the less strenuous tasks that wouldn't interfere with her recovery. With no core responsibilities of her own at Copernicus, she also got a jump on the mission debriefing she'd formerly expected to do back on Earth: typing up mission documentation, writing reports and lessons-learned, and doing technical and geological debriefs with Houston. She had also been extensively debriefed by the CIA on the two ground attacks, and asked lots of questions in return that they couldn't answer.

She had been invited for dinner in Zvezda several times with Belyakova, Okhotina, and a couple of the other high-ranking cosmonauts, and been convinced they'd been sounding her out for information just as assiduously as she was working on them. Vivian gave up nothing, for she had nothing to reveal, and acquired no useful intel herself.

Early in the lunar night, and true to their original schedule, Feye Gisemba and Christian Vasquez had left the Moon. That had been a very odd day and a somber parting. She'd expected to complete this mission with Feye, splashing down together in the Pacific. And Vasquez and Dobbs were to have been a team in a second Command Module, along with their own dedicated pilot. But that didn't work out either, because Dobbs was still at Daedalus and would remain there for at least another month while he continued to recuperate.

Lakontsev had also been flown home by the Soviets in the second week of lunar night, leaving Vivian Carter and Katya Okhotina the only remaining members of LGS-1 at Zvezda-Copernicus. Okhotina's departure date had not yet been determined. Vivian strongly suspected Katya was being kept on the Moon to grease the social wheels between Vivian and Starman on the one side, and Belyakova and the other Soviets on the other.

Tensions had lifted a little at the joint base, and not just through Vivian's and Katya's efforts. The thieving had stopped almost entirely. Their latest US supply shipment had shown up in a locked container and included a lot of new surveillance equipment besides. Belyakova had allegedly performed her own shake-up on the Soviet side. Plus, the kidnapping of Casey and stealing of the MOLAB had at least made it more credible that an outside group was at fault, rather than the existing members of Zvezda-Copernicus. Movement between the US and Soviet sectors was increasing again, though Checkpoint Charlie was still guarded twenty-four seven, or more accurately twenty-four twenty-nine, by both sides.

As yet, Starman had not assigned Vivian a firm departure date, though it was accepted that it was less than a week away. Her attempts at "diplomacy" had gone as far as they were likely to go, and her shoulder and ribs could hardly be an excuse for much longer. Plus, she was suffering from serious cabin fever and was agitating with Ellis during her daily calls with him to apply some pressure to get her home. It was definitely time to leave.


"Let me show you Kopernik."

Vivian's jaw dropped open. "The crater?"

Svetlana blinked. "Yes. Of course, the crater. There is another Kopernik? We can go down there, explore it. It will get us out of this place for a while."

"You're offering me a tour of the crater where I almost died?"

"I believed that you were interested in all of the Moon. You do not wish to walk Kopernik in the daylight?"

Vivian considered. "You're not planning to kill me down there, right?"

"Once again, you have a strange sense of humor."

"Seriously, Svetlana. You've thought through how suspicious it would look if I were to have an accident while in Copernicus Crater under your protection? Even if we were attacked by a convenient outside force?"

"You believe that is what I am planning?"

"Well, not really, but I've been wrong before."

Belyakova sighed. It was becoming her trademark sound when dealing with Vivian. "I am confident that there will be no assailants in Kopernik. If I was not, I would hardly risk the journey myself. As Kopernik is almost equatorial, we regularly scan the crater for activity from orbit. The last scan took place less than one hour ago, and I studied the images myself. It is likely that your people also keep a close watch on this area. By day, at least."

"Obviously not close enough, under the circumstances," Vivian said.

"I think there is no blame. The attack on you by night? The attackers would need to have been very careless to be seen from orbit, and I think they are not so careless. By day, it is harder to hide."

"And yet, hide they do."

"Vivian, are you coming to Kopernik or not?"

Starman had recruited Vivian to stay close to Svetlana and learn whatever she could. This was surely the best way to do that. But it would mean going out on an extended EVA on the lunar surface, and her last outside trip—over two weeks ago, now—had not gone well.

Much to her surprise and mild irritation, Vivian realized she was nervous at the prospect.

Perhaps Svetlana read her mind. "I would not like your last memories of the Moon, and of Kopernik, to be of violence. Just as I did not wish my own final memory of the Moon to be of a bad injury combined with a spacecraft emergency, both of which I was lucky to survive. And believe me, I have no wish to see harm come to you. I will watch out for you just as I would for Nikolai, if he were here."

"Well, that's quite the declaration."

"But if you wish, we can take guards with us. As long as we may still talk candidly. For that is my goal, as well as exercise."

Vivian decided quickly. "Guards won't be necessary." They'd just ruin the mood. And also make this a bigger deal because then Starman would have to take men off some other duty. And if Svetlana wanted to talk candidly, then Vivian wanted to hear whatever the Soviet was planning to say.

She really should take this opportunity to see the crater properly. And Svetlana was right. Vivian didn't want her last memories of the Moon to be bad ones. "Today? Now?"

"Certainly."

"Sure, but …" Reality crept in. "Uh, I'll need to get medical clearance. And I can walk just fine, but I probably can't go a very long way. All that kangaroo-hopping will eventually start to hurt."

"We can take a Lunokhod. And we can stop and return if you experience pain." Belyakova studied her. "But you look all right to me."

Vivian stifled her first response. Svetlana had, after all, taken bullets to the abdomen and thigh, been bound up by field medics in lunar orbit, and then suffered a Soyuz hard landing in central Asia less than ten days later. Belyakova defined toughness.

That didn't sound like any fun, though, and Vivian had no desire to emulate her. "I'd still better check. I don't want to piss off my people even more than I already do."

"Very well. Let me know when you are ready. To drive to the central peaks and back, it will take six hours, perhaps a little more, all told. But we can take a shorter journey if that is too much."

Vivian's eyes widened. "The central peaks? Wow." Her enthusiasm for this trip took a sudden step upward.

"I have only been to them once before, myself." Svetlana half-grinned. "If you wish, you can bring your core drill."

Vivian tried to imagine operating a drill in her current condition. The percussive vibrations alone would likely hospitalize her. "Maybe just a sample bag or two."


The Moon had three different types of craters. Most ubiquitous were the simple bowl-shaped craters that were *everywhere*, of varying widths and depths, and width-to-depth ratios. The shapes of their rims varied, since crater shapes depended on the angle the offending rock had come crashing in at.

The second type consisted of much larger craters with a central peak complex, like Tycho and Copernicus. In these, the crater floor was relatively flat, and the inner rim areas tall and steep. Here the impacting asteroid had penetrated deep into the upper crust; the peaks were formed by a central "splash" of liquified material, and molten rock then flowed back in from the crater edges. Type Three consisted of those rare craters like Schrodinger, near the South Pole, which had a peak-and-ring structure, sometimes called "walled plain" craters.

Carter's Convoy had explored Schrodinger, through a break in the "wall," and Vivian had seen literally tens of thousands of the regular bowl craters. But she'd never been inside one of the major central-peak craters, aside from her brief nighttime ride to Downstation.

Tycho had been one of the largest that LGS-1 had visited, but Vivian hadn't gone down into it. They hadn't had that kind of time, nor that kind of risk tolerance, and besides, the floor of Tycho had already been explored by Apollo 19 on a targeted mission of exploration.

Nor had LGS-1's schedule allowed Vivian to go down into any of the other "difficult" craters with high mountainous rims. She'd sampled the ejecta blankets on their outer slopes and looked down into several from the safety of the rim.

But *Copernicus?* A supergiant crater, a naked-eye object from the Earth's surface? One of the biggest, and also, by the way, the jewel in the Soviets' lunar exploration crown?

So, yes: Vivian now desperately wanted to see it properly.


Once Vivian had gotten the flight doctor's grudging okay, she checked in with Starman. His immediate response was, "No way."

Then he thought better of it, while Vivian was still opening her mouth to respond. "Wait. If you want to go somewhere alone with Belyakova, you must have good reason. And she must have good reason for asking you."

"Exactly. If Blond Svet is being this friendly, she wants something. Maybe I should find out what that is."

He nodded. "And Copernicus Center is somewhere Peter went, where you haven't been."

That hadn't occurred to her as a motivation. "Peter saw plenty of the lunar surface that I didn't."

"Uh-huh. I trust you'll have no objections to me keeping watch on you on your travels?"

Her face fell. "You want to send a chaperone along?"

"Not unless you want one. I was thinking more of keeping you in telescopic view from the crater rim for as long as we can."

"Which telescope is that?"

Starman grinned. "Not all the really good optics are in space. And not all of them are obvious. At dawn I had a robotic LRV sent west around the crater rim with a couple of my new telescopic cameras, optical and IR, and sat it there to watch over the Annex. It also scans the rest of the crater floor regularly."

"Ah." Vivian's Lunar Rover on Apollo 32 had been the first with remote-drive capability. She'd never really considered them as tools for surveillance. "How many more IR cameras and spare rovers do we have?"

"Since the last supply run a few days ago, quite a few. As we speak, I have two more rovers out on remote patrol looking back at the base from the south and east. Checking for any unauthorized incursions. We won't get surprised again."

"Closing the stable door after the horse has bolted," she said ruefully.

"Or learning from our mistakes."

"If our crypto-friends are smart—which they are—they won't try the same trick twice."

"But we do what we can. And you're not to share any of this with Belyakova, since it might be a way we detect Soviet thefts from us, if they start up again."

"Okay."

"I guess our two MOLs in orbit could also peer down on you on whatever cadence they have and snapshot the rest of the area for intruders. I could alert them to be aware."

In the past the photographic film exposed onboard the MOLs had been dropped back into the atmosphere in film buckets, to be grabbed in midair by a Lockheed C-130 Hercules transport plane and taken home to be developed. That was still how the USAF operated for the bulk of its routine imaging. But Vivian had recently learned that for specific targets of interest, they could now develop the film onboard the MOLs and scan it electronically, then transmit the images directly back to Earth or to US-Copernicus. Meaning that Starman might get a real-time photo of Vivian and Svetlana on-surface in less than an hour. But also, the MOL jockeys were extremely well trained and could look through the eyepiece of the giant DORIAN cameras their own selves and could often pick out what was going on in *real* real time, especially when the astronauts or their vehicles were the only things moving in an otherwise gray and immobile landscape. And since there was no atmosphere to blur and muddy everything, their view was really good.

Then again: "That seems a bit dramatic. And I don't think I want to overturn whatever other priorities Night Corps have, to watch over me on a joyride. Might be bad optics. If you see what I mean."

He nodded. "Okay. I think that's fine. The Soviets are not going to risk *Belyakova*, of all people. First woman on the Moon? One of their greatest propaganda weapons of the century. Staying close to her might be about the best insurance policy you could have."

"And speaking of weapons, we'll both be armed." She and Svetlana had already agreed to that.

Starman rocked back. "Whoa, Nelly. You and Belyakova, going out alone together and both packing heat? *That* sounds like a swell idea."

"It'll be fine."

"Just hope you're quicker on the draw than she is."

"I doubt it'll come to that. We're mostly playing nice, these days."

"Okay. I'd rather have you armed than not, anyway. So, off you go. See what you can find out."

"Will do."

"And try to have fun."

"Fun is the name of my game," she said.

"Sure it is, Vivian," Starman said. "Sure it is."


"I got the okay," Vivian said. "We're on for Girls Night Out."

Svetlana paused, taking a moment to decode this. "All right. Good."

"If nothing else, I'd like to just see the crater walls by daylight from close-ish up in the gondola; they expose about four vertical kilometers of the lunar crust. I'm sure other geologists have taken pictures, but I'd like to take my own set. And the mix of hummocky and smooth areas on the crater floor presumably indicates a high degree of compositional variation. The peaks may have brought material up to the surface from quite the depth. Maybe uplifted crushed breccia from the rebound after the crater was formed. And there are some small bright-halo craters ..." Vivian paused at the amused expression on Belyakova's face. "Sorry, aside from my crew I've spent the last three months with only geologists to talk to."

"Vivian, Kopernik has been studied in detail by geologists from both our countries. I doubt you will learn anything new today."

"Oh, sure. But at least I can take data that's consistent with all my previous samples. I presume someone has done seismic and gravity profiles around the central peaks area?"

Svetlana shook her head, perhaps bemused by Vivian's enthusiasm. "I presume so too. Shall we go?"


Vivian adored the vastness of Copernicus Crater. Even after circumnavigating the entire Moon, Copernicus had something Vivian hadn't seen before. A deep crater, surrounded by a high, mountainous rim, seen from the inside. And those tantalizing spires, still ahead of them.

Krater Kopernik was just under sixty miles in diameter, rim to rim. So, from the crater floor near the Annex, a spot almost two and a half miles beneath the mountain rim, it was a twenty-five-mile journey to the central spires.

Even having been down here once before, Vivian wasn't ready for just how *deep* it really felt. She hadn't considered the math: Mons Hadley, the second-highest mountain on the Moon, had loomed two point eight miles above Hadley Plain. The depth of Copernicus was comparable, so being down by the Annex was the equivalent of having one of the largest mountain ranges of the Moon right behind her. And also, Vivian was now lower beneath the mean lunar surface level than she'd been anywhere other than in the South Pole-Aitken Basin.

Even after traveling all around the Moon, Copernicus Crater still felt new.

"Thank you, Svetlana." She nodded to her spacewoman companion. "I really appreciate this."

They did not go into the Annex, which certainly didn't bother Vivian. "There is not so much to see. Inside, the Annex is just like a smaller two-hall version of Zvezda. But with more people."

Having done her time in Zvezda, Vivian had no desire to spend time inside an even more claustrophobic version, and no wish to be indoors when there was a giant crater to explore.

Two cosmonauts, anonymous in orange suits, their faces hidden behind golden visors, were outfitting and checking out a Lunokhod Rover. On Belyakova's approach they stepped back and saluted. Vivian heard clipped Russian on the Soviet channel; they talked fast but seemed to be telling Belyakova that everything was in order.

This Lunokhod was similar to the one that had been part of the first ground attack on Hadley Base. Yet another sour memory for Vivian, but by now, those were becoming almost routine. Larger than an Apollo Lunar Rover, it was big for just the two of them. In the rear she saw emergency pop-up tents, spare suits and batteries, spare everything. Unless Belyakova was just trying to show off, it appeared that the Soviets were finally learning how to mitigate risk.

And the rover was pretty fast. For the first hour they covered the miles quickly, and Svetlana's keen reactions kept it away from any serious boulders and smaller craters. For all Vivian's misgivings about Belyakova, she had to admit that the Soviet had keen lunar skills.

They did not talk, not right away. By unspoken agreement, for the first half hour they exchanged few words and merely enjoyed the

199

freedom, the separation from the rest of their fellows. On her lunar circumnavigation, Vivian had never been as far from the MOLAB as they were now from the Annex. It felt oddly freeing.

The crater floor they were traveling across was made of impact melt that had cooled and hardened. It was difficult to visualize the sheer quantity of energy in the impact that had made a basin of this size. Central peaks were only created in lunar craters more than twelve miles in diameter. The uplifted central peak material came from deeper in the crust than any of the other material around her.

And the Copernicus crater itself defined the youngest geologic period in lunar history. The Copernican Period. Eight hundred million years old. *Recent*, in Moon terms.

It wasn't all easy going. The floor of Kopernik was scarred, cracked, and pitted. Several times, Svetlana had to take the long way around. But that just added to the adventure; by now, Vivian's initial nerves were gone.

If this was to be Vivian's lunar swan song, at least it played a pleasant tune.

Svetlana's voice pulled her out of her reverie. "You would like to drive for a while? I think perhaps you have driven more on the Moon than I have."

A clear understatement, although Belyakova had been doing great. "Well, sure." Who knew when the ability to drive a Soviet rover would come in handy? Well, probably never. Though as it turned out, aside from the usual difficulty in decoding abbreviations in Cyrillic, it was straightforward.

Peter had hated Copernicus Crater. He'd talked about it many times, and Vivian had listened patiently while he'd reviewed his ordeal. She understood. She'd been through plenty of ordeals of her own, and Peter had sat through her recounting of those as part of her own personal therapy, so it was only fair.

But when Peter had traversed Copernicus, he had thought Vivian was dead and that he was partly responsible for that. And, for bonus points, he'd been stoned out of his gourd on amphetamines. Whereas for Vivian, Copernicus was her cool, calm place. At last.

"I was born in Ukraine. My parents, though, were Russian, in the Army. Most astronauts from Ukraine are actually of Russian background. Karpov, Beregoyov, Volk. And Marina Popovich. All born in Ukraine, too.

"The Russian and Ukrainian languages, they are similar but different, and the people too. They say that the heads of Ukrainians are larger and rounder, and perhaps their bodies as well. I have not really noticed this. I am Russian when I need to be, for the space program, and Ukrainian when I need to be, for my family."

"How very Svetlana of you," Vivian couldn't help saying.

"To be what I need to be, when the situation calls for it? Are you not the person you need to be, depending on the people you are with? You do just the same. Will you deny it?"

Vivian thought about it. "Okay, I guess you win that one. Touché."

She searched around for a safe topic of conversation. "So, Nikolai did not come with you?"

"Sad to say, no. Nikolai is retired. At least for now. He is still a cosmonaut, technically, but nobody expects him to fly again."

"I'm surprised he let you come alone."

Belyakova shook her head. "Let me?"

"That he didn't want to come with you, is all I meant."

Her lip twitched. "I, too."

"I thought … let me be honest, Svetlana, I thought that maybe Nikolai had some affection for you. And that perhaps you might return that feeling."

"Ridiculous."

Belyakova had said that very quickly, though. Vivian just nodded. "I'm sure you're right."

Yet another flashback: Belyakova in agony, shot multiple times, on the edge of unconsciousness, still finding the energy to reach up to Yashin in Columbia Station when he was threatening to take Makarov with him as a hostage. Svetlana, pleading: *Do not take him. I beg you, Comrade. This one thing. Give him back to me.*

It was the most human Belyakova-moment Vivian had ever witnessed.

Well. Who knew? And how was this any of Vivian's business, anyway?

Because it was Nikolai who had kept Svetlana in check. Nikolai who had finally made her choose the right side. When Vivian first saw Belyakova on the Moon without Nikolai, it had scared the crap out of her, and she was still trying to figure out what was in Svetlana's head. That was why it mattered.

Svetlana broke her train of thought. "Nikolai is in his dacha, with his family. He is living the life he wants to live, with the people he has chosen. He has his children, who he loves. I respect that about Nikolai. I always will.

"We flew together. And that will always be special. But that is all." Belyakova glanced at her, almost playfully. "There was nothing, then, between you and Ellis Mayer?"

*Here we go again*, Vivian thought. But, after all, this time she'd started it. "No. Ellis is a great friend, and a great crewman. But Ellis also has a very sweet wife and family. I never saw him as anything more."

They were silent for a long time. Until Vivian said, after a lot of thought: "Svetlana ... I have to know. Cards on the table. You seem ... more well-disposed to me now. Are you trying to play me again?"

"No," Belyakova said.

Vivian waited. "Elucidate, perhaps? Clarify. Tell me more."

"I have said that much has changed in the last three years. Today, we are not commanded to be enemies. There is much to admire in what you have done, especially in your journey around the Moon. And also, Katya Valeryevna gives you high marks." Svetlana looked at her sideways. "In all matters."

"That's good of her," Vivian said calmly. "I think highly of Katya too."

"In truth, you likely saved Katya's life as much as she saved yours. And Andrei's as well. And you have argued the American case reasonably, in ways others have not."

"Hmm."

"Perhaps we have more in common than you think, Vivian Carter. Despite all the ways in which we are clearly very different."

"Well, maybe."

"And why should we not continue to work together?" Belyakova said. "And work better? I am curious."

"Well ..."

"Because of Zvezda, the first time?"

"Since you mention it ... you *were* complicit in my torture. I have to admit that I've found that difficult to get past."

"That, still?" Belyakova shook her head. "There was nothing I could do about that, Vivian. Nothing at all. I had to obey orders."

"And you think that's a defense?"

"It is merely the truth. You would have preferred to see me shot in the head by Yashin, for not doing what I was told? Where would we all be by now, if that had happened? And I did save your life."

"You did? When was that, again?"

"When your heart stopped, at Zvezda Base. It did stop, Vivian. All the way. For a brief while, you were dead. I moved quickly, and shocked you with a defibrillator, a crash cart, and brought you back to life."

"Well." Vivian couldn't exactly deny that had happened.

Belyakova looked at her sideways. "So perhaps you might say your heart belongs to me?"

"Svetlana. Manipulative?"

She grinned. "Sometimes I am, yes. Or, persuasive, rather."

"Back then, you told me my torture made you cry. Was that true?"

Belyakova barely hesitated. "No. It was not. Then, I did say that just to manipulate you."

"Well, thank you for your candor, at least."

"And as for you? All this while, *you* were 'complicit' in a United States plan to bombard my country with nuclear weapons. To destroy millions of lives."

"No," Vivian said firmly. "I was not. When I found out about it, I thought it was a terrible, horrible idea. And I worked to stop it."

Svetlana paused, and eventually nodded. "I suppose you did."

"Damned right."

"And yet, for a long time you denied it."

"Yes. Because I believed my denial was true. And, technically, there were never any US nuclear weapons on the Moon. You do know that, right?"

"Merely the capability of launching them," Belyakova said dryly. "Once Dark Driver was operational, I am sure the weapons would have arrived promptly. Am I wrong?"

Vivian sighed. "No. I'm sure you're right."

Belyakova was silent a long time. Then she said. "However we see it, all of that is in the past. And so I feel that you and I must meet in the middle, somehow. Or at least try."

Even before Vivian's capture, Belyakova had also been on that second ground attack, the one on Hadley during which Vivian had been captured. And Vivian knew nothing about what Svetlana's role might have been in that battle. Several men Vivian knew well had died; it was possible that Svetlana had killed them. Norton, even. Or maybe Svetlana had even piloted one of the craft that had captured Vivian. Perhaps that made more sense: after all, Belyakova had been right there when Vivian first took her helmet off at Zvezda Base.

At this point, Vivian would prefer not to know, and would never ask. Whatever the answer, it was unlikely to be helpful.

Vivian hardly held the high ground. She had shot a Soviet woman in the head at Zvezda. A ruthless KGB agent who'd just tried to kill her, but still. And on an occasion prior to that she'd drilled through a Soviet soldier's helmet until it cracked like an egg. In addition to her recent surface kills near the South Pole in the heat of battle.

Wasn't it better to have Belyakova as an ally than an enemy? Even if some of it was an act? Even if some of the past could never be erased or forgotten?

"Perhaps you're right."

Belyakova nodded. "I will take that 'perhaps,' for now. Vivian, we may never trust each other. Perhaps that is impossible, as we have different loyalties. But maybe that does not matter. We must continue to work together, and I think we will."

*Except I'll be back on Earth by mid-February*, Vivian thought. But, "I guess we'll see," was all she said.

"Being on the Moon with someone changes everything," Belyakova said. "Whether we agree with each other or not, whether or not we see eye to eye … we are still two people who have been on the Moon together."

"Yes. We are."

To her surprise, Vivian found herself moved by that simple statement. Because it was true. The Moon encouraged strong bonds.

No one who had been on the Moon with Vivian was immune. She was bound to them all on some level. She, and they, would never be the same again.

The central peaks were sharp. High, compared to their width. Not truly spires, as such, but definitely mountains of a very different appearance than Vivian had seen close-up anywhere else on the Moon. Most mountains on the Moon were attached to other mountains, as part of a range or at least a ridge, but these were not. Just a complex of three peaks, two close to each other and a third separated off to the west, jutting up from the flattish plain that was the crater floor.

*Yes, I've been all around this giant rock in space, traveled thousands of miles of its surface, and there's still something new to see.*

Vivian took samples. Clambered up the slope of the eastmost peak as far as she could go—which was not far at all, given the incline—and took another sample from there and scanned the view. Took a whole bunch of photographs. Clambered down again and found Svetlana on her knees noodling around in the dirt with her own geologist's hammer, investigating the strata in a broad crack in the surface and looking completely absorbed in the task.

Another sign that perhaps she and Belyakova weren't all that different, once you got past all the history and politics?

They hadn't spoken for some time. Vivian had been aware of Svetlana's quiet breathing, but not much else. As she arrived at the Lunokhod and swung herself back into her seat, she also realized she'd been unaware of the residual pains from her injuries for the entire trip so far. She'd had more important things to focus on.

She continued to say nothing, just sat and surveyed the view all around her from the center of this giant crater, burning it all into her mind.

Presently, Belyakova looked up, checked her suit pressure and remaining oxygen supply out of the same long habit as Vivian, and then made her own way back to the Lunokhod. She, too, sat and looked around.

They had spare oxygen, spare water, and plenty of batteries, and it was clear that neither of them was in any hurry.

Eventually, Vivian said: "That center peak has an interesting stripe of darker material running down its side. Definitely a breccia mix. Lots of dark silicates, I'm guessing olivine."

"Yes, that is correct," Belyakova said unexpectedly. "Olivine and low-calcium orthopyroxene. I have quite a nice sample, from over there."

Vivian raised her eyebrows. "Well. You really do care about rocks. Uh, do we have time for me to go grab myself a piece from where you just were?"

"Of course," said Belyakova. "Be my guest."

Once she got back, sample bag in one hand and geologist's hammer in the other, Belyakova glanced down inside her helmet. From Vivian's

205

time in Soviet Moon suits, she knew that was where the time display was located. "I suppose that soon we must begin our return journey."

"Guess so."

The Soviet looked up and around. Vivian heard a long sigh in her headset. "And yet it is nice to retreat from Zvezda for a while. One matter on which I am sure your Starman and I can agree is that it is hard work, being the commander of a base on the Moon. And often, not very much fun." She tilted her head back to look up at the peaks again. "This is fun."

Another silence. Vivian looked upward too.

"But, to business, I suppose," Svetlana said.

The business of returning? Perhaps.

Then she heard a sudden click. "Vivian, look at this."

Svetlana's tone had changed. Vivian lowered her gaze warily, to find the Soviet holding up a cable, one end of which she had just plugged into her own chest console. "Hmm. Interesting."

"Well?" Belyakova raised her other hand to her radio controls, waited.

*She wants me to turn my radio off. And if I do that, no one at US-Copernicus will be able to hear me any longer.*

*Moment of truth, I guess.*

Vivian considered. Her machine pistol was in her thigh pocket. Where was Belyakova's weapon? She had no idea.

And they were hours away from Zvezda-Copernicus, quite possibly beyond the range of Starman's optics.

*What if I'm a gullible idiot, and Svetlana has—for whatever nefarious reason—decided to kill me after all? If so, it'll be right now.*

That would be stupid, though. If Belyakova really was one of the bad guys, after all this, she'd had plenty of other, far less suspicious opportunities to terminate Vivian. Right?

So Vivian nodded and put a smile into her voice. "Sure."

And turned off her radio.

# CHAPTER 16

## Copernicus Crater: Vivian Carter
## February 27, 1983

**SVETLANA** beckoned. The cable was only five feet long, and Vivian had to lean in to accept the other end. She looked down, located the socket, jacked in.

The Soviet raised her gold-coated visor to show her face and regarded Vivian thoughtfully. Vivian did the same. The Sun was bright, but not playing directly onto Vivian's face. "Hi there, fellow spacewoman. Alone at last."

"It is good that we have this time, when I can no longer worry that I am ..." She looked at Vivian appraisingly. *"Govoriu kak so stenkoi."*

"Talking to the ... walls? No."

"Yes. Usually in Russia, in Ukraine, it just means talking to someone who does not care, is not paying attention and will do nothing, no matter what you say. Some of us in the cosmonaut corps twisted it, used it to mean that we speak deliberately, always, knowing that others may hear us."

"Okay."

"You understand? You speak as if you are private, while knowing well that the KGB will be listening to your words and making decisions based on them."

"You believe that Zvezda is bugged? That your own government is spying on you?"

"It does not seem impossible," Belyakova said, patiently.

"So … every night I ate dinner with you and Katya and the others, we were being listened to?"

"It is always best to assume so."

"Well, that sucks."

"Yes." Belyakova gave her wry half-smile again. "That sucks. Vivian, I have your word? That you are not recording this conversation, and that none of your people, or anyone else, can hear what the two of us say, now?"

"You have my word, Svetlana. I'm completely off the voice loop. They'll be reading my vital signs, my suit telemetry, so they'll know I'm still alive. But that's it."

"You really let them see your heartbeats and your breaths?"

"And you do not?" Vivian could play this turn-the-question-around game, too.

Svetlana shook her head. "I am the Commander. If I say they do not see my vital signs, then they do not. No one is monitoring me today, in any way."

"It's just my breathing. Not my speaking."

"All right." Svetlana looked at her. "I think that perhaps you do not realize the very narrow line that I must walk as a cosmonaut, and especially as a woman cosmonaut."

"I'm all ears." Vivian paused. "Um. That means, whatever you'd like to tell me about that, I would be happy to hear it. I might have a story or two to share as well, once you're done."

Svetlana nodded. "In the Soviet Union, all cosmonaut candidates must be assessed by three committees. These are military, and political, and of the administration. One must pass through all of these committees to be considered. And a part of our training concerns ideology. This, for me, was not a problem. I am from a good family of workers, and we have no bones in the cupboard."

"I'd hope not …?" It took Vivian a moment. "Oh, skeletons in the closet, gotcha."

"Many cosmonauts have encountered difficulties because of ideology. A cosmonaut who refuses to join the Communist Party is immediately suspected. Or sometimes a serious problem will be discovered later. For one cosmonaut, the KGB revealed that his father had been jailed in the 1930s for anti-Soviet activities. Another, his father was sentenced to death by Stalin, and he was found to have relatives living in France besides. And beyond that, several male cosmonauts have been removed from duty because of their divorces." She looked over at Vivian. "None of the women, though. The women are a great deal more careful, it seems. The female cosmonauts are required to be agitators for communism just as actively as the men. Perhaps more so because in the degenerate West we are more in the public eye. We cannot allow any scandal to touch us."

"The degenerate West. Got it. So what you're saying is, you couldn't leave your husband even if you wanted to."

"I do not want to, of course."

"Of course not. And you have to be careful what you say to me, in case I were to reveal it and damage your flawless reputation."

"As a Westerner, you would not be believed. Unless corroborating evidence were found. Which would never be found, for it does not exist."

"Just so you know, Svetlana, anything you told me in confidence, I wouldn't reveal to anyone."

"I regret that I cannot make you the same promise. My duty is to the Rodina. So, have some care what you tell me." Belyakova looked at her thoughtfully. "Or what you tell Katya, or any potentially incriminating actions you might perform."

Vivian's face felt hot. "Can we drop that? Whatever you may have heard, Okhotina and I merely did our duty as crewmates."

Belyakova considered. "We have learned that there is one astronaut at NASA, a woman, who prefers the company of other women. This is not spoken of widely but has not prevented her from becoming an astronaut. She is spoken of very well and assigned to a flight for next year. This could never happen in the Soviet space program." She looked straight at Vivian. "There must be no hint of degeneracy. At least, not publicly. You understand, I am sure."

"I do understand." *I think.*

Belyakova nodded. "And now perhaps it is safer to change the topic. Yes?"

"Yes," said Vivian, attempting not to give away her relief. "Safer by far. And yet … that your Communist system treats you like that? And it doesn't piss you off? Not even a little bit?"

209

"I think you said that you, too, have stories?"

"Well, yes, but I didn't have to sit in front of a committee and explain my ideological views and my flawless worker background."

Svetlana hissed in irritation. "Always, you must poke at me."

"'Needle me,'" Vivian said.

"See? Again, you do it. Needle me. I try not to get angry with you, Vivian. I am doing my best, but you do not make it easy."

Vivian relented. "I suppose not. Um. Sorry. I can be a jerk sometimes, I know."

Belyakova breathed for a while, and eventually spoke again. "Perhaps let us not argue about politics, at least not today. Let us just talk like reasonable people."

Sun blazed down. Vivian adjusted her suit cooling, took a few moments to let Svetlana cool off too.

"Okay," Vivian said. "That's fair. I apologize. Please disregard. Carry on."

"Very well. Perhaps we should drive while we talk?"

Vivian looked up and around again. It had, perhaps, been too much to imagine that harsh realities would not intrude into today's excursion. "Sure. Let's make tracks. Unlike the cryptonauts, who don't."

"Indeed."

They arranged themselves in their seats, strapped in, and Belyakova set off driving away from the central spires. From this distance they could not even see the Zvezda annex, the gondola station at the rim, or any other evidence of human occupation of Copernicus. Their outbound wheel tracks, though, and others like them, pointed the clear way home.

"And so." Belyakova collected her thoughts, as the Lunokhod bumped its way across the lunar surface. "Let us turn to the main matter. Vivian, I now believe it is possible that you are right."

Vivian waited.

"I do not like to say this. But I am becoming convinced that the cryptonauts are indeed either Soviet, or Soviet-supported. Much to my unhappiness. Unfortunately, I cannot tell you my reasons." She glanced over. "I can only be honest with you to a point, Vivian Carter. I am sure that you understand."

"I guess so."

"I should not even tell you this, but I am telling you, and I am putting myself at risk to do so. I trust you not to … embarrass me in this matter. I believe I have explained why, adequately enough."

"Indeed you have. Do you know where they are?"

"No. I have as little idea of that as I had before."

"Okay. And you can't tell me what changed your mind?"

"No. Because if I tell you, and you tell others, it will be obvious where you received the information, and my life would be at risk."

"I see. All right."

"Always in the Soviet Union there are the two factions, the men who take the hard line, and those who are more moderate. In America, you might call them the hawks and the doves. Reagan is a hawk. And I do not believe I am a dove. But there are many in the Party who are more hawk than I am."

"Oh, I'm sure."

Belyakova looked at her again, appraisingly, slowing the vehicle as she did so. "It also seems clear to me that Commander Jones has instructed you to stay close to me, when you can. To talk with me as much as you are able, and discover as much as you can, in ways that he cannot."

"Can neither confirm nor deny," Vivian said. "Which means yes, Svetlana. Of course he has."

"He would be foolish not to. And if he had not, you would be foolish not to tell him, or others, what you know, where the safety of United States astronauts may be concerned. If our countries are not at war, they are not exactly at peace, either."

Vivian felt a chill. "You're saying there's a future danger to US astronauts?"

"'Can neither confirm nor deny.'" Belyakova gave her a rueful grin. "Which means, this time, that I do not know. Whatever the cryptonauts' future plans are, I do not know them. But I also know they are still here, and not far away, and you have faced dangers from them before.

"And yet, I hope that you will not tell Commander Jones this directly. That I told you so, today, now, in my own words. And it makes little difference, no? He already believes the Soviet Union is responsible. It changes nothing, for him."

Belyakova paused, considered her words carefully. "You understand, I think, how delicate my situation is. If I volunteer information to the Americans, then I am grounded, perhaps arrested. Perhaps even sent to a gulag. If you tell anyone what I told you, I shall be forced to deny it. But if I were to tell you more details of what I know, my people would not believe my denial, for it could be proven false. You understand?"

"And yet you are telling me."

"Yes. And I am doing so to try to gain your trust, to convince you that I am a reasonable person, for when I tell you the next thing."

"There's a next thing?" Of course there was. "Okay, shoot. So to speak."

Belyakova looked at her thoughtfully. "Katya Okhotina has convinced me that you are a reasonable person, for an American. I, also, have sometimes found you reasonable, and so did Nikolai. Our opinions of you are similar. But Katya's is more important, for she has spent a great deal longer in your company than either I or Nikolai. And her trust is hard to win, even harder than mine, I think. And yet she believes you to be a good leader, and a good friend."

Vivian nodded. "I'm grateful for that."

"You were willing to lie for her. On her behalf. To protect her against retribution by her own people, for protecting your LGS-1. Your concern for your crew and your friends was the most important matter for you. That means a great deal to me. I, also, am protective of Katya Okhotina. She is sometimes impulsive, just as you are. I would not like to see her in trouble.

"My real message is that you are on the right path, but that you must discover the truth for yourself. And so now, let me tell you the next thing. I believe—no, I am *convinced*—that the United States is doing something secret, again, on the Moon. Not this, not the cryptonauts. But there is *something* taking place here, something your people are keeping secret. Something that requires many flights. This we know, for a fact."

"I ..." Vivian hesitated.

Belyakova let the rover slow to a halt, turned to face her. "You agree. I can feel it."

Well. Nothing for it but to be honest.

"Yes. I agree, Svetlana. Something is going on. But they won't tell me what it is, either. I honestly have no clue."

Belyakova searched her face, and then nodded. "A pity." She looked around them, taking in the view of Copernicus. The peaks were well behind them now, but the crater wall ahead looked almost as distant as when they'd started back. "Maybe we should try to find out."

Vivian just shook her head. Belyakova looked frustrated. "I would rather explore than fight, and I know that you would, also. But both our nations are deceiving us, as well as each other. I believe that perhaps we have common enemies, you and I. Or at least, enemies that risk our fragile peace on the Moon." She took a breath. "I believe we should try to get to the bottom of both these matters, together. And for that, you will need to stay on the Moon. There is simply no other American who I can trust."

"Oh, God."

Vivian might have known. She should have guessed that it would come to this.

Belyakova reacted with surprise. "You wish to leave the Moon?"

"Yes. Yes, in fact, I do." No reason why Belyakova would have known that. Vivian had never told her. "It's not that I particularly want to go home. I'm sure that once I'm back on Earth I'll get depressed again and feel there's nothing left in my life ... sorry, I have my own grief about all this, and it's complicated, and I shouldn't inflict it on you. But I also think that my time is up here. I've pushed this life, this Moon life, as far as it can go. The Moon has hurt me enough. Nearly killed me enough times. I now have a bit of a love-hate relationship with it. Bottom line: it's time for me to go."

"There is more," Belyakova said.

"Jeez, really? More?"

"More Russian military are coming to Zvezda Base. Just as we expect US military will come to US-Copernicus. You have not been informed?"

"No. But I'm not surprised. By now the pattern is pretty clear, isn't it? Automatic escalation, as soon as there's trouble."

"Unfortunately, yes. I hope that this time we can maintain the peace. I have asked that Yelena Rudenko be assigned to return to Zvezda. I believe that managing a more populated base will take the energies of us both." She looked at Vivian. "I also asked for Nikolai. He would be good at this, better than I. People respect him and listen when he speaks. But who knows whether he will be willing to leave his retirement?"

"Makarov might return to the Moon? Despite what you said earlier?"

"If someone can drag him away from Olga and his children."

"Well, if anyone can do that, it would be you." Vivian said.

Belyakova nodded. "But the combination of you and me would be even stronger, I believe. You, me, Nikolai, Katya."

"I'd love to see him again," Vivian admitted. "Nikolai is a good man. But that's still not enough to keep me on the Moon. I'm not staying, Svetlana."

"And is that because of Peter Sandoval?"

"No," Vivian said.

Again, Belyakova assessed her. "I should tell you this: I have been informed that you and Colonel Peter Sandoval became … closer friends, once you were back on Earth."

"Dammit." Vivian raised her eyes to the skies. "Okhotina. Obviously."

"No. Not Katya. She has said nothing of it."

"Oh." *Shame that I just revealed her discretion, then.* "Well, good. Then because it's in my file?"

"Yes, it is in your file. Which has grown lately."

Vivian felt a little sick. "Because Soviet spies were watching me the entire time I was back on Earth."

"In fact, they were watching Colonel Sandoval. They got you 'for free,' as you say."

"Terrific."

"I am sorry." Belyakova seemed genuine. "I, too, do not like being watched over. But these things I have been told, I do not plan to use for any bad purpose. I know such matters are hard."

"They sure can be."

"I just thought it important for you to know what my country knows. I cannot say what use *they* might make of the information."

"Ha. Then your country, and you, presumably know that it didn't last."

"Yes. I am sorry."

"Not his fault. I was just having a bit of trouble being back on Earth. After … this."

"And … you did not like him?"

"Oh, I liked him just fine. But … I wanted the Moon more, right then."

"I see."

Was Belyakova trying to play her? Or was she just trying to be normal?

214

It didn't really matter. Vivian had trekked hundreds of miles across the lunar surface, for days, never taking off her suit, and with no company. And then nearly gotten nuked. And then, well, all the rest of it. This? She could do *this* shit all day. She apparently wasn't giving anything away that Belyakova didn't already know. And the view was still amazing.

And turnabout was still fair play. "How about you?"

"Me?"

"Since the radio's off ... *You're* back on the Moon. And you're married. So I guess you're fine with the separation, and all?"

Belyakova thought about that for a surprisingly long time. Eventually, she said: "It was a good marriage for both of us. Useful. It opened doors."

"Doors?"

"For us both. And, yes, I suppose that I love Georgi. But I have never been sure how much I like him. Or whether he is the right person for me. He is a good man." She grinned at Vivian through the visor. "He has his uses. Certain skills which I ... deeply appreciate."

"Uh, okay. Good to know." All right, fine. Maybe Vivian couldn't do this all day after all.

"And yet. What my husband really wants is children. Children, children, children."

"And you don't?"

Svetlana looked at her sideways. "And you do?"

"Uh, no. I never have. But everyone tells me I'm weird."

"Me, too." The Soviet nodded. "And my husband and I, if we had children, who would raise them? Who would be in command of *that* mission? I would. And that is not what I am here for." She looked around. "I do not mean *here*. I mean, not what I am on Earth for, let alone the Moon. At least, that is what I believe."

"You're unsure?"

"And you, you are sure you do not want children? How can you be so certain, deep down?"

"Because I never dream about them," Vivian said. "I mean really dream, when I'm asleep. My dreams are always about what I want. Or maybe about what's worrying me. Always. So I dream about flying." She laughed. "My God. So much flying. And I dream about the Moon, even when I'm here. And I have the usual weird nonsense dreams that

215

everyone gets. But I've never once had a dream that I can remember, where I had kids. When I dream, I mostly dream about space."

"So do I. And so, I believe my answer for you is that I love my husband ... but my real true love, I think it is space as well."

"I think it's the women that do," Vivian said. "Really love space, I mean. For some of the guys, it's often just a job to do. But you, me. Terri Brock. Katya. We're all really *into* it. Because up here we're all equal."

Belyakova looked dubious. "Equal?"

"Or at least more equal. And, hey, sometimes we're the bosses. Right?"

"Sometimes we are." Belyakova slowed the rover and turned to face her. "Earlier you spoke of cards on the table. Here are my cards. I can keep you on the Moon, Vivian Carter, if you wish. You only have to ask."

"Uh. Except, you're not my boss. NASA is my boss."

"I am sure we can come to some arrangement. We need you here, and I have already said why. Both your people and mine might benefit."

"After which, I'd be beholden to you?"

"Beholden?"

"In your debt. I would owe you something for that."

"No. There would be no debt. Because the arrangement would only last as long as it was useful to us both."

"Okay. Good. Then, no debts. But seriously, what are you suggesting? Spell it out for me."

"Of course." Belyakova steered around a large clump of rocks. Vivian resisted the urge to ask her to stop for a sample. This conversation was more important.

"No one else is as deep into this matter as you are. And none has the ability and is willing to work with the NASA people, and Night Corps people, and Soviet people involved. You are a bridge, and," Belyakova shook her head, "I do not see any other bridge. Commander Jones is not close, not understanding. He is too stiff. I could never talk to him as I talk to you now. With him it is all negotiation and games. He expects the Accord to break tomorrow, and he has thought this for several weeks. If it does, it will be no more than he expects. He will be ready and will not particularly care. And even once he rotates home, Daniel Grant will take over as Commander of US-Copernicus, and Grant is an idiot. But I know that *you* care."

Belyakova paused again. "You *do* have influence, whatever you claim. I believe your influence can help us here. And you have clarity of thinking, and we need that too. So, will you stay?"

They both fell silent. Belyakova let her think. Eventually, Vivian said, "Part of me really does want to get to the bottom of this. I'd love to get my hands on the people who shot at us. Nearly killed my crew and me. But staying on the Moon any longer makes it feel like I'd be tempting fate. And not just my own. It's starting to feel like wherever I go, other people get hurt." She shook her head. "It's time to get on with my life. Whatever that even means."

As if Vivian hadn't spoken, Belyakova said, "It may even be that the Lunar Accord can only survive if you continue to be involved. Continue to help us work together." Svetlana laughed, a little bitterly. "Even now, of all the American astronauts we deal with, *you* are the only one who has taken the trouble to learn Russian so well. Have you noticed it? Just you, in all of US-Copernicus. No other Americans will take that one simple step, on a base that is supposed to be a collaboration between our countries."

Vivian would not have claimed that learning Russian was simple. But it was undeniable that she was the best Russian-speaker among the lunar astronauts, and that the average Zvezda cosmonaut spoke much better English than the average US-Copernicus astronaut's understanding of Russian.

"We'll see," Vivian said. "I hear you, Svetlana. And I thank you for this, uh, odd trust you appear to have in me. But honestly, there's nothing I know about this situation right now that you don't already know. And your theory about the mighty influence I wield is entirely misguided." She thought for a few moments. "But I also can't deny that I may have a slightly better chance of keeping matters civil than Starman does."

Belyakova nodded. "And for that, the USSR will undertake to provide you with the necessary food, even accommodation if the US requires it, and to also provide your transport back to Earth at the end of the arrangement. After all, it would not be your first time in a Soyuz."

Vivian frowned. "Wait. If you can promise me all this, it means you've already cleared it with your bosses."

"Yes, I have. Which will prove to you that I am serious."

"Wow."

"Well?"

"I'm thinking, babe," Vivian said. "Stand by one."

Once—just a couple weeks ago—Vivian would have found this a tempting offer. One that would keep her on the Moon after all. And one that might, oddly, provide an improved promise of personal safety.

And ... "Well. I really don't like leaving things this way. With Casey lost."

Belyakova did that full-torso nod again. "I, too, liked Buchanan."

"You did?"

"Yes. He was the only American here with the ... balls? to flirt with me."

Vivian nodded. "'Balls' is correct in that context. But ... you *liked* that about Casey?"

"Of course. It was refreshing. You do not like men to flirt with you?"

"Well, not on the Moon. I mean, not when I'm working. But anyway. Let's not say *was* just yet, about Casey. Maybe we can still get him back."

"He may already be on a ship back to Earth, but I do not think so. We have been paying close attention to the vehicles that launch from the Moon. We cannot guarantee that we have not missed anything, but I think it unlikely."

"Your Almaz stations?"

Belyakova said nothing.

"Interesting." Vivian wasn't sure the US had that kind of capability. Then again, she wasn't entirely sure Belyakova could be believed either.

She looked around again. By now they could see the square bump of Upstation on the high crater rim, the line of the cable. This ride would soon be over.

One thing was for sure, if Vivian was really going to stay any longer, she'd need to get out more. Being stuck inside US-Copernicus all the time would drive her crazy.

God *damn* it.

"When do you need my answer by?"

"Not today. Of course. But soon."

"Good. And, um, thank you. I appreciate it. All of it—this trip, and the offer." She sighed. "Which I will think about."

Belyakova nodded, satisfied. "That is all I ask."

They dropped the Lunokhod off back at the Annex, hiked the short distance back to Downstation, and took the ride up to the crater rim mostly in silence, looking back out over the expanse of Copernicus Crater, Vivian studying the peaks again from a distance that she'd just visited close up.

When she'd begun this EVA, she'd anticipated it would be her last exploratory hike on the Moon. Now ... it seemed that might not necessarily be the case. Vivian still couldn't figure out how she felt about that. She'd sleep on it. Maybe talk to Ellis, before raising it with Starman.

As she crested the rim, the lights on her suit radio console flickered on. Line of sight reestablished with Zvezda-Copernicus.

And ten seconds later, she heard Starman's voice in her ear. "Carter, I need to speak with you immediately. Don't stop to doff your suit."

Immediately all her senses went on red alert. She scanned the area quickly, surface and sky, but saw no obvious threats. "Starman, Vivian. Is it an emergency?"

"No, but treat it as time-critical. Enter at US Airlock 2."

Not at Joint Port, then. Vivian raised her eyebrows, glanced at Belyakova. "Guess I need to hurry. Thanks again for the trip. I'll be in touch."

Vivian leaned forward, pushed off hard, and loped down the long slope that separated her from Zvezda-Copernicus.

Starman was waiting on the other side of Airlock 2. Just him, no suit tech. Vivian had already shucked her gloves and dropped them, and now unlocked her helmet, lifted it off.

"Vivian. Nice of you to drop in. Where the hell have you been?"

Starman was seething. His whole demeanor radiated irritation. Rage, even? What the hell? "Uh, sorry? I've been down below, in the crater. I cleared it with you. What's up?"

"You didn't tell me you'd be gone for *nine hours*. Or that you'd be out of contact for most of that time."

Nine? "It wasn't *most* of the time—Starman, what the hell's going on?"

"There's been a schedule change. You're launching today."

"Today? Uh, hold up a moment on that." Vivian took a deep breath. She'd expected to have time to collect her thoughts before having this conversation. "Starman, Svetlana has asked me if I'd be willing to stay on the Moon a while longer."

"Belyakova did *what*?"

"To stay. To help out, diplomatically, between the Soviet and US contingents and to keep working on the cryptonaut problems …"

He laughed bitterly. "Belyakova wants to put you in as a layer between me and her? Not a chance."

"Starman, that's not how she put it at all."

"Forget it, Carter." He shook his head. "Not going to happen."

Vivian drew herself up. "Look, *Commander Jones*, I'm not trying to *compete* with you here. I'm not angling for your goddamned job. I don't want it, trust me."

"You work for NASA. Not the Soviets. Especially, my God, not for Belyakova, however much you admire her."

"Admire? Jesus Christ. That is a million miles away from being the right word."

"The very first time we discussed her, didn't you tell me she was 'personable?' And you sure spend enough time with her now."

"I asked if *you* thought she was … jeez, that was a joke, you *know* it was a joke!"

"Well, I thought so at the time. But rumors are spreading about you, Vivian. Sad to say. Specifically, about you and that even more 'personable' cosmonaut, Katya Okhotina."

"Oh, for—" Vivian swore, mightily, using words she hardly ever chose to express with her professional colleagues.

"Mouth like a sailor too." He shook his head. "Nice. Anyway, none of that matters now. It's irrelevant."

"The hell it doesn't! This is all bullshit. I *respect* Belyakova's achievements, but that's as far as that goes. And whatever dumb scuttlebutt you're hearing about Okhotina, that's BS as well." She forced herself to calm down. "Look, Belyakova's idea isn't without merit. Could we discuss it more calmly?"

She backed up to the wall, ready to unstrap and hang her PLSS on the wall-frame. Starman stopped her, his hand on her arm. "Belay that.

Didn't you tell me just the other day that you were ready to leave the Moon forever?"

"Yes, I did. And I still have mixed feelings about it. But maybe I shouldn't be leaving so much unfinished business here. And by that, I mean the cryptonauts, who have nearly killed me several times now, and kidnapped—"

"But it took your long private chat in Copernicus with Belyakova to tempt you into this decision?"

"She made a lot of salient points. And the Soviets are willing to foot the bill for my continued accommodations here, plus my ride home."

Starman paced. Striding back and forth with anger rippling off him in waves wasn't easy in lunar gravity, but he gave it a great shot. "I'm sure. And all this had to be discussed with your radios turned off? A private chat, overheard by no one?"

"We had a lot to discuss."

"Like what?"

"Several topics. It was a private conversation."

"Private. With a Soviet."

"Yes, sir. With a fellow astronaut—who happens to be a cosmonaut."

"Carter, good Lord. Use your head. If Major-General Svetlana frigging Belyakova wants you to stay on the Moon, then there's a darned good reason for that, and not one that we're going to like. Maybe she sees a sympathetic ear she can pour misinformation into. Maybe she wants to use you to help twist the knife against us. Perhaps they even think they can turn you. You don't have strong family ties on Earth. Did she ask you to defect?"

"No! No, sir. She did not. She merely—"

"Skip it." He was shaking his head again. "Doesn't matter. Request denied. This is not the road you want to go down, Carter. Trust me. Even if that were possible, and it isn't. Because you leave today."

"Let's at least push the idea upstairs. See what NASA thinks, the Astronaut Office, JSC, HQ—"

"Let's not. They won't buy it."

"Goddamn it, Starman, *stop interrupting me!*"

Jones raised his hands. "All right. I'm sorry. But, Vivian, there's no point in discussing this. You've been ordered aloft. You launch in under three hours. I know you don't like it. Believe it or not, I don't like it either. I'm not just being vindictive. You've been ordered off the Moon."

221

"By whom?"

"Vivian. Come on. Who the heck do you think?"

"But three hours? You can't be serious." It would take a bare minimum of four to get aboard whichever LM had been allocated to her, activate it from scratch, align it, set the guidance computer …

"Well, if you'd gotten back sooner …"

"How could I have known I needed to?"

"You'll be taken up to Eagle Station by Fisher. He's already prepping his LM for launch."

"And who the hell is Fisher?" Gone were the days when Vivian knew all the NASA astronauts by name, service, and reputation. She'd skipped teaching or socializing with two astronaut candidate classes almost completely, between her Hadley and Marius visits to the Moon, her proposal-writing, and the training for LGS-1.

"Don Fisher. He's fine, competent. Apollo 49, plus various taxi runs into orbit and back. He'll get you where you need to go." Starman made a show of looking at his watch. "Vivian. Time's a-wasting. Put your helmet on and go."

"I don't even get to collect my things?"

"I'll have them sent on up."

"For God's sake!" Vivian stepped forward. "Starman. Please. Look at me. What happened to 'as friends?' What happened to 'not leaving mad?'"

Something fluttered behind Starman's eyes. It looked more like pain than anger. He said nothing.

"Starman?"

"Maybe we still can be friends. Eventually. I hope so. But … Vivian, frankly, honestly, that might be a while."

"Great." Vivian found she was almost on the verge of tears. But she would not cry, not here, not in front of Starman. "Thanks a lot."

"I'm sorry this has to be so abrupt. But you're done here." Starman stepped back. "All this comes from way above my head."

"Seriously?" she said. "*That's* how you're playing this? You always were a walking cliché."

Starman closed his eyes. "Vivian. Please. Just go. Right now. Clock's ticking."

# PART THREE: SKY-HIGH

March 1983

# CHAPTER 17

## Apollo 53L: Vivian Carter
## February 28, 1983

**VIVIAN** loped across the lunar surface, glancing to left and right as much as she could while still hustling. These would be her very last glimpses of the Moon from ground level. This chapter in her life was closing. Ironically, today was almost the exact three-year anniversary of her Apollo 32 landing at Marius with Ellis.

*Ah, those were the days.*

And now, in three hours she'd be launching off the Moon with someone she'd never even met.

How would that go? If either of them could launch into orbit separately, then they could surely work through it together. But Vivian would have liked at least one sim with the guy first—even just a conversation, an exchange of notes and experiences before they were tossed into a launch. Crews developed their own distinct rhythms and understandings over time. She and Fisher wouldn't get that opportunity.

But it would probably be fine.


Even before Vivian boarded, she recognized the craft as a three-person LM Taxi. Would someone else be riding into orbit with them?

No. The storage space behind the pilots was piled high with rock bags. This would also be another LGS-1 cargo run, one of the many flights that would be needed to gradually transfer all Vivian's rocks up to Eagle Station, and from there back to Earth. She eyed the bags uncertainly as she got to her feet in the LM, hoping they were well tied down. If any of them came free during launch, or once they hit weightlessness, it could make one hell of a mess.

Her pilot was already aboard, suited up, and standing on the left side of the cabin—the commander's position. Which was fair because this was his LM, but it still felt odd.

Soon after she cranked the hatch, the guy who had to be Fisher reached up and repressurized the LM without speaking. Well, a few moments of silence were fine with Vivian. She needed a few moments to regain her composure, as well as literally getting her feet back under her. The last few hours had been a whirl.

She watched the pressure rise. Once it got to 4.5 PSI and stabilized, she slid off her gloves and popped her helmet, and her new companion did likewise. He glanced at her briefly, without expression, then returned his attention to the instrument panels.

"Hey there." She reached out a hand. "Vivian Carter."

"Sure." His eyes never left the board. "Don Fisher. Good of you to join me."

"Nice to be here," she said automatically, though it wasn't. She glanced up at the circuit breaker box, scanned the boards. "Good to meet you, Don Fisher. Where are we on the timeline? Well ahead, by the looks of things."

"Actually, a bit behind where we should be, with an hour to wheels-up. Thanks to you."

"You're kidding." Vivian checked the clock on the panel, glanced at her wrist, scanned the boards again. "*One* hour? I was told three. We're launching an orbit early? Why?"

"If you don't know, I'm damned if I do. They moved my timeline up again. Guess the Commander really does want your ass off the Moon pronto."

"Well, shit." So much for a well-organized departure, the chance to set up and savor the last launch of her career. Fine. Whatever. "Ascent PADs are already loaded, then?"

"Yes, both in." Two sets of Pre-Advisory Data for their guidance computer. The first PAD would contain the parameters for a direct ascent to docking, requiring several corrections in-flight but arriving at

Eagle Station within a single lunar orbit. The second PAD was a backup, the burn times and parameters necessary for a longer, more leisurely but safer flight to a coelliptic rendezvous, requiring over four hours and two lunar orbits. Vivian was guessing this one wouldn't be leisurely.

"And you tested the rendezvous radar on Eagle?" He'd need to have done that on Eagle Station's previous pass overhead, two hours previously.

"Yes. Nominal, though we expect tweaks when we reacquire."

"I'd have liked to be here for that. Seriously, man, I'd have gotten here sooner if I'd been able. This was sprung on me, and when it was, Starman clearly said I had three hours till launch."

"Thought maybe you were happy enough to skip the grunt work. Being a hotshot TV star and all."

Vivian stared. "That's one hell of an attitude you're carrying, soldier."

"Yes, ma'am," he said. "But on this ship, maybe call me Commander. So, Pilot: you going to help, or what?"

Well. Vivian swallowed down her anger. They didn't have time for this, and technically Fisher wasn't out of line. "Of course, Commander. My apologies. Where are we?"

"Coming up on the inertial platform alignment."

"So you've already done the RCS hot-fire test?"

Fisher glanced down at his clipboard. "No. You're right. I got ahead of myself, damn it. RCS hot-fire is next. Thanks."

Well. They sure were behind. But even so, haste was the killer. "If I may?" Protocol be damned. Vivian plucked the clipboard out of Fisher's hand, scanned it. Checked the settings of various switches. Everything looked nominal, as far as she could tell.

"Satisfied?" He took it back. "Then let's get rolling."

"Roger that."

"And let's hope you're not about to get me killed."

Vivian couldn't control her exasperation. "You know I've launched one of these babies off the surface solo, and with no backup from Mission Control, right?"

"Sure. Three years ago. During your insubordinate period."

"Yeah, well, I still remember where everything is, trust me."

"When was your last sim?"

"I ran three dry-sims a few weeks ago with Feye Gisemba. The guy I thought I'd be flying home with."

"Dry-sims." During the night, without power to any of the instruments. "The kind where you follow along in the binder and point to switches rather than flipping them."

"And a bunch more full-up sims at Johnson and Kennedy prior to the mission." Time to come off the defensive. "And you?"

He just grunted. "Hope you have a good memory."

And Vivian was going to be with this jerk all the way back to Earth? That was going to be a bundle of laughs.

They did the hot-fire checks, firing the RCS thrusters in opposing pairs, checking all the positions of the hand controllers. Despite the balanced thrusts, the firings shook the whole spacecraft pretty good.

"All thrusters nominal," she said.

"I confirm." He pushed-to-talk. "Houston, Apollo 53L. Hot-fires complete. Are we okay to bring the ascent batteries online now, or do you want to wait till T-minus-35? We could sure use the time buffer."

Vivian nodded. Smart. Anything they could do to claw themselves ahead of the nominal timeline, buy time for later, they should do.

A crackle. "53L, Houston. Stand by … Yes, okay, now is good. Bring them on."

"Will do." Fisher glanced over, but Vivian was already doing it. He gave her a quick thumbs-up. *Okay, great, we're being professional at last.*

"53L, we have a couple of accelerometer bias updates to read up to you."

"Roger that, CAPCOM." He looked at Vivian, who nodded. "Ready to receive."

Numbers flew through the air, some of them acting as verbs, others nouns, still others load addresses for the onboard computer. Fisher watched and listened carefully as Vivian wrote them down, entered them, read them back to Houston.

"Okay. Alignment is next." Fisher launched into it, the P57 gravity-vector measurement and star sightings for the fine-tuning of the inertial platform. So that the LM would know exactly where it was. Which was critically important, when hurling yourself into space.

And he did it well. Despite his snark, he was quick and practiced about taking the measurements, and he read them crisply to Vivian. Aside from that first RCS-fire bobble, where she'd arguably distracted him, Fisher was solid, and Vivian might not have been able to take the readings as fast herself. Of course, for all Vivian knew, Fisher did this ten times a month. Taxi drivers spent a lot of time behind the wheel.

"Apollo 53L, we have some rendezvous radar angles for you to upload."

Fisher gave her the nod just as Vivian said, "Go ahead." She took them, entered them into the guidance computer.

Fisher double-checked her, which was a routine precaution, and nodded again. "Okay, Houston, we're on Line 8-12 of the checklist, waiting to don helmets and gloves again in about ten." They'd be fully suited for the launch. Though it was low probability, there was always a chance that the pressure wave from combustion might compromise the LM's fragile hull.

"We caught up well, Commander," she murmured.

"We did at that, Captain."

She scanned everything. "Houston, our AGS lunar align is about half a degree off the PGNS."

"We copy. What axis?"

"Pitch."

"Good," Fisher said. "No worries." He paused. "Hey. See the 16mm camera back there? Want to configure it over your window to film the ascent?"

"Is that still protocol?"

"No. Hasn't been since Apollo 40. Just figured you might want the reel, since this is your last launch off-surface. Keepsake, and all."

"Good point," she said. "Uh. Thanks, man."

"No problem."

Vivian set it up. Getting close, now. Ten minutes till they pressurized the fuel tanks. Twenty minutes until launch. And those last minutes would be *busy*.

He picked up a glove, offered it to her. She could have done it herself, of course, but she appreciated the gesture. They briskly finished the re-suiting, and cross-checked.

"Okay, Houston, we're suited and locked. Moving to LM O$_2$ and H$_2$O."

"Roger that. We're recommending PGNS for direct rendezvous."

"Copy." They were going up the fast way, then.

Vivian glanced at the clock. "Ready to pressurize tanks now. Houston, are we good?"

"Roger that. We're standing by. You have the Go for press."

"Okay, here comes Tank One. We'll pause before Two."

"Master Arm switch is set to Arm," said Fisher. "We have two lights. Selector switch set."

At his nod, Vivian opened the valves to release high-pressure helium into the tank. Houston would be monitoring the tank pressure to make sure all went well and that there was no pressure decay due to leaks.

"This part was dodgy without Mission Control," she said. "When I was bailing out of Hadley."

"Yeah. Must have been." He pushed-to-talk. "Tank One pressurized. Manifold pressures look good. Confirm?"

"We confirm, 53L. Go for Tank Two."

"Roger." Fisher studied readouts. "Okay, there's Two." She could see his shoulders relax a little.

The numbers looked good. If anything had been about to go wrong, to hand them a launch abort and give Vivian a few more hours on the Moon while they rectified it, it would have been the tank pressurization. But it was going smooth as silk.

"Tank Two, confirm nominal. You're go for liftoff. Congratulations again, Vivian Carter, on a successful circumnavigation of the lunar surface. Safe trip home."

*Oh, hey, someone remembered.* "Roger that, and thank you Houston. I've had a blast."

Awkward silence. Perhaps they were remembering the nuclear blast from her previous trip.

But in the closing minutes everything was business, and she and Fisher fell into a steady rhythm as if they'd been working together for weeks.

Vivian: "Attitude control, three, to Mode Control."

Fisher: "Okay."

"PGNS and AGS to auto. TTCA, two, to jets."

"Copy, two, to jets. Vivian, we need to get the rendezvous radar AC closed at T-minus-5, yes?"

"Yep, copy." She typed, waited, watched. "Okay. Confirm closed."

"Phew." Fisher rocked back. "Standing by on two minutes, on my mark. Three, two, one, mark."

"Master Arm is coming on," Vivian said. "AGS needles deflected, alignment looks good. Guidance steering is in."

"Roger that," CAPCOM confirmed.

Only now did Vivian begin to feel a little tension, that apprehensive tickle in her gut. Was she that blasé about a launch off the Moon's surface? Apparently so. And yet Belyakova's offer to keep her here longer still niggled at her, damn it. An opportunity missed?

"One minute," Fisher said. "Confirm Master Arm is two lights, A and B both on. Average-G is on. Engine Arm to Ascent. Thirty seconds till launch."

The clock ticked. Vivian started the camera over her window. "Standing by for ten seconds."

Ten seconds left on the Moon.

He looked at her. "Ninety-nine PRO."

At T-minus-five seconds, Vivian's display showed ninety-nine, asking her to confirm engine ignition. She pressed it. "And: PROCEED. It took. Three, two, one, and—ignition."

A kick from beneath them, surprisingly light, but Vivian had been expecting that. Liftoff from the Moon was nothing like liftoff from the Earth.

Just like that, Vivian Carter had disconnected from the Moon.

"And we're away." Fisher glanced out the window, then back at the consoles. "Auto start, engine start. Seven, eight, nine ... Automatic, yaw left, pitch-over."

"Pitch-over. Stable around 306."

The engine made so little noise. Dave Scott from Apollo 15 had referred to it as sounding like the wind blowing through a window. The rocket firing beneath them made more of a swishing sound than a blast.

It was only half a G, but it felt like more. "Lot of wallow," she said.

"Afraid so. That's a feature of this ship, and we're heavy-loaded today."

"Okay." Vivian checked. "She's right on the H-dot, though." Their upward acceleration was nominal. "Thirty seconds. Fifteen-hundred-plus feet of altitude. 308 looks good."

"Cool beans," Fisher said. "Great job, partner."

"You too."

CAPCOM came in. "You're still Go at one minute."

Vivian checked. "336 feet per second. At one minute twenty we're at seven thousand feet and change."

Already, the Moon was far below her.

"AGS and PGNS tracking together, Houston," Vivian said. "V-sub-I is good, H-dot is right on the money." Total velocity, acceleration upward, all nominal. "Height is fine, fourteen thousand three hundred feet at two minutes."

"Trajectory looks perfect, per FIDO."

"Appreciate it, Houston."

"You're go at three minutes."

They just stood and swayed and watched as Oceanus Procellarum retreated away from them.

"Trim the AGS, in-plane only."

"Roger," Vivian said. "In-plane only on AGS."

They came up on seven minutes. "Seven hundred to go." Seven hundred feet per second, the remaining speed they needed to achieve rendezvous. "Main valves are open …"

"Main shut-off valves open, ascent feeds closed." Fisher grimaced. "Sorry. Spoke over you."

"No problem. Three fifty, two hundred. Fifty, forty, thirty, ten, shutdown." And the engine shut down right on schedule, abruptly freeing them into weightlessness.

"Roger, trim the PGNS, all axes," said CAPCOM.

"Roger that."

"Ascent burn terminated," Fisher said. "Nominal." He breathed out a long sigh of relief. "Just another day at the office."

And nothing had blown up. Given Vivian's record on and around the Moon, she could hardly believe it.

Still time for her to screw up, though. She looked back at the numbers, like she was supposed to be doing. "Coming up on sixty thousand feet, and the residuals are good. We're at minus 0.2, plus 0.8, minus 1.1." Those were the velocity residuals—the differences in all three axes, in feet per second, relative to the plan.

"Guess I typed the numbers in right after all."

"Guess you did. Go you. Sorry. I'm just … you know."

"Used to being in control. I get that."

"I was going to go with 'naturally snarky.' But, yeah. That too." She looked at Fisher sideways. "Sorry again."

"You remind me of my wife." Fisher checked himself. "Sorry, sorry, not in a bad or a weird way, that was just …. Please disregard."

Vivian grinned. "It's fine. Houston, standing by for tweak burn."

CAPCOM read up the time and parameters, they typed them in, did a flawless three-second trim burn—and that was that.

The Moon was literally behind Vivian now, and she was well on her way to Eagle Station.

And then to Earth.

Vivian reached up to the window. "Camera off."

"Copy. Houston, we're going to take five, okay?"

"Roger that, Apollo 53L," said CAPCOM. Fisher flipped the switch to toggle the comms off, blew out a breath.

Vivian turned to him. "Uh, hey. We got off to a bad start, and I regret it. But since we're going to be sharing this space quite a while longer, maybe we could take it again from the top? So, hi. I'm Vivian Carter, US Navy."

"And I'm still Don Fisher. Sorry I gave you such grief when you first came aboard. I had my nose a bit out of joint. I don't know what the hell was going on with those last-minute replans, but I was *not* happy about it. Figured it was maybe your fault, but it sounds like you got burned by it same as I did. Plus, it's always edgy doing a launch with someone you've never trained with. And setting up alone."

"Ain't it just," she said.

"But you did a bang-up job. Textbook."

"You too."

He glanced at her. "By the way, when I made that crack earlier, I wasn't casting doubts on your experience. It's just ... well, you know. Flying with Vivian Carter. Bad things tend to happen where you are. To be honest, I wasn't jumping for joy at this assignment. But it's good to meet you in person. And you're not at all what I expected."

She grinned cheerfully. "Well, sorry to disappoint. But yeah, I'm a bit of a trouble magnet, can't deny it. So, I'm guessing we're going to be together all the way back to Earth?" By now, Vivian was actually okay with that.

"That's the plan. But not just us. We'll be picking up a Command Module Pilot at Eagle, rotating him home." He shook his head. "I don't know who, sorry."

"Par for the course, today." She glanced down at the Moon beneath them. How could she be both relieved and miserable to be leaving?

He was studying her. "You all right, Captain?"

"Oh yeah. Sure thing."


"Apollo 53L, Eagle Station. We're ready for your state vector."

Vivian looked up from the DSKY keyboard, pressed the comms button. "Working it, Eagle. Stand by."

Fisher pointed. "There she is. Twelve o'clock, dead ahead. Bright star."

"Roger that. We have you in sight, Eagle. Visual acquisition."

"From our angle you're still lost in the inky black. But we'll see you soon, Apollo."

"That you will, Eagle Station."

The radio crackled again. "Apollo, Houston. Hi, Vivian."

She grinned. "Oh, hi, Ellis. Good to hear your voice. And I guess I'll be seeing you in person in a few days."

"Yeah," he said, and her ears immediately pricked up at the strained tone in his voice. "About that?"

Vivian and Fisher exchanged glances. She lifted her finger off the Push-to-Talk, and Fisher said, "Did I speak too soon?"

"Maybe you did."

Vivian glanced at the fuel indicators. To keep the weight down with all those rocks aboard, the LM had only enough to get it off-surface and to Eagle Station. Landing again without refueling wasn't in the cards. There was literally nowhere else they could go. She opened comms again. "Houston, this is 53L. Spit it out."

"Proceed to dock at Eagle. Vivian, you'll be transferring. Remain suited. You'll be briefed there."

"Uh. Transferring to Eagle? Why? Give me a clue, maybe?"

Vivian could almost hear Ellis shrug. "If I knew anything, I would."

She shook her head. "Ellis ... what the heck?"

Fisher cleared his throat. "Houston, Ellis, this is Don. Got any updates for me?"

"Hey there, Don. You're to hold at Eagle Station for a day or two. We're apparently readjusting your crew assignments for the Earth-bound leg. We'll get back to you when we can."

"Oh. Swell." Fisher's face was wooden. "Roger that."

Vivian turned off the mic and looked at him. "Sorry."

"Wow. Revolving door crew assignments. I hate it." A long sigh. "I was *really* ready to go home, you know?"

"Me too. Sort of."

"My wife's prepared me a welcome-home party. All the neighbors. Then it's my kid's big game. You know, all the usual clichés, but this time they're actually fricking true." He looked over at her. "You honestly have no idea what's going on?"

"Not the foggiest. Pinky swear."

He shrugged. "NASA, eh? Go figure."

"Yeah," Vivian said. "NASA."

Unless, of course, it wasn't NASA at all.

Slowly, slowly, Apollo Lunar Module 53L crept up on Eagle Station. Vivian called numbers. Fisher performed the small thrusts with the RCS jets. Neither of them had to work all that hard.

As they approached, the bright Venus-sized dot grew out of the black and resolved out into a collection of linked spacecraft, some of which Vivian was intimately familiar.

Her LGS-1 team had not stopped at Eagle Station on the way to Zvezda-Copernicus to begin their trip, so this was Vivian's first sight of Eagle since she'd left it on Apollo 32. It was still shiny and well-maintained, the cross of its solar panels still in one piece. In sharp contrast to the remains of Columbia Station, to which it was linked by a retaining spar.

Columbia was the previous Skylab that had suffered so much damage during the Hadley conflict. Some of that damage had been repaired: there was no longer any sign of the Soyuz that Vivian had crashed into it, nor the remains of the Soviet Progress vessel she'd slammed it into. Minerva, Apollo 32's Command Module, was long gone, of course: no longer pinned in place by the Agena rocket that Dave Horn had speared through Columbia's waste management area. Columbia's fabric had been refurbished, with two new solar panel blades and a new thermal blanket across its midsection. But it was still a mess, much of its outer shell blackened and bashed and patched. It looked about a hundred years old. Vivian knew that it was still basically functional—still had its own power, still held pressure—but it was largely being kept around for storage space and being cannibalized for spare parts.

Speaking of storage space, here was another blast from the past: Vivian's Apollo 32 third stage from three years back, now mated to Eagle Station's axial port. They used half of that big cleaned-up open volume for recreation because flying around in a large empty space in zero G was always fun and good for TV. The other half housed some industrial prototypes for the various chemical processes that they were working on: experiments in refining lunar material for the L5 Project.

Finally, jutting out to the right and left of Eagle at the Adapter Module level was the inevitable boom, with the Command and

Service Modules of Eagle's crew moored along it like a line of jewels on one side and half a dozen Lunar Modules attached to the other.

"That's ... actually quite impressive," Vivian said.

"You haven't seen pictures?"

"Not since they got it all together like this, only schematics. I've kind of avoided paying attention. Other things on my mind."

Fisher nodded. "Bad memories?"

"That too."

"Big old jury-rigged, patched-together space station."

"Sure is. How many people aboard it now, the whole thing?"

"Don't recall. Twenty, maybe? Two dozen? But I guess we're about to find out."

"Maybe," she said. "If that's what Ellis meant by 'Transfer.'"

"We'll see. Okay. Last bit." He paused. "You want it?"

She shook her head. "Your command, sir."

He half-grinned. "Roger that."

For docking, Fisher had to look upward through the top hatch window, and his controls and displays were ninety degrees to his line of sight. Vivian had always found that counter-intuitive, but to his credit, Fisher adjusted smoothly. He'd likely had a lot of practice.

She looked back at Eagle Station. "Oh! Oh, holy living shit."

"What?" Suddenly alert, Fisher scanned the boards, looking for red. Glanced around him, then back at Vivian. His initial irritation returned to his voice. "Vivian, what?"

"What is *that*?"

Fisher's eyebrows went up. "Huh. Well, that's a first."

On the far end of the boom hung a USAF Blue Gemini craft. It was small enough and dark enough that it'd escaped her notice before.

All of a sudden, Vivian wished she could sit down.

"Fascinating." Fisher looked at her. "Are you thinking what I'm thinking?"

"Yeah," Vivian said. "Afraid so."

"Ooookay."

They glided in to a smooth dock at the boom, at the point where Eagle had directed them. Made the LM fast. Waited. Nothing happened.

"Well, anyway. Good job, crewman. This was fun." Fisher held out his hand.

She shook it. "You too, man. Hope you make it back for your kid's big game."

"And good luck with whatever the hell is going to happen next for you. I don't envy you."

Vivian shrugged, a little helplessly. "Thanks."

Finally, they heard a voice on the loop. Male, but not Ellis. No one Vivian recognized. Southern accent. "Captain Carter? By now, you'll have seen your smooth ride just waiting for you."

"I guess so." She paused. "You want me to get over there?"

"Sure. Just as soon as you're ready."

"And why? What's going on?"

"We'll talk later."

"Roger." She pulled out binoculars for a closer look. "Ingress point? Please don't tell me I have to crawl in through the, uh, rear end."

"No, ma'am. You get to board like a lady."

She could see him now, the guy talking to them. One of the Blue Gemini's forward hatches was swinging open and there he was, in a gray spacesuit, doing a stand-up EVA from the left seat of his ridiculously small spacecraft.

Fisher looked at her. "Guess you're reassigned."

"Guess I am."

Fisher looked perplexed. "Forgive the indelicate question, but: rear end?"

"The NASA Geminis have two crew hatches, one for each crewman, on that conical area of the capsule directly above each seat. Like, where he's standing right now. But the Air Force Blue Geminis, you generally go in through the ... backside. The heat shield."

His eyebrows shot up. "They cut a hole in the *heat shield*? You've got to be kidding."

"Excellent idea, right? Apparently, that hatch melts shut during reentry, so *that's* fine."

A headshake in disbelief. "Perfect."

"Some of the Blue Gems only retain those two crew hatches for final egress on splashdown. Apparently my ... new smooth ride retains both hatchway capabilities." She thought about it. "Which for lunar orbital ops has to be a really smart move."

"Guess so," Fisher said. "Well, enjoy your spacewalk, okay?"

"I always do," she said.

He gave her a look. "You're kidding, right?"

"Yes," Vivian said. "About that, I am most definitely kidding."

# CHAPTER 18

## Blue Gemini: Vivian Carter
## February 28, 1983

IT *did* make a big difference to be doing a zero-G spacewalk that wasn't an emergency. Every other time Vivian had been outside a spacecraft in orbit she'd been in fear for her life, one way or another.

This trip felt calm and sedate. Vivian even had time to look around her, at star fields so bright that it was difficult to pick out the familiar constellations. She wished her helmet visor didn't distort the view so much. The universe was really quite majestic.

And the closer she got, the better she could see the Gemini that she had apparently, somehow, and for whatever reason, been reassigned to.

Just like NASA's Gemini craft, the USAF Blue Gemini variant consisted of two parts. The upper part, the pressurized reentry module where the crew sat throughout their mission, was indeed a deep blue-gray color—NASA's Geminis had been a darker gray. This was the only part of the spacecraft that would return to Earth. Behind it the adapter module flared out, colored a dirty silver-white. But the whole craft was *tiny*, especially next to the bulk of Eagle Station, and even more so when compared to an Apollo. The Apollo CSM combination was just over thirty-six feet long, of which the Command Module made up eleven and a half feet. The Gemini capsule, both modules together, clocked in at a scant eighteen and a half feet from the tip of its nose through the base of the adapter module. The Command Module's base was almost thirteen feet in diameter, the Gemini's just ten, and even from a distance that difference was very significant.

Simply put, the Gemini looked like a toy. Even once Vivian got right up next to it, at the end of the boom.

Which led to her next problem: getting herself into it.

First, she had to connect an umbilical that her new pilot floated out to her to provide her with oxygen and water. There was no space to bring her PLSS inside the Gemini, and the pilot had to help her unhook it and fasten it to the boom for someone to retrieve later. That was a finicky multi-stage operation in itself.

Next, Vivian needed to contort herself to wriggle in through the hatch. It was surprisingly difficult.

Back in the 1960s, Ed White had done the first spacewalk from a Gemini, followed on later missions by Gene Cernan and Michael Collins. Buzz Aldrin had performed three EVAs as part of the final Gemini 12 mission. All had managed to get themselves back inside afterward, with varying degrees of difficulty. Vivian was smaller than any of those guys and had a more sleek and modern spacesuit tailored to fit her, so it ought to have been easy enough. Right? Wrong.

Part of it was due to Vivian's fear that she might bang into the instrument consoles, or against a man she didn't know, and either do some harm or just look like an idiot. But mainly, it was just a really tight squeeze. Clambering in, the effort overwhelmed her environmental system. Her faceplate fogged, and she grew embarrassingly sweaty.

In the suit and the unfamiliar cockpit, Vivian initially had difficulty bending at the waist and knees and sliding in, but she eventually made it into the right seat. Just like on Apollo, the commander took the left seat with the pilot to his right. Neither NASA nor the USAF formally used the term "copilot" for any of their astronauts. Nor did the Soviets, for that matter. Not that Vivian expected to be doing much piloting on this trip.

And then she finally got the oxygen line from her chest pack plugged into the Gemini's systems and could free up the umbilical.

"Hi," her companion said, once that was done. "Kevin Pope, United States Air Force. Good to see you."

"Vivian Carter. Navy. Man, umbilicals are a total pain in the ass."

"You got that right, ma'am."

239

She could close the hatch easily enough, but when she attempted to lock it, the torque just rotated her around in her seat. How could she brace herself with both hands on the hatch handle? She struggled to brace herself with her knees and wedge her shoulders in place.

"Not to be too forward, but it'll work better if I hold you in position while you do that. May I?"

"Sounds good. Go ahead. But I sprained my left shoulder not so long ago. Don't put any weight on it."

"Hmm." Naturally that was the shoulder closer to Pope. He held her left arm instead, and awkwardly reached around her neck to anchor her on the right. Vivian locked the hatch.

The Air Force astro looked at the telltales, flipped a switch. "Good and good."

She flopped back. "Wow. That was a bear."

"Yes, ma'am," said Pope. "Here comes $O_2$."

"Copy." And none too soon.

Pressurizing the cabin collapsed their suits enough for Vivian to be able to relax and look around her, and eventually she could take her helmet off and check the place out properly.

The Gemini cabin basically consisted of the two seats for the crew, plus a large wraparound instrument panel in front of them and to either side, with another panel of switches and circuit breakers over their heads. Compared to an Apollo, the instrument panels were *close*. In between their seats was a central console with a control stick, and most of the panel in front of Pope was devoted to the velocity indicators, range/range-rate displays, altimeters, and other instruments related to maneuvering. Both the Commander and Vivian had maneuver controllers within reach; the controllers managed the Gemini's fore and aft thrusters, while the joystick served for manual attitude control. Vivian could already tell by watching Pope that he controlled attitude with his right hand while firing the translation thrusters with his left. If for some reason Vivian had to drive this bus, she'd need to control attitude with her left hand and master the translation thrusters with her right, which would require a bit of thought to get right. She found her fingers moving instinctively, trying to imagine it. Fortunately, her years of training on both sides of the LM had made her at least partly ambidextrous.

The Gemini was far too cramped to switch seats. That wasn't happening, not without opening the hatches. If she ever did have to fly it, she'd be doing it from where she was.

The console to Vivian's right was dominated by the guidance computer keyboard and console. For Pope's solo flight to Eagle Station, Vivian was guessing that a lot of the guidance information must have been preprogrammed; if not, Pope must have spent a lot of time leaning across an empty seat. She was hoping that similar programming had been preloaded for his return trip, and that she wouldn't need to operate a whole new guidance system because she could tell immediately that it was very different from the Apollo DSKY and console she was used to.

In the spare space she saw racks of other switches, and recognized much of their functionality: comms, water management, environment control—plus lockers for more rudimentary life support: food storage pouches, water, etc.—all packed closely together.

It was pretty clear where everything was. But, heck: it would take her a long time to be fluent on Gemini to the point where her fingers would instinctively move in the right directions.

While she was still looking around, they crossed the terminator into lunar night. Lights turned on automatically behind her, along with white and red floods on the instrument panel, bathing them both in a blood-red glow.

The big fuel cells behind her would generate potable water as well as oxygen; for as long as they had power, they wouldn't run short of $O_2$ and $H_2O$.

The sharp tang of pure oxygen in her nostrils and the hiss of its circulation in her ears, the crackle of the intercom, the constriction of her suit: yes, this was very much like the fighter jet experience. Aside from the guy sitting next to her, that is.

Pope had been flipping switches, setting dials, quickly and competently getting them ready for flight, and Vivian had been leaving him to it. Now, he turned and grinned at her. For sure, this guy had a genuine Southern twinkle. She liked him already. He said: "So, I'm told you're really looking forward to going back to Earth."

"Sort of. It's like a double-edged sword."

"Well, I'm truly sorry to hear that. Apparently, we need to borrow you for a while."

"Night Corps, I presume."

"Naturally, I can't comment on that." But he nodded solemnly.

Pope's name meant nothing to her, but his face seemed vaguely familiar now. "We've met before, right?"

"We have indeed. I'm impressed you remember."

"Except I don't know where. Were you at Daedalus Base?"

Pope waggled his fingers. "Well, technically, yes."

Something about the way he said that. "Oh, right. You work for, uh, Colonel Sandoval. And you must have been with Apollo Rescue 1 at Hadley because you were one of Sandoval's MOLAB crew when he arrived at Dark Driver after that bonkers trip halfway around the Moon."

"Bonkers? From the woman who went *all* the way around it? Doesn't that make you twice as bonkers?"

"Sounds accurate." Vivian had paid scant attention to the four Night Corps grunts who had arrived at Daedalus with Peter. At the time, she'd been more concerned with Ellis, Terri, Casey Buchanan ... "So, okay, Kevin Pope: please tell me we're not going all the way back to Earth in, uh, this."

Pope looked wounded, affected a pout. "What, you don't like my ship?"

"It's really more like a backpack than a ship. A spacecraft you strap on."

"Gosh," he said. "Devastatingly rude."

"Hey, man, I call 'em like I see 'em."

"But at least you didn't call it a capsule," he said. "We hate the C-word in Night Corps. I mean, the Air Force."

It was only luck that Vivian hadn't said the word out loud. It was impossible to see a Gemini, from outside or in, and not think "capsule" rather than "spacecraft."

"Either way, I know nothing about this vehicle. Wherever we're going, I won't be much help to you."

"No worries. I've got it. It's really a one-man machine. One and a half at the worst of times."

She leaned toward him. "Tell me, Kevin—you can be honest. Does it really have a hatch in its ... you know?" She pointed behind them.

"Butt? Rear end? Yes, ma'am, it does."

"Kinky." Vivian thought about it for a few minutes. "So, we're going where, exactly?"

Pope just pointed upward. "Higher."

242

"Okay." Vivian swallowed. "And, why?"

"I wouldn't know," he said.

She looked at him. "Right. Everyone keeps saying that, but in your case it's a little hard to believe."

"Truly. I have no idea. All I know is that the USAF flexed and told NASA they were pulling you away, just a few hours back."

"'Told NASA.'" She nodded. "Okay, that explains at least part of why Starman—Commander Jones—was so pissed."

He nodded too. "NASA hates being overridden by the Air Force. Hates it in clubs, hearts, and spades. So naturally my bosses try to do it just as often as they possibly can."

"Kevin. You really don't know what's going on?"

"I do not," he said. "But welcome to the Dark Side."

Vivian looked out at the nighttime lunar surface below them. "Thanks."

He glanced at her. "Dark side? Darth Vader? Guessing you're not a Star Wars fan."

Star Wars again? Vivian shook her head. "Guessing I'm the only astronaut who isn't."

"I find your lack of faith disturbing."

"Oh well," said Vivian, lost.

He paused. "All right. Try this, then: welcome to military space."

"Thanks—I think."

"Okay," he said. "Gonna disconnect us from this complicated mess of NASA habs and do some free flying. Buckle up."

"Sure, man," she said. "Take me higher."

Pope applied a burn. It felt gentle in terms of G's, but the Blue Gemini reacted very sportily. Then again, it was pretty light. He glanced over. "Sure you don't want to fly it?"

"Maybe not today."

"Piece of cake. You'd get used to it in no time."

Well, Kevin Pope was certainly different from her last crewman. "Uh-huh."

"Seriously, if you can fly that tin can," he gestured back at the LM, now retreating into the distance behind them with the rest of the Eagle and Columbia Station combo, "you can certainly fly this. I can fly both myself. Besides, didn't you once fly a Soyuz?"

"That wasn't quite flying," Vivian said, and stopped there. It had frankly been more like crashing, but that was another C-word that astronauts tended to avoid.

"Apollos are fine in their place, I guess," he said. "But Gemini is a pilot's spacecraft."

She looked at him sideways. "And I'm an aviator." To the air Navy, "pilots" were guys who steered sea-Navy ships past shoals and into harbors.

"Okay," he said, companionably enough. "So if you think of Apollo as a bomber, and Gemini as a fighter jet, you'll be about right."

Jets had much more cachet than bombers among real flyers, naturally, but since Vivian used to fly Navy jets for a living, she didn't exactly feel the burn. "It's a tight fit in here, sure enough. Even for a skinny chick like me. How does Sandoval pack himself into one of these?"

"Beats me. Those broad manly shoulders and all? Must be hell." He glanced over and grinned.

*He knows. Damn it. But at least he's too polite to bring it up.* "So, Kevin, back to why I'm aboard. You must know *something*."

"All I know is, you're reassigned from NASA to Night Corps for an unspecified length of time, for an unspecified mission. And if I knew any more than that, I would tell you. Seriously." He looked over again. "So, for all I know you might actually *need* to know how to fly one of these, someday. Even soon."

"Why would I?"

"Damned if I know. I'm just speculating. I'm being straight with you, Vivian: Sandoval wouldn't brief any of us until you arrived."

"Why?"

"Well, if I knew that, then I'd know something, wouldn't I?"

"Whoa. Wait a minute. Peter Sandoval *himself* is here? In lunar space? Up there, wherever we're going, presumably one of the MOLs?"

"Yes, ma'am."

"Holy shit ... excuse my French. I never thought I'd see the day. Peter *hates* the Moon. I just assumed he'd be radioing orders in from Earth orbit." Vivian breathed. "Not to be weird, since you and I only just met, but to be honest, I'm not quite ready for this. What's our flight time?"

"Oh, you have plenty of time to process. We won't be there for another thirty-six hours."

That earned him a double take. "*Thirty* ... What?"

"Do you see an Agena parked on our nose? We don't have one. And we need to effect a big orbit change. We'll be using the Gemini OAMS, the main engine, to push us real high up into a halo orbit, and then we'll kind of meander around and then loop back down. Energetics. We're taking the slow road to MOL-B. It's the only feasible mechanism to work our way up and back down into a lunar almost-polar orbit without burning a shit-ton of fuel." He grinned at her yet again. "Pardon *my* French."

Polar orbit? Okay, yeah. But even at that, the Blue Gemini OAMS—Orbit Attitude and Maneuvering System—must have been beefed up by quite a bit since the mid-sixties.

Well. Maybe that was obvious. The military didn't hang around when it came to technical upgrades. The USAF space program was dark, funded out of the Defense budget. They likely had more money than God, and certainly more than NASA.

But still. "I'm stuck in this ... absolutely marvelous flying machine for nearly *two days*? I thought we were in a hurry."

"Making haste slowly. Catch up on your sleep, maybe? While you're getting ready to see, uh, that guy again?"

"I guess."

"Count your blessings. It would have been forty-two hours, but we found a better orbital solution at the last minute."

"I'm guessing it was one that required you to initiate the burn from Eagle Station two hours earlier."

"As a matter of fact, it was."

Vivian nodded. Many of the oddities of the past few hours were starting to make sense.

He looked at her sideways. "Better than going back to Earth, maybe?"

"I don't yet have the data to make that call."

"Fair enough."

She took another look around. Thirty-six hours? That made this Blue Gemini seem even *more* cramped. Vivian would never complain about a Command Module again. A CM was luxurious by comparison.

And that meant sooner or later she was going to have to broach the question of ... bathroom facilities, with a guy who seemed very nice, but whom she'd only just met.

*Yeah, maybe later rather than sooner.*

"I hope to God we have some food in here?"

245

Pope looked as if he was considering it. "Food that doesn't suck?"

"Uh, preferably."

"Cannot confirm. That's in the taste buds of the beholder. And this *is* the military. But we do have MREs." Pope opened a cupboard behind him by feel and pulled out a plastic-wrapped pouch. Reached back again for a hot water jet. "You be the judge."

*Sleeping simultaneously. Not together.*

Vivian was used to jet fighter cockpits, but nobody ever slept in one. Tonight would be an interesting challenge.

At least she and Pope would take their rest periods at the same time because a staggered sleep schedule was impractical in a cabin this small, and they allegedly had sufficient fail-safes and alarms to wake them if something bad happened. Vivian did find it a little odd that their telemetry wouldn't be monitored from the ground while they slept, but their Blue Gemini wasn't in touch with USAF Mission Control at all, or with anywhere else, lest their transmissions be tracked by the Soviets. The Gemini was running dark, with only occasional and very brief directed transponder chirps between it and the MOL ahead of them as navigational checks, but this seemed to be standard operating procedure for Night Corps. Pope was clearly unconcerned, so Vivian went with it.

They fastened metal plates over the windows to keep out the blinding sunlight that would otherwise stream in through over half of each lunar orbit, and those shades fit well. When Pope doused the lights, the cabin was dark, aside from some reassuring green telltales from the instruments. Sleep, however, was elusive for a while. The sitting-up position wasn't Vivian's customary sleeping posture, and she eventually had to wedge her head into a corner to stop her neck kinking. Another potential issue was that Geminis ran an $O_2$-rich atmosphere at 5 psi, and pure oxygen tended to keep Vivian awake and alert when she wasn't used to it. But as it turned out, tonight it wasn't a problem. Post-adrenaline exhaustion had finally hit.

Vivian jolted awake all at once, her neck stiff, her hands constrained. Strapped down? Trapped again? *Goddamn it.*

She opened her eyes, disoriented, to see covered windows and instrument panels now lit an eerie red from a faint nightlight. Apparently, she'd tucked her hands into her seat restraints to stop them floating up in front of her in the zero gravity and maybe touching some of the toggle switches on the disconcertingly close instrument panels around her.

"Hi there." Pope was reading a novel with a penlight. "Sorry, am I turning pages too loudly?"

"No." She glanced at her watch, automatically compared it to the time reading on the panel in front of her. "Huh. I guess I really can sleep anywhere."

"Or you were really tired." He peeled the coverings off the windows to reveal the inky black of space, studded with a billion stars. The Gemini was rolling slowly, and thirty seconds later a gibbous Moon swung into view.

They were really high up above the surface now. "Wow."

Easy to see why the USAF wanted their MOLs at such an altitude, though. From up here, Vivian could see a much broader swath of the lunar surface, and given the Moon's lack of atmosphere, she was sure that their angular resolution for studying the lunar surface was still amazing, even from this altitude.

"How much higher are we going?"

"This is almost it. Couple thousand more feet. In twenty minutes at our absolute high point, I'll need to fire a short plane change burn and then a second burn four hours later to insert us into a circular orbit similar to MOL-B's. And then I get to read some more, and we both eat godawful MREs and stare at the view some more and maybe sleep again, while we gradually catch up to it."

She glanced at his book. *Tinker Tailor Soldier Spy*. "John Le Carré? Hmm."

"It's this or *Day of the Jackal*. Only books aboard. I've read them both three times."

Vivian looked at the instrument panel, glanced down in between them to the binder containing his flight plan and procedures. "Actually, if it's all the same to you?" She patted the binder, waved around them. "Professional interest. Assuming your checklists aren't above Top Secret."

"Sure, knock yourself out. After all, like I said: one day you might have Need to Know."

"If I ever need to fly one of these, everyone's in trouble," she said.

He grinned. "Stranger things have happened."

Later: "Hey, Vivian, I hear you don't get these babies as standard issue in Apollos?"

It was a sextant. A standard, handheld, honest-to-God bronze sextant. "Nice! There was a time I would have killed for one of these."

He nodded, didn't ask, probably knew when she meant. Her long hike across the lunar surface after her crash with Gerry Lin would presumably be well known to all the Night Corps folks.

Her fingers itched. "Can I play? Ten to one you have a slide rule in here as well."

"Oh, that would be a sucker bet." He produced one instantly from the seat pocket beside him. "I hadn't heard you were an orbital rendezvous junkie."

"Me? Ha. No, I'm absolutely not. But any navigating math that I can do with just a sextant and a slide rule, I want to be confident that I can do it." She didn't mention that this had been her evening project for several weeks back on Earth, between missions.

"Seems fair, given your interesting lifestyle."

"Uh-huh." Vivian looked around the night sky, hunting for constellations, and started figuring out which stars were close to the lunar horizon. "Bright star catalog?"

"Here."

"Great. Okay, man, buckle up: let's have some fun."

He looked at her in admiration. "Gee, you're a stone-cold nerd, aren't you?" She looked quizzical, and he quickly added: "Just like the rest of us. Peter always triple-checks his computer with a slide rule if he has time."

*I know.* "Survival skill. Make an, uh, emergency landing on the Moon sometime and try to do math without a computer. It's a life-changing experience."

"Oh, God, no. I'll skip that first step, if it's all the same to you. But if it's good enough for Buzz Aldrin, it's good enough for us."

"Then let's dig in."

Presently, Pope said: "Much easier to measure angles above the lunar horizon than it is above Earth."

"Yep. Very tricky to do with any accuracy, with the atmosphere getting in your way."

"Man," he said. "That gosh-darned atmosphere, messing everything up. Hate it."

"I *know*."

Okay, fine. This beat going straight back to Earth after all. Vivian was thoroughly enjoying herself. She could stand even this confined space for another fifteen hours, with Pope for company.

She was sure the other shoe would drop eventually, and she'd realize what the next hell was likely to be. Probably in fifteen and a half hours. But for right now, Vivian had math to do.


Much later: "Those guys in Gemini 7 really spent *fourteen days* in one of these? I mean, I love your ship, man—love it to death, best ship ever—but … damn."

Pope was already shaking his head. "Yeah, I'm all about Gemini, but … concur. Borman and Lovell, spending two weeks cooped up in one? True American heroes. Apollo 8—even 13—had nothing on *that* ordeal. This trip right now will be almost the longest I've ever spent aboard a Blue Gem. Just as well I have such terrific company."

She grinned. Sharing such a small space with a guy she didn't know, a comment like that might have felt … off. But Kevin Pope was fine. Ridiculously easygoing and engaging. "Thanks. Likewise."

"So, um …?" He gestured at the controls. "Like to give my girl a spin? Literally. No harm in playing with the attitude control jets. If it works out, maybe you could give some active help during the docking phase. I wasn't kidding about the training. I mean, who knows? Who knows anything anymore?"

Vivian hesitated for only a femtosecond. "If she's a fighter jet, in space? Okay, you've finally talked me into it."


It was still weird to see—to be *in*—a Gemini capsule in lunar orbit. Obviously, Vivian associated them with NASA's pre-Apollo missions. The original NASA Gemini missions had been ten crewed flights during an action-packed twenty-month period in 1965-1966. They'd been essential learning experiences for astronauts to practice maneuvering in orbit, rendezvous and docking, EVAs, and long duration flights. But the USAF had also used Geminis to covertly fly crews to their Earth-orbiting MOL stations, for years now.

Vivian did recall that Gemini had once been suggested by some at NASA as a fast-track option for the United States' first flight around the Moon. And for the USAF space program, Gemini craft were the workhorses, and they paired well with the existing MOLs. Given a booster to get them all the way to the Moon—needing less thrust than a Saturn third stage because Gemini was way less massive than an Apollo stack—then, why not?

The body of this Blue Gemini might look like a relic of the 1960s, but its guts were bang up-to-date. For their docking with MOL-B, the active interrogator/transponder system that helped them with range, rate, and angles was just as good as the Apollos, and maybe better. And with the Gemini being lighter, it was absolutely more responsive than an Apollo. After turning it in three axes and later on firing a few correction burns under Pope's instruction, Vivian could certainly see the appeal.

Now, just thirty-some hours after seeing the NASA Eagle Station complex, Vivian was coming up on another collection of disparate spacecraft, this time loosely linked together in a much higher lunar orbit.

She was expecting the MOL, Manned Orbiting Laboratory. She had never seen one before—as far as she knew, no NASA astronaut ever had, no reason for them to, and every reason for them to be kept clear—but she'd seen schematics. A MOL was essentially a tube some eighty feet long and ten feet in diameter that held a crew of four plus a gigantic DORIAN optical telescope and all its associated hardware peripherals. Plus, the MOL was outwardly similar in appearance to the CORONA, GAMBIT, and HEXAGON strategic reconnaissance satellites that Vivian was also familiar with from briefings.

MOL-B had a boom extending out from it on either side, just like the NASA Skylabs. Attached to it were two Blue Geminis and three USAF Lunar Modules, similar to NASA's but a little chunkier and heavier and with larger RCS jets and differently-placed antennas.

Floating in space nearby were three more cylinders that were clearly boosters, plus a Cargo Carrier, and just coming into view behind the MOL was something that looked like a Gemini, but … bigger. With an inflatable and flexible docking tunnel connecting it to the MOL, presumably allowing shirtsleeves transit between them.

"So, Kevin. What the hell is *that?*"

"Figured that might catch your eye. Technically, it's an Advanced Gemini, though we all just call it Big Gemini or Big G. It's basically a stretch Gemini that can take twelve people."

"Twelve? Holy cow." Vivian looked again. "Must be hellish cramped in there. Damn, that's really something. And … those aren't Agenas. Are they?"

He shook his head. "Centaurs. Centaur-G upper-stage boosters. We shoot them all the way here fully fueled."

They looked heavy. "Shoot with what?"

"The same Titan IIIM that we launch the MOLs with, but with an additional Centaur for the trans-L5 injection burn."

"Using a Titan to launch a Centaur that launches another Centaur." Vivian shook her head. "Station-keeping all this stuff must be a bear."

"Luckily, Cheyenne handles most of that." USAF Mission Control, in Cheyenne Mountain, twenty miles from Peterson Air Force Base in Colorado. "Though we do have someone on duty here around the clock, using eyeballs and radar to check that nothing crashes into anything else."

And scanning the lunar surface, checking comms, monitoring chatter, and keeping an eye on telemetry from all these ships as well, Vivian had no doubt. In space, it was rare for an entire crew to all be asleep at the same time. Aside from aboard this Gemini, of course.

"The glamor of spaceflight."

"Tell me about it."

Now, they fell into the hardcore technical chatter of a rendezvous. Even though Vivian had zero prior Gemini training, that hardly mattered—the physics was all the same, and by now she'd picked up on the locations of all the critical dials and switches, so it was relatively straightforward for her to read numbers to him. After all, Pope had done all this solo when rendezvousing with Eagle Station, though he did admit he'd had his hands more than full.

Vivian even had time to use his sextant to take measurements of the angular size of the MOL from their vantage point, check how that changed with time, and turn those numbers into crude rate and rate-change numbers that they could compare to the "official" transponder numbers. They were darned close, and Vivian quietly thought they might have been able to dock with the MOL purely on visual data, given enough time.

251

By now, they were in a very different orbit. Circling the Moon in polar orbit, they were currently moving south to north across its surface. To Vivian, well used to equatorial orbits at much lower altitude, it felt unusual and disconcerting. Her instincts kept trying to warn her that something was wrong, though it obviously wasn't.

Although still being in orbit around the Moon, when she'd expected to be halfway back to Earth by now, did mean that *something* was going on that might be very wrong. And soon, Vivian—and Kevin Pope, too—would find out what that was.

# CHAPTER 19

MOL-B: Vivian Carter
March 1, 1983

**POPE** latched the Blue Gemini onto the boom by its front docking rig and flipped switches to power off the thrusters. "And that's how we do *that*. Welcome to MOL-B."

She nodded. "You're right. I likely could have done it."

"Told you." He'd offered to let her do the dock, but she'd demurred, not wanting to screw up. "But anyway, here we are. Your long ordeal with me is over."

"No ordeal. It was a cool flight. Thanks."

He dipped his head in the closest to a bow that anyone could achieve in a Gemini cockpit. "High praise."

She sighed. "Okay. Guess we should get our butts out there and find out what the bad news is."

"Hey, you never know. Maybe it's good news."

She gave him a look.

"… Yeah. That was a joke."

Once they were helmeted and gloved once more, Pope opened a valve, spilling oxygen out of the craft to begin the depressurization, then handed her a crank. "This? Slides in there. Apply torque to the hatch that way. But don't do that before we're at complete vacuum, or the hatch'll fly out of your hand and might get damaged."

Which was a lot different from the Apollo hatches, so Vivian was glad he'd mentioned it. "Roger that. I'll await full purge."

Transfer into the MOL involved another spacewalk, this one less than thirty feet. Once Pope had vented the cockpit atmosphere into space, Vivian pulled herself out of the Gemini hatch, triple-checked her tether and umbilical, and steered herself hand-over-hand along the MOL's boom behind Kevin Pope. She thoroughly enjoyed the wide vision field she could see now, compared to the narrow field that had been visible through the Blue Gemini's windows. It was good to see that bright sky again that she loved, radiant with stars. And the bright Moon far beneath them.

Oddly, it was the only one of Vivian's almost countless EVAs in which she'd had the security of a tether and umbilical throughout, so it felt weird. The umbilical in particular had a life of its own and kept trying to wrap itself around her torso like a python.

They made it into the MOL-B airlock without incident. Unhooked their umbilicals and tethers and left them to drift outside, relying on their in-suit oxygen for the few moments of repressurization.

The inner airlock door opened, and Vivian Carter floated into a USAF Manned Orbiting Laboratory for the first time. Another place she could never have imagined she'd be.

There was just one guy to greet them, which was perhaps just as well given how confined the MOL Adapter Module was. The guy, José Rodriguez, shook Vivian's gloved hand politely and then helped them both out of their helmets and suits. "Welcome aboard MOL-B, Captain Carter. I've heard a lot about you."

*Hasn't everyone? Apparently.* "Unfortunately, I'm not sure I can return the favor."

"Yeah, well, I'm secret." He grinned.

"Were you another one of Sandoval's crazy around-the-Moon Night Corps guys?"

He bowed his head in acknowledgement. "I sure was. That ride *was* crazy. Also, mind-numbing."

"What? Boring? Seriously?"

"Uh …" But Rodriguez was rescued from the need to reply because here came Terri Brock, soaring into the Adapter like she'd been born in space. "Hey, girlfriend. You making trouble again?"

Vivian rocked back. "Wow, holy crap!"

Terri gave her a mock-stern look. "Not happy to see me?"

Vivian grabbed her into a hug, and her momentum sent them bouncing off the wall. Rodriguez retreated prudently. "No, Terri, I am freaking *overjoyed* to see you."

Terri returned the hug and stabilized them before they could bang into Pope. Vivian held her at arms-length, taking her in. She hadn't seen Brock for years. "So, wow. Look at you. All hot and Night Corps-y and still in space."

"Nowhere else I'd rather be." Terri tilted her head to one side at Vivian's pause. "But not you?"

"Damned if I know. It's complicated. People keep trying to kill me."

"Well, sure, that would be a bummer."

"No one tries to kill you?"

Brock shrugged. "Not much, lately."

"Well, damn. Maybe I should transfer to military space after all. It might be safer."

"I guess we'll see. Hey, I wanted to be the one to come fetch you from Eagle, but I'm not solo rated for Gemini yet. So *this* lunk got all the fun instead."

Pope shook his head. "Terrible chore. Hated every second."

"I bet."

Vivian sobered. "So, Terri? Guys? What the hell is going on? Why am I here?"

"Beats me. Peter wanted to wait for you to be acquired before briefing us."

"Acquired? Nice." The less Vivian found out, the more apprehensive she became. Casually, she said: "So, where *is* the boss?"

"In the shower. He's been sleeping. Briefing's on the hour." Terri looked at her sideways, bonked her on the shoulder. "Guess he wants to be all squeaky clean when he greets you."

"Terri. Stop."

"Sorry. Uh, you want the tour while we're waiting? We have twenty-five minutes. Except this MOL is tiny, you don't have need-to-know on the DORIAN optics and operation, and you're not cleared yet to enter the Big G, so it'll probably only take seven or eight."

"Okay, sure. After that flight I need to stretch and get the blood flowing again anyway." Vivian looked around. "So. Entertain me."

Terri was right. The MOL had its tiny airlock area in the Adapter Module, which the crew also called the Forward Compartment. Beyond that was the Observation Deck where all the control panels for the DORIAN telescope lived, plus all the comms equipment. Then came the middeck, containing the galley and exercise gear, and finally the crew sleeping quarters and personal hygiene area. And while that sounded like four rooms, they were really four damned small spaces.

While Brock, Rodriguez, and Pope were briefing her, two other Night Corps troops came in to staff the DORIAN console. Vivian wasn't introduced to them, and didn't introduce herself, but they looked young. As they spun verniers, flipped switches and pressed buttons, and spoke to each other in quiet sentence fragments peppered with incomprehensible three-letter acronyms, Vivian heard the occasional *chunk* sound reverberating through the station. "If that's a shutter I hear, that's a *large* camera."

One of the men glanced across at her, so quickly that it was almost a facial tic. "Yup," Terri said solemnly. "Large camera."

"How long have you been here?"

"Our team rotated in a week ago." She paused. "I guess I should explain. We work in teams of four. Peter, Rod, Pope, and I are a unit. But due to the Big G build-up we have another three groups of four, one rotating off, two more in training."

*Chunk.* There it went again. Jeez, that was loud. How did anyone sleep on this tug?

Terri gave her a broad-brush functional rundown: the panoramic camera that was always taking wide shots of whatever was directly under the station, surveying the Moon in stripes; the big main camera, steerable by the crew to focus in on specific areas; and the two side-view aspect cameras that took pictures of the stars to help calibrate and orient the lunar images.

Terri also pointed out the seats, verniers, spotting telescope, and binocular eyepiece for the DORIAN. The TV screens and ranks of switches on the instrument panels, the console and the intercom, the teleprinter. The wall pockets crammed with binders and logbooks and who knew what else. And around them, all of the open duct work, the blue-painted metal walls.

The USAF certainly had its own style. Vivian kind of liked it.


And before she knew it, here he was, cruising through from the mid-deck in a crisp blue jumpsuit, his hair still wet. "Oh, hey, Colonel Sandoval."

"Hi there, Captain Carter. Glad you could make it."

"I got an offer I couldn't refuse."

He grunted. They shook hands without making eye contact. Vivian was keenly aware of the other three deliberately not looking at one another and making efforts not to grin. "So, Carter. Everything in here is super Top Secret, right? You're approved to be in here and get a general overview, but … don't poke around too much, okay?"

"Roger that." Now, of course, Vivian wanted to poke around big-time.

"Let's let these guys work." He scooted backward, through the hatch into the mid-deck, and the rest of them followed him.


"What's the resolution of these pictures?" Vivian looked around as no one answered. "Oh, come on, I wouldn't be here if I didn't have need-to-know. Right?"

Terri looked at Sandoval. "Isn't Vivian one of us now, for the duration of whatever this is?"

Sandoval shook his head. "Still classified, even for her. Wish it wasn't. Sorry."

"She knows the Moon. She can do math. Probably figure out the answer herself to within ten percent."

"Okay, but …" Sandoval considered. "Fine. Vivian, for today's purposes, assume we have a resolution of a few feet."

Vivian nodded, impressed. That had been her rough guess, anyway, based on their altitude and quick barnyard math. The original Lunar Orbiter pictures that NASA used to plan Moon landings, like Apollo 32's at the Marius Hills, had had resolutions of over two hundred feet, and the ones in her hand were *much* better.

Peter looked wry. "Which is good, but it sounds better than it really is. The Moon's albedo—the surface reflectivity—is highly variable based on direction and illumination."

Vivian widened her eyes. "You don't say?"

He raised his hand. "I know you know; this is your thing. But that scatter ... the same square of lunar terrain can look completely different on Friday than it did last Tuesday because the solar illumination has changed completely. Which makes it hell for the boffins on Earth to compare the images."

"I'm sure."

"Plus, the Moon is all pretty much the same color."

"No, it isn't."

"Well ..." Sandoval closed his eyes, then opened them again. "Sure, okay, so not really, but it certainly is when you compare it to the Earth. It's *much* easier to pick out objects on the Earth. Often because they're straight-edged, man-made. And there's a big contrast and color difference between water and land, and between various types of land usage. On the Moon, everything is curves and shadows, gray and brown, with some misleadingly straight features that are actually natural. Plus, something happens to the surface twice a day as the terminator moves across it, which I'm sure you two understand better than I do."

Terri nodded. "Electrostatic effect. It's due to ..."

"Doesn't matter, but what it *is* is an effect that blurs photos of the Moon at high solar inclinations and makes everything worse. And then there's small meteorite hits. Even smart-asses like you two might be surprised how often that happens, across the Moon's surface as a whole.

"Bottom line: it's difficult for us to pick out any small-area, low-level changes in the appearance of the surface that might help us locate the cryptonauts' rover in transit."

Vivian blinked. "You call them cryptonauts too?"

"The usage spread," Pope said.

"We're a bit sad that none of us thought of it first," Terri added.

Sandoval soldiered on. "For right now, it sure looks like they're undetectable. Provided they don't block anything large, like a distinctive crater rim—which you can bet they don't do for long—and can successfully smear out their tracks after they've gone by—which they obviously can. The folks at NRO have spent a great deal of resources hunting for signs of the cryptonauts' passage. We know they've come and gone from the South Pole. We know they've come and gone from

Zvezda. But even knowing that … we haven't been able to latch on to any of their tracks."

Pope raised his eyebrows. "They're good. We knew that."

Peter nodded. "But a change in position of a pretty large object, that jumps out right away." He separated out another four photographs of various sizes from his stack and handed them to Vivian first because she was closest. She fanned them out, held them so that the others could see.

Peter pointed. "These first two are of Rimae Bode II. Landing site of Apollo 28. There's the descent stage, and the ALSEP package laid out, and all the rest. So, who can tell me what the—"

"The LRV has moved," said Pope. "The Lunar Rover they left behind has shifted between these two pictures. And its … color has changed. Or is that just an illumination effect?"

"Good eye," Sandoval said. "Yes. It's moved slightly, and the color change is likely because someone swept the dust off it. Probably when they scavenged the batteries out of it, and other stuff."

"The experiments have been disturbed too," Vivian said. "Not much. Maybe I'm imagining it. The angle's different, but I'm thinking … oh, look over here. They took the RTG off the leg of the descent stage, and in doing that they must have tugged on the whole mess of power cables and pulled some of the experiments askew."

"You guys would make great spies," Sandoval said ironically.

"So, Rimae Bode II is …" Vivian looked at Terri. "Quite central, right? About ten degrees north of the equator, a little to the west of center."

Terri's eyebrows went up. "So kinda-sorta right next to Mare Vaporum."

"Well," Vivian said. "Isn't *that* interesting."

Pope and Rodriguez looked at each other. "Is it?"

"Vaporum is where …" Vivian suddenly remembered who she was talking to and shut up.

"You can say it out loud." Sandoval said. "Mare Vaporum is where Carter and Lin came down, three years ago."

"Of course it is. Damn." Rodriguez turned away. Terri looked down at her feet. Pope's and Sandoval's expressions suddenly became professional masks, revealing nothing.

After a brief pause, Peter said: "So, Vivian. Could you identify the area where you came down, if you saw it again?"

"I've seen a lot of lunar terrain since then. A *lot*. And the horizon was pretty flat all around me. It was a mare, after all. Uh, why?"

"Would you know it from above?"

"No. Well, wait." She closed her eyes, trying to visualize it. "I guess I do have a mental impression of how the craters looked in my immediate vicinity while I was assembling all the supplies for my cart. But, more than that: around the crash site the area would be all scuffed up. And I did a bunch of arithmetic with a rock in the dirt, jotting numbers down. I guess that would still be there." Which was a weird thought. "And there's a big gash where the LM impacted and skidded across the surface. Why are we talking about this?"

Sandoval pulled out another large-format photograph, eighteen inches on a side, and handed it over. It looked like just a random piece of lunar terrain. "Did it look like that?"

Vivian looked more closely. Just the usual lunar mess of boulders and small craters. Nothing else. She shook her head.

"That's your crash site."

"Well, no, because if it was we'd see the wreckage of the freaking LM I augered in aboard."

"Exactly."

Vivian looked up at him with incomprehension. "Sorry. I don't get it."

Pope took the photo from her, and he and Rodriguez bent their heads over it. "You're saying the crashed LM *itself* isn't there anymore?"

Rodriguez glanced at Vivian. "Or that it was never there in the first place."

Vivian felt hot around the collar. "What the hell?"

Everyone started talking at once. Peter raised his hands for calm. Pope let go of the photo and let it float in front of him. Vivian snatched it out of the air and looked at it again. "That's not possible. You must have the wrong coordinates."

Peter handed her a second photo. "Here's one from two and a half years earlier, taken from Eagle Station using the wide-format camera you originally brought up. Those were the best optics we had at the time, so the resolution is degraded relative to the one you just looked at. What do you see?"

Vivian's heart lurched. "You want me to say it aloud? Christ. I see the wreckage of a Lunar Module, and some hint of parallel tracks heading north away from it. From my cart."

She quickly compared the two images and after a few moments her practiced eye made sense of the patterns, figuring out the constellations of craters and large boulders in the smaller photo and mapping them to the large photo. "Holy cow. When was this taken? The newer DORIAN photo?"

"Three months ago."

"And Night Corps didn't clean up that wreckage?"

"We did not."

"You've known for three goddamn *months*? Before I even came here with LGS-1?"

Vivian was startled by the depth of her own anger. So was Sandoval, rocking back away from her. Terri interposed herself. "Vivian, no. The MOLs have been in lunar orbit less than a year. They expose a hell of a lot of film, which needs to go back to Earth for developing and processing, and a lot of calibrating and applying coordinates—it takes forever. They're only now on hurry-up because of the cryptonaut activity, trying to find their surface bases. They're blinking the images with those obtained on previous passes, or with the Eagle/Columbia images or the Lunar Orbiter images—which are way worse—looking for differences. We don't know exactly what we're looking for, maybe a base-like shape, or maybe their rover in transit. They have literally *hundreds* of people working on this on Earth, but it all takes time."

"Maybe thousands of people," Sandoval said. "And Terri is right. This anomaly wasn't detected until a few days ago."

"Oh," Vivian said. "Okay. Uh, sorry."

She should have realized. Film was still better resolution than electro-optics, and scanning and digitizing photographs was a chore. Maybe ten years from now, or twenty, they could do that kind of stuff quickly and easily, on a big mainframe. Until then, well, that's why the highly classified National Reconnaissance Office had entire buildings full of computers in addition to—apparently—thousands of people.

What didn't make any sense at all, though, was that the LM that she and Lin had crashed in had vanished completely, as if it had never been.

"The cryptonauts are scavengers," Vivian said. "They scavenged the damned thing."

"They'd likely call it salvage," Peter said.

"I'd call it stolen," Terri said forcefully. "Just like all the stuff filched from US-Copernicus."

Vivian shook her head, unsure why Terri was getting riled up. "The cryptonauts went to Mare Vaporum, loaded up the wreckage of my Lunar Module onto a rover, took it away, and cleaned up after themselves?"

Terri looked at her with more irritation than Vivian had ever seen from her before. "Uh, Vivian. Point of order. That wasn't *your* LM. It was *my* fricking LM. Lin requisitioned our Apollo 25 Module from Hadley for that mission."

"Oh, God. Right. I'm sorry."

Vivian knew how she'd feel if her Apollo 32 LM, Athena, had been blown out of the sky by a Soviet missile, even if she hadn't been aboard it at the time. She could almost taste that feeling on a visceral level. "Sorry, Terri. I hadn't made that connection. What did you call her?"

"Lucy," Terri said, so mournfully that Vivian instinctively put her fingers on Terri's arm to comfort her.

The guys had fallen silent. They all understood. Peter looked at Vivian as if to say, *Well, go on. Fix this.*

So Vivian did her best. "So, 'Lucy' … Like Linus and Lucy?"

"No, like the first woman. The three-million-year-old one found in, um, Ethiopia, I think. Get it? First named woman on the Earth, first US woman on the Moon. Also, Lucy in the Sky with Diamonds. The girl with kaleidoscope eyes?"

Vivian grinned. "Ah, it's coming back to me now. NASA hated the name, am I right?"

"With a fiery blazing passion. But we had the *best* mission patch."

Vivian saw what might have been tears in the corner of Terri's eyes. She reached out to bump her companionably on the shoulder. "Really sorry, Brock. Lucy was a good ship. We did our best to save her. We just couldn't."

"Understood." Terri nodded. "But I'm just so *mad as hell* that someone *stole* her remains, as well as …"

Silence fell. No one mentioned Lin's name out loud.

Eventually, Vivian turned to Peter. "Okay, so now we're all caught up … what next?"

He nodded, relieved. "We've been directed to go down and take a look, get some ground truth on all this."

Vivian raised her eyebrows. "Land in Vaporum?"

"Land in Vaporum. Salvaging that LM wreckage must have been a big operation. Maybe they didn't tidy up after themselves completely. We may be able to spot debris or clues at the site that we have no way of detecting from this altitude. We're to do a full forensic analysis. Aside from when LGS-1 was attacked at the South Pole, this is the only opportunity we've had to examine an almost-pristine area after the cryptonauts have done their best to clean up after themselves. So we'll be taking soil samples and so on, looking for, I don't know, chemistry or burned-on volatiles or something. Any material that doesn't match the material around it. Not my field, but I already have people in my crew here, Rod and a couple others, who are professionals at all that. We're to find out as much as we can.

"We might be able to get more on how they cover their tracks. Like, literally, how they wipe their wheel prints clean behind them. We developed our own method of doing that at Night Corps a while back, but it's not perfect. Theirs might be different. If we can figure out a way of identifying what their tire-track-redacted terrain looks like, maybe we could even follow that, use it to track their course across the Moon."

"You'd think it ought to have *some* recognizable signature," Rodriguez said.

Pope grimaced. "Seems like a long shot."

"Sure," said Sandoval. "But worth a try. And if it works, we can just follow the breadcrumbs all the way to their base."

"You're thinking that might be nearby? Somewhere in the general area of Rimae Bode II and Vaporum?" Vivian looked at Peter. "Tell me that the National Reconnaissance Office is focusing an intense, dedicated search on that area."

Sandoval grinned. "They are indeed. You've correctly identified our second objective."

Pope was sketching out notes on a yellow pad. "So, y'all. We were already aware that their ground transport was large enough to carry the flyer that attacked Vivian, plus the Lunokhod-sized rover and other stuff. But now we know it's got to be big enough to carry a Lunar Module."

Rodriguez nodded. "Even smashed, the LM would have a lot of cool stuff they could use. Or reverse engineer, whatever."

"We don't even let the Soviets ride in our NASA LMs in case they pick up some tech intel they can use," Vivian added.

"Then maybe we shouldn't have left one just lying out there in the dirt for three years," said Pope.

"And we likely wouldn't have, if the Soviets had the equivalent of MOLABs. But they don't have anything like the major overland capability that the US has."

"Until now," said Rodriguez.

"For goodness sake, guys," Terri said. "This was a crash site. A war grave. A man lost his life there. Some things are supposed to be sacred."

"Apparently not to everyone."

"Wait," Vivian said. "Were any of the other expeditionary Apollo landing sites looted? Or just Rimae Bode II?"

"I love working with you people. You're all top-notch." Peter nodded in satisfaction and waved the photos again. "Once the NRO discovered the disappearance of the Apollo 24 LM, they naturally took a look at all the other expeditionary Apollo sites, from Apollo 11 on. Those sites all contain the LM descent stages that were left behind, with their RTGs, the ALSEP experiments, the rovers from Apollo 16 on, and all kinds of other stuff abandoned in place. The NRO looked very carefully. The only Apollo site disturbed was Rimae Bode."

"Apollo 28," Vivian said. "As it happens, me, Ellis and Dave were the backup crew for that mission."

Terri nodded. That made sense to her, at least: backup crews trained with the prime crews, then got their own missions two or three Apollo launches later. It'd been that way since the start of the Apollo program. Heck, back through Gemini.

"That's great," Sandoval said. "So you know that terrain, too?"

"Sort of. I trained for it, like five or six years ago. I doubt that's worth a whole lot by now, though."

"We'll see." He looked at his watch. "I need to take a break now. Work some timelines, and deal with the other admin crap that's raining down all around me. But Carter, Brock, you two have homework: I'd like some options on where we should aim to put down. We've all been on the surface, but you two are the experts."

Pope grinned. "He means the biggest Moon nerds."

"Guilty as charged," Vivian said.

Peter ignored them. "I can see two considerations, but there may be more. We'll need to land far enough away that we don't disturb either of the sites we're there to examine. And, just in case we hit the jackpot and the cryptonauts' base *is* at Rimae Bode II, we need to land far enough away that we can deploy quickly before any hostiles arrive to spoil our day. It won't be helpful if we get blown out of the sky or attacked as soon as we reach the ground."

"Not helpful," Vivian said. "Concur."

Terri floated over to the bookshelves, pulled out a large-size binder full of photographs, checked the contents page. "Okay, not too close because we need to deploy. Not too far. Somewhere just right."

"Yes, thank you, Goldilocks."

Vivian grinned. "We'll work it."

Peter nodded crisply. "Once you have, give the candidate sites to Rod or Pope to work with the mission planning guys at Cheyenne, and we'll get this show on the road as soon as we can. Class dismissed. I'll be back in a couple hours."

He kicked off, shot through the hatch into the Observation Deck.

"Well, that's my cue for a shower." Pope gave Vivian and Terri an ironic salute and headed in the opposite direction. Rodriguez also exited, heading forward. Vivian stared at the lunar photos adorning the walls and shook her head, dazed.

Terri eyed her. "What?"

"Whiplash. I keep thinking I'm all-done with the Moon. And yet …"

Terri grinned tightly. "Guess the Moon's not all done with you."

Vivian didn't say the second reason out loud. *So, now I work for Peter Sandoval. The one thing I said I'd never want to do.*

*This isn't going to be weird. Nope, not at all.*


Terri pinned a photograph onto the corkboard in the Observation Module, pointed. "Here. Right on the edge of Sinus Aestuum which, for whatever it might be worth, is Latin for 'Seething Bay.' It's mostly level, not highlands, which makes it good for landing, a quick deploy, and level habitation. We did consider highland terrain to the east, in between Aestuum and Mare Vaporum, but it would be better to keep it simple. It's close to equatorial. We can land there easily enough, and it allows for egress to either polar or equatorial orbits, which is good for extraction."

Pope studied the photo, checked with the map book he was holding. "Not actually in Mare Vaporum, then?"

"Vaporum is tiny, as mares go. One hundred fifty miles in diameter. Vivian came down in," Terri grinned at her, "*my* LM in the middle of it, pretty much central."

Vivian took over. "We drop at the location indicated, at the edge of Sinus Aestuum. Eleven point five degrees north, five degrees west. We deploy and head north to Rimae Bode II, thirty-three miles away, to take data on the disturbance at the Apollo 28 site. If you feel we need more margin than that thirty-three miles, which is about two hours travel time, we can land however far south of there you like, it's all good. Then, after we're done at Bode II, we head into the center of Vaporum, which is a hundred sixty miles from Drop. Eight hours, a bit more, so some of us get a sleep shift on the way."

Terri took over again. "Drop is two hundred eighty miles from Copernicus. Not super close, but not far. Less than a day's travel, if we need to get there, but far enough away for safety."

"We can move closer to Copernicus if you're willing to sustain more travel time to Vaporum," Vivian said. "That's an operational choice. It's basically all mare, we can be anywhere in there."

Sandoval nodded. "Okay. So ... you basically picked a site two-thirds of the way between Zvezda and the center of Mare Vaporum?"

Terri glanced at the map. "Right. Just south of that line."

"Seems fine." Sandoval nodded. "Good enough. Let's make it happen."

"Yes, sir."

"We're still going to call it Vaporum Base, though. Because whatever that Sinus thing was, it's a tongue-twister."

"Vaporum it is, sir."

Vivian chimed in. "If you're willing to hit very slightly farther south, there are a whole bunch of small craters in the Schröter complex that would be fine locations for, uh, Vaporum Base. It's a cool area geographically, with an area of dark mantle deposits that have the lowest albedo on the Moon. It's likely the result of pyroclastic deposits from volcanic eruptions. You know, just in case we have some spare time and sample bags."

Sandoval frowned. "This isn't a joyride."

Unseen by Sandoval, Pope winked at Vivian. "Actually, boss, that's not a bad idea. By using Schröter as the drop we can claim this is a joint military and scientific expedition. It might provide us a bit of extra coverage when this comes out."

"Uh … Okay, I guess." Sandoval frowned. "Wait, Schröter? Didn't one of the early Apollos already land at Schröter?"

Vivian gestured at Terri. "You go. I've already pissed him off once."

"Sure." Brock took over. "Lunar naming is unreasonably complicated, sir. Apollo 18 landed at Schröter's Valley, which is twenty-five degrees north of the equator and fifty degrees west. The craters Vivian is talking about are named after the same guy, some German astronomer, but are almost at the equator and only around ten degrees west. So …" Terri waved her hands, stalling while she did some quick mental arithmetic. "So the two different Schröter sites are eight hundred, maybe nine hundred miles apart."

Pope was looking at the photos. "It's really six of one and half a dozen of the other. Their Schröter craters are about a hundred miles south of the canonical drop site the ladies first mentioned, but it's the east-west positioning that's critical. And if the Russkies really are based near that strategic Rimae Bode II area, this would put our landing drop farther away from them. Less chance of them seeing us come down, and more time for us to get our act in gear prior to any potential attack." He turned. "I say we give the lunar dorks their pyroclastic deposits and ourselves a bit of wiggle room and come down that little bit farther south."

"Sure. Whatever. Okay, thank you, people. Let's get this done, so we can go home." Peter had clearly had enough of this conversation.

*Home.* Vivian had no idea when she'd ever see home again.

"Roger that," she said.


Bunks on the MOL were two-and-two rather than individual quarters, and really more like hammocks with restraints to stop them floating away, or their limbs flapping around in weightlessness. Vivian ended up next to Terri Brock. Admittedly anything else might have been awkward, and it did give them time to talk, quietly, in tones the men couldn't hear.

"Terri, I'm so glad you moved to Night Corps."

Brock eyed her, quizzical as ever: "Because?"

"Because it means you're still in space. And so you can watch over Peter's ass, stop him getting into too much trouble."

"Can't say I've done too well on that score so far. But thanks. And, on that topic," Terri scooted in closer. "I have some privileged information, that I'm not sure whether to share with you. About Peter." At Vivian's expression, Terri added quickly: "Not about you. Directly mission-related. And you may know it already."

"Is it that the Moon scares him shitless?"

Terri blinked. "Oh. Okay. Yes. That's it."

"I didn't know that was a secret. I mentioned it to Kevin. Whoops."

"Vivian, I think that's what's overwriting all of his circuits right now. He's not usually this cranky. Likely, he doesn't even realize. He just … doesn't dig the Moon. At all. Even from this height above it. Once he gets on surface, we may need to watch out for him. Get my drift?"

"Sure. We're on the same page there. This mission, though? Not sure I really buy it."

"You don't think we should be going down?"

"Not that. I think we should absolutely go down, look for clues and do forensics and all. And it makes sense for me to come with you. But seriously, what are the odds that the cryptonaut base is close to where my—our—uh, to where the Apollo 24 LM came down? With the whole Moon to choose from? It just seems like a hairy coincidence, is all."

"Unless they deliberately sited themselves there."

"If I was the boss cryptonaut, I wouldn't be creating two major anomalies visible from space, close to where I've sited my top-secret base."

"Well, okay. Then again, it is a good location for them, well-placed. Two and a half days from Copernicus, easy trip there and back. But far enough away that they won't be accidentally discovered during a foray from Zvezda. It's well beyond the easy radius of a MOLAB or rover excursion from US-Copernicus. And it's still a large area, if we do have to search it looking for them."

"I guess so."

Terri shrugged. "Okay, then, try this. Why do they need a base anywhere?"

Vivian considered. "Huh."

"What if their rover is a real rover? No fixed address, they just keep rolling along. That means they can maneuver to keep themselves in sunlight for more than fourteen days out of every twenty-nine. All they care about is supplies and daylight. We already know their rover has some cunning camo to make it hard to see from above. Maybe they don't need anything more than that. And then they can choose to situate themselves a couple days from *anywhere*."

"I don't know." Vivian doodled on a notepad, thinking about it.

"Nomads, wandering the lunar plains."

"Poetic."

"And in that case, we might never find them. Ever."

Vivian made a face. "Well, not never, I hope."

"Well, not easily."

"Not sure it works." Vivian totted up a column of figures she'd been scribbling down. "I just finished a grand tour of the lunar plains myself, and the logistics were a pain. They'd at least need some drops, some places to stash stuff. Somewhere to rest. They can't carry everything they need, all the time, for weeks on end. It's not feasible, especially when they're also carrying the mass of other vehicles."

"Could be a convoy, just like LGS-1?"

"They'd still need a stash," Vivian said. "A depot, somewhere."

"So, fine, they have a stash. Maybe at the South Pole, then? Maybe they found water there, where we didn't. That would be a huge help with their mass margin. Water would also give them oxygen and fuel, if they could figure out an easy way to process it."

"Meaning that they attacked LGS-1 from a base close by? They must have known we'd go over that area really carefully."

"Again, 'that area' is hundreds of square miles, and it's not well observed by the MOLs. And some of the peaks have access to a lot of solar power, and they have a whole lot of always-shadowed crater areas to hide in."

"They do." Vivian slid the notepad into a wall-pocket, stretched out, sighed. "But we're not going to solve this tonight, and I need to sack out. I'm beat. Ever tried to sleep in a Blue Gem?"

"Nope."

"Don't. At least, for more than one night." Vivian sighed. "So, now Peter's my boss? I'm really not sure how I feel about that."

"For this trip, anyway." Terri searched her face. "Is that going to be a problem?"

"I guess not. Long as I can speak my mind when I need to."

Terri grinned. "None of us are exactly renowned for our deference. It's easy enough to tell when he's in 'sir' mode and when he just wants to be one of the guys. He mostly has a first-among-equals style, at least with this unit. I speak my mind a whole damn lot."

"Okay then. We'll see if he takes it as well from me as he does from you."

"I've got your back," Terri said. "And it sure looks like Pope does, too."

Vivian grinned. "Thanks, Army. Or I guess it's Air Force now."

"No prob, Navy." Terri hit the lights. "Goodnight, Carter. Sleep tight."

" 'Night, Brock."


"Morning, sir."

Sandoval looked up, reflexively blanked the TV screen above him, and then shook his head and turned it back on. "Sorry. Just used to being secretive."

"Well, you are Super-Secret Agent Man."

He glanced around, said nothing.

"Yeah, I know. We're on the job. No fraternizing."

"That's best for now. Let's keep it simple."

*Nice goal,* she thought. *Wonder if we can do that.*

She studied him. "Frankly, I'm surprised you're here. Surprised you accepted the assignment. I thought you'd sworn off the Moon forever."

He nodded. Maybe a quarter of an inch. "I didn't get a whole lot of choice. It's fine. I can hack it."

She glanced casually behind them. They were still alone on the Observation Deck, but it was a small ship. "You're sure?" she murmured.

He met her eye. "I'm sure. No problem."

"Well, if No Problem turns into Problem, let me know."

"Copy that."

"Or Brock."

"Will do."

Pope came through the hatch from the mid-deck, still buttoning his shirt. "Oh, sorry. Am I too early?"

"Right on time," Peter said. "In fact, the others? All late. Going on report."

"Oh, right." Brock slid though the hatch on Pope's heels. "Like *that's* going to happen."

"So, we're going down in the LMs, then? Who do you want at the helm?" One of them would be Vivian, surely. That would have been one of the reasons Sandoval had "acquired" her. He'd already said the others hadn't been down on-surface since the Hadley-Daedalus days. And if so, Vivian wanted to check out a USAF Lunar Module as soon as possible, to accustom herself to any differences from the NASA LMs she was used to.

"No," he said. "Not the LMs."

Aside from the LMs, all they had was the Big G, the boosters, and the MOL itself. "And … what's our other choice?"

"You're not going to like it. And neither am I, by the way. Not at all."

"Wait." *Please, no.* "You're saying it might be more of a, well, controlled impact?"

"Yes, in fact I am."

"Oh God. No, Peter. Seriously, just no."

"Sorry." Sandoval looked at his watch again. "It should heave into view any time now. Soon as it docks, I'll introduce you to your crash couch."

# CHAPTER 20

## The Brick: Vivian Carter
## March 2, 1983

IT was already just a few hundred feet away and cruising in to rendezvous. Square, black, and silent.

"Hey, cool," said Terri. "A flying brick."

"Brock in a Brick, real soon," said Rodriguez.

She gave him a look. "You just had to go there, didn't you?"

"Afraid so."

The approaching craft really did look like lot like a brick. It was similar to the Cargo Containers that NASA used to stock their surface bases, but more bulbous and with more definite corners. Flat topped and flat bottomed except for a conical rocket nozzle sticking out beneath it. RCS jets—thrusters—at each corner. It was colored a very basic black, and at this distance, Vivian could see no other hatches, no windows or portholes, no markings at all.

She lowered the binoculars, handed them to Terri. To Peter, she said: "When you arrived in one of those for Apollo Rescue 1, you called it 'the Bunker.'"

"That's what it's called officially, when it's not being called a Contingency Lunar Facility. But if it looks like a brick, quacks like a brick, flies like a brick ..."

"Fair," she said. "That rocket nozzle retracts on landing?"

"Immediately before contact."

"Seems like a questionable design. If you don't mind me saying so."

"Hasn't failed yet. In fact, it can't fail because if the nozzle doesn't retract, it just breaks, punches up into the main body, so we still land level. But that's messier."

"I bet."

"We need them to sit much lower to the surface than a Hab. Easier to cover with camouflage netting and regolith. Much less detectable. And they're modular; you can attach them together at the ends, sides, whatever."

"Like actual bricks."

"Building blocks."

Rodriguez spoke up. "Most of the original buildings at Daedalus were put together from these."

"Huh." Vivian looked again. "Oh, right. Okay. Six of them attached together. Two rows of three." Once Rodriguez had pointed it out, it was obvious. She looked around at the others. "So, break it to me, guys. Daedalus aside, where else on the Moon does Night Corps have these?"

"Nowhere. We don't have standalone Night Corps bases anywhere on surface. Until now."

"For real?"

"There's this thing called the Lunar Accord," Peter said, deadpan. "So we hardly want to be caught putting clandestine facilities on the Moon. Covertly dropping military-only bases anywhere on the Moon might kick off another superpower confrontation mess. We're keen to avoid that."

"Until now, apparently."

"Well, now a peaceful joint US-USSR geological survey has come under fire. Astronauts at an equally peaceful US base at Copernicus have been attacked and one of them captured. And meanwhile, all through this, a substantial quantity of important US matériel—some of it of high strategic value—has been stolen. We need to investigate, and we need to do so securely." He pointed at the Brick. "And those things are *damned* secure."

"And we're about to drop one into Mare Vaporum, or close enough."

"We are."

"Let's say 'onto,' not 'into,'" Brock objected.

"And we'll naturally inform the Soviets of this through usual diplomatic channels, so this doesn't get out of hand?" Vivian's tone was sardonic.

"I think you mean 'any more out of hand,'" Pope said.

"Yes, we will. In due course. We'll send formal notification of a single landing—Soon. Ish. We won't reveal our location immediately because that would place us in potential jeopardy. Once we're out, we'll tell 'em the full story. Unless, of course, something else hits the fan in the meantime."

"What are the odds?" Rodriguez muttered.

They saw the brief sparkle of thruster jets at one corner of the Brick, adjusting its attitude. "Is that thing crewed?" Vivian asked.

"A dozen troops. There's room for more, but the rest of the space is packed with supplies. And our MOLAB, of course."

"Back to the surface," Vivian said. "*And* back into a MOLAB. Sheesh."

Rodriguez shook his head. "I still have nightmares about the last time."

"What goes around, comes around; you know it," Terri said. "At least for us, I guess."

Vivian looked at Terri. "Did *you* ever think you'd end up back on the Moon?"

"No. I absolutely did not."

The Brick floated closer. Slowly and smoothly, but it was nowhere near as cautious as a NASA docking approach. "And have you been in one of those before?"

Brock nodded. "Once. In Earth orbit, as part of my training. Just for a few hours in zero-G. No crashing involved."

Somehow it looked smaller floating in space than Apollo Rescue 1 had on the Moon's surface at Hadley. "I'm not going to enjoy this, am I?"

"Doubt it," said Terri. "They're a little tight."

"No," Rodriguez added. "You absolutely are not."

A thought struck her. "Uh, question. How do we get off-surface again after this mission? Presumably the Brick only goes in one direction."

"Down." Sandoval nodded. "And once it lands, it's a bunker. These are single use. But that's okay. While the current crisis persists, we need forces on the ground anyway, within easy reach of Copernicus in case we're called to defend our people there or to respond to another hostile action in the area. So we'll be setting up shop there for a while."

Vivian did quick math. "Vaporum is like, what, a week from sunset right now? So we'll be staying there into lunar night?"

"We will. That's factored into our energy budget."

"Oh, lord," she said. "Another lunar night?"

Sandoval checked his watch. "Speaking of time, it's a-wasting. Let's go pack up, get ready for the drop while these guys close the rendezvous."

So when they'd been calling it a "drop" earlier, they really weren't kidding. "Who's piloting this ... descent, anyway?" Vivian held up a hand. "Actually, you know what? Just don't tell me. It may be better that way."

"It won't be me," Terri said. "I'll be shivering and puking in the crash bunk right next to yours."

"Awesome," said Vivian. "Can't wait."


Calling the Brick "a little tight" had been an understatement. "Majorly claustrophobic" would have been more accurate.

From viewing Apollo Rescue 1 from the outside, Vivian knew that the end walls of the Brick could telescope outward once it became a Bunker, creating more open space, and that they could add even more pressurized space using inflatables. But for right now, there was barely enough room to survive, none to thrive, and definitely zero to spare.

The rocket engine was the centerpiece, with the MOLAB packed in close on one side and the environmental controls and a bunch of other machinery balancing it on the other side. Not that the MOLAB was visible right now. Every square foot of space above, under, around, and inside it was packed with exosuits and other spacesuits, plus supplies of various kinds. The available breathing space for the crew consisted of two extremely small dormitory areas, A and B, with bunks stacked six deep on either side of a two-foot-wide walkway. The "bunks" were, in fact, fairly sophisticated couches; for flight they were padded, sprung, and customizable to provide full support for both high G's and heavy impact. The Night Corps crew and Vivian would make moonfall strapped into these couches. Each dormitory also contained one extremely small toilet facility, and the two dorm areas were connected by a crawlway—not a walkway, but a tunnel only three feet high. Easy in weightlessness, of course, but it would be a pain on the Moon, scooting along it on hands and knees, until they got the expando-walls set up and cleared out some of the other supplies out of the way.

Also, needless to say, the Brick had no windows aside from those in "CC & C," Central Command and Control, a tiny bridge area front and center on the Brick where Sandoval and the still-nameless descent pilot would be strapped into very similar couches for their barely controlled plunge down onto the Moon.

It was all very utilitarian. Very military. Very grunt. Compared to the stripped-down functionality of NASA vehicles, the Brick had a different feel. Almost Soviet in its spartan discomfort.

Vivian figured she wouldn't say that part out loud.

As they prepped for the drop, even among the Night Corps crew you could cut the tension with a knife. Night Corps might be an elite unit, but at least half these troops were space rookies on their first tour of duty, and most were considerably younger than Vivian, guys in their twenties and early thirties. One of them vomited neatly and then just as calmly disposed of the evidence prior to strapping in. Everyone else ignored the incident, mostly lost in their own thoughts. There was almost no chatter beyond the functional, and especially not to Vivian, whom most of them regarded with curiosity but showed no inclination to talk to.

Vivian and Terri were the only women aboard. Vivian was assigned the second-to-lowest bunk in Dorm Area B, with Terri next to her. Pope and Rodriguez were in Dorm A, and the rest of their bunkmates were fresh from Earth, so the women were surrounded by strangers. As the relative expert, Terri had given Vivian the tiny tour of the new space and helped her adjust her couch and strap into it. Vivian was only slightly amused to find she was sharing her bunk space with a rifle, seven boxes of ammunition, her gloves and helmet, and a PLSS backpack. She had no idea where the rest of her Moon suit was, but this seemed like a smooth and well-organized operation, so presumably someone else had that under control.

So Vivian tightened her straps, looked at the blank underside of the couch above her, mere inches above her nose, and tried not to worry about a Moon landing she would not even see, let alone have any hand in. Vivian wasn't great at trusting other people's flying.

Their only source of information was a loudspeaker in the ceiling, which had been quiet ever since they'd boarded and remained silent for a good forty-five minutes after they were all strapped in. Clearly Vivian was back in the "hurry up and wait" military mode.

As the clock ticked remorselessly up to the hour, the speaker finally crackled, and a voice she didn't recognize came on the line. "Brick pressurized and under internal power. Be advised, we disconnect from Orbital in ten." For some reason, Night Corps referred to the whole complex of the MOL, Big G, and all their associated hardware as "Orbital."

The Brick yawed sickeningly, presumably to duck it under the Big G, and then swung again. Next moment, Vivian felt the unmistakable judder and shove of a translation thruster. "And away we go." So, ten seconds rather than ten minutes, then.

Terri's hand crossed the eighteen inches that separated their couches, to clasp Vivian's. Vivian glanced across in surprise, but Terri was just staring upward, outwardly calm. A few moments later, she closed her eyes.

Probably a good plan. Not that anyone would be getting any sleep in the next thirty minutes, but a few moments of quiet contemplation on their insignificance in the cosmic scheme of things might be in order. If for no other reason than to relax the muscles that were likely to be taking a pounding between now and the time the Brick arrived on the lunar surface. So Vivian awkwardly squeezed Terri's hand and closed her own eyes.

They were on their way down. Even flying blind, there could be no doubt.


Not knowing when to brace herself during the descent was inconvenient, to say the least. They heard no further announcements over the Tannoy, and no one else seemed to expect any, so this was apparently standard protocol for Night Corps. Meaning that none of them had any warning of the vertiginous swings and slews that the Brick underwent as its pilot completed the initial deorbit burn, and the various other tweaks and attitude adjustments along the way.

At least Vivian didn't need to maintain a stoic calm. Others among her new crew shouted out often in surprise or alarm, and no one seemed to think the worse of them. Mild oaths and pithy comments also seemed tolerated, but true profanity would be greeted by a growled "Keep it down, soldier," or "Steady, man," from the top bunk.

"Reminds me of boot camp," Vivian muttered.

"Yeah," was Terri's only response, followed by "Ack, what the hell was that?" as the entire Brick swung all the way around under them.

"Damned if I know." Lacking visual cues, they had no way of telling gravity from acceleration, and as yet had only the vaguest idea which direction was "down." Vivian raised her voice so that everyone would hear. "So they don't even give us a projected time-till-landing?"

"Best not to know," came the growly voice from up top. "Trust me on that."

"Yeah, I'm not so sure," Vivian said.

"Well, suck it up, soldier," said the growler, and then after a hesitation. "Uh. My apologies, ma'am. I forgot you weren't a member of my squad."

"No worries. Sucking it up, roger that."

Vivian could almost imagine the lunar surface coming up toward them. Looked at her watch, and realized she couldn't even remember what time they separated from Orbital. It hardly mattered anyway. She wiggled and adjusted herself, so she'd be ready if they hit something. As ready as anyone could be, anyway. Though if they hit something without decelerating first, her exact posture wouldn't make much difference.

Even as that cheerful thought crossed her mind, the Tannoy crackled. "Braking burn in five, people. Be ready."

"Seconds or minutes, this time?"

"Like, now-OWWWW," Terri said, as the punch of the forced deceleration slammed into their backs.

"You okay? Don't … bite your tongue, babe."

"Didn't. Slammed my … teeth together real good though."

The G forces on them rose. After so much time in one-sixth G and then none at all, Vivian couldn't gauge how much. Likely not as much as an Apollo Earth splashdown, so less than four G? But more than enough.

When Vivian had watched Apollo Rescue 1 come down into Hadley, they'd decelerated brutally right at the end. Was that this?

It sure was. "Landing in ten," said the Tannoy, the voice sounding strained, and that was that. Vivian relaxed her muscles completely, closed her eyes, and tried not to think about …BAMMM. The couch crumpled beneath her—by design—partially absorbing the intense shock of impact. A roar of oaths erupted from the berths around her, and this time no one tried to quiet them.

The Brick shook, rang like a bell and quivered with a much deeper vibration, seemed to stop moving—then lurched suddenly and slid sideways. Quite far. Banged into something, spun horizontally maybe ninety degrees, then its slide was arrested.

Everything stopped moving, for real this time. Thank God.

Terri coughed and gasped beside her and eventually choked out, "Viv, okay?"

Vivian's still-healing ribs and shoulder were aching like hell again, but she didn't feel like sharing that. "Sure. Fine. How are you?"

"Just winded. I hope. Oh, boy."

"Jesus H. Christ, that sucked."

"Yeah, I hear you."

Vivian held up her other arm, her left. Relaxed it, and watched it gently settle back down onto the couch next to her. Yep. Definitely the Moon.

Sandoval's voice over the Tannoy. "In case there's any doubt, we've arrived."

"Smartass," Terri coughed again, then cleared her throat as Vivian peered over anxiously. "I'm fine."

"Yeah, you sound perfect."

From the Tannoy: "All burns nominal, descent nominal, landing bang on time and on target."

"Yeah, 'Bang' is the word, dude."

"Yes, boys and girls, it was actually *supposed* to feel like that. And we're exactly where we'd planned to be."

Which was miles away from anywhere, really, but that was good to know. At least no one had shot at them yet. Yet. What was the over-under on that?

Sandoval, at least, sounded calm. Despite being on the lunar surface again. "Everyone just stay put for a moment. We'll punch out and get ourselves deployed, get you some more breathing space, as soon as we can. For now: roll call. If you or anyone near you is having a medical emergency, you should have shouted out already. Do so now. Otherwise, when I say your name, respond with 'Here' if you're fine, 'Injured' if you require prompt but non-urgent care, 'badly injured' if something is really-the-hell wrong, and if you're dead, don't say anything."

Vivian shook her head. Even by her own rather wonky standards, Night Corps had a very ... *specific* sense of humor.

279

"Okay, here we go. Brock?"

"Present."

"Carter?"

"Terrific."

"Doyle?"

"Peachy."

"Godfrey?"

"Bruised."

"Jeez, I really hate every one of you. Jacobson?"

The call went on. Twenty names. Twenty troops in this tiny Brick, plus Sandoval himself and whoever the pilot was, sitting next to him. No wonder it smelled so bad in here. But at least no one came up injured, badly injured, or dead.

"Cool. Hang tight, people."

"I gotta pee!" Brock called out, and everyone laughed, including her.

"Hold it in, lady."

"Roger that, Commander. Legs crossed."

Vivian just shook her head and rested it back against the couch.

*Well, here I am. On the goddamn Moon.*

*Again.*

"Smoke 'em if you've got 'em," some wag two bunks above Vivian said, and people laughed again. Clearly *that* wouldn't be happening. In their current pure oxygen environment, even steel would burn.

Since Vivian was now back in the real military, there was a *lot* of hurry-up-and-wait. It took over an hour to stabilize the Brick, run diagnostics, and get to the point where they could start unfolding themselves from the crash couches. And nobody played favorites; they unloaded from the top bunk down, so Vivian waited patiently while the guys above her all clambered out in turn, stretching and bouncing out of the dorm, many of them crashing into the bunks on either side or banging their heads on the ceiling due to their unfamiliarity with one-sixth G and the Bunker having settled at an odd angle.

When it was their turn, Terri clambered out first and claimed the head. Vivian just lay where she was and let the guys beneath her clear out. For a brief moment she was alone in the dorm with her thoughts.

Terri exited the facilities. "Jeez, get your ass out of there, lazybones." She hauled Vivian up onto her feet, looked at her. "Phew. We made it down without getting broken into a thousand pieces. Holy crap."

"God *damn*." Vivian was bruised in a dozen places, but likely everyone else was too. At least her shoulders and ribs didn't seem to have sustained any additional damage.

Terri leaned against the bunk and shook her head, and they both just breathed for a moment. Eventually, Brock said: "Okay, fine. Let's go shove those rookies away from the portholes and see where the hell we've ended up this time."

It was an anonymous-looking area. Craters and boulders. No signs of hostiles. At this Sun angle there wasn't much evidence of the lower albedo this area should have. But that was likely patchy.

After stabilization, setting up defenses, and chow, their next task was to break out the MOLAB. Vivian joined the Night Corps grunts in unpacking all the crap that was shoved in around it and moving it all to where it was supposed to go. Once the MOLAB was unpacked and out, she had no doubt the sergeant-major types who were calling the shots in here would have the grunts moving everything back in to where the MOLAB had been.

Of course, by that time, Vivian and the others would be on the road to Vaporum. Which was good because even with its walls now extended, this Bunker was entirely too crowded for Vivian's taste.

# CHAPTER 21

## Mare Vaporum: Vivian Carter
## March 3-5, 1983

THE Night Corps MOLAB was thoroughly military. Rocket launchers, antennae, and a periscope on the roof. Gun racks on the walls. A very utilitarian single trailer with a three-cylinder stack of extra supplies and emergency equipment, and two of the ubiquitous Moon bikes strapped to it, each with a sidecar for a gunner. In the past, Vivian had only seen those sidecars attached to Soviet dirt bikes.

This definitely wasn't a vehicle designed for scientific exploration. Sandoval's MOLAB was loaded for bear, and lumbered rather than rolling, so its armor had probably been tweaked up a notch or two as well.

"Sure didn't expect to see the inside of one of these again." Vivian glanced behind them into the main body where Brock, Pope, Rodriguez, and Doyle were doffing suits and stowing gear, and lowered her voice. "Shame we have a bunch of chaperones."

Sandoval grinned. "Remember the good old days at Hadley, when people used to keep leaving us alone together?"

It was the first sign of the old Peter she'd seen so far. "I do. Kinda liked that."

"Shame it doesn't happen more this time around." He looked at her, looked away. "I really wish we could talk more, Viv. But we have work to do."

"Yep. I hear ya."

He just nodded, then turned back to the controls to set the circuit breakers and power up the engines. "These controls: same as your MOLAB?"

"Close," she said. "Aside from that whole rack and panel there."

"That's for the weapons systems. Plus maybe a couple surprises."

"Good," she said. "I like surprises."

He looked dubious. "Might ask you to drive quite a bit, since you have the recent experience. We'll handle most of the outside patrolling and the comms. You're certainly capable of doing all that too, but ... you know."

"I'm not one of you. Understood."

He grinned a little. "Right."


Visiting the Apollo 28 landing site at Rimae Bode II was all kinds of weird. The original astronauts had landed here back in 1977, but since very little ever changed on the lunar surface, it looked like they'd only just left.

Here, Vivian saw Night Corps move into top gear. Rodriguez was the lead operative for this part: Doyle and he spent three hours out on the surface before Sandoval would let any of the others egress. They began by separating and circling the area fifty yards from the abandoned descent stage, then much closer, in a twenty-foot radius, moving quickly but efficiently, photographing and mapping the area, and taking samples. They discovered no tracks made by either boots or wheels, aside from those expected from the seven EVAs of the Apollo 28 crew. After that, they stepped up to the descent stage itself, using devices that looked to Vivian like spectrometers.

During this work, Rodriguez and Doyle talked quietly on their own loop, comparing notes and cross-checking each other, working their way down a long checklist monitored by Pope from inside the MOLAB. Eventually Rodriguez turned back to face the MOLAB and came back on to the general loop. "Okay. Time to send NASA out."

Vivian and Terri were already suited up. Sandoval gave them the high sign, and out they went. It was their job to look around with their NASA-trained eyes and look for any variances from what they'd expect. Terri had the Apollo 28 logbook detailing exactly what the

283

original astros had done, and left behind, and the final configurations of all the instrumentation.

Six hours into their time at Rimae Bode II, Terri finally said, "Taking five," and pulled herself up onto the abandoned descent stage to sit down.

"So that's it?" Sandoval said.

"That's it," Vivian pulled herself up beside Terri on the LM, feeling odd even as she did it. Off in the distance in opposite directions she could see Rodriguez and Doyle patrolling on the dirt bikes, guarding their perimeter. From this distance she couldn't tell which was which.

She held her checklist where Terri could see it too. "So, they came for the RTG, and they took the Lunar Rover batteries, as we suspected. They also unbolted and took the camera and comms equipment off the rover. And three of 28's unused oxygen tanks, and their toolkit."

She waved at Terri to go on and paused to take a sip of water from the straw at her neckline, bite into the protein bar that was also conveniently located at mouth height, and look out over the expanse of Sinus Aestuum to the rille, Rima Bode, that the site was named for. She had no doubt that if she asked to go over there and take a sample of the talus, Peter would deny the request.

Terri was saying: "Other than that, the only equipment we're dead sure about is the PLSSs. They'd have been thrown out at the end of the final EVA to get rid of the weight, like usual, along with their trash and other stuff that wasn't needed. Those PLSSs are gone. There's a bunch of other stuff tossed randomly under the lander, like those messy exploratory astronauts always do," at which point Vivian elbowed her in what would have been her ribs if she hadn't been protected by multiple layers of spacesuit. "There may be other smaller items missing, but it would take much longer to figure out what those might be. I doubt it's worth the effort."

"I can take inventory," Pope said from inside. "If we're staying here a bit."

"Sure," said Sandoval, to Vivian's surprise. "We'll take a rest period, eight hours, before heading east. Me and Doyle, and maybe Terri, we get a sleep period. Pope assumes command while I'm off duty. Everybody else, rest up, as long as two of you stay vigilant at all times, and at least one of you monitors comms with Cheyenne."

Vivian and Terri looked at each other. Terri said, "Is my sleep period mandated, or can I stay out here and buddy Carter?"

"Why, where's Carter … Oh. Silly question. Sure."

So, for the next few hours Vivian got to play what-might-have-been. Walking around the site, taking her own samples—because by now she just couldn't help herself. Once Sandoval was safely in his bunk, Pope slipped them the wink and they even got to bike over and check out the rille, while Rodriguez monitored them from the MOLAB and Pope kept a weather eye out from his station on the descent stage.

"Hey, Vivian, before you come in …" Sandoval's voice. He'd obviously cut his sleep period short. "Go take a look behind the MOLAB."

"Uh, roger that."

She walked around the big truck, past the trailer, and peered off into the distance behind it. "What am I looking for? I don't see anything out of the ordinary … Oh. Oh, wow."

"Since you're big on sampling, can you take a six-foot-wide sample parallel to the rear of the trailer? Mix it all in together, doesn't matter. Just want to run a couple of tests on the aggregate."

Vivian shook her head in admiration. "You cunning bastards."

She heard Sandoval's laugh in her headset. "From you, I'll take that as high praise."

Behind them, the Night Corps MOLAB had left no tire tracks. Under the back of the trailer was some … mechanism. Even staring straight at it and knowing what it did, Vivian couldn't tell how it worked, at least not while the MOLAB was stationary. She made a note to look more closely the next time she was on bike duty, if she ever was.

"You did figure it out after all." She shook her head. "You guys."

"This is its first field trial on the Moon itself. Testing it was one of the side aims of this trip. MOL-A and MOL-B have both confirmed that our tracks are as invisible from the orbit as from the ground. They can see the MOLAB itself, of course, because we don't have a camo wrap on it; we're not trying to conceal our presence. But—provided we're not shedding something behind us in that sample, which is why I need it—when the day comes, we're confident we can be as elusive as the cryptonauts."

"You do realize that if I had a suspicious mind, this might strike me as pretty solid circumstantial evidence that Night Corps could have been behind the attacks, after all?"

"Us?"

"In some kind of false flag op. Once the Soviets realize you have this technology, I wouldn't be a bit surprised if they folded that into their accusations."

"Sure," said Sandoval. "But Night Corps didn't attack you, Viv."

"Well, *I* know that," she said.

*At least, I think I know.*


Onward. Once they got over the short stretch of highlands and onto Mare Vaporum proper, Vivian went down for a five-hour nap, followed by a bumpy shower. Fortunately, the shower cubicle was so small there was really no room for her to fall very far without a wall stopping her, and crumpling to the floor would have taken rare talent. But she wasn't quite sure she'd gotten the shampoo out of her hair.

"Vivian, come take a look," Rodriguez called from the driver's cabin. "There you are."

He slowed the MOLAB, and Vivian came forward out of the main body and leaned on his shoulder to stabilize herself while she peered past him.

Sure enough, they were coming obliquely upon a line of boot prints in the regolith, mostly placed between two parallel grooves.

"Wow, crap," she said. "There's younger Vivian, hiking the hell out of Vaporum."

"Your boots, and the tracks of your cart." Rodriguez peered. "And from the depth of those wheel indentations, that sucker was heavy."

"You have no idea. And look how close together my boot prints are. That's not my usual Moon stride. Must have been tired." Then again, she'd been tired most of the time.

Nothing like the normal lope of an unencumbered astronaut. Many of the boot prints were scuffed, like she'd been dragging her feet. And this had been in the *early* part of her Trek of Death. What the heck had her trail looked like once she got really weary?

She cleared her throat. "How far are we from the crash site?"

Rodriguez looked down at the drive console, up at the clock. "Maybe fifteen miles. I'll need a better NAVSTAR fix to be any more accurate. We're due for that in about eight minutes."

" 'Kay," she said. "I'll go suit up."

"Suit up?"

"Yeah." Vivian had a lump in her throat. "I need to get out. And I may be radio quiet for a bit."

"Out?" Sandoval pursed his lips.

"Recommend you just let her do it, boss," Brock said quietly. "Not worth the discussion."

Sandoval's people looked at him. He paused, nodded. "Fine. Concur. EVA for Carter. Do I have a volunteer to go with?"

"I can," Pope said.

"I don't need a chaperone."

Sandoval looked uncomfortable. "This is my op, Vivian. So, my rules. Everyone buddies on surface, even you. Sorry."

"Fine. But I'll need my space, okay?"

Pope gave it to her. After walking thirty feet behind her for about a quarter-hour, he waited for the MOLAB to catch him up and hopped onto the running board, leaving Vivian to walk by herself.

She could easily ignore the MOLAB trundling a couple hundred feet behind her. Vivian just walked, retracing her steps of three-plus years ago in reverse, back to the site of the crash that had nearly killed her.

An indulgence, of course. They should really get the job done and get back as soon as possible. But this was something of a pilgrimage.

Then, dead ahead of her, her three-year-old footsteps vanished, along with the wheel tracks from her cart. Apparently pristine lunar surface stretched away from her.

Without looking back, she stopped and raised her hand above her head. She didn't feel quite able to speak yet. Then she turned in a complete circle, looking around carefully.

"No more tracks. But … this is not where we came down."

"Um," Sandoval's voice in her ears. "I thought you didn't have perfect recall. And don't all mares look the same?"

287

"True, and true. But now I'm here, I do kind of remember how the horizon looked when I first crawled out of the wreckage of Lucy, and that isn't it. Can we get a NAVSTAR update?"

"Not right now, but I'm triangulating off a MOL plus Eagle Station, hang on." She heard Rodriguez punching buttons over the loop. "Okay, looks like we're still some three miles out."

"They covered *my* tracks, for three miles?"

"Maybe while covering their own?"

"Could be. Or just to mess with us. I'm going on."

Vivian walked on for another half hour, keeping her eyes glued on the dust and dirt around her looking for clues, and occasionally scanning the horizon.

But when she did arrive at the site, it was obvious after all. A lump rose in her throat, and she felt the prickle of sweat on her neck and all down her spine. "Uh, guys? Guys, you likely want to stay back."

At her tone of voice, Sandoval cut in immediately, his worry evident. "What's up?"

"Gerry is here," she said flatly.

"What?"

"They left his .... Uh. Crap. He's just still here, okay?"

*They didn't take him along.*

Was she going to be sick? No. Not in a helmet, usual drill. She swallowed. And besides, she'd seen death before. This death, even. But still.

They'd taken Gerry Lin's suit, because of course they had. But they'd left his body behind.

He lay there on his back, looking for all the world as if he was staring up at the stars, until Vivian got close enough to really see his face. He'd suffered violent decompression, and the damage from that was ... very obvious.

This was exactly how he'd looked the day he died. It was truly spooky. Vivian remembered it vividly: the broken visor, the face beneath bloody and puffy and almost burned-looking, and none of that had changed in the slightest, despite all the day/night cycles his corpse had gone through in the time since. His hair was maybe a little bleached, his face a bit washed out by the UV. But all the blood, and everything else, looked just the same. Vacuum was one hell of a preserver.

The dispassionate, logical part of Vivian's brain said: *Freeze-thaw cycles won't have as much impact on a corpse once all the water has boiled away.*

They'd taken his liquid-cooled garment as well. Stripped off the backpack, removed the helmet and gloves, and the LCG, and so there he was in his goddamned skivvies. They'd at least arranged the limbs so that his body was straight, and partially scattered regolith over him. Was it this world's most half-hearted burial attempt? Or just to make it less obvious to the US orbiting surveillance?

It made a harsh kind of sense. Why take a corpse with them? Why add the weight to their load, and then just have it to deal with when they got home?

At least she had now resolved the mystery of where the cryptonauts had got the NASA suit she'd seen aboard the flyer at the South Pole. A new helmet, and it had been good to go.

"Peter, Kevin, José …. It's frankly kind of macabre. They took his suit but not, well, him. His underwear hasn't been bleached by the Sun yet. He looks just as if …. Ah, shit." She had to turn away.

"Vivian?" Terri's voice, worried.

"Sorry. I'm okay. Well, I'm not okay, but I'm functional. Just give me a minute."

Terri had known him too, of course. She had copiloted for Gerry Lin when he'd taken her LM up for a training run at Hadley. But that likely wasn't the same as augering in with a guy and then needing to manhandle his shattered corpse around the cabin. And it wasn't the same as serving with him for years, either.

The MOLAB trundled up beside her, came to a halt. She peered up at its front window, but couldn't see anything through its reflective coating, of course. "So. What do you want to do? Want to take him back?" she asked.

Neither NASA nor the USAF took dead bodies back to Earth. That protocol was already established. Die on the Moon, stay on the Moon. Vivian was asking whether they wanted to take Gerry's body back to Night Corps Vaporum Base, and inter it properly there, with honors.

Or even Zvezda-Copernicus? Back to where the people who'd killed him had been based. Vivian didn't say that part out loud.

"The scientists would want us to," Terri said eventually. "Examine the damage to his … to him, from lunar exposure, or some shit."

"Yeah, well, they can find someone else for that," Pope said, perhaps a little too forcefully.

"Copy," Vivian said. "The scientists aren't in charge here. This is up to us. To Peter."

"I was … just saying." Terri's voice was very quiet.

"I know," Sandoval said. "It's okay. But screw that. We're burying him here where he died, once we've done a full forensic sweep around him. Vivian, trade places. We're coming out. Pope, we'll need the pick-axes, probably the drill."

"I can help, guys." Vivian said.

"Vivian …"

"Let me." Pope took over. She could imagine his hand on Peter's arm. "Vivian, we were Gerry's crew. We worked together as a unit for years. Went through a lot of stuff together, the bad and the good. We need to be the ones to take care of him, okay?"

She paused. "Of course, man … Obviously. Sorry."

"Not to minimize what you went through with him … and we appreciate the offer. But you get it, right?"

Vivian blinked away her emotions. "Understood."

Doyle cleared his throat. "Uh, sorry guys. But … forensics?"

"Sure. Knock yourself out."

The men came out. Vivian went in.


As Sandoval, Pope, and Rodriguez dug into the lunar soil, and Doyle began his lone sweep of the perimeter, Vivian checked the instrument board out of habit and then looked up at the sky out of the cab window. *Jeez.*

She looked behind her. "Hey, uh, Brock?"

Terri didn't look up. "Yeah?"

Was Terri crying? It was unclear. She certainly wasn't happy. Vivian cleared her throat. "Frankly? Not to be a big wuss, but I could use a hug around now, if you'd be okay with that?"

"Copy." Terri got up briskly, came over without meeting her eye, scooped her up. *Wow. Brock is strong.* "To tell the truth, I was kinda feeling the same."

Twenty minutes later the airlock cycled, and Sandoval came in. He looked at the women now sitting quietly in the cab, arms around each other, dry-eyed but somber and each of them staring into her own space, then took his helmet off and moved back into the main cabin to give them privacy and get out of his suit by himself.

# CHAPTER 22

Vaporum Base: Vivian Carter
March 6–12, 1983

BY the time they got back to the Bunker, it looked substantially different. The Night Corps crew had levelled it and attached two inflatable extension areas and tidied it up considerably. A radar dish now sat on top of the Bunker, constantly scanning the sky, and a rocket launcher stood at each end protected by shielding. A hundred yards away sat a cube that was presumably some kind of radioisotope power system, covered with regolith weave, and the area was crisscrossed with boot prints and tire tracks from lunar dirt bikes, two of which Vivian could see parked on either side of the airlock while an astronaut patrolled out to the east on a third. It was quite the transformation, considering the short time they'd been out on the road.

"Home sweet home," Vivian said. By now, she was beginning to lose count of how many lunar bases she'd been on, and for how long in total. Someday, she'd do the math.

But Pope was frowning. "We're less than forty-eight hours from lunar night. They should have already piled soil up against the walls and have the roof insulation ready to go."

Sandoval's expression was grim. "Vivian, Rod: can you put the MOLAB to bed and bring in all our crap, while the rest of us go kick some ass?"

The interior space had been revamped too, with equipment and supplies organized and packed away in blocks. It was a ruthlessly efficient use of space, and needed to be, considering the Bunker needed to house twenty-two people through a lunar night in a total volume not a great deal larger than a small single-person apartment. Considering the limited space, and that some of this work must have been done with the living space depressurized and everyone suited up, Vivian thought the troops had done well. But Sandoval was clearly in a mood and had everyone jumping for the next nine hours.

At the end of which he came to knock on the "door" of Vivian's microscopic cubicle in the Brick.

The Vaporum troops each had their own makeshift personal spaces by now, but they were even smaller than the Pod, or the sleep spaces in US-Copernicus. When Vivian put her bunk down, as a test, it filled the whole cubicle aside from a two-foot square area of floor by the door. Once the bunk was stowed, the only furniture was a fold-down chair and tiny desk area. The walls were thin and plasticky, and the bathroom facilities were shared, but it was still better than sharing a dorm with a bunch of stinky guys she didn't know.

"Captain Carter."

Noting his dour expression, Vivian stood immediately. "Yes, sir?"

That earned her a grin. "At ease, Captain." He glanced at her desk curiously as she slid a piece of paper on top of the one she'd been writing on. "What are you doing?"

"Reading about lunar surface albedos and trying to make sense of my Schröter measurements." Which she'd been doing for all of ten minutes and would likely only do for another ten before sleep claimed her. Apparently, Peter's crews couldn't expect a whole lot of downtime. "So, what's up?"

"I've been informed that you're to have a physical."

"A what?"

"While we were away in Vaporum a message came in from NASA through channels. It's clear they've got some kind of stick up their

292

asses that we took you away from them at such short notice. And they want my medic to give you a complete check-up, run your blood work, and take a look at your shoulder and ribs. They wanted a full report by six hours ago, but they'll get it when they get it."

This was alarming. "Why? Some problem I should know about?"

"None that was relayed to me."

Vivian shrugged, tried to act casual. "Okay. I guess it's nice they care."

Peter eyed her critically. "When you did that, one of your shoulders went higher than the other. Aren't you supposed to have been doing physical therapy this whole time?"

"Uh, probably. But in the MOLAB, and now in here ..."

"God, Vivian. Okay, stay here. I'll send our medic in to see you, and we'll get this done." And he left about as abruptly as he'd arrived.

Vivian shook her head. A full physical, right at the end of a busy day on the Moon? That sounded *awesome*.


Lunar night came to Night Corps Vaporum Base with its customary suddenness. The base had been ready for it long before time and would have been even without Sandoval barking at everyone, but maybe it made him feel better.

Another lunar night Vivian hadn't expected to see .... *Whatever. I guess at this point I should just stop expecting anything at all.*

Despite Sandoval's concern, the Night Corps medic had been impressed with the strength and range of motion of Vivian's healing shoulder. He'd also given her a much more thorough physical than she'd expected. He'd taken a urine sample as well as the blood draw, given her an EKG, tested her vision and hearing, and checked out her lungs, reflexes, and many other aspects of her health. He'd even looked at her teeth. Vivian had protested, mostly through weariness, at which point he'd shown her his written orders from NASA and Cheyenne and offered to fetch Sandoval. Vivian had acquiesced. It was good to know whether she had a clean bill of health, right? Though, even if those tests found something, Vivian likely wasn't going anywhere in a hurry.

Perhaps it should have freaked her out more, that the crew of Night Corps Vaporum had no way of getting off the Moon in an emergency. Except that Vivian had had no way of getting off the Moon during her hike from Vaporum to Hadley, and no easy way of leaving the surface during her circumpolar journey.

In fact, now Vivian came to think of it, she'd spent more time stuck on the Moon with no way off it than she'd spent with a launch capability nearby. It was an interesting thought.

Also interesting: the Brick required much less lunar-night maintenance than any NASA site. Its Night Corps crew spent much of their time doing lab work on the forensic materials they'd collected at Rimae Bode II, Vaporum Base, and the LM crash site, and freely allowed Vivian and Terri to use the same gear to analyze their own rock samples from Bode and Schröter. A lot of the rest of the time they spent exercising, doing outside drills in exosuits, and generally training.

Meanwhile, Vivian spent her spare time reading, doing even more physical therapy, and talking to Terri Brock. They had a half-assed idea of writing a book together once they got back to Earth. The first US woman on the Moon, plus the first mission commander, along with the first circumnavigation? They wouldn't be able to publish it until Vivian left NASA, whenever that might be, because of ethics rules. And neither of them would have the energy to do it separately, but together … maybe? Could be fun.

And then, four days into lunar night, NASA reached out for Vivian again.


"Hello, this is Vivian Carter, reporting in from an undisclosed location on or near the lunar surface. What's up?" She'd been firmly instructed by Sandoval to say it that way, though anyone with a clue could see she wasn't weightless.

Vivian peered at the screen, which was small. She was back in the Night Corps MOLAB, by herself this time. Once again, Peter Sandoval had been ticked: NASA had demanded to speak to Captain Vivian Carter, today, no excuses, and in strict privacy. A direct feed, no monitoring, and we really mean it. *We need to talk to our astronaut, right now.* And Cheyenne Mission Control had pushed the request right on through.

Vivian was peeved again too because she'd been working all day, and this was the beginning of her rest period. And by now she was getting freaked out. What the hell did NASA want? Was she sick? And if so, why hadn't the Night Corps medic told her that right away?

The blue placeholder test card on the display went away, and all of a sudden Vivian found herself face-to-face with the NASA Administrator.

*Okay. That was unexpected.*

James Beggs was a kind-faced and quite attractive man with salt-and-pepper hair, perhaps approaching sixty years old, but still fit and lean. He'd been Navy too, Vivian recalled, shortly after the war. Following that he'd gone to Harvard Business School, then worked for General Dynamics and Westinghouse, among others. He was likely a really smart guy, so maybe Vivian should get her act together.

She sat up straighter. "Good evening, sir." Then she checked the clock and subtracted for Washington, DC time. "Morning. Good morning, sir."

"Good morning, Captain Carter."

"What can I do for you, sir?"

Beggs half-grinned. "Well, that's an even bigger question than you know."

The view changed to a different camera with a wider view. It was the Administrator's office in downtown Washington DC. Vivian had been in it twice. It was nice.

Sitting with Beggs were John Young, head of the Astronaut Office, and ... Dave Horn.

*Whoa. What?*

"We have been assured that this is a private conversation, and that Night Corps is not monitoring it. Can you confirm?"

The Moon-Earth-Moon time delay was useful because it gave Vivian a couple of extra moments to compose herself.

"I'm afraid I can't. I mean ... this isn't my radio gear. Night Corps owns this whole facility. I have no way of telling whether this is a secure line. I'm inclined to trust Colonel Sandoval's word, and his inclination to obey orders, but I can make no assurances." She shrugged. She was confident that both her shoulders were level that time.

"I suppose that will have to do. How are you, Captain Carter?"

"I was about to ask you the same, sir. But as far as I know, I'm fine and healthy, and suffering no ill effects from any recent activity." And since she didn't see a doctor in Beggs's office, maybe that was a good sign.

"Your recent physical confirms that."

Vivian blinked. "So, there's nothing wrong with me?"

"No." Beggs glanced back at John Young as if to say *I told you so.* "You're in good health, your numbers are fine across the board. I'm sorry if we gave you cause for concern. That was not our intention."

"Good to know, sir."

"There's no need to keep calling me 'Sir.' May I call you Vivian?"

"Yes, of course."

"Vivian, we'd like to bring you up to speed on a major project that NASA has been pursuing quietly and offer you the opportunity to participate in it."

The cogs in Vivian's brain started spinning. "Oh?" She glanced at Horn. "Does this have anything to do with the L5 Project, by any chance?"

"Tangentially." Beggs nodded to Young, who took up the tale. "The L5 Project provides a useful cover story, and the location is a good place to prepare, away from prying eyes."

Vivian pursed her lips. Dave Horn leaned in. "At this point, you'll want to reassure Captain Carter that this is not a military operation."

Young nodded. "Correct. Not military."

If not military, then …? What were the other big-ticket items on Apollo Applications?

Light dawned. Vivian's jaw dropped. "You're kidding … sirs."

Young studied her expression. "What's your guess, Vivian?"

"You're asking me to speculate?"

Young met her eye, from a quarter million miles away. "Sure. Why not?"

There really weren't that many "major projects" in the Apollo Applications program beyond cislunar space. And if it wasn't L5 …

Vivian took a deep breath. "You're preparing a craft for Venus flyby?"

Maybe Young grinned. Or maybe not. His eyes crinkled, anyway. "You're close."

"Okay, then maybe … Mars flyby? Dynamically Venus makes more sense—it would be a shorter mission, right? But I have no clue where we stand for launch windows to either planet. I'm willing to be educated on that point." *In other words, sirs, just freaking tell me.*

"You're sort of half right," Young said.

"Better than my usual odds."

"Which half?" said Dave Horn, ironically.

*Oh, holy shit.*

Vivian waited.

Young left it a couple more seconds, enjoying her suspense, and then said: "It's both."

*"Both?"*

"Venus flyby. Slingshot around it, take the gravitational assist to get to Mars. Fly by Mars, and then back home." Beside him Horn nodded, adding: "Manned. Naturally. Crew of eight."

*Naturally.* Vivian choked back the saltier words that had almost escaped her lips, and instead came out with: "Holy cow."

A Venus flyby had been one of the stated long-range goals of the Apollo Applications Program from the very beginning. But it had seemed like a wild dream, so far down the road that it was almost hypothetical. Go to *Venus*, using Apollo technology?

And then add in Mars? *Sure, why the hell not?*

These guys either had more powerful imaginations than Vivian, or a shakier grasp on reality.

Worth noting: Vivian's circumnavigation of the Moon would have seemed laughably ambitious just three years ago, and the Chief of the Astronaut Office and the NASA Administrator were hardly men to play practical jokes. And Dave Horn was one of the most pragmatic and careful orbital mechanics guys NASA had.

And they wanted to talk to *her*. And had pulled a lot of strings to set up this little chat.

"I'm listening. Tell me more."

Horn moved in closer to the camera. "This would obviously be an extended-duration mission with a challenging schedule. Even if we just do Venus, a typical duration for the outward leg is around a hundred and twenty-three days. Flip around Venus, and then it takes about two seventy-three days to return, for a total of just under four hundred days. For some launch opportunities we can shave a bit off that, but it would still be over a year in deep space."

Vivian had almost started giggling at "flip around Venus." A classic piece of Dave Horn understatement. "Okay." She was absorbing, thinking, calculating.

"The exact numbers depend on the departure date, effectiveness of the course corrections, and all that. If everything is going fine on the Venus approach, and nothing is contraindicated, we adjust the trajectory and use the slingshot effect to take us on to Mars. We pick up quite the turn of speed at Venus, so the round trip, Earth-Venus-Mars-Earth, comes out to around five hundred eighty days."

"Five hundred and eighty." Vivian whistled. "Hoo, boy."

"Over a year and a half," he added.

Well, yes. Vivian could do that math. "And this is what you've been working on the whole time, while pretending it was just about L5?"

"L5 is a serious project in its own right. That'll continue, and I've been working that too. But, yes, I've known about this since soon after we came back from Apollo 32."

This whole conversation seemed unreal. "Right. So how close to Venus and Mars will this mission get? Close enough to make all this worthwhile, I assume?"

Horn nodded. "A minimum altitude of three hundred kilometers, for Venus. Probably two hundred, for Mars, which has a less dense atmosphere."

"Impressive." A couple hundred kilometers was *close*. Closer to the surface of Mars than low Earth orbit was to the Earth's surface.

That would be quite the view. Briefly. How briefly?

"How long would the craft be near Venus?"

"During the course of an hour, the ship would pass within three Venus radii, do its closest approach, almost skimming the cloud-tops—that's a slight exaggeration—and be out to three Venus radii again. Mars, same-ish. So that'll be a very busy hour, in each case."

It was brain-spinning. Vivian barely knew how to respond.

"If that doesn't sound like a lot, here's two more ways of looking at it: we'll spend four hours in total inside eight Venus radii. And thirty hours in total, closer to Venus than the Moon is to the Earth." Horn waggled his hand. "Very roughly. Lots of variables in there."

Beggs nodded crisply. "We need to be close enough to take good pictures and do good science, while going fast enough not to get caught. We just need to stay above enough of the atmosphere that we don't suffer braking and negate all the fun gravitational slingshot stuff that we need."

She wasn't fooled by the royal *we*. Beggs himself would hardly be going on this trip.

But Vivian might. Right? Why else would they be talking to her?

She held up a finger, grabbed a water bottle, chugged and swallowed. "Do I understand you correctly, gentlemen?"

"By now, I'd hope so," Young said dryly. "You're under consideration to command the mission."

A startling excitement gripped her. Vivian had the sudden urge to run and jump and smash things with ferocious joy. It was like nothing she'd felt since getting her Apollo 32 flight assignment. A deep throat-catching, stomach-churning feeling, with an undercurrent of fear, because anything this thrilling would absolutely be as dangerous as hell.

She tried to visualize the solar system from above. The Earth and Moon rotating around their common center of gravity, in their mutual orbit around the Sun. And then Venus and Mars in their own orbits, inside and outside the Earth's orbit. And the distances involved in going from Earth, to Venus, to Mars, while all three planets rolled around the Sun. It would be an unfathomably long trip.

*Wow.*

Calm, logical Vivian took over again. She wondered how much her facial expression had changed over those last few seconds.

"I see. Thank you. I'm flattered by the offer. But how big a vehicle are we talking? Because Dave Horn might be just fine stuffed into a cabin the size of a Command Module for an indeterminate period, but that might be a bit much for a normal person. Or even me. Even for Venus."

Horn stifled a grin. "We can do a bit better than that."

"And did I hear you say *eight* people? Wasn't the original Bellcom Venus flyby study for a crew of three?"

Beggs looked impressed. "Good recall. Yes, that study was done in 1967, and allowed for a three-man—three-person—crew, in quite a restricted space. The concept has evolved since then. We'll be using an Apollo-Skylab configuration."

"A Skylab?"

"Yes"

"To Venus, and on to Mars?"

"A Skylab with some really big boosters attached," Horn said.

"Sure," Young said. "Why reinvent the wheel? We've spent years developing Skylabs, Apollo Command Modules, Geminis, and all. They're mature and reliable. Practically off the shelf by now. We have high confidence in the designs, and massive experience. The bugs are all ironed out."

"Mostly all," said Horn.

"And our experience with them lends confidence that we can achieve the mission."

"It's not just that," Beggs said. "The actual cost of the human space program is relatively minor once all the tech development has been done. We can continue to use Apollo-based technology for a small fraction of the development costs of starting something new. And for a new start, we'd need Congress to approve the money. This, we can do this with pocket change as part of the existing program."

"Pocket change." Vivian nodded back, tried a grin. "Nice."

"Relatively speaking."

After she'd gotten over her initial surprise, it all made sense. NASA could already throw Skylabs into lunar orbit, and the USAF could get MOLs there too. Getting the mass up and out of Earth's gravity was most of the battle, and after that, it got a lot simpler. After all, early in the Apollo program many of the depleted Saturn V third stages had just kept going past the Moon and into orbit around the Sun. Hell, if one of the early Gemini spacecraft had bounced off the Earth's atmosphere wrong when angling in for reentry, it would likely have ended up in orbit around the Sun too.

The trick was getting into the *right* orbit around the Sun. But if NASA could plan flybys of multiple giant planets for the two Voyager spacecraft currently making their way through the solar system, presumably the math of getting a Skylab to Venus and then looping past it to Mars was already well understood.

Presumably.

"Would you default to a free-return trajectory around Venus in case a problem occurred? Like we used to do for Apollo 8 and the other earlies? If the SPS, or whatever the engine is called for this sucker: if the main rocket motor doesn't fire up for whatever reason, you wouldn't want the craft to just keep going into the wild black yonder."

Young was already nodding. "Free return, yes, that's exactly the plan. And we'll try to set Mars up the same way. Once you're on the way, you'll need to do correction burns at various times, but for the planetary encounters we'll be aiming to give you a default trajectory that brings you back to the Earth's vicinity with little or no further delta-V."

*The Earth's vicinity.* Vivian noted the phrase. Well, that was better than *not the Earth's vicinity.*

She'd follow up on that later. *Vicinity* was good enough for now. If Dave Horn was in the mix, she could be sure that all of the orbital calculations and maneuvering math would be meticulously planned. Plenty of time later for her to get arms-deep into the equations and mission details herself.

Wouldn't there?

"Venus has limited launch windows, right? It's only available sometimes? I, uh, don't remember how this works, sorry. I never needed to know, until now."

"Correct. Because of the ratio of the Venus year to the Earth year, Venus launch windows recur about every nineteen months. But the math is different if your goal is to use Venus to get to Mars, and the launch opportunities are fewer and farther between."

"Sure. So which one would we be aiming for?"

"Next one up is in early July. If we miss that, the one after is in 1985. But we don't plan to miss it."

Her jaw dropped. *"This* July? This *actual July?* Less than *four* months from today?"

"That a problem?" Young asked ironically. "I heard you were a woman who didn't like to wait. Has trouble sitting still."

"Well, that's true, but, holy sh— Uh, hell's bells." Vivian was having to do a lot of euphemizing. But for Venus? Maybe it was appropriate. "So you already have the hardware ready to go?"

"The Skylab is already at L5. We're still finalizing some rocket motor decisions, but they're expected to follow shortly, and the stack will be assembled there."

Vivian found herself blinking rapidly. *The Skylab is already at L5.* That was quite the sentence, all by itself.

Vivian took a deep breath. "Gentlemen. I thank you for the honor, and for your faith in me. But ..." She stopped. *Why am I even questioning this? Just say yes!*

But she had to know, and she needed to be honest.

"I have to ask: why me? I've already had ... a lot. Apollo 32. LGS-1. And now I get another plum?" They just stared back at her. "There must be a dozen other astronauts experienced enough to lead this. And it's a quick turnaround. To make a July launch window I'd have to scramble,

301

big-time. You could have had someone training for this for the past two years. I'd only have four months to get my shit ready. Uh, forgive me: I mean, to do all the necessary study and sims to be prepared. So, seriously: why this approach?"

Beggs deferred to Young. "Your advantages should be clear. In fact, you need very little training. You have a deep spaceflight experience base that you can bring to bear on this right away. You're already current on all the necessary hardware, software, and procedures. You have intimate familiarity with Apollo and Skylab. You're one of a very small number of NASA astronauts who've piloted spacecraft solo, should that be needed, which we hope it won't be. You've already proved yourself in every one of the mission areas critical for Apollo Venus Astarte."

Young gestured to Dave Horn. These guys had a nice round-robin style going. Horn said: "You're used to extended missions. You have almost unparalleled EVA experience. Resourceful under pressure. Courage in a crisis."

"Stop," she said. "I'm blushing."

"Oh, I'm just getting started. Familiar with isolation—"

She shivered.

"Experienced in command. And—forgive me for raising personal issues—but …"

Horn looked uncomfortable, so Vivian helped him out. "I'm single with no family ball-and-chain, and gullible enough to say yes to something as nutty as this."

Beggs raised his eyebrows. Young stifled a grin.

"Independent, fancy-free, *and* usefully gullible." Horn nodded. "I'd say that sums it up. So, you're pretty much ready to go, right out of the box. The mission-specific stuff you don't already know, we can teach you quickly. The hardcore science, we have other people already trained up in that, and you'll have lots of cruise time to study up."

"Good grief."

"You're also good on camera," Beggs said. "Your ratings on your round-the-Moon jaunt were very respectable. We got a lot of letters. Public interest was higher than anything else NASA has done in space for a long time. You already have public name recognition, and something of a following."

"A what? Gosh."

He studied her face. "And despite your understandable trepidation, I note you haven't turned us down yet."

"Oh, I'm interested, you can count on that, but ... two—no, three—more questions, if I may?"

Beggs glanced at the clock but gestured her to continue.

"Today is the first time I'm hearing about all this. So you're keeping it very quiet?"

"Correct. You can't tell anyone about this. Nobody, aside from the people in this conversation, until we tell you different. No one else in the astronaut corps or outside it. And definitely no one currently on the lunar surface, or around it, of either nationality. We've been concerned about listening devices and espionage activities at US-Copernicus for some time. So, should you find yourself back there, this topic is off the table. And you can't discuss this with your current Night Corps colleagues, either."

That was almost funny. "Even Colonel Sandoval's clearance isn't high enough?"

"If 'need-to-know' is good enough for the USAF, it's good enough for NASA. And they jerk us around all the time. They deserve a bit of payback." Young paused. "Although, if you and Sandoval are ... still involved, I suppose we might need to consider an exception? If his opinion might affect your decision. But he would need to keep this strictly under wraps."

"Sandoval is extremely good at keeping secrets, but we're ... no longer romantically involved." Vivian took a breath. "There's no need to bring him in on this."

"Good." Beggs nodded, relieved.

*Huh. I really did just blow Peter Sandoval aside in a couple sentences, didn't I? I'm sure he'd be thrilled. Nice going, Vivian.*

Maybe he'd understand. One day. Vivian stole a breath. "Let's move on. So ... we're keeping this quiet to steal a march on the Soviets? We're going to betray the trust we've worked so hard to build by doing this behind their backs? Is that really such a great idea?"

Beggs smiled faintly. "Betray trust? Surely, it's not that bad."

"Or maybe it is."

"We're only required to collaborate on the Moon," Young said. "The Reds have their own independent missions as well. They're planning further Mars landers, for example."

303

"Sure. Unmanned landers, and doing so publicly."

"Who knows what aces they might have in the hole? We'd be naïve to think they're being open about everything. If they were, it would be the first time. And they're not required to be, we can each pursue our own projects in deep space, as long as there are no military implications."

Beggs nodded. "As soon as we launch, we'll tell them. Likely beforehand. We'll tell the whole world. The exact timing of the announcement hasn't been finalized yet. The President will want to have his say."

"I'm sure," Vivian said. "But here's the thing: the Soviets have caught on that we're planning something. They're well aware that the US is hatching some scheme behind the scenes again that they're not being briefed on. They've asked me about it directly on several occasions. Not telling them breeds distrust and suspicion, and just invites them to jump to the conclusion we have another covert military project underway, and—if I may speak freely—the President's rhetoric on Star Wars and space lasers and the Evil Empire and all isn't exactly helping anything."

Dave Horn raised a hand. "I'll take this one, if I may? Are we worried the Soviets would try to scoop us on this if they knew? You bet. We've been dueling with them on planetary exploration just as much as the lunar stuff. People just notice less because there are no human flights involved. Yet."

He glanced down at his notes. "The first unmanned Venus flyby was by a Soviet probe, Venera 1. It never got closer to the planet than about a quarter of the Earth-Moon distance, but that was pretty good for 1961. They crash-landed Venera 3 on its surface in '66 and sampled its atmosphere in '67. Venera 7 landed in December 1970 and survived on the surface for almost twenty minutes. Just about everything we know about Venus, its temperatures and pressures and atmospheric density profile, the clouds and high winds—most of that was discovered by the Soviets. And they don't announce their launches beforehand. There's every reason to assume they're planning to go back, maybe even during the same launch window we're aiming for."

"But the US has been to Venus too, right? Didn't we send some Mariners there, or something?"

"Three." Horn looked down again. "Mariners 2, 5, and 10 in the '60s and early '70s. But no landers, so far. We think we have the expertise, but it's not a slam dunk. Venus is hard.

"And Mars is even harder. The Reds sent a bunch of probes, had a bunch of fails, but managed the first successful orbiter and the first soft landing in 1971. They've sent Zond craft there, too. You know the interesting thing about the Zonds? They're damned similar to their Soyuzes and Progresses. They use the same spacecraft bus. It takes very little to convert one to carry humans, and we think that's the idea. The Soviets came *real* close to sending cosmonauts around the Moon in a Zond ahead of Apollo 8. That's why NASA changed the mission profile so late in the game and sent Borman, Lovell, and Anders on a Moon-orbit mission. That wasn't their original flight plan."

"Right ... but Dave, I've been inside a Soyuz, and not even the Soviets are going to send cosmonauts on trips of hundreds of days around Venus or Mars in something that small. Unless it's some kind of sadistic gulag punishment for political prisoners."

"No, but they might if they send something the size of a Salyut along with it, in the same kind of configuration as we're planning to use with Apollo Venus Astarte. A Soyuz-Salyut combination is similar in capabilities to an Apollo-Skylab combination."

"Do we have any evidence at all that the Soviets are planning to do that? Throw a Salyut around Venus?"

"No, nothing solid. Just as they have nothing solid on us. But no one wants to be reading in the newspapers this summer that a Soviet manned spacecraft is beginning a planetary trip, if the US has the opportunity to send one sooner."

Young chimed in. "They've been training people for it for years, don't think they haven't. In their appealingly named Soviet Institute for Biological and Medical Problems, they've been studying the problems of long-duration isolation since 1960. They did a year-long space-flight simulation there, where they put a crew of three guys into the same kind of living space as they might get on an interplanetary flight. And that was about fifteen years ago, from the end of '67 through the end of '68. Since then, they've had some very-long-duration Salyut crews around Earth, unsupplied for months at a time. They're going at this seriously on the tech and human side, and they're at about the point where they might actually be able to do it. So guess what: the US is going to make damned sure we get it done first."

"Okay." Vivian shifted her gaze back to Horn. "So who else would be on the crew?"

305

"We'll talk about that soon. I'm the only confirmed crew member, at present. We have a bunch of people in training, but we haven't made the final assignments. We needed to solidify the Commander selection before going any further. For a trip of this duration, in a confined living space, we need to take every care to ensure crew compatibility. You'll have options. I'm confident you'll like a number of them."

Vivian nodded. "No good flying by Venus if the crew have all throttled one another by the time we get there."

After a brief pause, Young started writing: "I'll add 'dark sense of humor' to the list of desirable attributes."

Beggs gestured upward at something off-camera. Likely a clock because Young nodded. "We'll have to draw this to a close now, the Administrator has a ten o'clock he needs to run to. Why don't you sleep on this, get with Dave later on—which will be tomorrow for you, early evening for him—and talk through the details we don't have time to get into here? He can run through the crew candidates with you then."

Vivian had forgotten she was supposed to be tired. "Okay, sure. Yes, sir."

"We'd like a decision soon. As soon as tomorrow, if you can."

"Um. Point of order. You should note that, right now, I'm stuck where I am. Physically, I mean. If this does work out, it may take a little effort to, uh, get me to wherever I need to go next."

"Understood." Young was still scribbling notes. "We'll work that as necessary, after we get your decision."

"And where would that be? Where do I need to get to?"

"L5," said Horn. "No point in taking you back to Earth prior to the mission. All the action will be in space. Easier to train in situ."

"Ah," she said. "Right."

"But lunar orbit would be a good start. We'll work this more later. This channel, seven o'clock tonight?"

Vivian checked her own clock. Nine hours from now. That was good, because it might take her a while to get to sleep.

"Roger that," she said. "And thank you."


"Colonel Sandoval, Vivian Carter."

"Please hold for Colonel Sandoval."

Peter had a receptionist now? Nice. Even if it was a guy with a very brusque military tone.

Sandoval came on ninety seconds later. "Vivian, Sawbones."

She paused. "You love that, don't you?"

"It's kind of a cool call sign. Piratical. So, what's happening?"

"Permission to sleep over, here in the MOLAB? It has enough pow-er, and a couple meal trays, and I need to be on another call with NASA soon after I wake up. May as well save time by staying put. In fact, why aren't we using the MOLAB as extra sleep space already?"

She could hear him thinking it over. "Good point. Vivian ... is everything okay? You're all right?"

"I'm fine. Clean bill of health."

"Good. Sooo ... what's the deal with NASA?"

"Nothing bad. I'm not being court martialed yet. We're just chat-ting about my future."

That earned her another pause. "You'll be staying with the Agency a while longer, then?"

*A while longer.* "Looks like that's in the cards."

"Okay. Houston or Kennedy? Or somewhere else?"

"TBD. It's complicated. And they want to keep it under their hats a bit longer, while we're still tossing ideas back and forth."

"Intriguing," he said, and when Vivian didn't respond, added: "Okay, sure. Permission granted. Enjoy the MOLAB."

She looked around her. "To be honest, it's a bit odd having one all to myself. I keep looking around for Feye or Bill." Or Katya. "Or you. But, you know, it's actually kind of nice."

"Roger that," he said. "Guess we'll see you tomorrow?"

"Guess you will." She paused. "Looking forward to it, Peter."

She could hear the smile in his voice. "Me too, Vivian. Vaporum, out."

He broke the connection, and Vivian immediately grabbed a yel-low pad and a Sharpie and started scribbling notes.

# CHAPTER 23

Vaporum Base: Vivian Carter
March 12, 1983

**VIVIAN** had done quite a bit of damage to that yellow pad by seven p.m., Houston time, when Dave Horn's face appeared again on the TV screen. "Hi, Viv. Sleep well?"

"What do you think? But I sure as hell have a lot of questions."

"Questions are good. I had a whole bunch myself."

"And they all got answered to your satisfaction?"

He spread his arms. "I'm here, aren't I?"

"Okay, first question. Under cover of the L5 thing, you've obviously been planning all this for some time. Years, rather than weeks or months. Who was originally on the hook to command it?"

"Me," he said.

"You?"

"I never *wanted* to command it, but I sure as hell want to go. And I'm picky about my commanders. I only want to work with the best. Luckily, they'd already decided that you were their top selection."

Vivian looked dubious. "Seriously?"

"Yep. God's truth. They just didn't want to distract you from LGS-1 and, to be frank, some of the less convinced were considering LGS a trial run. Manage a Moon circumnavigation, and you can likely manage a Venus flyby. If you'd screwed that pooch, we wouldn't be having this conversation. Turns out you didn't screw the pooch."

"Only by the grace of God," she said. "I could have died. Easily."

"But didn't. Either way, you're the one. So we were waiting till you finished LGS-1 safely. Then, after all that, you went and put yourself on the injured list after all." He shook his head. "Dumb. So then we had to hold off and see how *that* played out.

"Then, finally, it looked like you might be okay, and we had you manifested to come up to Eagle Station, where we could talk to you under secure conditions. Only for fricking Night Corps to steal you away to do whatever the heck it is you're doing now and throw our whole program into an uproar. My boss's boss had to talk to Sandoval's boss's boss to try to get some clue when we might get you back, and also make a hundred percent sure you were healthy enough to do what we needed you to do."

"Hence your sudden and annoyingly comprehensive medical exam. Which, by the way, made me worry something might be seriously wrong with me."

Horn nodded. "Sorry about that."

"So Starman knows nothing about Venus flyby?"

"Correct. He knows we're doing something special, but not what it is. Johnston at Daedalus is the only person currently on the lunar surface who knows a single thing about Apollo Venus Astarte."

"Catchy name."

"But Starman *does* know that NASA is incredibly pissed off with him about you getting injured. John Young is a good guy, but he can be damned biting when he's angry. I'm guessing Starman thinks his career's in the toilet, but John's calmed down a bit now. He—Starman—also knows NASA wanted you back urgently enough to override his own Apollo scheduling plans. And he knows the Night Corps folks were ordered to intercept you at Eagle for their own nefarious purposes and are jerking him around even harder, and that no one will tell him a goddamned thing."

Vivian nodded. That would explain some of Starman's anger, outbursts, and unpredictable mood changes. Wheels had been turning all around him, and everyone had been stonewalling his questions about them. All that, plus the stresses of running US-Copernicus in close confines with the Soviets … no wonder the guy was fried and all set to quit.

Horn studied her. "So. You want this, right?"

"I have more questions. You're still the backup commander?"

"Yes. Second-in-command, overall."

"And who else are you recommending for the crew?"

"How d'you feel about Josh Rawlings? I have him penciled in as Skylab captain. In the naval sense that you're the commander, but he's the one with the deep Skylab expertise?"

"Wow."

He looked at her, likely trying to decode her expression. "Okay?"

"Better than okay. So perfect I'm almost emotional."

Horn nodded. "Thought so. The only other one you know well is Marco Dardenas, also from Columbia Station."

"I don't know him quite as well, but what I do know is impressive. And presumably he gets the Josh Rawlings seal of approval?"

"He does. And those two guys have already worked their tails off on this for a year or more. Josh is already at L5, and Marco is at Houston kicking everyone's ass. Between the two of them, anything that breaks in a Skylab, those two can fix it—while complaining a lot. But in an entertaining way."

"Sounds great."

"We'll need to talk in much more detail about the other four. Those will be the solar physicist, two planetary scientists, and the mission doctor. I don't think you know any of the candidates personally, so we'll have to do a deep dive into their resumes, set up some calls."

"Are some of them women?"

"Yes. Several, in fact."

She nodded, satisfied. "Good."

"I do have strong recommendations, but I have almost a dozen people for you to consider. Crew selection for this one is extremely important. We need a strong science bench, but we also need everyone to get along. We're going to take all the time we need to get it right … as long as we're ready for a launch in four months."

Vivian shook her head. "You're a funny, funny man. So if we were to miss this launch window, the next shot would be 1985? I bet I know why it's key to go right now, and it's not just the fear that the Soviets will do it first."

Dave Horn grinned. "Reagan wants this launched and on its way during his presidency."

"Bingo. Politicians: so predictable."

"But it's not all just about the big boss. The longer NASA leaves it, the more chance our budget will get axed to the point where we can't do it at all."

"But if we hurry so much we kill ourselves, that's also not good."

"It only feels like a rush to you because you're the last to know," Horn said. "I mean, not to be a jerk, but I've been working, eating, and sleeping this mission night and day for over two years now, and so have a ton of other people."

"I know. And suddenly I'm going to leap in from nowhere and take charge of all that?"

"That's the plan."

"Dave. Be straight with me. Who's going to resent me, if I take this command? Are you?"

"Nope. Being commander isn't really my thing. I like flying. I don't like being the boss. I'm very happy for you to take responsibility for all the politicking and paperwork." He grinned.

"And the credit?"

Horn snorted. "I don't give two shits about *credit*. Never have. You know that."

"That's okay, I'll make sure you get it anyway."

"Which is one of ten reasons why you're a good commander. I'd much rather work under a good commander than have the stress of trying to be one myself."

Vivian thought about the changes in Starman since he became the US-Copernicus base commander and nodded. "All right. But back to my question. If I take this, who am I forcing out? I don't want to screw anyone else over, just because Beggs and Young and whoever else have now decided I'm their public face for this because I bring them good TV viewing figures or some crap."

Now, Horn looked uncomfortable.

"Dave. Spit it out."

"No one."

"What? Don't shit me, man."

"Well, not exactly no one. But no one with your experience at the command level. Seriously. Not for this gig."

311

He seemed sincere. She shook her head. "Come on, keep talking. Tell me all of it."

"Including the final in-flight checkouts prior to launch, this is a two-year commitment. Two years is a *long time*, Vivian. Most folks aren't prepared to put their lives on hold for two years, just to fly around a planet or two they can't possibly land on, and then come home. It's a looong way to go for two quick and intense flybys."

"What about you?"

"I want to see Venus, close up, with these eyes. And Mars. And I want to work on the gnarly math to get us there and do all the nifty engine fires and course corrections." He grinned. "I'm not 'most folks.'"

Vivian nodded. "And that's a fact. Okay, what are the technical unknowns? I assume we have all the flight dynamics and orbital mechanics for this already finalized."

"Long, long ago. I started working on them soon after we came back from Apollo 32, and other people had already been working it for a while by then. All the trajectory and burn options, everything, figured out to a T. There are books and books and books of tables and figures I can talk you through."

"Sure. Later. We're really talking about a standard Skylab?"

"Sleep quarters are twice the size and there are two hygiene cubicles, for redundancy. Lots of extra storage space. Freezers for food. Some extra windows, one of them large-format. And a literal ton of instrumentation and experiments. Other than that, you'll float aboard and feel right at home."

"Piloting?"

"Two Command and Service Modules attached to the side. Identical, again for redundancy. They also serve as survival pods in case of contingency."

"Eight people in two Command Modules, for however long? Hope we're never facing *that* kind of contingency."

"Well, me too."

"Propulsion systems?"

"The CSMs have their own, of course." He fell silent for a moment. "But for the main engine: how do you feel about nuclear propulsion?"

Vivian rocked back. *Shit.* For some reason, that possibility hadn't crossed her mind.

She knew well enough that NASA now had a Nuclear Assembly Building (NAB) at Kennedy Space Center, in addition to the usual Vehicle Assembly Building. Nuclear launches went off from a pad well away from Pads 39A through 39D where the conventionally powered Apollos were launched from. But she'd thought the efforts were still in their infancy, and largely intended for unmanned interplanetary missions.

"Vivian?"

"Just mentally processing. We're using a nuclear rocket?"

"Maybe," said Horn.

"Dave. It's nuclear, or it isn't."

"Both are possible. Both will work. We haven't made the final choice between nuclear and conventional yet. Really."

"Four months to go, and you haven't *decided*?"

"We're pursuing parallel development. The NERVA engine has been extensively tested in cislunar space and it's doing quite well." NERVA: the Nuclear Engine for Rocket Vehicle Application, a nuclear thermal rocket designed to replace the conventional third stage. "Tests are ongoing. We have two candidate flyby engines getting a workout right now. One's doing loops around the lunar L2 point in some weird halo orbit. The other's at L5."

"Just so's they're a long way away from me."

"Vivian, they aren't bombs, they're just thermal engines that use nuclear reactions instead of chemical reactions. In principle we can get twice the amount of power out of a NERVA third stage."

"Okay. But didn't I just hear you say, 'both are possible?'"

"Yes. The mission will work either way. We don't *need* nuclear power to get to the planets, if we don't have to launch from the bottom of the Earth's gravitational well. The delta-V requirement is really very modest, once we're already out of Earth orbit and at L5 ... and if everything goes nominally. But if we get into trouble and need a lot of push for a serious trajectory adjust, the nuclear stage would be a much better way to get it."

"Okay." She studied his face. "But?"

"So that's the plus side for nuclear. On the other side, I'm not yet convinced we have enough in-flight experience with the NERVAs. Every other component is tried-and-true, long heritage, lots of experience. I'm letting the engine boys do a few more tests and hoping the answer becomes obvious. We already have a conventional third-stage engine in lunar orbit, ready to be pushed out to L5 if we need it. We can bolt either onto the ship with a few days' notice, and then we just switch out one set of tables and PADs for another. It's not like building a stack in the Vehicle Assembly Building back at Kennedy."

Vivian shook her head. "All the procedures and protocols would be the same? Even the switches on the racks?"

"Well, no. But nothing we can't handle. This is a long trip, remember. It's not like Apollo, where we're always finalizing everything just in time. On Astarte we'll generally have *weeks* of lead time before we have to do any particular burn or correction. More prep time than we could possibly need."

"Planning the mission while we're flying it?"

"I wouldn't put it quite like that. But yes."

"Okay. But if you had to decide today, which way would you go?"

"If we were leaving tomorrow, I'd say chemical. For nuclear, they're *really* going to need to talk me into it."

Vivian thought about that for a moment. "No."

"No to which?"

"No, because I doubt a couple months more is going to increase your confidence to that extent, and having to worry about it will just waste time and energy we could be spending on more important things. If we put our foot down right now and declare we're going with conventional, would that resolve it? Or would we still end up in all the same meetings having all the same conversations, trying to persuade people?"

That earned her a grin. "I'd want to socialize it a bit, not make it an ultimatum. Let me talk to the powers that be, quietly. Figure out a way to let the nuclear engineers down easy, and not make enemies. Never know when we might need them."

"I surely don't need any more enemies." She leaned forward. "Dave, this goes for other areas, too. Let's just nail down all the easy variables right now, to free up our heads for the rest of it. We don't need the most cutting-edge answers. Cutting-edge might well be the death of us. We need reliable tech we can trust, with the least effort. July will be here before we know it. Let's limit the number of things we fret about."

"Sure, but … Vivian, you're acting like we're the ones who have the power here."

"Because we *do*. We're the ones they want to man—or woman— this, with the relevant experience. If NASA wants a Venus launch this summer, for the love of God, and with no messing? It's you and me, or it's nobody. We put a good well-thought-out plan in front of them, and they'll take it." Vivian shrugged. "Or, if I'm wrong and they have a B-team ready to step in, then Godspeed to them. But if you and I are going to do this, we do it our way or we don't do it at all."

"Okay. Roger that." He paused. "Sure sounds to me like you've made your decision."

Vivian hesitated and gut-checked herself. Took a big breath and blew it all out.

Horn grinned. "A week or so ago you wanted to go home. Back to Earth. Back to normal."

"Times change."

"That's it? Times change?"

Dave Horn was about the most careful and competent pilot Vivian had ever flown with, and he was a genius at orbital mechanics. Even putting that aside, Vivian respected his opinion immensely, and his confidence—plus his direct experience peering into the guts of this project and fixing anything he didn't like the look of—went a long way toward persuading her.

"I'm in," she said, triggering a heady dose of adrenaline.

"Good."

A long pause, and they both laughed. "So, that's that, then?"

"Dave," she said, "I'll only tell you this once, but: despite how exciting this is, you are the only person I'd do it with. I wouldn't have the nerve to fly across the fricking solar system with anyone else."

"Now *I'm* blushing."

"You should be. Now, forget I said that. I'm guessing I have a steep learning curve to sprint up, if I'm to do this thing."

"Yeah. But you're Vivian Carter. And, more important: you have me to help you, and I'm awesome. So I don't really think you have much to worry about."

"Easy for you to say."

"It really is. I can send you all the reading material you want, if you have a way to print it out securely."

A facetious thought crossed her mind. Vivian's assignation to command a trip to Venus and Mars would solidify Svetlana's opinion that Vivian yielded one hell of an influence on the US space program.

If it ever came up, Vivian would likely skip telling her that no one else with anywhere close to Vivian's level of experience actually *wanted* the gig.

"How soon can you get away from Night Corps?"

"Unknown. That'll take some interagency diplomacy high above our heads, But, frankly, we're just sitting around at the moment."

"Where?"

She grinned. "Nice try. I can't say. So, now I've agreed, Dave, tell me honestly: is this Apollo Venus Astarte scheme safe, or is it insane?"

Horn considered. "I can only pick one?"

"Eight people. Six hundred days. Traveling more tens of millions of miles than I know how to add up right now. And being *really* far from Earth."

"It's challenging," he said. "But we can pull it off. We really can."

She glanced down at her notepad again. "So. How about we bring Ellis in on this?"

"Ellis? He's never going to leave his family for two years for a harebrained adventure like this."

"No, he sure isn't. But I trust his opinion, and he's a demon planner. We need him on ground support. Math, logistics, safety. Especially safety. Sell it this way: you, me, and Ellis have a proven track record of success at Hadley and Marius, and Ellis and I have a proven track record with LGS-1 in addition. It's a no-brainer."

He nodded. "Okay. I'll run that by John."

"And Dave, seriously? If we're going to do this, then you have to use headphones for all that Elvis Presley shit you play, or I'm pushing you out the goddamned airlock."

"Oh, I've moved on now. What do you think of Aerosmith?"

"Oh, dear God."

"Paul McCartney?"

"Tell you what, you go to Venus, and I'll go to Mars."

"You don't even like Paul McCartney and Wings?" Horn shook his head. "Okay, fine, what are *you* listening to?"

"Duran Duran. Flock of Seagulls. Blondie. And David Bowie."

He shuddered. "Okay. Headphones for both of us, then. Adding it to the inventory list." Horn looked at his watch, started pushing buttons. "Okay, let's bring the Houston folks into the loop for the crew conversation."

"Right now?"

He paused. "Sorry, you have other plans?"

She glanced out of the MOLAB window at the Earth-lit lunar surface, and the faint lights of Night Corps Vaporum. "Not exactly."

"Because the sooner we can finalize the crew, the better."

"I get that." Vivian ran her fingers through her hair. "Okay, may as well, I guess. No time like the present. Can you give me half an hour to freshen up and let, uh, my local teammates know I'm still alive?"

"How about fifteen minutes? Because they're waiting for my call."

"Twenty," Vivian said. "And that's my final offer."

Horn nodded. "This mission is going to go *great*, isn't it?"

"Hey, you knew what you were getting when you asked me. I'll be back with you soon."

And then, with three loud blips, a second screen lit up to Vivian's right, and Terri Brock's face appeared on it. "Vivian? Sorry to intrude, but you're needed in here. Matter of urgency."

On the first screen, Horn's eyebrows raised. "Is that Terri's voice?"

"Dave? Hi there," Brock said. "And bye there. Sorry, but we need our astronaut, right now."

"*Your* astronaut?"

"Now, Carter. Boss's orders."

Were they under attack? Vivian glanced out the window, saw nothing. If they were, surely Terri would have said that straight away. "Uh, Dave? I'll have to call you back."

"Vivian …"

"Sorry." Vivian hit the button, swiveled to the other screen. "Horn's gone, can't hear you anymore. We're alone. What's up?"

"We've found the cryptonaut base."

"You're kidding." Vivian rocked back. "Shit. Wow. Eureka."

"Immediate conference." Terri paused, pursed her lips. "And, Vivian, brace yourself because you're really, *really* not going to like it."

317

# PART FOUR: STRIKE FORCE

March 1983

# CHAPTER 24

Vaporum Base: Vivian Carter
March 13, 1983

"THE Marius Hills." Back in the Bunker, still in her spacesuit but minus the helmet and gloves, Vivian leaned forward and sank her head into her hands. "For God's sake. Of all the places on the entire Moon the bastards could have chosen, they *had* to pick Marius?"

"Sorry, Vivian." Brock sat down next to her. Pope and Rodriguez sat nearby, eyes downcast. "Peter's on the horn with Cheyenne. He'll be out in a bit."

"Okay." Vivian looked around them all: Brock, Pope, Rodriguez. "You've been fully briefed already? We're quite sure about this?"

"We are," Rodriguez said. "And, ironically, it was a photograph you took on Apollo 32 that helped to blow their cover."

Vivian frowned. "How's that?"

"Remember this, by any chance?" Rodriguez took a picture out of a folder and passed it across. It was a Hasselblad photo taken on the lunar surface, showing two volcanic domes on the right, and the beginnings of a long ridge reaching off to the left of the frame. Lunar Rover tracks and boot prints were evident in the foreground. One of their standard record shots.

"Sort of," she said. "I mean, not this picture specifically—we took hundreds—but I know the area. Our EVA-3, or perhaps EVA-4.

Anyway, it was one of the two days Ellis and I drove up onto that ridgetop to peer down into the lava tube skylight and take detailed measurements. Those were long days. Exciting, though. What about it?"

Rodriguez handed her another photograph. "Compare and contrast."

A much larger format photo, obviously taken by a DORIAN camera from high orbit, looking across the lunar terrain at an oblique angle, and covering a more extensive area of the Marius Hills. "Uh. Okay." She held them side by side, trying to figure it out. It wasn't easy.

Pope slid in on Vivian's other side. "Those two domes on your picture are these two."

"Well, yes, because the ridge is .... Wait. Is that ...?" She just stopped, looked at Pope.

He grinned at her reaction. "It is."

The steep slope of the rising ridge that appeared gray-smooth on Vivian's picture was much darker on the DORIAN picture, and the pattern of the darkness appeared roughly circular. Vivian looked more closely, peering at the craters and the domes to figure out the Sun angle. "No, come on, that could be anything. They're taken at completely different times of day. Early lunar morning for mine, and this one is mid-to-late lunar afternoon with the Sun coming from partly behind the ridge. Most likely it's a trick of the lighting. And if it's not that, there could have been a rockslide in the meantime exposing material of lower albedo. The contrast is cranked on the MOL image."

"Or," Pope said, "it could be the egress point from a lava tube. A circular hole, knocked out long after you left."

"It could be, but it isn't," Vivian argued. "We're seriously thinking the cryptonauts broke through the end of a lava tube and then concealed it with an overhang so that it couldn't be seen from above, but the DORIAN happened to catch it from the side? What are the odds the lava tube even goes that near the surface? Most don't. Anyone want to place a bet on this?"

"Keep your money," Rodriguez said. "There's more."

He reached into the folder for more pictures. "Look at that."

Vivian shook her head. It was just a high-resolution image of what looked like a random spot on the surface. "Regolith? I don't see anything. What am I supposed to be noticing?"

"This was taken from right above the proposed cryptonaut location. It's the area at the foot of the ridge, the one spot they'd need to drive in and out over, repeatedly—their maximum traffic area, at the maximum imaging resolution the DORIAN is capable of."

"And I still don't see anything."

"Because there's nothing there," said Terri. "Very few areas of the Moon this size have so little in the way of features. It's literally a blank slate, right? See the larger rocks and divots at the edge of the area? When was the last time you saw an area of the Moon a hundred feet square with so few craters, rocks, boulders, cracks, whatever?"

"All the time."

"Not statistically, and not at the foot of a scree. This area has been regulated and reordered several times by their track-removal system."

Vivian glanced between them. "Guys, you're all awesome and I respect the heck out of you. But, for real: your clinching evidence is literally the *lack* of evidence? A nice clean patch of lunar surface?"

Rodriguez leaned back. "I've spent a ton of time looking at all this. This kind of forensics is my thing. It may look circumstantial, but I'm convinced. And I believe we'll prove it beyond doubt, very soon."

"How?"

Rodriguez grinned. "Soon."

She shook her head. "Man, I hate you Night Corps people."

"Yeah, you really don't."

Vivian leaned forward, thinking it through. "So, if this pans out, and the cryptobastards really are located at the Marius Hills, does that fit in with everything else we know?"

Pope looked at her sideways. "Like what?"

"Well, it's a long way, for a start."

"From where?"

She stood up, stretched out her back and neck. She was carrying a lot of tension there. *Go figure.* "Marius and Zvezda are about five hundred fifty miles apart. At twenty miles per hour that's a twenty-eight-hour trip, nonstop. But that's a fast MOLAB-level average speed. We've been guessing their original ground crawler is heavier and slower, taking them longer to get anywhere. Eight miles an hour might be a reasonable pace, if they're cleaning up their tracks as they go. So if they drive around the clock, Marius to Zvezda, five hundred sixty-nine miles, eight miles an hour is … seven eights are fifty-six, so about seventy-one hours."

"Under three days," said Terri.

"That's still a lot, if you're regularly commuting in and out to steal things. Does that work with the timings of the thefts at Copernicus?"

"We don't know those timings all that well," Pope said. "And anyway, an agent at Copernicus might be collecting stuff for them and leaving it out for them to pick up."

"You mean someone at Zvezda?" said Terri.

"Maybe," Pope said. "One or the other. We can't rule anything out."

Vivian frowned. "Given the timings of their attacks on us, they'd have to be doing a lot of their driving at night."

"Must be hell driving for that long wearing night-vision goggles," said Rodriguez. "Because they obviously can't use headlights. But that's what they must be doing."

"And popping a lot of aspirin," Vivian said.

"Or the Soviet equivalent."

She sat again, started scribbling on a pad. "And then, Marius to the South Pole? About eighteen hundred miles. Ninety hours at twenty miles an hour. Two hundred twenty-five hours at eight miles an hour. Which is just over *nine days* and driving around the clock. So it might have taken them as long as eighteen days there and back, to come hit us at the South Pole."

"Maybe," Pope said.

She looked up. "Okay, what's the 'Maybe' this time?"

"Maybe the vehicle and crew were landed near the South Pole initially. So they were fresh from Earth when they attacked you, and then only had to get themselves to their Marius hideaway afterward."

Pope glanced over her shoulder at the pad. "So Team One sets up Marius Base, starts thieving from US-Copernicus and other soft targets. Team Two lands near the South Pole, attacks LGS-1, heads north to Marius afterward." He stopped, scanned their faces. "That case would require them to have at least two vehicles. But maybe they do. Who knows?"

"We don't," said Terri. "Nothing about either scenario is impossible, except that once they put a big vehicle down on the surface, it's staying on the surface, not about to be taken off again. Even we don't launch items the size of a MOLAB off the surface once they're down. We airlift stuff back to lunar orbit bit by bit."

"None of this is impossible," said Rodriguez. "It's just ambitious enough to be impressive."

Pope glanced over at Vivian. "And again, you're shaking your head."

"Not at any of the technical stuff," Vivian said. "Just the human cost. Rolling across the Moon for weeks at a time? We've all done that. But, doing science with your friends in a big comfy MOLAB is one thing. Even doing a single long overland haul, like you did. But what these guys are doing, repeated trips, just to attack *us*, or to scavenge enough supplies to live, well …"

"Maybe that's why grabbing your MOLAB and some of your other gear was so attractive to them," Pope pointed out.

"Still. They must know they can't get away with it forever."

"Forever? No. Just long enough to do their damage. Blow the Accord apart. Get whatever they need out of Casey. Mess things up good up here."

Terri reached out, touched Vivian's arm. "Hey. You realize that if all this checks out, we're going to need you, right? You spent a week and a half in the Marius Hills. You have ground truth on it. You know the whole area better than anyone else."

"I absolutely do realize that," Vivian said bitterly.

"Uh. Sorry."

Vivian leaned back and took a long breath. "I know how odd this sounds coming out of my mouth, but I was *really* looking forward to getting off the Moon."

"I know."

"And even more so, right now."

Brock looked at her face. "Because NASA has something else waiting for you."

Vivian didn't answer that. She couldn't tell Terri and the guys that she was scheduled to fly to L5 and then on to fricking *Venus*. Though, if Brock had still been working for NASA, Vivian would have tried like hell to coax Terri onto her crew. Which would have been doomed to failure, of course. Terri had a ball and chain at home. She wasn't as independent, fancy-free, and usefully gullible as Vivian, even if NASA HQ had been willing to risk their first US woman on the Moon on a trip to the planets.

"I need coffee," she said.


Finally, Sandoval emerged from the comms room. He was frowning. "So, Vivian, you've been briefed? Good. And, yes: Cheyenne wants you on the team. I have full authority to conscript you, and the Air Force will take its lumps with NASA later. But ..." He paused and looked at her. "Uh, I'm not about to force you to come with us. If you really want to leave, I can make that happen."

She stared at the wall, thinking about it.

"Vivian?"

It somehow made it worse that Peter had picked up so quickly on her mood and was trying to give her an out. Vivian shook her head. "Who else will be on the assault? You all?"

"Of course. This is my team. Plus several dozen more troops, maybe even about fifty in total. We're a ways from finalizing the manpower and assault plan, but we're not going to short-change this. We'll go in with what we hope is irresistible force and try to minimize casualties."

"A night attack? It's dark at Marius now."

"God, no. Much too dangerous. Too many factors we can't control. We'll go in at dawn." He grinned. "Fly in at them out of the sun. Just like the good old days."

"Then why do they even call you Night Corps?"

"Hell if I know."

"But that means we can't go in for another two weeks, right? If we're going in at dawn, or just after, that'll be ..." Vivian did quick mental arithmetic. "Something like March twenty-sixth? Oh, holy crap."

Gently, Terri said: "What's significant about the twenty-sixth?"

"Nothing, specifically. I'm just trying to figure out what the heck to tell NASA about my availability, without giving the game away."

Sandoval waved it off. "Not your problem. I'll take care of it."

"Yeah, but ..." Vivian would miss another *two weeks* of Venus Astarte training. And she only had four months left. Less. "I need to talk to NASA again. Same secure line. Same privacy requirement. If I'm going to stay for an assault on Marius, I'm going to need several large chunks of lone MOLAB time between now and then. Plus unmonitored access to a printer. I'll obviously continue to say zip about the cryptonauts, Marius, what we're doing, whatever, but I absolutely need to do concurrent preparation for my next thing. Will that work? Because it'll have to."

"Whatever it takes," Sandoval said readily.

She thought a while longer. "Let me check in with NASA again, right now. I just had to cut them off kind of abruptly."

Sandoval paused. "Let me know if I can be any help."

"Will do."

Terri looked at her watch. "It's getting late in the US, now."

Vivian glanced at the wall clock. "It is. Damn." Yeah, Dave would likely have freed up the folks at Johnson Space Center by now.

To Sandoval, Brock said: "Then, in the meantime, let's get Vivian out on surface, stat."

Vivian raised her eyebrows. "Outside? Why?"

"Because if you *are* coming along on this raid, we need to give you a crash course in how to handle a Night Corps exosuit. They're not like NASA Moon suits. At all. And the sooner we start the better, especially if you'll have time constraints later."

"Okay, I guess. So, how are they different, exactly?"

"In every way. The balance, the way the weight is distributed. How the joints feel. Where the controls are. And especially the boot power-assists."

Vivian stared at her. "The boot what-nows?"

"Don't get your hopes up, it's not quite like *Starship Troopers*, but it's still pretty cool."

"Oh. Okay."

"Yeah." Terri stood up. "So, no time like the present. Let's get you wrapped and out the door."

Because it was Terri, Vivian allowed herself to be hustled out toward the airlock area. "I sure hope you're a quick study," Terri murmured.

"Me too." In front of her now was an array of exosuits, hanging from racks in a ghoulish display. Terri pulled a suit out of the rack, turned it around to show Vivian the back, raised a metal flap. "See? More like a hatch than anything else."

Sure enough, the exosuit appeared to have a hatch in the back. "Damn. This really is a suit of armor, isn't it?"

"Pretty much." Terri grinned. "You need to be limber. Us ladies can generally shimmy in and out of 'em quicker than the menfolk. It helps to have real hips."

"Sure."

Terri put her hand on Vivian's arm. "Wait a moment. Be straight with me: are you really going to be okay?"

"Probably."

"Vivian, come on, this is *me*. I used to be NASA. What the hell's going on?"

"Can't tell you. And that hurts." Vivian shook her head. "I think I owe Peter an apology."

"Because?"

"Because I was always down on him, for keeping secrets from me. But it *sucks* having to keep secrets from everyone. It fricking *sucks*. It's not glamorous, it's not cool. I hate it."

"Hey, at least you're in demand."

Vivian just looked at her.

"Sorry."

"And now I'm torn two ways. Trust me, both are critically important. And both the NASA and Night Corps people are going to resent me because I can't tell either of them what the hell is going on with the other one."

"Good times," said Terri. "But you still have friends. And we understand."

"Do I? Do you?"

"Yes, yes, to both," Brock said. "Okay, let's go. But before you get into this crazy suit of armor, let me point out a few things …"

Terri hadn't been kidding her. The exosuit was *heavy*.

# 25

## Vaporum Base: Vivian Carter
## March 16, 1983

**VIVIAN'S** descent stage was still at Marius, untouched, sitting exactly where she and Ellis had left it when they'd launched their ascent stage off the Moon on March 10, 1980, on the first leg of their journey back to Earth. The ALSEP, Apollo Lunar Surface Experiments Package, and other instruments they'd laid out on the surface also looked undisturbed. If the cryptonauts really were based at Marius, they were not so foolish as to advertise their presence by messing with something so obvious. They hadn't gone anywhere near the Apollo 32 landing site. The boot and rover tracks Vivian and Ellis had made in various directions during their excursions were still in place, and outside their EVA locations the surface looked pristine.

Their rover wasn't at Marius anymore, though. The Apollo 32 LRV had been equipped with remote operational capability, so at the end of their final EVA Vivian and Ellis had loaded it up with their unused supplies, plus all the equipment they wouldn't need any more and didn't have the mass margin to take home. As was now traditional, Horn, orbiting in the Command Module above them, had remotely steered the camera on the rover's nose to keep them in frame as their ascent stage blasted off, and after that Apollo 32 had handed control of the rover back to Mission Control. Shortly afterward it had departed the scene, its driving seats empty, controlled telerobotically from Eagle Station and Houston. First, it had completed a photographic survey of the Marius Hills area, documenting the extended region in more detail than Vivian and Ellis had time to do. Then, after lying dormant through the lunar night, it had been powered up again to begin its overland trip to US-Copernicus. It had been another success for the mission, the first long-haul test of a teleoperated US Lunar Rover.

Which meant that, to everyone's chagrin now, the rover wasn't in the one place where it might have been invaluable as a remote surveillance tool.

But by now NASA had other, similarly equipped rovers at US-Copernicus that could be controlled from either Copernicus or Eagle Station through the NAVSTAR system. And so Night Corps had requisitioned two of them, irritating Starman even further by declining to brief him on why. From Copernicus to Marius overland was an almost straight shot: off the Copernicus highlands, across Mare Insularum, and then curving north of Kepler Crater onto Oceanus Procellarum. Constantly on the move, rotating the remote driving teams and keeping the speed down to reduce the risk of accidents, it took a little over forty hours to get the rovers in place.

And the video coverage they achieved once they arrived on-site in the Marius Hills confirmed the cryptonaut presence there once and for all, just as Rodriguez had predicted.

It was almost comically easy. From orbit, the cryptonaut base was well hidden, but from close by on the ground, looking across the surface, it stuck out like a sore thumb. The hostiles really had made use of the existing lava tube that connected to the deep pit visible from space, its far end now carefully bored out to give them rolling access into the tube from the surface, while leaving an overhang to help disguise its existence. And from beneath that overhang came a faint glow in the optical, and a fifteen-degrees-Celsius infrared excess. Vivian owed Rodriguez an apology.

They couldn't drive the US rovers too close without tipping off the hostiles that their base had been discovered, so Sandoval ordered them left where they were, close to the local horizon, with their stereoscopic view of the tube opening from the northeast and southeast. Occasionally a moving shape was visible in the tunnel or out on the surface, presumably a suited soldier or vehicle moving around.

So, a hostile base, hidden in a lava tube. If not for Casey Buchanan, who might just be still alive in there somewhere, Night Corps could have just bombed the lava tube ceiling down and entombed the enemy combatants: not very sporting, but immediately effective. But, as they still had hopes of bringing Casey home, a more complicated plan was in order.

They'd removed some of the interior walls in the Bunker to create a meeting space and set up some cameras so that the briefing could be broadcast up to the MOLs orbiting overhead. All the Night Corps crew were assembled there, with those for whom it was the "off" shift blinking and sucking down coffee.

At exactly sixteen hundred hours, Sandoval walked in and pinned a huge photographic print onto the wallboard. It was four feet wide by three feet high and still glistening slightly wet, which meant that somewhere in the Bunker they had an enormous printer that Vivian hadn't seen yet. She wondered what else Night Corps had squirreled away that she didn't know about.

Of course, she recognized the image immediately.

Sandoval gestured to Vivian. "Would you like to introduce us to your friends?"

"Uh, sure." Vivian stepped forward. "Ladies and gentlemen, the Marius Hills, the site of the ten-day Apollo 32 expeditionary landing in February-March 1980. Originally scheduled for late 1979, but we ran into hazardous circumstances beyond our control."

A ripple of amusement. Everyone there knew exactly what had happened three years ago. Terri had told her there was even a course module about the Hadley War in the USAF astronaut training these days. Which was a surreal thought. Terri herself had helped to write it.

Vivian often caught Night Corps astros scoping her out, looking at her out of the corners of their eyes. Appraising her. Probably wondering how this skinny and rather unremarkable-looking woman had survived being attacked, captured, tortured, and nearly blown to bits several times, plus hiking across the Moon by herself, stuck in a suit with no food and limited water for more days straight than she cared to be reminded of.

That was cool. Vivian liked being respected. It made a nice change after her young aviator days, when any respect she'd earned was grudging and hard-fought. Just as long as none of them expected her to ever do any of that shit again.

Vivian had hardly looked at the photograph, which was effectively a large-scale map of a substantial area, so even she felt like she was showing off when she said, "Apollo 32's landing site was here," and pointed straight at it without squinting or double-checking. "During our sojourn at Marius, Lunar Module Pilot Ellis Mayer and I conducted ten EVAs, totaling a hundred and sixteen hours, and thoroughly explored and sampled this whole area, sometimes traveling as far as fifty miles away from the LM." She grinned. "Which doesn't sound like a whole lot anymore but was actually a record for an *expeditionary* Apollo at the time and wasn't exceeded until Apollo 39. And, yes, I know there are several people in this room for whom that distance is peanuts. I'm one of them myself."

She looked back at the photograph. "So I've walked or driven a lot of this terrain. And we have now confirmed that this is where our hostiles, almost certainly Soviet but often referred to as cryptonauts for political correctness, have their main base."

She glanced at Sandoval, but he gestured her to continue. *Okay, sure, guess the NASA chick will just brief freaking Night Corps on their upcoming military action. No big deal.*

"The hostiles are holed up, quite literally, in a lava tube at least a mile long, but likely a heck of a lot longer. It has at least two potential points of ingress and egress. One of them is the lava tube skylight that you see right here that we'll now call the Pit. Our Apollo 32 third and fourth EVAs took us across this whole area.

"Despite its apparent circularity, the Pit is natural. The hostiles didn't make it. The roof collapsed somewhere around three and a half million years ago. Our guess is that the cryptonauts landed themselves straight in there on their first arrival on the Moon, then scoped out the lava tube."

Peter swung in and stuck up another photograph next to the first. "Here's their new side door. Not visible from above, this is a slant-shot of the point where the cave egresses onto the lunar surface. The hostiles knocked out the end of the tube, but again, the circularity is basically natural, originally made by, uh, the flowing magma or something."

"Lava," Vivian said helpfully.

"Yes, of course. Hence the name. Lava, that drained out onto the lunar surface. On the original photograph, this egress is …" He paused to get his bearings, and Vivian resisted the urge to undermine his authority again by helping him. "Here. So the tube definitely runs between the Pit and this point, and for all we know runs beyond the Pit in the other direction a ways."

It definitely ran in the opposite direction. The original lava had needed to come from somewhere. "Okay," Vivian said. "Maybe let's back up and talk about this area a bit more generally. I know you've all had basic training on lunar terrains, but the Marius Hills are not typical of the Moon as a whole.

"The shallow dome-like objects you see all over this picture were created by volcanic activity. If you've seen so-called shield volcanoes on Earth, on Hawaii or a bunch of other places, that's kind of what these are. They're roughly circular, with gentle slopes, created from what was probably very fluid lava, not the really thick viscous stuff. Marius Hills has one of the richest concentrations of such volcanic features anywhere on the Moon.

"Okay. These long winding chasms, the rilles: these we *do* see all over the Moon. They can be miles long, even hundreds of miles. A lot of them likely started out as fractures in the lunar crust, where the surface materials collapsed inward. They can also be made volcanically, when the lava that made up the big mares—the seas—cooled and contracted. Maybe some are rivers that carried lava from big volcanic vents.

"Lava tubes are a little bit different. We see those on Earth too. They form when the surface of the volcanic flow has cooled, but lava is still flowing under the surface. If those tubes drain out, then they become caves."

She looked around at the troops again. "The Marius lava tubes aren't the only ones we know of. There are other skylights in Mare Tranquillitatis and Mare Ingenii, and those are potential targeted destinations for in-depth study by future expeditionary Apollos, to compare them with the data we took from Marius."

A question from the floor. "That area's not still volcanic, right?"

"Right," Vivian said. "There have been no volcanic eruptions for tens of millions of years. Most of the volcanic activity happened three *billion years* ago or more."

Another hand went up. "How big is that Pit? What's inside it?"

"Good questions. That feature is two hundred feet seventy feet across, and the floor inside is just over three hundred feet down. We

333

did not enter the Pit on Apollo 32—rappelling down into an underground cavern was out of scope for an unsupported two-astronaut team—but we did lower cameras, sample scoops, and various sonic devices that allowed us to determine the diameter and direction of the lava tube that extends off underground to either side. The inside tube diameter is about two hundred feet, and the tube stretches off to the southeast and northwest. As you can see, the surface opening is roughly southeast of the Pit."

They were all watching her intently. Good students. Then again, their lives might depend on these details.

She went on. "This is actually just one of four lava tubes that we detected at the Marius site, based on seismic and gravimetric measurements, but the others did not possess skylights, let alone ground-level entrances. Most of the Moon's lava tubes are completely underground. Some may be quite deep. But, based on Earth lava-tube analogies there's no reason to assume that this is just one single tube with two ends. Like any river, the river of lava that made it may have split into streams. The inside of the hostiles' lava tube might have junctions, tributaries, offshoots, whatever. There may be a whole system down there.

"It's reasonable to assume that the Soviets haven't deliberately stuck their main base miles into the tube—they'll want easy in-and-out access. So we're expecting their living quarters and all to be just inside the entrance we know about, but we can't rule out other installations deeper in the tube, or even another exit. And just because we don't see anything in the Pit by looking down into it from orbit, we can't assume there isn't anything at that location, tucked away out of easy view from above."

She paused. "All of this information about the Marius lava tubes has, of course, been published in the open scientific literature, and so the Soviets would have known about it for the last couple of years.

"Bottom line: we should likely expect Soviet assets or installations at the entrance, and maybe others close to the Pit overhang or in surrounding areas. Landers or flying craft might be stationed in the Pit, though flying in and out would be hairy. We have no way of telling how those assets are distributed, or how many troops they have."

One of the Night Corps men raised a hand. "Why didn't NASA follow up with further investigations at Marius? Seems like there might be a lot to learn from going inside. Or maybe the US could have stuck a base there to control it, and not let the Reds take it."

Vivian nodded. "A Marius return is in the NASA plan, but not soon. There's obviously the risk of structural collapse. The hostiles have apparently accepted that risk, but NASA is a little more cautious. The first deep investigation of the Marius lava tubes was to have been performed with an autonomous rover. Various NASA and university groups are already assembling instrument suites to help map and explore them: an environmental package to measure the internal conditions, temperature and radiation level and dust and so on, plus other modules for ground-penetrating radar, spectrometers, and ... uh, acoustic tomography, and so on."

Hands went up.

"And no, I don't really know what that is. Something to do with bouncing sound around between a network of sound sources and receivers."

The hands went down again.

"But we're still at least two years away from a scientific return to Marius. I always figured that if I was still working for NASA by then, I might get to CAPCOM it. But the point is that the bad actors know that Marius is safe to hang out at for quite a while to come."

The questions were coming fast now. "How thick is the roof of the tube? Is there a chance it might collapse in on top of us while we're inside? Since it was considered too risky for NASA astronauts, and all."

Too risky for NASA, but of course a good number of the men and women in front of her were about to take that risk. Invading an underground area stuffed with hostiles? Vivian was glad she wouldn't be one of them. Vivian might have tiptoed into a lava tube on her Marius trip, if they'd found one with a walk-in entrance, but she'd have been damned careful about it. These soldiers wouldn't have time for caution.

"Excellent questions. The roof is likely between fifty and a hundred feet thick, from inner ceiling to outer surface, but there may be areas where it's thinner, especially close to the Pit entrance. If the roof was precarious, sensitive to vibration, it would presumably have fallen in already on the hostiles. They had to drill or blow out their egress point from the tube from the inside, in the first place. And it seems like they've been driving vehicles in and out for weeks, at least. That implies a robust structural integrity. But the risk is not zero, especially if a firefight breaks out in there." *When* a firefight breaks out in there. Vivian didn't say that out loud though. "Be alert, and remember you won't hear it breaking, though you might feel the vibration." She smiled. "Sorry. Stating the obvious, I know. But sometimes it's good to drive the obvious home."

Yet more questions. How tall were the volcano domes? ("Anything from 600 to 1600 feet above the surrounding plain.") How far apart, typically? ("Well, as you can see, that's highly variable. They can be right up against each other, or miles apart.") What was the gradient on their outer slopes? ("Again, it varies. Generally, not as steep as other lunar ranges, but no picnic to clamber up, either. The smaller ones tend to have steeper slopes.") Is it possible that the hostiles might have put camouflaged gun emplacements on top of the ones near their base, for defensive purposes? ("Probably not. Even the small domes can be half a mile to a mile across. Might be good places to site a surveillance scope or something, but otherwise the height wouldn't lend them much military advantage.") Are all those rilles and gullies going to be a problem for a ground attack? ("No, not if we come in from *here* and *here*.")

It was a long afternoon.

The Night Corps attack would be three-pronged, from what they were calling "land, sea, and air" for convenience. Although there was no literal air, and in this case the "sea" was the area from tens to thousands of feet above the surface.

In other words, where the attack Lunar Modules would be operating. All of which, as it happened, would be commanded by naval aviators.

"So," Sandoval said, once the briefing was over and he'd reconvened with his core team: "Doyle and Pope, and Jaffe and Godfrey, they've been crewing together on LMs and Blue Gems forever, and it doesn't make sense to split up established teams for this action."

"Oh?" Vivian glanced at Terri.

"Yes," said Peter. "That means the two of you get to fly together."

"Okay, cool," Vivian said.

"Girl power," Terri added.

Sandoval leaned forward. "Listen, you both know the BS as well as I do. 'No women in combat situations,' is still the official line from above, believe it or not. Even though I have several women on my own force. My bosses know Vivian will be spotting for the assault, but my plan for you is a little more … active than I've been advertising. I'm not supposed to do this. So please try not to get killed."

"Stay alive, roger wilco," Vivian said.

"We'd hate to embarrass you by dying in a fireball," Brock added.

Sandoval blinked. "Right. Thanks. So, we need to decide which of you gets to command. Actually fly the bird."

"Vivian does," Terri said promptly.

"I do? Okay."

"I expected that to be harder." Sandoval made a note. "Rationale?"

"Vivian has trained and flown LMs more recently. She landed one on the Moon just weeks ago."

"Kinda months now," Vivian said.

"Whereas I haven't flown a LM since Hadley, plus our expedition to retake Columbia Station. Equally important, Vivian also did the requisite hundred-plus hours of simming before she left Earth for LGS-1 to make sure she had all her flying chops back in place, on top of being one of the most experienced LM jockeys out there to begin with. Me? You already know I've been busy training on MOL, Dyna-Soar, and Blue Gem, plus a bunch of other tactical and technical stuff. There's a limit to how many things I can focus on at once."

"Okay." Sandoval kept writing.

"There's more. The USAF LM controls are identical to the NASA LMs—the weight distribution of the bird is different, with the armor and all, but the flight controls are the same. But there are significant differences in the panels and readouts, and additional programs in the guidance computers that the NASA folks aren't familiar with. As the Lunar Module Pilot, I can handle all that *way* faster than Viv. Plus, she knows the lay of the land. So she gets the left station. I get the right."

"You can stop now, I'm convinced." Sandoval looked at Vivian. "Are you convinced?"

"Sure." She turned to Terri. "It'll be a pleasure to fly with you."

"Hah." Sandoval shook his head, still scribbling. "You might rethink that once you've actually flown with her. Brock can be a royal pain in the ass."

"Thank you, sir. I've learned from the best." Terri paused for effect. "I meant Allen Collier, of course. My Apollo 25 commander."

"Nice save. Okay, fine, it's official. You're a team. Go get your shit together."

"Will do, sir. Gonna get our rhythms aligned, right now."

Vivian laughed. Peter glanced over. "Meaning?"

"Uh, nothing, sir. We're on it."


The first time Vivian saw one of the modern USAF LM assault-craft variants they'd be using for this attack, she said flatly, "God, what a monstrosity."

What would have been the ascent stage on a NASA LM could only be separated in the direst emergency on the USAF model, in the sort of "cut and run for orbit" event that Vivian and Gerry Lin had attempted after he'd arrived to give her a ride as she fled from Zvezda. The fragile skin of the NASA LMs had been replaced by a bulletproof metallic shell. The pilots would fly fully suited up, with the cabin de-pressurized and in full vacuum. The hatches above and in front of them were much larger—no slow backward crawl to exit a USAF LM. The front and top windows were also larger.

The biggest change, though, was the addition of the gun turrets. One on each side of the craft for balance, as if the LM had two side-cars. Vivian would be flying with a gunner on each side, armed with grenade launchers and machine guns, "out in the open" but with ar-mored protection.

It was about the saddest perversion of a Lunar Module that Vivian could imagine. But the gun platforms weren't even the oddest part.

"Well," Vivian said, looking at her boots on the cabin floor, and past them. "That's … interesting."

Terri grinned. "Afraid of heights? Hope not."

"That's not the problem. What the hell is that *made* of?"

Beneath her, the floor of the USAF LM looked just like glass. Com-pletely clear. Eighteen feet below her own feet was the scuffed-up surface of the Moon, only partially blocked by the LM descent engine nozzle.

"Pyrex," Terri said with a straight face.

"Oh, come on. You're shitting me."

"Only a bit. I know it's some kind of specialized borosilicate glass made by Corning. But I'm not a chemist. They assure me it won't melt, though."

"Sure, lots of glasses have really high melting points. I'm more worried about it softening or fracturing under differential temperature stress, being that close to the fricking rocket." She thought about it. "Or cooking my feet. Isn't glass a good heat conductor?"

"Uh .... Aren't metals better heat conductors? Vivian, I have no clue. But it'll be neat to be able to see beneath us as well as in front, no?"

"When we're flying over a battlefield, I guess it might have its plusses." Vivian moved to the left station, checked out the robust support structure that would hold her in place. NASA LMs had waist straps to hold their pilots in position, but then NASA LMs weren't designed to operate in combat situations. "Well. Shall we take it for a spin?"

Terri grinned, and began strapping herself in. "Sure."

# CHAPTER 26

## Kepler Advance Base: Vivian Carter
## March 25, 1983

*NINE days later ...*

It was amusing, in hindsight, that Vivian had thought Kopernik would be the first and last giant lunar crater she'd ever be deep inside. Because here she was, almost in the center of Kepler Crater.

And, yes, she'd already taken regolith samples and sealed them into her little Teflon baggies.

Kepler Crater was twenty miles across, and almost two miles deep. It had a clump of hills in its center that hardly deserved to be termed "peaks," just a couple miles from where Vivian now stood. As best, she could tell from looking out the LM windows on their arrival, the crater outer rim had terracing similar to Copernicus, and beyond that a prominent ray system that extended into Oceanus Procellarum to the west and Mare Insularum to the east.

The advantage of Kepler Advance Base for the approaching assault was clear. Night Corps Vaporum Base was almost a thousand miles from Marius. Kepler Advance Base was a mere two hundred and fifty. The closer to Marius the assault LMs took off from, the more maneuvering fuel they'd retain, and the easier it would be to coordinate with the rest of the attack. And they wouldn't have to fly over—or avoid—Copernicus, which was three hundred fifty miles east of Kepler, which reduced the risk of tipping off someone at Zvezda, who might then tip off someone at Marius.

Kepler was far enough from Marius that the cryptonauts would hopefully remain ignorant that their forces were massing, and that any seismic equipment they had wouldn't detect the landings, but close enough to be an easy one-day drive for the slowest component of their attacking force: the Night Corps MOLAB.

Which was so slow that it had yet to arrive. So the only people currently at Kepler were the twelve crew of the assault LMs, plus the four hardworking engineers who took care of logistics and fueling and such. Everyone was competent to a fault, but no one was particularly chatty. Sandoval's people were there to do a job. And Vivian was NASA and not Night Corps, so whenever someone outside Sandoval's core team spoke to her there was always a detectable air of over-politeness. Vivian didn't quite belong.

Which was fine. She'd suffered worse things than politeness.

If Vaporum Base was spartan, Kepler Advance Base was downright rudimentary: the three USAF Lunar Modules, a small fuel dump that had arrived shortly before Vivian and Terri had brought LM-1 in, the two rovers the engineers had arrived on, and two inflatable habs.

Fortunately, these habs were a lot larger than the emergency inflatable that Vivian had survived inside for all those days, while the radiation from the Hadley nuclear blast was fading along its exponential curve. The Kepler Habs had six rooms each and decent headroom, though their air handling was dodgy at best. Condensation constantly trickled down the walls and they smelled a little funky too, with that sour-sweet odor of rot that no one could quite pin down.

It was military, contingent, and cramped. But at least Kepler Advance Base was well-guarded. Vivian could always see two of the gunners or engineers out on dirt bikes patrolling the perimeter.

They'd only be here a couple of days more. Lunar night was nearly over, here, and dawn would come to Marius one day later.

Vivian had spent most of the past week studying her Venus flyby material and talking with Horn about personnel and logistics, finalizing their crew and getting hip deep into the flyby science, objectives, and instrumentation. When she wasn't practicing flying the USAF LM, that is. Because the other advantage of a crater that was almost

341

two miles deep? You could fly around inside it at altitudes of five thousand feet or more, and no one outside the crater could see you doing it.

By this time Vivian was in such a smooth operational groove with Terri Brock that the two operated as a single unit. Taking off. Landing. Swerving around inside the crater to practice taking evasive action. Scooting over the surface at a gut-churningly low altitude, really quite fast. And at night.

This definitely wasn't Vivian's normal gig. And there had been a couple of heart-stopping moments when she'd thought she was doomed to plow into the lunar surface again, roll and wreck another LM, embarrassing herself in front of Night Corps and Peter, and likely delaying the attack on Marius all by herself. But she never quite screwed up badly enough.

And then there were the additional bouts of surface training in the Night Corps exosuit, which was *seriously messed up*. It was so heavy that it held her down onto the lunar surface much more tightly than an Apollo Moon suit. But also with those crazy power-assisted boots that could throw her into the air if she kicked them up without taking care.

Add the weapons training and strike planning, and she was experiencing a lot of wild stuff—and that was before the assault even happened. But Vivian still managed some time alone to process her thoughts, time she badly needed.

In those interludes between Night Corps training and Apollo Venus Astarte training, the magnitude of what she was planning to do in a few more short months was really sinking in.

Terri had been the first US woman to walk on the Moon, and Vivian absolutely didn't begrudge her that. The bright glare of publicity, the intense press scrutiny of everything Terri Brock had ever done in her life: Vivian would have hated it. She'd endured enough of that herself, but Terri's experience must have been an order of magnitude more grueling. But this, Venus? To be not just the first woman, but the first *person* and commander of the first mission of exploration to go outside the Earth-Moon system? Just the publicity pressure alone was going to be intense. The only saving grace was that it would all be happening at a distance, rather than in person.

Eventually, a *considerable* distance. Vivian now knew from her detailed mission preparations with Dave Horn, that after her July 4 launch, she'd be over seventy million miles from Earth when she passed Venus on November 14, which would mean a massive delay on roundtrip communications of over twelve and a half minutes. On passing Mars in late May 1984, the Apollo Astarte would be a mere fifty million miles from Earth, with about a nine-minute latency on communications.

With luck, they'd return to Earth on February 5, 1985, on what for them would be Mission Day 582. Vivian and her crew would be a *long* way away during this mission, and for one hell of a long time.

Such extreme isolation would be a high price to pay. But for that cost, Vivian Carter would earn the experience of being one of the first people to visit another planet, let alone two planets. Even though she'd never touch down, that would still be huge. And who could ever touch down on the surface of Venus and survive, anyway?

Look at how Apollo 8 had made history. People talked about Apollo 8 almost more than Apollo 11, probably because Apollo 8's manned lunar orbits had been an American first, and Apollo 11's landing had been an embarrassing second best. But still. Apollo Venus Astarte would be Apollo 8 on steroids.

All Vivian had to do was survive yet another lunar conflict, and Venus and Mars could be hers.

*All I have to do. Oh, God.* Vivian took a deep breath, then leaned forward and put her head between her knees. No one could see her in here. It was fine to have a little private personal reaction time.

*Vivian, for the love of God, do not screw this up.*

*Get through this. Survive.*

*Because, after you're done here, you can have something awesome.*

*Or? You can be dead, and feeling really stupid about what you've missed out on.*

The stakes had gotten a lot higher. Before, Vivian had just been risking a boring future life on Earth. Easy enough. But now? *Jeez.*

Vivian was essential to this military strike on Marius—she was the only one of them with firsthand knowledge of the area. And, ideally, she and Terri would be calling the shots from on high, and not facing enemy fire. At least not immediately.

Ha. As if, with Vivian's luck, that was even *remotely* likely to be true.

# CHAPTER 27

## Marius Hills: Vivian Carter
## March 27, 1983

**THE** days seemed to speed up as the critical date approached, and now it was upon them.

D-day. Zero hour. Time to go.

They were up and out of the crater, flying just a few hundred feet above the surface but at serious velocity: Vivian at the controls with Terri by her side, swaying in her restraints and calling numbers at a brisk clip. Though the only number Vivian was paying attention to was their altitude, as measured by their front-facing radar.

Because, unnervingly, LM-1 was flying largely face down. Out of their front windows they could see only the regolith beneath and slightly ahead. Craters were whizzing by *fast*, flickering bright-dark-bright-dark as they were thrown into sharp relief by the dawn Sun almost directly behind them, just a few degrees above the horizon.

Fortunately for Vivian's gunners, their seats were gimballed. They could be sitting up level if they chose, not staring down at the fast-moving lunar surface and hanging from their straps. Though at this altitude, that might not be any less unnerving.

Somewhere ahead was Peter Sandoval, doing his own version of a forward sprint in the MOLAB, which had now been even more up-armored to become a literal tank, and equipped with a half-dozen of the skeletal roof-mounted rockets besides. The uncrewed rovers were

344

creeping forward as well, controlled from Eagle Station, as additional sets of eyes on the ground.

Night Corps was moving in for the kill.

A few miles behind Vivian's craft and to the south was LM-2, with Doyle commanding and Pope in the LMP position. A couple of miles back and to their north was LM-3, with Jaffe and Godfrey. Vivian couldn't see either of them and had no time to keep track of her own coordinates, let alone theirs—she had other people taking care of that.

All three LMs had camera gear slung under them, controlled directly from USAF Mission Control in Cheyenne and the MOLs in orbit. Cheyenne would be studying the real-time images, correcting for motion control and vibration, and helping to map the ground situation at the strike zone as best they could. Vivian didn't want to know how many buildings full of computers and analysts were on the case right now, enabling them to do all that magic.

Meanwhile, on the high ground, the USAF equatorial MOL-A would begin overflying the area any minute now, ready to call in whatever they could see, and MOL-B, in its polar orbit, would be swinging in from the north to take over in about twenty-five minutes.

Beside her, Brock switched circuits and continued to talk quickly. Vivian could still hear Terri's voice in the cabin, but not through her headset. For the attack, she and Terri would mostly be monitoring different loops. Brock was talking mainly to Sandoval and the Strike Command and Control team at Cheyenne. Vivian was linked in with the other LM pilots and her gunners, plus a separate coordinating flight ops team at Cheyenne. This meant they were often both having loud conversations with different people at the same time, while breaking off to snap numbers and directions at each other. The cabin was *noisy*, and Vivian was glad that they'd piled up so many flight hours at Mare Vaporum and Kepler crater in preparation. The Vivian of 1979 could never even have flown with such precision so close to the ground, let alone do it while being buffeted with this level of clamor and chaos.

Terri broke into Vivian's channel briefly to say, "T minus six," then dropped out again. "T minus six minutes," Vivian repeated, passing the word to her outside crew.

"One, Left, roger that," came the response. The LM-1 gunners were Jeff and Steve, or at least that's what Vivian had been told to call them on the ground, but during the operation they'd simply be Left and Right.

A new, sudden crackling in her ear. An override. "Vivian, come in?"

It was Belyakova's voice. "*What the hell?—Damn* it, how did you get this frequency?"

"Vivian?"

"Kind of busy right now. Later?"

"No, now. Listen, please. You are attacking Marius, yes?"

"Shit." Fear flooded down Vivian's spine. "How do *you* know that!"

"You have been betrayed, Vivian. You and your people. The cryptonauts know that you are coming."

"*What?*"

"They have an agent in US-Copernicus. A double agent, an American. Did you know this?"

"Of course not!"

On the other loop, Terri was saying: "MOL-A has visual, reports significant ground activity outside the Door."

"Oh, holy crap." Vivian glanced at her altitude, jerked LM-1 up by about a hundred feet. She needed more height margin, with all *this* going on.

Belyakova was still talking. "Where are you now?"

"Not saying. But Svetlana, you need to talk *real* fast."

"All right. We monitor all radio traffic out of your sector. Of course we do. It is almost all in the clear, although some you encrypt. Yesterday we detected a transmission from your side of Zvezda-Copernicus using a very old Soviet encryption method, an obsolete code we have not used ourselves in a long time. Naturally we could decipher it, though it took time. It was a message to the Marius cryptonaut base, warning they would soon be under attack."

"Svetlana, no one at US-Copernicus knows! This op is Night Corps only!"

"They do know. The message talks about intercepting a rover signal. Do you understand this?"

The signal from the teleoperated rovers was sent in short bursts, bounced off the NAVSTARs to Night Corps in a tight beam on a restricted frequency. Could a well-equipped double agent at US-Copernicus have detected that?

Perhaps it hadn't been such a great idea to borrow those rovers from Copernicus, after all.

Vivian thought quickly. "What else can you tell me? How many of them there are, what weapons do they have? Any idea of the layout inside the lava tube? Any clue where they might be holding Buchanan?"

"No, Vivian, I know none of this. The message made no mention of these matters."

"And why would you tell me this? … Wait. How could someone even get a message to Marius from US-Copernicus? They couldn't have bounced it off a NAVSTAR, and the Soviets don't—"

"—have our own satellites, no. Vivian, the message was bounced off Earth. Sent there and was retransmitted back. We detected it both ways."

"Again, why warn me? If they're your people at Marius …"

"They are not."

"Then who the hell are they?"

Svetlana hesitated. "You should not find out from me. But I think you will soon learn this for yourself."

"No, come on—"

"Good luck, Vivian. They are ready for you. Be safe."

"Uh. Thanks. Talk again soon, okay?"

Vivian broke the connection and realized that Terri was looking over at her with ice in her expression. "That was *Belyakova*?"

"Affirmative."

"Vivian. You cannot trust anything that woman says."

So much to unpack. No time to unpack it. "Who mentioned trust? Patch me into Sandoval."

Brock hit her comms button. "Control, priority one." And to Vivian, as she punched another button: "Go."

"Sawbones, this is LM-1."

He responded immediately. "Sawbones. Talk."

"The Marius cryptos know we're coming."

"Source?"

"Soviets. Blond Svet."

Sandoval didn't ask for details. No time. "Confidence?"

"Ninety percent plus. More."

"Got it." Sandoval toggled a comms switch, came back into her ear on the wide loop. "Team, heads up. Confirmation: hostiles have been alerted. Prepare to face stiff resistance."

Vivian glanced at her board as an orange light flashed. Three miles out. *Jesus H. Christ, that was fast.* "Pilot! Go for tilt-up."

"P105, proceed." Brock said at almost the same time.

"Proceed, proceed!"

Terri pressed the PRO button. They both rocked back in their straps as the LM engine gimballed and pushed them up and away from the ground on a preprogrammed trajectory. Gaining altitude at last.

And there they were, sliding up into view through the big forward windows: the Marius Hills that Vivian recognized and loved, arrayed in front of her once more.

Last time, they'd been her mission.

This time, it was war.

Vivian knew exactly where she was, without even having to think about it. She'd memorized this terrain over four years ago, simulated it before launch, and then explored it in depth and written one of the longest and most comprehensive mission debriefs about it afterward that NASA had ever received.

If she'd had time, she might have cried. But in that first glance, Vivian's trained eyes had already identified the ridge and rough location of the hostiles' lava tube exit. "Navy, I have visual on target."

"Roger."

"Roger." Behind her and to her left and right, Doyle and Jaffe responded from LM-2 and LM-3 respectively, fast and terse.

Ahead, between her and Ground Zero, maybe a mile out, Vivian could now see Sandoval's MOLAB powering in at full speed, bouncing and bumping on the harsh terrain and kicking up all kinds of dust.

And ahead of the MOLAB? *Wow. Shit.*

"Visual contact with hostiles. Gun emplacements, defensive capabilities. Armored foxholes. Repeat, you're running onto guns."

"Maybe a dozen," Terri added. "No, even more. Fanned out in a ninety-degree pattern outside the Door."

"Roger, LM-1."

The foxholes were all low to the ground, installed inside craters. Some glinted in the early Sun, and others Vivian had to squint to see, but neither she nor Terri were in doubt about what they were looking at. The hostiles had been damned clever to get all that out there without being spotted by the surveillance rovers.

Then again, the rovers would have had a tough time seeing anything in the deep shadows and bright scattering right after lunar dawn. And, of course, it must have helped that the hostiles apparently already knew exactly where the rovers were. And if the enemy was that smart and well-informed …

Vivian felt another gut-pounding flash of fear. But only for a moment, before that icy battle-coldness returned.

*Steal Marius from me? Corrupt my dream? Steal Casey, and my MOLAB, and even some of my Aitken Basin rocks? Shoot at me and toss me into a fricking crater?*

*So help me, I'll kill you all stone dead, wherever the hell you came from.*

Vivian took over manual control again and rocked the LM forward so the engine could push her farther and faster, over the top of them. Still half a mile out from the enemy base.

"Incoming shells," Terri said calmly. "Evasive action."

"On it." Sure enough, the hostiles were firing on them. Tracer flew by to their left and right. Viscerally, Vivian could almost feel the explosive shells that were likely interspersed in between those tracer rounds, but by now she was weaving the LM erratically left and right, up and down, and it would be hard for the hostiles to get a fix. She was vaguely aware of a rocket erupting from Sandoval's MOLAB and arcing up and down beneath them and blowing the shit out of one of the hostile gun emplacements.

*Night Corps for the win. Thanks, guys. Just don't hit me, okay? No friendly fire deaths here, if you'd be so kind.*

The damned rocket explosion made quite a crater. And hopefully it had rattled the enemy as well. Then Vivian was past the strike zone, beyond the ridge, and throwing LM-1 into a hard left turn to loop them back around.

She tuned back in to Terri, who was alternately looking out the front, side, and floor windows and rapping into her microphone, giving further ground-truth details of the site. "… change Drop One, four down three right to compensate."

Sandoval's voice in her ear. "Four down three right, confirm?"

"Roger."

"Wilco. Drop Two remains nominal, confirm?"

"Affirmative. Drop Two on-plan," Terri said.

"Got it." Sandoval clicked off.

Brock looked at the instruments. "Okay, straighten, you're over-cooking, lose height fifty. Don't overfly again, not till my mark."

"Fifty, roger." Vivian eased up on the throttle, and LM-1 bobbled downward. At the same time, they felt a murderous vibration through the ship's hull as the left gunner let loose. Vivian came very near to jerking the controls and shook her head. "Shit! Damn." She didn't know what Left was shooting at, hadn't really thought through how crazy it would be to fly into a war zone and not even be able to see it properly.

Brock: "Up-up, correct for reaction, keep her steady."

"On it. Maintain forward?"

"No, half-on. Yes, like that. Drop One is imminent. Dead ahead of us." Brock glanced at her computer, then back at Vivian. "Don't flinch, babe. It'll be quick. Five, four, three—"

Something gigantic fell past their front windows, plummeting toward the surface at a rate that seemed in excess of lunar terminal velocity. "Holy frigging …. Gah!" Vivian shouted involuntarily.

"—Zero," Terri said. "Sorry. Best numbers I had. Good job not putting us into a death spiral, though."

"You're so goddamned welcome."

Brock grinned. "Okay, up-and-back, up-and-back, let's take a look."


Over the comms on all NASA and Soviet frequencies, essentially all the radio channels commonly in use on the Moon other than the ones Night Corps was actively using for this assault, a recorded message was going out in Russian, Ukrainian, and English. The message told the hostiles that they faced overwhelming, deadly force—just in case they couldn't guess—and exhorted them to surrender immediately and they would not be harmed. That any attempt to break through the blockade that Night Corps was imposing would be futile. And that any craft attempting to launch would immediately be shot down.

The Brick that Vivian and the others had ridden to the ground close to Mare Vaporum had been the most packed-up that a Brick could be. It had contained almost no empty space, and they'd needed lots of time to unpack and effectively deploy all the people and equipment. Apollo Rescue 1, in 1979, had been a little less densely packed, meaning that Sandoval had been able to exit right away while his other folks were still getting themselves up and out. They'd brought no MOLAB on that first drop, of course, and so had more room to move.

The Brick that had just fallen past Vivian in LM-1 and crash-landed to the south and east of the lava tube entrance was different again. It was set up in assault configuration, with lots of free space for a fast deploy. It could be repurposed as a Bunker habitat later on, once the assault was complete, but that wasn't its primary role. It had come down depressurized, with the Night Force troops inside it already suited up, armed, and armored. Now, as Vivian rocked LM-1 back and oscillated it in an erratic, constantly moving hover, she could see those troops had already blown open the walls of the Brick and come pouring out.

Six of them were on dirt bikes, skidding them out to the right and left to get clear of the Brick and establish positions. Although she couldn't see them from this altitude, she knew that all were armed with both grenade launchers and recoilless rifles. Another fourteen were on foot, some leaping on those power-assisted boots and firing rifles from the peak of their arcs, others in a kangaroo-hopping sprint to gain distance. Vivian saw one of them get blown out of the air in a bright flash by a hostile shell, saw two more dive headlong into craters of their own and prop their weapons up on the crater edge, firing steadily.

Certainly, a lot of ordnance was being expended, but no one was gaining or losing ground. Sandoval's MOLAB should have been here already, but was only now entering the battleground, and from farther east than Vivian had been expecting.

Beside her, Brock was talking in her fast, clipped technobabble with lots of letters and numbers, relaying information quickly, and now and then breaking off to direct Vivian one way or another.

Then suddenly Terri stopped speaking, then swiveled and pointed. "LK Lander rising."

"Confirm," said Right through her earpiece. "Pit egress."

Sure enough, a craft had just shot up out of the lava tube skylight to their northwest, mostly rendered visible by the small plume of flame beneath it. Vivian pulled at the controls to slew LM-1 off sideways in that direction. "Negative on LK. Much smaller."

"It's a flyer," said Left.

It kept going, straight up, and as LM-1 roared toward it, Vivian could see it was identical to the one that had attacked her at the South

Pole. Its two pilots must have caught sight of Vivian's LM-1 because now the enemy flyer tilted away from them to streak across the lunar surface to the north, climbing at a steep angle. "Fleeing, not engaging."

"Go with," Terri said tersely, and Vivian hit the afterburners. Well, they weren't really jet afterburners, just two small additional rocket engines, but that's what Jaffe, Doyle, and Brock called them.

Yeah, that was a high-G turn, and now the LM was heading almost straight upward in hot pursuit.

Brock was checking the radar, shouting more jargon to Cheyenne. Then she turned to Vivian: "Missile!"

"Shit!"

The hostile flyer was firing on them. *Déjà vu*, Vivian thought.

"Drop, Viv. Down-down-down! *Fast!*"

Vivian cut the afterburners, but Brock was already shaking her head. "More, much more. C'mon, flip the bird."

"What?" But Vivian did it immediately, swinging the LM around. Now the engine was forcing them down toward the surface, powering them in. Vivian's gaze locked onto her altitude indicator, watching unblinking as the numbers plummeted. At five hundred feet she rocked backward, hauling at the controls.

"Into the Sun!" Terri shouted.

"Already on it, babe."

The LM powered upward again. Putting itself between the flyer—and its missile—and the Sun.

"Okay, dropping chaff. Once I do, hard left, okay?"

"Yes."

Brock punched a button, releasing a stream of aluminum strips from a compartment in one of the LM's bays. "Go! Fast evade!"

Vivian punched the LM to the left, two seconds later saw a brief but lurid flash out of her right window, and finally saw Brock breathe and relax. "Wow. Okay, we're okay. Missile neutralized."

"Holy *moly*," Gunner Steve said mildly from the out the right-hand side of the LM, and at that Terri laughed, a spasmodic sound that was almost a wail. She clicked the comms switch. "You can say 'shit' in front of us, you know."

"Yes, ma'am. Appreciate it."

"Then, sheee-*it!*" came the voice of Gunner Jeff to her left.

"Okay, go-go-go, get back on the flyer's tail," Terri said. "We don't let it escape. Gunners, send them to hell."

Vivian hit the gas again, almost straight upward. Wow, that extra rocket power was fierce. And the flyer couldn't compete with it. Leaning back to look out of the top hatch window, Vivian saw it growing rapidly as LM-1 overhauled it.

Then came that unholy vibration of gunfire through LM-1's airframe again as her gunners poured shells into the flyer, and almost immediately Left shouted "Got it!" at the same time as Right snapped "Kill! Evasive!"

Vivian twisted and shoved at the controls, swinging the craft facedown again. Its engine drove them southward and away from the flaming debris that soon showered down, visible behind them through the transparent floor.

"Gunners, report. Okay?"

They responded instantly. "Left, roger."

"Right, confirm okay."

Phew. Vivian hadn't gotten either of her own guys killed yet. Outstanding.

She glanced quickly out of each of her windows. Where were they now, relative to Ground Zero? "Height, pilot?"

"Fourteen thousand feet, H-dot thirty high. We're looking good. Let's go back down."

Vivian and her crew had just killed two more people. How many did that make? Eight that Vivian could immediately think of, that she'd either scored or directly assisted on. *Eight kills. But who's counting?*

"Initiating P64," Brock said. "Okay to proceed?"

"Sure, proceed. Get the computer to take the strain for a change." The preprogrammed P64 would pitch them upright and bring them into final approach for a landing. Not that they would actually land, but it would take the pressure off and give them both time to breathe before they got back down into the battle zone. "Eyes peeled, though."

The LM stabilized. "Twelve thousand feet, H-dot nominal," Brock said. She switched circuits to banter incomprehensibly in jargon with Cheyenne, then said: "We're to descend half a mile north, come off P64 to manual at eight hundred feet, then sweep the zone again."

"Roger that. How's my fuel?"

"Fine," Terri said, and went back to her Cheyenne code-talking.

"Thanks." Vivian scanned her board, checked her fuel and other vitals herself. They were, indeed, fine.

"Gunners, still keeping eyes out for incoming, right?" Her artillery men had much better all-around vision than she did.

"Roger that," came the call. Of course they were. They were Night Corps. Vivian allowed herself to relax for a moment. She wished she could wipe her hands on a towel, but that would have meant ungloving, which didn't seem like a swell idea.

So. Two cryptonauts had made a run for it. Abandoned the rest of their men and bolted, rather than staying to fight. Interesting strategy. And they could easily have gotten away scot-free if LM-1 hadn't been in the right place at the right time.

"Brick Two, incoming," said Terri. "Nowhere near us this time."

"Makes a change."

Terri pointed, and they saw it make landfall a quarter mile from the Door and north-northeast of it. Again, the Brick seemed to erupt as soon as it touched the lunar surface. Two more bikes, this time with sidecar gunners, moved forward and out. Six more troops loped out on foot, running not toward the battle but up the northern slope of the ridge. A few more, deploying larger guns, rolled them clear of the Brick. "Artillery's arrived."

Vivian shook her head. "Crazy shit."

"Okay," Terri said. "Phase Three is a go. Up and to the right."

Vivian scanned the boards. "I'll need numbers, Pilot. A *lot* more numbers."

"Sure. Up two hundred, right twenty-five degrees. Fast as you can."

"Ridgetop, confirm?"

"Affirmative."

"Then away we go." Vivian twisted the controls, and the LM leaned forward and powered away from the battlefield and toward the ridge ... and the Pit.

# 28

## Marius Hills: Peter Sandoval
## March 27, 1983

**THE** MOLAB was bucketing over the lunar surface at a really unhealthy speed, sometimes lurching sideways as it banged off rocks the driver couldn't quite avoid in time, and even occasionally skipping up off the Moon's surface, despite its weight. Sandoval was strapped in tight and facing forward, sitting at a console and trying to study it rather than staring out the front window in horrified fascination. He was pretty damned sure today was going to end up with this MOLAB on its side. Luckily, even if that did happen, he'd still be able to collect his battle-field intel and fire his missiles. But if it rolled all the way onto its roof, decommissioning all his missiles at a stroke, they'd be up shit creek with no paddle in sight.

Rodriguez was driving with a manic desperation that he usually saved for cruising around Mexico City. Jacobson was sitting next to him, also strapped in, calling numbers as calmly as if he was playing a video game.

Sandoval was supposed to be guiding the action from his console, but that was impossible in this mess. It was Cheyenne who had the top-down view and could combine it with the scatterings of intel they were getting from the LMs, the MOLAB, and the riders and ground troops out of the Brick. Sandoval would just have to hope that the two-and-a-half second message propagation time wasn't going to be the death of anyone.

For the first time, he gained an appreciation of just how difficult the Soviet assaults on Hadley Base must have been. When you were defending, sitting still in one place, you could gain a much better idea of the battlefield than when you were piling into it pell-mell, attacking from several directions at once, bouncing over craters and throwing up dust and rocks and trying to keep track of where a few dozen people, three flying machines, two Bricks and one semi-tank were … and that didn't even take into account what the enemy was doing.

And the enemy was firing at them. Four of Sandoval's ground force were down already. Dead? Merely wounded? No time to think about that. But Night Corps had taken out half a dozen of the enemy gun emplacements already in return, and were still storming in like crazy people.

But, shit, this was some heavy action. All in all, Peter Sandoval would much rather have been in a fighter jet over 'Nam again, facing a MiG-17.

So … the lava tube entrance faced southwest, and the enemy troops were fanned out in front of it, each in their own little armored foxhole. Weapons? Sandoval hadn't seen rockets yet, just bullets and shells, but that didn't mean the Soviets didn't have any. They might only have a few and were saving them for when they really needed them.

Bullets were ricocheting off the front of his MOLAB in a steady din. And those hostiles weren't using tracer, which was smart because that would have told his Night Corps guys which emplacements were crewed by real human hostiles and which ones were dummies, if any. Surely some of them had to be dummies. No?

The Sun glare was making all of this fiendishly difficult. What had seemed straightforward on paper was far from it in real life. Even though the sunlight was coming in from directly behind his MOLAB, they were getting substantial reflected scatter and glare off the regolith in *front* of them. Sandoval didn't know how that worked, and when he asked Rodriguez, the words "zero-phase lighting" meant nothing to him. Perhaps he should have done some serious, honest-to-God dedicated Moon training at some point after all, even though he had been 100 percent dead set against ever coming back here. He should have known that Murphy's Law would plonk him back down on the lunar surface again, sure as shootin'. God had a strange sense of humor.

"Beginning evasive pattern." Now, Rodriguez started jerking the wheel irregularly to the north and then to the west. It threw the MOLAB around in a nausea-inducing fashion, but it did help to mitigate some of the illumination effect, as well as making them trickier to hit, in theory. The clatter of bullet impacts wasn't attenuating by a whole lot, though.

If the Sun was making it hard for Night Corps, Sandoval could only hope it was making it even harder for the enemy, who would need to stare straight into it to aim at them.

The MOLAB was now spearheading the attack, literally bounding in over the rough terrain, one or more wheels off the ground more often than not. Spread out around the MOLAB on either side were the dirt bikes from Brick One, riding from foxhole to foxhole to annihilate the resistance within each one. At least, Sandoval hoped that was what they were doing. The battle was becoming increasingly chaotic. His three LM spotters above the battleground were supposed to be helping to call the shots and direct the MOLAB and bikes, but they were having their own problems. Cheyenne had directed LM-1 skyward to take out the enemy flyer, and both LMs 1 and 3 had come perilously close to being shot out of the sky by the hostiles. The way all three craft were skidding back and forth, sometimes doing runs fast and low to shoot at the enemy, and then breaking off to loop around and come back from a different direction was making their input less than helpful, and the folks at Cheyenne weren't getting what they needed from the LM's cameras. Their best intel was coming from over a thousand miles above, where the USAF MOL-A operatives were sending pictures and doing their best to describe what they saw. Unfortunately, they just didn't have the bandwidth to send along a movie feed with high enough resolution.

Sandoval was focusing on all these battle logistics with a dogged intensity. Firstly, because it was his job right now, damn it. But secondly, because somewhere in the airless skies above him Vivian Carter was taking enemy fire and desperately trying to stay alive, and he was going mildly insane with worry about it.

Vivian. And Terri, of course. In the heat of battle. And he, Peter Sandoval, had ordered them there.

No choice about that, of course. None whatever. The two of them were the best. Vivian knew the terrain; she was a stone-cold pro flyer, and Terri was cool as ice under pressure and smart as hell besides. He couldn't have done this any other way without compromising the mission, but *shit*, if he'd known the Soviets would be ready and waiting and he'd be sending them straight into the lion's jaws, he might have, well, at least *tried* to consider other options.

Sandoval still wanted Vivian. Of course he did. It was like a constant dull pain at the back of his mind, every minute they spent together up here. But they were on a mission, with critical activities and conversations that had to take precedence literally every time he spoke to her.

And now here they all were, in battle, with all their lives on the line. So this wasn't the time to be thinking about his love life. And Vivian had made her position very clear anyway, back on Earth.

So he wasn't thinking about any of *that* at all, right now.

*Damn it.*

Whatever. Sandoval wasn't stopping. His goal was to plow the MOLAB straight through the battleground to the lava tube entrance and secure it, if at all possible. The bikes and the men on foot were also supposed to make their way there. Killing the enemy troops in the foxholes where they could, but with their main goal being to get behind them. The shielding in their foxholes was, logically enough, facing outward away from the Door. Sandoval was banking on the fact that he was facing a numerically smaller enemy and that most of them would be deployed on the plains outside the entrance.

If they could secure the Door, the enemy combatants would be cut off from their safe haven and in deep shit. After that, Night Corps could mop them up at their leisure.

It was a great plan, but it ended up not working worth a damn.

They couldn't have dropped the Brick any closer in, or the men inside it would have no time to deploy before it came under heavy fire. A Brick was solidly armored, but a few good rocket hits would still be more than enough to take one out. And his men were better than awesome, but even they couldn't get up and out instantaneously. If it took them any more than a few seconds to get up and out of the Brick, it would likely be the death of them and the end of the attack. Bottom line: they had to drop the Brick far enough back to keep his people alive in the time it took them to egress, which meant storming the enemy defenses from the front.

Land, deploy, fight; that was the only sequence that worked on the Moon.

And, as the Soviets had found out years before Night Corps, sometimes that sequence didn't work worth a damn either, if the opposition was expecting you.

"Eyes up, there's their big truck," said Jacobson from the MOLAB cab, and in seconds Sandoval got confirmation of that from two other directions: "APC spotted at egress point," from MOL-A, and "Be advised, tank in the Door," from one of Sandoval's spotters on a dirt bike. Sandoval himself couldn't see anything, not yet, and he had no idea how Jacobson had been able to make it out with the MOLAB bouncing around like this. Then he got a console visual: sure enough, this must be the cryptonauts' major ground rover, now catching the early sunlight at the egress point from the lava tube.

To Sandoval it looked like more of a truck or an APC—armored personnel carrier—than a tank, more industrial than military. It was a wide flatbed with either three or four pairs of wheels down its side, and a small cab at the front.

"You'll need to slow up if you want me to blast it," said his gunner, the guy at the rocket-launcher console behind him. The rockets on the MOLAB roof were really surface-to-air missiles; they'd shot one into the battleground right at the start to try to dent the adversary's morale but been too far away to engage with the flyer that LM-1—Vivian's LM!—had destroyed.

His gunner wasn't wrong, but Sandoval was in no mood to stop, and the big guns at Brick Two might do a better job anyway. "Artillery station, target the APC, fire when ready," he said, and almost bit his tongue as the damned MOLAB went briefly airborne again and crashed back down to surface at an odd angle, presumably the fault of some errant boulder that Rodriguez had chosen to disregard. "Holy shit," he said, with feeling, even though his mic was hot. He was sure no one was about to disagree.

"APC has halted," said MOL-A.

"Providing cover's my bet," said Rodriguez. "Plenty of hostile fire coming from behind and around."

"Shit."

They'd been hoping for the element of surprise, and they hadn't got it. They'd also been hoping that they'd arrive in overwhelming force, that the Night Corps force would outnumber the cryptonauts to such an extent that the ground action would be simple and over quickly. And that clearly hadn't happened either.

This time Sandoval flipped the comms switch so only his in-MOLAB crew could hear him. "Goddamn it, how many people do they have?"

"Too many," said his gunner, and "More than we thought, that's for damned sure," said Jacobson—

A horrendously bright flash illuminated the MOLAB interior, just as an invisible giant punched the vehicle from underneath. Sandoval was aware only of a sudden violent headache and a feeling of yawing vertigo, and then the MOLAB crashed down onto its left side and rolled, rolled, rolled, bouncing as it did so. "Shiiiiit!"

Sandoval could hear himself but no one else: all communications had gone out at the same time, and when he opened his eyes again, he could see absolutely nothing. "What? Rod!"

A sudden buzz and a click as comms came back up on the backup circuit. In the darkness, he heard Rodriguez's voice. "Peter?"

"Rod! Here! What happened?"

"Rocket hit. Right side."

"Dang … Rod, I'm blind. Are you blind?"

"No. Hit the override on your chest. Your suit flash protection automatically opaqued your visor."

"Oh, for crying out loud." Sandoval felt too stupid to live. He hit the suit reset and could see again.

Sort of. It took him a moment to make sense of it. The MOLAB had spun several times, throwing stuff everywhere. He was hanging upside-down, his truck clearly resting on its right-upper side. So, like, crushing those deliberately skeletal missiles. Exactly what Sandoval hadn't wanted to happen. *Great.*

"Everyone okay?"

"Looks like," said Rodriguez. "For now. But we've got to get out of here."

"No kidding." Sandoval punched the quick release and fell down onto, well, the ceiling. The gunner had already cut himself loose and scooted to the back of the truck. Behind Sandoval were Rodriguez and Jacobson, piling out of the cab. Good. "Blow the airlock, both." They'd been driving depressurized anyway, so opening both doors at once was possible.

"Airlock both, aye," said the gunner.

The MOLAB rocked again as more ordnance hit it. "Out, out, out!" Rodriguez shouted, and scooted past Sandoval on hands and knees, rifle in hand.

Rifle. Good idea. Sandoval was an airman, damn it; Earth orbit was his natural environment, and maybe that godawful explosion had fried his brains. "Go on, go on," he said. Rodriguez hit Moon dirt and kept running. Jacobson handed Sandoval a rifle from the wall rack, and the two of them surged out the back of the MOLAB together, Sandoval half-tripping over all the crap strewn on the "floor" beneath him.

All at once, he was out on the lunar surface. The place he hated the most.

And as soon as his boots hit the ground, he was taking enemy fire. Bullets clanged off his torso. A bright shell ricocheted off his shoulder so hard that it knocked him off balance. Well, even further off balance.

He may as well make the most of that. Sandoval threw himself into a horizontal dive, hit the dirt and skated forward. There was zero chance of his exosuit cracking or tearing under that kind of action; it even had small skids mounted on his chest to make the move more effective. He'd been holding his gun out ahead of him, and as he skidded to a halt, he flipped forward what they called the "kickstands," small rods that became a low tripod. He was ready to fire in seconds and did.

Damn. This hot zone was *hot*. Were Vivian and the rest of the LM crews okay? Sandoval had no clue. And no time to ask.

*Damn the Moon.*

And also: *focus, man.*

He was alone. Jacobson had run on, presumably following Rod and the gunner. Far to his left, other Night Corps troops had also hit the dirt, lying prone and setting up rifles or other projectile weapons.

Panic started biting at the edges of his mind. He felt the sweat forming on his neck and forehead, his breath coming short.

*Oh, come on. Not now. Not now. No.*

Someone leaped at him from his right. Gray suit. Not one of his, then.

*Move. Move!*

Peter rolled sideways, jerked up his weapon and opened fire at the hostile from point-blank range.

# CHAPTER 29

## Marius Hills: Vivian Carter
## March 27, 1983

"WE'RE to land by the Pit." Terri looked over. "Secure it against hostile egress."

"Sure. Distance from rim, preferred direction? Give me precision!"

"Jeez, girl, be cool. Say, fifty feet from the opening? Facing it. No cardinal direction given. You choose."

"Okay. Advise we face southeast. That way we're not looking straight into the sun, and we also have a view across to the battlefield."

"Great, do that."

Vivian was already looping past the Pit and turning to approach it again from the northwest. "Do we expect any hostiles to poke their heads up? Or come running over the top?"

"Who knows, why?"

"Need to know whether to stay stable enough to not freak the gunners out so they can provide prompt response to active threats. If not, I'll go for speed over stability."

"Speed. Just get us there."

"Can do."

Scary how almost-comfortable Vivian felt doing all this crazy maneuvering so close to the ground. "You're watching my fuel, right? And my temperatures? Because I'm totally not."

"Affirmative. Still half a tank. Nothing in the red zone. We got no worries."

"Ha," Vivian said. "If only." She scanned the area beneath them for boulders—that glass floor was coming in handy after all—and curt-seyed the LM down onto the surface in what was, to her surprise, her softest lunar landing to date. "Contact light. Touchdown."

"Nice," Terri said, and babbled to Cheyenne.

Phew. It *was* nice not to be moving. The last ten or fifteen minutes had been nuts. Vivian realized she was soaked with sweat from neck to thigh and nudged up her suit cooling.

More déjà vu: Vivian's boot prints, and Ellis's, were still visible on the terrain around her from their exploratory visits, three years before. Amazing. Freaky.

Everything around them was comfortingly still, but that could change in a heartbeat. Vivian hit Comms. "Left and Right, watch our six and our sides, remember we have no rearward vision from in here. We won't see anyone sneaking up on us. That's on you."

"Wilco, ma'am," said Right.

At the same time, Left said, "On it."

Brock stopped talking, rolled her head from side to side. Vivian heard two loud cracks. "Holy cow, Terri. Tense, much?"

"What do you think?" Terri grinned. "Cool flying, by the way. You're a beast."

Vivian nodded sagely. "That's me. I am a beast."

Brock suddenly looked attentive, put her hand as close as her ear as she could get in a helmet and gloves. "Incoming friendlies. The six Night Corps troops from Brick Two are close by. And LM-2 will land any second now."

"Roger," Left and Right both said at the same time.

Vivian could already see the half-dozen Night Corps soldiers, bounding in *fast*, power-assisted boots flinging them up into arcs high even for the Moon's low gravity. As they got closer, she also saw the rifles flung over their shoulders and other gear in their hands. "Okay, so what are we doing? Which option?"

Terri held up a hand, still listening to her headset. "Stand by one, babe."

Beyond the troops Vivian could see the firefight a mile or more away, the muzzle flashes and the occasional explosions of grenades. No way to tell how it was going from here.

363

"Roger that," said Brock. "LM-1: friendly craft incoming."

Doyle's LM-2 swooped in and eased to a landing to the south-west, a quarter turn around the Pit from LM-1. His left-hand gunner jumped down and loped toward the Pit edge, a rifle slung over one shoulder, holding something else over his head.

Vivian looked to Terri. "Shit, what the hell's he doing?"

"First up? Peering into the hole."

"He knows the lava sheet around the edge of the Pit is thin and attenuated and might break beneath him, right? I briefed you all on this."

"Damn it. Yes." Brock pushed-to-talk. "Connor, freeze, hold up." LM-2 Left skidded to a halt, raised his gun and looked around quickly. "New orders. Tether up before approaching the Pit and beware of potential subsidence."

"Roger, wilco."

"Randy, you'll support, be ready to take his weight if he falls through."

"Yessir." LM-2 Right—Randy—jumped off, connected up a tether and handed the other end to Left on his return. LM-2 Left—Connor—clipped on and approached the Pit edge more gingerly this time. Ten feet from the lip he went down onto hands and knees and crawled forward, pushing his weapons and a lamp ahead of him.

Belly to the ground, Connor rocked his head forward then immediately back, sneaking a quick peek. Seeing no threat, he leaned in more slowly to peer over the edge, then brought up his lamp, turned it on, and held the light over the abyss.

"Here, shoot at this," Vivian said sardonically. Brock frowned, maybe holding her breath, and didn't respond.

No one shot the light out. Connor leaned out over the Pit again, played his light around, scanning the Pit bottom.

"Report," came Doyle's terse voice from LM-2.

"Abandoned equipment on the floor around the perimeter. Scuffs, footprints and tire tracks all over. No sign of a threat."

"Right, because it's an ambush," Vivian said.

"Or because all the hostiles are at the other end of the tube," Brock said. "We're directed to capture and hold this end of the tunnel, trap the remaining hostiles in between us."

Vivian frowned. "This end?"

The six Night Corps troops arrived, halting twenty feet from the Pit edge. One raised his arm, and Vivian saw it had a blue band around it. Likely the squad leader then. Terri flipped a comms switch and Vivian heard a new voice: "Alpha Team here. My troops are to descend to the Pit floor and secure the area."

"Holy crap. Rather them than me," Vivian said, and then suddenly made the connection. "Huh. Major Alpha! We meet again."

"Yes, ma'am," he said, a little impatiently.

Terri took her finger off the Push-to-Talk. "You *know* him?"

"South Pole. He led our escort home."

"Ah. Okay."

"Depth of floor?" came Doyle's voice.

Connor: "Two, three hundred feet?"

Vivian broke in. "Three hundred twenty-two feet. Measured it with a laser and a sample drop cable my own self. Did *none* of you listen to my briefings?"

"Level floor?"

"About as level as anything on this frigging rock."

Two of the Night Corps soldiers were already hammering pitons into the lunar rock, Alpha and one of the others laying out the rappelling ropes, plus reeling out a thin cable with an electronics box on the end that they'd dangle over the Pit rim to give them comms once they went over the edge and lost line-of-sight with the LMs. The final two troops were standing facing opposite directions, scanning the perimeter. All their movements were efficient and economical with almost no talking, and Vivian felt like she was watching an op they'd practiced a dozen times. Moon pros, obviously.

Nonetheless, she had no guarantees that they'd memorized her briefings, either. So she spoke up. "Once you go over the edge, the Pit widens out rapidly on either side. You'll be swinging in space, not rappelling down a cliff."

"Roger that, ma'am. Should be okay."

"And for the love of God, guys," Vivian couldn't help saying, "be careful in there."

"Will do, ma'am," said Alpha.

Terri suddenly sprang into action, her hands dancing over the boards and pushing buttons on the guidance computers. "Power up again. We're all going in together."

"*Which* us?" Vivian recoiled. "You mean we're *flying* into the Pit?"

"We are. Yep."

"You've *got* to be kidding me. That wasn't in the plan."

Terri nodded. "Correct. It was not."

"Hey, where's your sense of adventure?" came Doyle's wry voice from LM-2.

"Must be in my other pants."

Brock, still listening on the Command and Control loop, cut in quickly. "Hey-hey-hey, everybody listen up. We now have a siege situation. The surviving hostiles have retreated to the lava tube entrance. It's partially blocked by their ground transport, giving them cover. We're exposing that entrance to fire, but it'll be a tough nut to crack. But the tube has two ends. We're to secure this area in case the hostiles retreat this way, and fast, before they can get here. Trap 'em between us."

Vivian just shook her head.

"Alpha Team goes in first," Brock continued. "Once they hit bottom, LMs 1 and 2 drop to join them. But if the troops take fire on the descent, the LMs are to go in immediately to provide covering fire. We're to overcome any opposition, secure the Pit, await further orders, but be prepared to proceed down the tube as needed."

"Proceed down the tube?" *Oh, holy crap,* Vivian thought. *Really?*

Whose plan was this? Not Sandoval's, Vivian was guessing. This seemed like a call someone might make from, say, a quarter million miles away inside a mountain in Colorado.

She took in a breath to object, then remembered: this wasn't NASA. This was Night Corps. She was back in the military, and these were orders.

"Roger that," she said, and started checking her fuel, pressures, switch positions.

Then she glanced up at faraway Venus, burning bright and steady, just another beacon in the radiant sky. *Jesus H. Christ. I can't die here. I just can't. Can't even be injured.*

And realized that Terri was looking at her, worry in her eyes. "Hey. Carter?"

"Hey, Brock."

Terri flipped the switch to mute her mic and reached over to touch Vivian's hand briefly. "You've got this. Don't sweat it."

"I'm that obvious?"

"Tiny bit. Look, you're a kickass aviator, and those six seriously built dudes are rappelling in first anyway. It'll be fine. You'll see."

There was nothing else Vivian could say. *But Terri ... Venus!* Hardly.

"Sure. Sorry."

"I trust you. Because you're the best. Just breathe." Terri bopped her on the shoulder. "Now hush. I need to listen in." She went back to her loop.

Vivian used those moments to suck in a couple of deep breaths.

Okay. Fine. How was this going to work?

Height-wise, she'd already be in the Zone of Unforgiveness once the LM flew over the Pit entrance. Meaning, they wouldn't have time to abort to their ascent stage if their descent engine got shot out from underneath them. They'd land, or they'd crash.

The engine block on USAF LMs was more armored than on NASA LMs. But still.

And, just because they couldn't see any hostiles didn't mean there weren't any around. How dumb—or short-staffed—would the Reds have to be, to leave their rear unguarded? And they sure didn't look like they were hurting for personnel.

Vivian had the very, very strong feeling that this was a bad idea. But Night Corps had been ordered to secure the Pit, and for better or worse, right now Vivian was a member of Night Corps.

"LM-3 showing up soon. It'll stay up here and cover our rear. LM-1 goes in, LM-2 follows and provides covering fire. Leave a gap."

"Real short gap, if there's enemy action," said Alpha. "We'll want all guns in there fast."

"All guns, roger."

Just a few days ago, Vivian had thought she was all done with the Moon. Even before that, she could never have imagined she'd be flying into a lava tube, on the Moon—deliberately.

Especially not a tube that, despite Doyle's assurances, might still contain a significant number of active hostiles.

Alpha Squad was going in, and at speed. Having finished their preparations, one Night Corps guy just let himself topple into the abyss. And on the other rope, the second guy—the squad leader, Major Alpha himself—ran to the Pit edge and just *jumped* the hell in there.

*Well. Way to make himself a difficult target. I guess.*

The next two hooked up, approached the edge, and went over it with a little more finesse.

Vivian was plugged into the Night Corps loop now. So she clearly heard when the squad came under attack. The thumps and ricochets off their suits could be heard over the radio even before Major Alpha, calm as ever, said: "Taking gunfire."

Pope's voice: "LM-1, up and in, go-go-go. Doyle, we go in on their tail, quick as you can."

Brock: "Roger that."

Doyle: "Got it."

And almost before Vivian could take a deep breath or experience a conscious thought, she'd applied thrust, and LM-1 was off the ground and scooting forward to the edge of the Pit.


Beneath her feet, through that damned glass floor, Vivian saw their bright engine plume and beyond that … just a black hole in the ground. "Oh boy."

"Rock and roll, Carter." Brock's eyes flicked across the instrument boards as quickly and competently as Ellis Mayer's once had. "Go. Drop faster. Let's not just hang around up here waiting to be shot at."

Vivian twisted the controls. "Drop faster into a black hole in the ground on the fricking Moon, under fire. On it."

The rim of the Pit came up around them. "Give me numbers!"

Terri had already started calling them, even as Vivian admonished her.

Right now, Vivian could still see nothing through the floor except her own plume. Then bullets raked the LM. Some pinged off its outer skin. Vivian clearly saw two of them ricochet off the window in front of her. Some passed through the skin on the LM, and three bounced off her exosuit. "Gah! Wasn't this dumbass ship supposed to be bulletproof?"

"Sure, for some bullets …"

Both her gunners opened up with a barrage of automatic fire so heavy that it unbalanced the LM. Vivian compensated. The rain of bullets fell off. *Phew.*

"Getting multiple radar scatters," Brock said. "Difficult to gauge altitude."

"Yeah." Vivian had been worried about that too.

"Still a hundred feet up, maybe," came the voice of Left. "Seventy, fifty …" Then the clatter and swing as he fired again.

"Terri, accurate?"

Brock shook her head. "Damned if I know."

"Great."

"Got 'em on the run," said Major Alpha through her headset. "Hostiles disengaging."

But a moment later, Left opened up with his gun again.

"I call bullshit," Vivian said, and dropped faster.

Right shouted, "Whoa, Commander, slow down!"

"Seriously?" Vivian said but hit the juice to try and put them into a hover. Damned if she could tell whether she'd succeeded, though. She was doing all this on feel alone.

"Twenty feet," said Brock at the same time. "That's my best guess."

Vivian glanced down past her boots and through the glass floor. They were still about thirty feet from the lava tube floor in the reflected glow from the main engine. "Man, you all suck at this." She goosed the LM down, got the Contact light, dropped maybe four feet lower and then cut power. The LM swayed, then bonked down onto the Pit floor. "LM-1 down."

"LM-2 down," came Doyle's voice, two seconds later.

She waited, every nerve tense. No one was firing now. No more bullets came through the LM's skin, and the gunners to her left and right weren't giving fire either.

"Phew," Vivian said. "We didn't explode."

Terri scanned her. "You cool?"

"I'm cool. But I'd love to know where all those bullets went that smacked into us."

"Damned if I know. But we're Not Dead Yet!" Brock said it with a fake British accent and grinned fiercely, so … a cultural reference? Vivian was guessing Monty Python, Benny Hill, or Star Wars. She'd ask sometime. Not today—

"Hit the deck NOW!" shouted Right, and there was an unholy din outside in the dark. Vivian punched her restraint release and dropped to the floor, banging into Brock on the way down. She was glad she'd practiced extensively with the exosuits because attempting to curl up in one was a very different experience than in an Apollo Moon suit.

Shells punched through the LM's skin, then they saw a bright flash outside and the throbbing vibration of an explosion. LM-1 swayed, creaked, and ever so slowly tumbled over backward. The floor became the wall, and Vivian and Terri rolled back in a dogpile. A heavily armored dogpile, with Vivian underneath.

"Well," Terri said laconically. "This is different."

Doyle, over the loop: "LM-1 has taken a hit and rolled. Guys, you okay?"

"Still here," said LM-1 Right, as both gunners again started firing.

"Us too, inside," said Vivian.

"LM-2 still upright and returning fire."

"Give 'em hell for us."

Terri was already moving, twisting behind herself to pick up her rifle. "Blowing the top," she said, even while she was doing it. Pyros flashed and the top hatch—currently the side hatch, as the LM was horizontal—flipped up and out. Brock thrust her arms and rifle through it, and followed with her head and shoulders, and twisted to shoot.

Again, Vivian felt the vibration of automatic fire. Saw nothing at all through the front windows but the stars, framed by the circle of the Pit entrance.

She grabbed her own gun. "Blowing the front hatch."

"Roger," Terri said tersely.

Vivian pressed the button and sent the front hatch—which was now above her—on its own explosive trajectory.

LM-1 was vibrating, almost throbbing now. More bullets sprayed through the cockpit. Vivian saw the bright flashes of ricochets off her Night Corps armor. If she'd been wearing a NASA spacesuit she'd already be in extremely deep and probably fatal shit.

"Heading out!" Vivian took a deep breath, threw her upper body through the hatch just as Brock had: gun first, then arms, head and shoulders.

In front of her was the lava tube, and that was the direction Brock and Right were firing. Vivian saw sparklies: muzzle flashes, or perhaps bullets ricocheting off the walls.

They should have gotten out quicker. Blown the LM fully, whereupon it would have divided into fragments and fallen away, leaving them out in the open. Such a disintegration was allegedly designed to avoid injury to her Left and Right gunners, but even if that was true, one of those heavy, hot fragments might have hit LM-2 or one of the six Night Corps troops supposedly rappelling down around them, and they'd obviously never be able to take back off again. A disintegrated LM couldn't be rebuilt.

Not that the LM she was still standing half-inside could be in any great shape after all the fire it had taken.

Vivian saw a dim form running at her out of the tunnel behind the LM, gun blazing, and blasted right back at it, the gun jumping in her hands and banging back against her shoulder. From nearer the ground, Terri was also firing. Eventually the aggressor went down and was still.

"Cease fire!" That was Major Alpha.

"I think we're clear," said Right. Vivian glanced at her gunners, still physically attached to the LM in their gimballed seats, swiveling side to side.

"Let's check," said Pope over the radio. "Flare?"

"Flare, aye," said Alpha and fired one down the tunnel. It lit up bright as hell, and all it revealed was a bunch of crates, a small fuel tank, and maybe eight bodies scattered across the floor of the lava tube in those gray suits the hostiles wore that were becoming all too familiar.

Glancing around, Vivian did a quick head count of her own people. Their Night Corps squad was intact. Better suits, better armored. All that weight was worth it.

From LM-2, one of Doyle's gunners pointed a searchlight in the other direction, the northwesterly tunnel. The tunnel went a few hundred feet in a semi-straight line before curving away to the right. Nothing in that direction at all.

Vivian and Terri extricated themselves fully from LM-1. Vivian cast her eye over the craft. Skin torn, dented and banged up; front and top radar dishes both seriously bent; lots of other visible damage. "Holy hell."

"Pit squad, maintain position," said Major Alpha. "My people: scan around for booby traps."

Well, that was a good thought. Hadn't occurred to Vivian. Guess that was why Major Alpha was in charge.

The six-man squad prowled the area, checking the ground, shining those incredibly bright helmet lights everywhere, high and low. Vivian shone hers around too, switched to their private LM-1 loop to say: "Good grief, people—we're in an actual lunar lava tube!"

"Sure wasn't on my life bingo card," said Left/Jeff.

"Not going to lie," Terri said, "being underground on the Moon is a bit peculiar."

Right/Steve didn't say anything at all. He was unbolting his big gun from the LM and hefting it up in his arms.

"Oh, crap," said Terri, listening on the command loop.

"What now?" Vivian demanded.

"Okay, people, ears on me," Major Alpha said crisply. "New orders from on high. We're to divide into two groups. Group A proceeds to the southeast, with caution but all due haste. Clear the tunnel, squeeze the hostiles in between us and the main group. Kill or capture hostiles as appropriate. Group B holds the line here.

"LM-3 will continue to guard the Pit ingress from above. Here in the Pit, LM-2 Commander and left gunner will form Group B, stay put, keep the assets and Pit egress secure. My squad, the LM-1 crew, and LM-2 Pilot and Right will form Group A and proceed toward the Door to engage the hostiles from the rear. Understood?"

A chorus of assents.

"Shit," Vivian said, on the LM-1 loop.

Terri glanced over. "Gotta be this way. You're safer with the larger group than sitting here waiting to be attacked. And we need your smarts in the cave. Plus, our LM is toast and Doyle's is still in one piece."

"I know, I know."

Major Alpha went on: "My squad will lead out. Captain Carter, as terrain expert I need you right behind me. Advise me of anything I need to know. Don't wait to be asked. Clear?"

Vivian switched loops. "Yessir," she said crisply.

"Group B: If you find yourself facing overwhelming force, you'll blow up the debris from LM-1 and make a tactical retreat in LM-2. Lunar Modules do not fall into enemy hands. Am I clear?"

Doyle: "Yes, sir."

"Okay. Fall in."

There were twelve on the tunnel squad, with two holding the Pit and guarding their rear. So, they were operating on the thinnest of margins. And as soon as Group A went around the slow curve ahead of them, they would lose contact with LM-2, LM-3, and thus with Cheyenne Mission Control and Sandoval's battlefield command and control center in the MOLAB. Radio waves weren't about to penetrate this amount of rock. They'd be completely cut off until they got to the Door.

Pope stepped up to Vivian's left, and Brock to her right. The three gunners from LMs 1 and 2 brought up the tail of the group, guarding their rear.

"Okay. All lights off. Then switch to infrared and activate night-vision hardware."

Vivian dutifully cut her headlight and internal suit lights with the others and found herself in a deep darkness only slightly alleviated by the glow of starlight through the Pit aperture. She flipped another switch to bring Night Corps' version of night-vision goggles online, and her helmet visor closed up completely. A green-light projector came on above her head, projecting the view outside onto the inside of her helmet, and she hurriedly adjusted the brightness as Alpha turned on a low-wattage infrared flashlight.

They set off at a fast jog down the lava tube, IR light glinting off its freakishly clean walls.

*Never expected to be inside a lunar lava tube. Another first for my collection.*

And even if Vivian had somehow imagined traversing one, it would hardly have been as part of a goddamned Night Corps assault, with no sample bags, and a bloody great gun in her arms.


To anyone lacking infrared vision, the small Night Corps squad would now be invisible in the pitch black. Meaning that if Vivian's night-vision capability broke or lost power, she'd be blind and helpless unless she turned on her helmet white-light.

Best not to dwell on that. She had plenty else to occupy her mind.

"Watch the floor," she said. "It's smooth enough right here, but we can't rely on that. We'll find drops and bumps. Minor ceiling collapses will have dumped loose gravel that might make for treacherous footing. And the IR view tends to iron out boulders and dips."

That wasn't the half of it. The soldiers ahead of Vivian were mere dark hulks. Their exosuits were thermal-neutral, registering almost the same as their environment; Vivian could tell them apart from the background mostly because they were regularly shaped and moving, and occulted the light from Pope's IR beam. There was a real possibility she could run right into the man in front of her if she wasn't careful.

And sure enough, the uneven ground threatened to trip her at any moment. The lava tube was not a straight run, not at all: it twisted and turned, angled up and down, and contained random boulders and rubble in a pattern that felt very different from the usual distribution of obstacles at ground level.

Vivian did her best to hold those twists and turns in her mind and compare them to her mental map of the lava tube configuration. It was tough. Ground truth often felt very different from a graphic, and she was spending half her time swerving around boulders and other obstacles that the men in front of her had just encountered. But if she wasn't mistaken …

She wasn't. Up ahead, lava tube was splitting into two, the leftward spur perhaps fifty feet narrower than the one on the right.

Major Alpha slowed. "Carter?"

"Left," she said.

"You're sure?"

Was she? Yes. "Left, sir."

"Very well, Captain."

They went left.

One of the Night Corps guys slid on loose scree and tumbled base over apex, swore, and jumped back onto his feet. Vivian was glad that hadn't been her. It could easily have been.

She glanced quickly up at the ceiling. There really was a chance that the vibrations from their pounding through here in these heavy Night Corps suits could bring it down on their heads. Plenty of evidence of roof-falls all around them, and if another one happened right now, they'd have no warning.

"Carter?"

"Sir?"

"This feels too far. Are we really going the right way?"

*Shit.* "Give me a moment," she said.

"Group, halt. Take a breath. In your own time, Carter."

Major Alpha's sarcasm was clear, but Vivian could hardly blame him. She thrust that out of her mind and considered. Around her, men panted. Even the tough guys of Night Corps were finding this run a considerable effort. Beside her, Terri leaned on her shoulder. For comfort, or out of exhaustion?

Honestly, it did feel like they'd been running for two, three miles. Were they somehow going in the wrong direction, deeper into the tube, farther from the battle?

They had no compasses. The Moon didn't have a magnetic field strong enough to make them feasible. But Vivian had come straight down when landing in the Pit, without swinging around all that much, so LM-1 had still faced southeast, toward the direction they were supposed to go. Plus, their orientation inside the Pit had also been defined by LM-2, along with the rappelling point the ground squad had used. So they'd come the correct way in the first place. No doubt about that.

And now, yes. The left fork had been the right choice. It must just be that the map they were working off didn't have all the twists and turns of the real lava tube. Their Apollo 32 seismic and gravimetric scans just didn't have sufficient resolution. Which was why it seemed like they'd come too far and were running deeper into the Moon, further away from the rest of humanity.

Vivian was a hundred percent positive. Almost. Call it 98 percent. Good enough for government work.

"Direction is correct, sir. Another quarter mile or so—maybe a little more—and the tube will tilt upward. A slow turn to the left, and then we're at the Door."

"Better be right about that, Carter."

"Yessir."

They ran on. And as they continued to jog forward, even while she was monitoring their surroundings and keeping tabs on her squad-mates, Vivian couldn't stop the rest of her thoughts spinning out of control.

Heading into battle had a hell of a way of concentrating the mind.

Vivian was in a goddamned cave, a tunnel on the Moon, for the time being completely isolated from all that might be going on outside. Meanwhile, out there on the surface Peter Sandoval was in the thick of battle. Vivian had no doubts about that: if the battle was going on at all, Peter would be right in the middle of it.

God, she hoped he survived. God, she wished the two of them had had more time to *talk*. It was just easier in space, their interactions felt much more natural, whether they were up in orbit or on the Moon's surface. All those Earthly cares, all the baggage and crap that had crowded her brain after Apollo 32, just faded into the background now they were back up here ... except that their missions had given them almost no time to discuss anything, or even to just be together.

She should have tried harder. Back on Earth for all that time, while Peter had been busting his ass trying to make it work between them, Vivian had been staring into herself, feeling sorry for herself, and after that hurling herself into the LGS-1 planning. Surely, she could have spared a little more time to be a human being.

Vivian had to face it. She knew for a fact that if Peter Sandoval died today, if he was dying right now, she would regret shoving him away on Earth for the rest of her life.

Assuming she survived today herself, of course …

Vivian never did detect that upward slope, but with shocking suddenness they arrived on the enemy's rear. As they yomped around a gradual leftward bend, shallower than she'd anticipated, light—visible light—began to be evident on the right-hand wall. Major Alpha made a series of three fast hand-and-arm gestures, and his squad immediately slowed to a moderate lope. Alpha and two others bunched to the left, and the remaining three bunched to the right of the tube. Vivian, having been commanded to stay with Major Alpha, followed closely behind him, and immediately felt exposed when Terri Brock went the other way.

She turned the gain on her night-vision apparatus down to reduce the new, extra glare; it seemed bright to her, but it wasn't intense enough to cause the mechanism to automatically shut off. All their radios were set to receive-only. The only breathing Vivian could hear was her own.

Another gesture from Alpha, and Pope put his hand on Vivian's arm as Alpha began moving slowly forward again. She got the message. Alpha's original ground squad would go in first.

The six troops raised their weapons in what looked like a single movement. These guys were good. Major Alpha bobbed his head, once, twice, three times—and on the third bob the squad leaped forward, each of them leaving the ground in a high arc—their power-assisted boots set to max—and just kept going. At the top of his fourth arc, Alpha opened fire and his two buddies alongside him, a fraction of a second later. It took the other three troops, on the right-hand side of the tube, a few more long bounds to make visual contact with the enemy, but as soon as they did, they opened fire as well.

Pope let go of Vivian's arm, raised his gloved hand high in the air, pumped it twice, and began to run. The three Night Corps gunners and Terri joined him immediately. Vivian was slower off the mark, but soon stepped forward and took what felt like a huge leap off the ground. Came down, jumped again—in her case it was more of a kangaroo-hop than a giant stride, and it was only on her second madcap bound through the air that she remembered to shove the lever on her weapon that took the safety off.

In front of her, Pope's rifle exploded into bright and silent firing. All of a sudden bullets and shells were spraying toward them, many of them aimed too low—it looked for all the world as if the Night Corps guys were leaping over the missiles aimed at them, which technically they were. Once they started taking fire, several of them lowered their leaps while trying to maintain forward speed, to make their trajectories less predictable.

Then one was hit—Vivian was losing lock on who was who, but by his position she thought it was her gunner, Jeff. Airborne at the time, the shells put him into a roll. His legs kicked up ahead of him and he rocked backward. His gun flew through the air.

Vivian could see the enemy ahead of them now, or at least the muzzle flashes and explosions from their weapons, and several running forms, zigging and zagging. She also glimpsed her MOLAB and its Pod trailer sitting off to the left of the tube, their windows dark, a couple of empty and battered-looking Lunokhod-style ground vehicles, and what looked like some kind of habitat structure well beyond it to the right. And there was light at the end of the tunnel because past both of those was the Door, a slightly-more-than-semicircular hole with a starry sky beyond it, lit up with what looked like intermittent fireworks but was almost certainly Night Corps' main attack.

For a startled moment Vivian thought Alpha Team had vanished, but they had all dropped forward and were either lying prone or on one knee, continuing to fire. A war of attrition, this: Vivian already knew the Night Corps suits could take a number of impacts from shells and bullets, but that number was not infinite. The cryptonaut suits were less armored but still provided substantial protection in a firefight.

She canceled the power to her boots and dug her heels in when next she alighted on the surface, jarring her legs and spine in the process. Scooping Jeff's gun off the floor, she stepped over and knelt by him.

"I'm fine," he said. "Just winded. Gimme that. Uh, I meant, 'Sir.' Sorry."

"No problem." Vivian dropped the gun into his arms, then turned and leaped to the side as a stream of shells interspersed with tracer swept by them.

Alpha Team had all ignored the MOLAB and were now up and proceeding past it. It would take time to bring the vehicle online, of course, with its circuit breakers and all, and maybe they didn't know how to drive one. Or maybe it would just be an obvious target for shells and get destroyed quickly.

More likely, they were worried that it might be booby-trapped. But if Casey was anywhere around here, he'd be in the MOLAB, the Pod, or that large hab to the right of the door.

Okay, screw it. Having brought Alpha Team to the mouth of the lava tube, Vivian's responsibilities as terrain expert were at an end. Plus, she was NASA, and somewhere around here there might be another NASA astronaut requiring her assistance.

Vivian punched her radio on, switched to the NASA frequency. "Casey, Vivian Carter. D'you copy?"

And, to her amazement, Buchanan responded immediately.

# CHAPTER 30

## Marius Hills: Vivian Carter
## March 27, 1983

"**HI.** Vivian? Thank God. So good to hear your voice."

The voice in her headset sure sounded like Casey Buchanan, though even weaker and frailer than when she'd last heard it. Vivian scanned around herself quickly, checking for enemies. But by now there was no one near her. Gunner Jeff had picked himself up and scurried forward, regaining ground to enter the fray. Vivian was now well to the rear of her group.

She took a knee, rifle raised to her shoulder while she scoped out the vehicle. She saw nothing. "Casey, where are you?"

"In the Pod. You?"

She paused. "Close by. Any hostiles in there with you?"

"Negative. I'm alone in here now."

"'Now?'"

"I was under armed guard. I'm guessing my guard had been ordered to kill me if this position was overwhelmed. But we'd established something of a rapport. We're both prisoners here in our own way, right? So I guess he decided to let me live, and off himself instead. Just now when Night Corps came past from up the tube, he bowed to me and shot his own brains out."

"Shit. Uh. Okay. So that means you have his gun?"

"I do."

Vivian wasn't convinced. Again, she looked all around. This had to be too easy, right? "Why are the lights out in the Pod?"

"I turned them off. Last thing I want is someone killing me by mistake."

"You have a suit in there?"

"No. And I can't get into the MOLAB. I'm locked out of it."

"Turn on the lights. Wave at me from the window."

Someone did, briefly, and turned off the lights again immediately after. But Vivian sure wouldn't be able to recognize Casey from here.

Let's face it: there was a splendid chance that the Pod was booby-trapped. If it was, Vivian could die even this far away if it went off. Closer in, it would be a certainty.

"If it's really you, and everything's on the level, tell me what you told me when you didn't launch off the Moon three years ago."

"When I didn't .... Sorry, what?" A dry laugh that turned into a wet cough. "Oh, oh, yeah, I get it. 'Don't fly too close to the Sun, Vivian,' is what I said, or something like. Guess you're really bad at taking good advice."

"Guess I am, old man. Any hostiles hiding up front in the MOLAB?"

"Couldn't say. Not a clue. I don't hear anyone in there."

"Didn't think so." Well aware of her vulnerability, out here on her own, Vivian backed up and took cover behind a rock. "You know what? I think we'll just wait for the cavalry to show up. Sticking my head into that MOLAB might be a bit like those chicks in slasher movies who go down into the basement alone. Discretion, valor, and all."

"Makes sense. I'm fine in here for now. Are we winning?"

Vivian glanced toward the Door. "I'm seeing much less firing from outside. Listen, I'm going to head out there and come back for you in a bit. And even if I'm ... detained, someone else will be along soon enough."

"Okay."

She hesitated. "Casey, man. Are you really all right?"

"Well. I've been better, and that's for goddamn sure."

Vivian had never heard Casey even say *goddamn* before. He wasn't a swearing man. "I am so, so sorry. What happened to you? This is all my fault."

"Well, maybe. Yeah, okay—it is." A pause. "But, Vivian, if it makes you feel any better—it's just us here, right now?"

"Yeah, what?"

"I sang like a bird. Answered every question they asked me. Oh, it took a while, but they broke me, Vivian. They absolutely did. Broke me. Bad."

Vivian rested her helmet against the rock. "Sorry to hear."

"Not even sure I can remember everything I told them. But I am absolutely for sure that US intel assets are now at risk across the Earth, as well as on the Moon."

"Shit."

"Vivian ... If I didn't need to tell the CIA every single thing I've blabbed to these bastards ... if I didn't need to try to remember it all so that they can pull out any agents that are still out in the field, and ..." His voice spluttered for a bit, incoherent, before continuing. "They need to know what's compromised and what isn't. If not for that ... I swear I'd take this gun and blow my own brains out. I've been wanting to die for weeks. Months."

"Casey, no. Come on. For the love of God, don't even say that."

Now, he was silent.

"Look, hang in there, man. Don't think about any of that for now. Stay cool. Wait for me. Once we're out of here, we'll talk. Okay? Promise?"

"Okay." Buchanan's voice changed abruptly. "Vivian, eyes up. Hostiles."

*Shit.* Vivian rocked forward, risked a swift glance past the rock that was protecting her.

Right then, they appeared from behind the MOLAB, one from around the front and the other at the back. They'd already seen her, knew exactly where she was, and both were holding rifles of some kind.

"Sure enough," she said. *And the trap closes. Nice work, Vivian.*

She'd waited too long. Had they forced Casey to deliberately keep her talking, so that they could get out to her?

Maybe. Maybe not. But if so, under the circumstances, she could hardly complain.

"I didn't know they were there. Vivian, I swear. You hear me? God's truth, I didn't know."

"Okay. Keep talking, help me out, but I'm going dark so they can't track me."

"Roger. Be careful, Vivian."

*Hah.*

Radio off, Vivian shuffled backward, raised her gun. How to handle this?

She took another quick look and … crap, she even recognized one of them. Or his suit, at least.

From the red stripe around his upper arm, and the disheveled and dirty look of his spacesuit, she was pretty sure this had been the guy in command when they'd thrown her into Copernicus Crater.

Awesome. Vivian owed him some payback for that anyway. And she was damned if she was going to just sit here and wait for them, and she sure as hell wasn't going to run, either. If only because she didn't want her corpse to be found in an exosuit with extensive bullet damage to the back of it. Way too embarrassing.

Even more to the point, Vivian's life support system was on her back, and even though it was as heavily armored as the rest of her, she wasn't about to roll the dice and risk another dead-suit-certain-death scenario. *No way, José. If Death is coming, she can sure as hell meet me head-on.*

Head-on it was, then.

Vivian leapt up and ran straight at the hostiles. Pressed the button for the boot-assists but didn't expend all that energy on leaping high. Instead, she leaped *across*, driving herself forward in an almost-straight line, right for the enemy commander.

And … the guy with the red flash around his suit arm? Backed up and ran.

*Unexpected.*

But the other guy didn't. The other guy stood his ground and raised his gun. So when Vivian landed and pushed off again, she changed course and went for that second guy instead because he was now the bigger threat.

She slammed into him like a ton of bricks, her momentum knocking them both off the ground and sailing up surprisingly high.

The hostile hit first, thumping into the corner of the MOLAB's roof. A killing blow? Hardly. Somehow, he retained his grip on his gun. Swung it down, jammed it into Vivian's chest and pulled the trigger. Sparks flew, and Vivian felt the vibration of a half-dozen bullets, all in the same place, drilling into her exosuit.

Too many bullets would blow open even a suit as ridiculously over-protected as this one. She was already twisting away, grabbing the rifle and shoving it aside just as they both crashed down onto the ground, Vivian skidding left due to the torque she was applying to the enemy gun. She went down, and the hostile shoved and scooted himself back and away from her.

Stupid, stupid: Vivian should have retained her hold on her own gun rather than using her arms to break her fall.

But at least being empty-handed meant she could scoop up a rock. She flung it at the guy, full force. He tried to dodge, but the rock hit him squarely on the shoulder, sending his left arm flying upward and his body twisting back to slam into the MOLAB again. Great, finally someone other than Vivian was receiving shoulder wounds. That gave her a dark satisfaction.

She fell forward and grabbed his legs, and again keyed her boot assists to give her more leverage. They slid across the rocky, gravelly surface together, the cryptonaut scrabbling at the dirt around him in a vain attempt to arrest his motion. Didn't manage it, and the upper half of his torso slid underneath the MOLAB, between the second and third pair of wheels.

Vivian pushed herself up and glanced at his boots. Recognized the Soviet-style fastenings. And then she seized the left boot, flipped up the catch, twisted, and pulled.

The boot unlocked, slid partway off in her hand.

Which, of course, depressurized the hostile's suit immediately.

The cosmonaut jerked and tried to sit up, which was naturally impossible. She felt his helmet bang into the underside of the MOLAB as he began thrashing. *One, two, three …*

He was already dead and gone.

It had all happened real fast. The other hostile, Red Flash, had made it to the front of the MOLAB, arrested his movement by banging into the cab, and was only now turning to raise his gun against her. Vivian threw the boot at him, and he recoiled as if it was a grenade.

Not brave, this one, despite his apparent rank. But he still had a gun, and Vivian's was off behind her on the ground somewhere. She didn't exactly have time to go look for it.

*Hmm. Just maybe …?*

Vivian jumped to the right and overcooked it on her ridiculously over-power-assisted boots, thudding into the MOLAB herself, but her fist found the panel she was looking for and it sprang open.

Holy shit, it was still in there.

She grabbed the machine pistol, thumbed off the safety and swung it around.

Seeing this, Red Flash tossed his rifle away and raised his hands above his head.

"Oh sure, *now* you want to surrender. Asshole."

He dropped to his knees.

Vivian's trigger finger itched, but ... a live captive might be worth something. And, for all the adrenaline and anger that filled her right now, she couldn't just shoot a guy who was defenseless and surrendering to her.

She glanced around, super-quick. Still no one else in sight.

"Face down." She gestured at him. He didn't move. "Jesus fricking Christ." Vivian marched over to him, keeping the pistol trained on him. Grabbed his helmet, shoved him forward.

And the guy grabbed her gun and pulled, and Vivian went down on top of him.

*Damn. Stupid. Stupid! Again!*

Vivian resisted, but he was *strong*. The strength of desperation. So she let go of the machine pistol and hit a button on her chest. Blinding white light shot out of her helmet, and she steered it downward and flipped up the hostile's visor, dazzling him.

She felt him twist and squirm beneath her, wrestling with her. "Yeah, right. Bright, huh? Don't mess with me and my people, loser ..."

Now, of course, she could see his face.

Perhaps Vivian had been expecting a Sergei Yashin, or someone like him. Deep down, she was anticipating a cold fish with cold eyes and a bland face that betrayed little emotion and no humanity.

And so she got to be surprised in a different way: the face before her was Chinese. A man of indeterminate age, with black hair. He looked completely terrified.

Red Flash let go of Vivian's gun, reached up for his helmet valve, twisted it. Even in the vacuum Vivian could see the fast scatter of ice crystals subliming out near the valve. She slapped his glove away, twisted the valve back the other way, grabbed up her rifle. "No way, buddy—I'm taking you alive. I've got questions."

Vivian tried to say it again in Russian, but her adrenaline made her tongue-tied, unable to find the words. And she had no idea even whether he was listening to her frequency or even knew Russian, let alone English.

The man looked frustrated. Desperate. Sorrowful. He closed his eyes, and his lips moved.

Not communicating. *Praying?*

A chill swept her. Could this guy have an explosive device in his suit? If it went off, killing him, it might easily kill her too. Even a nifty Night Corps exosuit might not withstand a full-frontal explosion.

Frantic, she looked at his gloves, but his hands were stretched out to either side, his fingers looking as relaxed as fingers ever looked in EVA gloves.

The man's eyes opened. He nodded to her, calmly, in what might have been a faint bow if he weren't supine. Then he leaned his head forward and to the left in his helmet and bit down on something she couldn't see.

"Shit! Shit!"

Vivian jumped. Threw herself to one side, rolled.

She sat up, raised her weapon, looked back.

The guy hadn't exploded. He, too, had sat up, and was now regarding her with sad eyes.

And then his face constricted in agony. He began to gasp for breath, his cheeks reddening. And then ... he vomited into his helmet explosively and went into convulsions. Contorted, rocked, his flailing so spasmodic and violent that he lifted himself off the ground. Vivian recoiled away in horror.

Cyanide. Not a single doubt in the world.

The man continued to thrash in his suit, battering himself against the inside of it, his body twisting. Vivian thrust herself further and further away, watching the man's limbs jerk and get weaker and weaker, until finally he fell back and was still.

*My God. Horrible.*

Red Flash had taken his own life rather than be captured and interrogated. And taken it in one of the nastiest ways imaginable.

*Damn.*

"Vivian! Are you all right?"

"Yeah, Casey. I am." She pulled in a shuddering sigh of a breath. "Sort of."

"Thank God. That was quite a show you put on for me."

She peered toward the Door. Couldn't see firing any more. She flipped her radio to the Night Corps frequency and heard a brief snatch of what sounded like English, quickly cut off. Likely a line-of-sight issue.

"I *think* maybe we won," Buchanan said. "I don't hear anything over the radio except you. But if the Chinese had won, I'd be hearing chatter on their frequency. Right?"

"The Chinese," she said.

"Yes." Buchanan paused. "You didn't know?"

"Not until this moment." It was too big and complicated for Vivian to wrap her head around right now. "Uh. Hang tight, man. I'll be back. Need to see if my people are all right. Stay put, okay?"

At that, Buchanan half-laughed, though it was a raw and painful sound. "Sure. I'll be here when you get back."


As Vivian walked past the enemy hab and on toward the Door, the stars appeared to fade until the sky became the familiar and paradoxical deep black of daytime. And, as she approached, she picked up more and more chatter over the radio.

The hostiles were all down. Night Corps *had* won.

If this could be considered a victory. She saw several Night Corps exosuits among the fallen in the lava tube, some very badly damaged. It took a lot to breach an exosuit, but once you did, it was game over.

Peter? Where was Peter? Had he made it through? Vivian couldn't see him, or at least couldn't identify anyone in those anonymous suits. Peter's wouldn't be marked differently from anyone else's; Night Corps didn't identify their leaders, lest they stand out as a target …

Resisting the urge to break into a run to find him—to see for herself he was still whole—she switched to another loop, and then a third, and eventually she heard his voice, talking calmly to Pope and Rodriguez. He was alive, and so were they.

*Wow.* She breathed again.

*Okay, who's next?*

Vivian switched back to her crew frequency. "LM-1, report. Terri?"

"Oh, thank God. Where did you go?"

"Long story. Are you good?"

"Yeah, babe, I'm good."

"Happy to hear it." Vivian couldn't pick her out, didn't know which of the Night Corps people she could see was Terri Brock, but it was enough to know she was still standing. "LM-1 Left, check in?"

"Here. I'm ... okay, I guess." She could see him, waving to her from over by the enemy transport. She'd check that out later. Priorities.

"LM-1 Right, report?"

Nothing.

"Lunar Module One, right gunner, check in. Steve? ... Shit. Jeff, Terri, either of you have eyes on Steve?"

"Still looking," Jeff said. "I've been looking for you both for a while now. Stand by."

"Aw, crap," Terri said, at almost the same moment. "Steve's down." She paused a long time, and simply added: "Regret to inform."

*Oh, man. God damn it.*

"Roger that, Pilot," Vivian said. And then, "Sorry," because that was all she had left.

She turned off her radio, and as she stepped out of the tube entrance, and into bright sunlight once more, realized she had tears on her cheeks.

# CHAPTER 31

## Marius Hills: Vivian Carter
## March 27, 1983

**WEARY** soldiers reassembled on the gray and dusty lunar surface from all directions. Anonymous exosuits walked out of the black hole of the lava tube, turning off their suit headlights as they stepped out into the oblique dawn glare. Others walked down the gentle slope from the ridge or drove in slowly on lunar dirt bikes, all converging on Sandoval, Rodriguez, Pope, and the rolled and battered Night Corps MOLAB. By now the main communications loop had fallen silent. It wasn't a time for talk. They were all taking a moment to recover from what they'd just been through. Some might be feeling lucky to be alive, others might be second-guessing themselves, or mourning the comrades they'd seen die right in front of them. Always a broad range of emotions after a firefight.

Peter was counting his troops by hand, his arm raised, in addition to glancing down at a tablet device he held in his other hand. Perhaps the manual count was unnecessary. Or perhaps not. Some of his solders might have damaged radios or transponders. If so, people Peter thought were dead might still be alive.

The black visors on the exosuits would always look sinister to Vivian, but at least some of the names she saw on the suit chests were those of men and women she knew. Pope stepped up beside her, touched her on the arm briefly in welcome. Vivian returned the contact. Terri Brock found them, her suit looking scorched and a gun dangling from her arm. She touched gloves with them both and then leaned against Vivian. Vivian leaned back.

When it looked like everyone was assembled, Peter reached up to his chest. Vivian heard the crackle as the open loop went live. "Great job, people. Outstanding. No one could have done that any better. Take the rest of the week off." Vivian saw heads bob, presumably some people were snorting or laughing, but their microphones weren't on. *Only the dead will be getting the rest of the week off,* she thought, and was then mortified that she could think such a thing. Casey and John Young weren't wrong: she was definitely getting too dark.

After a few moments, Peter spoke again. "Just kidding, sad to say. We still have a lot of work to do today. Sorry. But for the time being, everyone take fifteen minutes to stand, or sit, or walk around, and breathe. Get your heads together. Fifteen minutes, and then I'll divide us up into teams and assign tasks for the mop-up, and for getting ourselves somewhere to sleep tonight."

Sandoval stopped. Leaned back against his MOLAB and tilted his head to look up at the Earth. Was he trying to compose himself? Vivian desperately wanted to go to him, to look after and find out if he was really okay. But she obviously couldn't. She stayed put with Pope and Brock and waited.

Eventually, Sandoval said: "The threat is eliminated. We accomplished our mission. Everyone here did great. But a lot of us died today—too many—and that's on me. This was hard, but I should have done better. I apologize."

People looked at one another. That was hardly military protocol. Colonel Peter Sandoval wasn't okay, not at all. Vivian glanced at Terri, who didn't look back, but just leaned a little harder. Vivian chose to interpret that as supportive contact, rather than a shove. God, exosuits sucked for conveying subtle emotion.

*Time for that later, I guess.*


Over the many hours that followed, the surviving Night Corps troops checked out the rest of the lava tube complex for further hostiles. Broke into the enemy habs and vehicles and searched them thoroughly. Collected weapons, studied the suit markings on the downed cryptonauts. Safed some unexploded ordnance and weaponry. Checked out Vivian's MOLAB and Pod for booby traps and drove it out of the lava tube into the sunlight so that its solar panels could start pulling power. Gave Casey the immediate health care attention he needed and put him on an IV drip.

They started cataloguing the stolen Soviet and American equipment and supplies, which were even more extensive than they'd anticipated, and found the remains of Lucy, Terri's Apollo 24 Lunar Module, now substantially disassembled, cannibalized for parts to study and materials to recycle into other uses. Before long, they prepped the two Bricks for pressurized habitation once everyone eventually went off duty, whenever the hell *that* might be.

And, grimly, collected up their own dead.

Accommodations for the cryptonaut squad had been spartan, even by lunar standards. The hostiles had been accommodated in the three inflatable habs. But, compared to the enemy habs at Marius, even Kepler Advance Base was spacious. Considering the number of hostiles here— close to sixty, to everyone's surprise—life at Marius must have been claustrophobic, unhealthy, and downright miserable. No one was keen to press the cryptonauts' habs into service for the Night Corps astros.

The same pattern held in the cryptonauts' big overland vehicle. It was a wide flatbed with four pairs of segmented wheels on either side. It had a surprisingly small, pressurized cab at the front and another at the rear, with an inflatable tunnel passing in between them, and just a couple of niches and a tiny mess area to accommodate the rest of the ten-man crew. The Night Corps astros were shaking their heads about it; even to guys used to living in confined spaces, the enemy rover looked horrifically cramped.

"Brutal design choices," said Terri.

"Made by people who wouldn't have to suffer it themselves," Pope said. "It's bare-bones, the absolute minimum needed for survival. The engineers who built this didn't give a single solitary hoot about the people who'd have to crew it." He looked around. "And another thing very much missing?"

Vivian and Terri both nodded grimly. It had been obvious to all of them, throughout the battle. "No landers," Terri said. "Or none that could extract these guys afterward." They'd discovered the remains of two wrecked objects similar to a Night Corps Brick, which had brought all of these people in stacked like cordwood, and that was that.

"They just had the two flyers," Vivian said. "Each of which could carry two people, and both of which I helped shoot out of the sky."

Of the lunar cryptonaut squad, there was no one left alive. No one merely wounded. Which had clearly been their savage contingency plan all along. Or *someone's* plan, at least.

Those who had not been killed by Night Corps had either killed themselves or been killed when a device in their suit had set off a small pyro charge, executing them instantly. No one was going to be giving Sandoval, Vivian, or anyone else any answers, by design.

And when they finally managed to survey all the downed hostiles, those in the Pit as well as those out on the Marius Plain and near the lava tube entrance: they were all Chinese, too. Every single one.


"China?" Vivian paused, trying to process it through her weariness. She ran her hands across her eyes, rubbed her temples. "Seriously? For real? *China* had astronauts on the Moon? We were attacked by the *Chinese*?"

"So it would appear," Sandoval said dourly.

Peter's team of four had convened in Vivian's MOLAB, since the Night Corps military version was still tipped over and being checked out for structural integrity before they attempted to winch it upright. Vivian herself was the last to arrive. Since Pope had been busy leading the group who'd searched the enemy habs, Peter had tasked Vivian and a couple of members of Alpha Squad to retrace their steps through the lava tube. They'd done a quick inventory of the cryptonaut equipment in the area, after which Vivian had run numbers for Doyle and helped him fly LM-2 out of the Pit and down to the central site outside.

LM-1 was a write-off, as Vivian had anticipated. Even if they could right it and patch it up, it would never fly safely again, though some of the avionics boxes might be salvageable. Later, Night Corps would strip it down and drive the pieces overland to Kepler, or Copernicus, or wherever. Gone were the days when they'd just leave Lunar Module ascent-stage hardware lying around on the Moon where someone else could claim it.

Vivian looked around at them all. Four men and women in sweat-stained jumpsuits, mostly just staring at the wall. "And Casey confirms it?"

Behind them in the Pod, Casey Buchanan was sleeping under medical supervision, having spent a while earlier being debriefed by Sandoval. Vivian wished she'd been there for that. She knew it would be hard on him to admit what he'd gone through. The secrets he'd given up.

"Chinese is the only language he heard them speak," Sandoval said. "Aside from when they were interrogating him, of course. They had at least two guys with really good English, and several others were passable. And everyone he saw was Chinese, the whole seven weeks he was in captivity."

"So we're really saying the *Chinese* had developed the capability to stay on the Moon long-term? Without us knowing?"

"You don't need to keep repeating it, Vivian," Terri said. "It's unexpected. We get it."

"Well, excuse me."

Rodriguez stirred himself. "They haven't been here long. Best we can tell from sifting through their garbage, they likely started arriving sometime in October. Around a month before you arrived at Copernicus to begin LGS-1."

"Which is about the time when items started going missing from Copernicus and Zvezda. They must have gotten right on the ball with that."

Pope shook his head. "I'm with Vivian. Chinese astronauts did their first landing on the Moon *and* got themselves established quickly enough to then mount an attack on LGS-1 at the South Pole, a quarter of the way around the Moon from Marius, just in a couple of months? On their first trip here?"

"They had help," said Brock, and didn't mean it as a question.

"Must have done," Sandoval said. "Of course, Andropov and the rest of the Supreme Soviet will deny it until their dying breaths, but it's dollars to doughnuts that at the absolute minimum, the Soviets gave the Chinese substantial technical assistance." He paused. "Beyond that minimum, it's also very possible that the cryptonauts weren't really *Chinese* Chinese."

"Weren't …" Vivian blinked. "Sorry?"

"I've checked in with Cheyenne and as best they can tell me, there are a hundred thousand or more ethnic Chinese living in Soviet territory. Mostly in the far east of Russia, near the Chinese border, like you might expect. The population of Vladivostok alone is about a quarter Chinese. But even Moscow and other major cities contain large groups of ethnic Chinese who are Soviet citizens."

"So. They were either from the People's Republic, but had major material help from the Soviet Union in getting space hardware, or they were actually *Soviet* all along?"

"Either way," Sandoval said, "the Soviets likely played a big part in this, but—of course—made sure they had plausible deniability. Andropov and the Kremlin have predictably thrown up their hands in outraged innocence. They've pointed out—somewhat legitimately—that their own cosmonauts at Zvezda Base were also targets of the cryptonaut thefts. They've pointed to the well-documented spying war between the Soviets and the People's Republic over recent years as evidence that the Chinese could have just stolen the technical secrets they needed, thrown money at the problem, and developed their own capability."

"And, you know, that could be true." Terri put her feet up on her bunk and massaged her toes, wincing. "Or at least it can't be discounted. There really was a full-fledged spying war between the Chinese and the Soviets, all through the 1970s. So, maybe they did scrape up enough military secrets from the Soviets to catch up. Or, maybe they really did just figure it out all by themselves."

Sandoval snorted. "Not a chance," Pope said at the same time.

"Except: maybe they did," Terri persisted. "Seriously. China was beginning to develop basic missile and rocket tech as far back as 1956. Same motivation as the US and the USSR: get left behind in the missile race, and you put your superpower at risk. They had plans to launch satellites, and after Sputnik, Mao Zedong announced publicly—to the world—that China intended to be the equal of the other superpowers. May have taken them longer, but they *did* launch their own satellite in 1970 and were already selecting candidates for manned flight ten years ago. We were *told* that Mao didn't really fund the program properly, and we were *told* that all this collapsed completely under the Gang of Four, but … all that may have been a smokescreen. Deng Xiaoping has always been a great advocate for this kind of high-tech stuff. And once the Soviets were landing people on the Moon, you can bet that the Chinese wanted to do it too."

Vivian frowned. "So … you really think they developed an independent lunar capability?"

"I'm just saying it's *possible*," Terri said. "The Chinese are smart. And because of that, lacking further evidence or an open admission by the Chinese, we really have no way of disproving the Soviet story."

"How about launches?" Vivian glanced at Peter and Terri in turn. "We have MOLs regularly peering down into their backyard, right? So, do the Chinese have a big launch center, or don't they?"

Peter nodded. "They sure do. Jiuquan, in Inner Mongolia, is their main launch site, and it's where most of their early comms and weather satellites were launched from. I've photographed it a dozen times or more. And they have a second launch site at Taiyuan, which is in ..." He looked at Terri.

"Shanxi Province," she said.

"Shanxi, right. Lots of ICBM launch tests from that one. And they're just finishing a third launch site: Xichang, in Sichuan, where they've thrown together a complete launch facility in fourteen months."

"Fourteen *months*?" Vivian's jaw dropped. "And we didn't think .... I mean, none of this rang any alarm bells?"

"Well, it gave us no reason to think they were sending dozens of people to the goddamned *Moon*," Sandoval said, with some irritation. "That would have been a stretch. No one knew they were even launching people into Earth orbit. The Air Force, NRO, CIA ... none of us. We had no idea there was any such thing as a Chinese astronaut."

"There isn't, really," Terri said. "They'd call them taikonauts. Or *yuhangyuan*."

"Well thank you, Miss Encyclopedia."

"You're welcome, Mr. I Don't Read My Intelligence Briefings."

Vivian shook her head. "What do the Chinese themselves say? Please tell me someone's asked them."

"Oh, sure. In fact, there's a huge international political ruckus going on right now, back on Earth. A big blame game."

"Again," said Terri.

"Predictable," Pope added, at almost the same time.

"The People's Republic freely admits they're training, uh, taikonauts and hopes to get them into Earth orbit soon. They also say they plan to eventually land Chinese people on the Moon, coming in peace and brotherhood with no military intent, blah blah blah. But they strongly deny having already sent a force here to attack US and Soviet assets. They deny any involvement with the Marius base. Of course they do."

"Sooo …" Vivian tried to think. "Everything in their garbage was Chinese? Chinese characters on everything, no Cyrillic?"

Rodriguez raised his hands helplessly. "Oh, their garbage pit contains all sorts of stuff, marked variously in Chinese, Cyrillic, and English. But since they were—allegedly—pilfering Soviet supplies up here as well as US materials, you'd expect a mix."

"Wow. They really did think of everything."

"Soviets are a lot of things," Pope said. "Stupid isn't one of them."

"So we'll never be able to prove any of this, either way?"

"Not today, anyway," Terri said. "And speaking of smart Soviets, what the heck was up with Belyakova and that so-called warning?"

"The deniability factor again," Sandoval said. "As soon as the Soviets realized the game was up, they got Belyakova to call Vivian. Now they have it documented that they warned us, which supports their attempt to point the finger at the PRC."

"Hmm." Vivian doubted this was the whole story. But she didn't feel like arguing the point, not right now. That would be a problem for another day. "Okay, so … if we can't pin down the Who, what about the Why?" Seeing Peter frown, Vivian clarified. "What I mean is: what were their motives?"

"Depends," Terri said. "If this really is Chinese-driven, then breaking up the Lunar Accord is the big deal. Getting the Soviets and the US back at each other's throats. Working together, we're both increasing our lead over the Chinese. Separately, at a minimum, we waste time and energy competing on things we could be collaborating on. If they can get us to start killing each other again instead, the Chinese can then effortlessly step into the lead."

"Oh!" Vivian snapped her fingers. "And then there are the rare earths."

Sandoval frowned. "Earths?"

"Rare earth elements," Vivian said. "On Earth, the planet, rare earth elements—metals important in electronics—are mostly found in, guess where? The People's Republic of China. They have a choke hold on an important strategic resource for the next couple decades. If the US—or Russia—find tons of rare earths on the Moon, it changes the game economically on Earth. To China's detriment."

Sandoval shook his head. "I'll take your word for it."

"So that's why they attacked LGS-1 when they did. It was the sweet spot. We'd finished our crossing of the South Pole-Aitken

Basin and had the maximum number of rocks aboard from the Moon's most interesting area, all well labeled. If there was a treasure trove of rare earth elements in there, the Chinese would have gotten themselves a big head start on figuring out its location and extent. Adding to the obvious tactical bonus that we were right in the middle of the zone with minimum comms coverage with Earth, US-Copernicus, and Daedalus."

"And minimum oversight from the MOLs in orbit," Pope added.

"That too. Giving China the best chance of success. They didn't just want the vehicle. They wanted the rocks, too. And to not lose their monopoly on rare earth elements. God, I need to sleep soon." Vivian rubbed her eyes. "But, you know, even if you're right and Andropov is behind all this, those motives still work. Andropov doesn't want the US and the Soviet Union being pals on the Moon. He never did. He was forced into that position. He'd much rather have us back in competition and reestablish Soviet lunar autonomy, than be running three steps behind us all the time. But he can't attack us directly, can't pull another Yashin, can't be seen to send up another bunch of Spetsnaz goons to smash shit up. So he conscripts himself some Soviet Chinese proxies instead, so he can disavow any knowledge."

"Sixty is a lot of people," Pope said. "Maybe they were building up for a major assault sometime soon?"

"Or getting ready to mine metals, if they found evidence for any," Vivian said.

"But what about Buchanan?" Peter said suddenly.

Vivian stared, thought about that. "Hmm."

Terri's forehead puckered. "What *about* Buchanan?"

Peter leaned forward. "The Soviet interest in Buchanan is obvious. But would the *Chinese* really have been so interested in acquiring him that they'd stage an attack on Zvezda-Copernicus to grab him?"

"Well, if they'd learned through their espionage on the Soviets that he was useful ..." Vivian said.

"No." Sandoval shook his head. "That's just one too many problems with the Chinese-led theory. This is a Soviet group. Got to be. So I'm guessing that the two *cosmonauts* you blew out of the air on the flyer, the ones that bolted out of the Pit, were the *Soviet* bosses of this group, abandoning their conscripted *Soviet* Chinese grunts."

"Leaving them here to get massacred," Vivian said.

Sandoval looked perturbed. "Vivian, I wasn't aiming for a massacre. Not my orders, not my intent. If they'd just goddamned surrendered ..."

"Which they couldn't do."

"I know, I know. Half of them blew themselves up so they couldn't be taken alive. Or someone else blew them up. Because it seems clear that our attackers weren't volunteers. They were coerced. I'm guessing they were told to win or die in the attempt because losing would mean very bad consequences for their loved ones back home. The usual thing."

Vivian shook her head grimly. "I really hope that doesn't happen."

"And that's what Casey's guard told him to say," said Pope. " 'Tell them you overpowered me. I died fighting bravely. Yes?' And, of course, Casey said 'Yes, yes, I overpowered you, that's right,' and watched the guy kill himself."

"That's bleak," said Terri.

"It really is," Vivian said.

Terri shook her head, closed her eyes. "To be very damned clear, if Commies were holding my husband hostage on Earth at gunpoint and told me they'd kill me if I surrendered, I'd have killed myself rather than be captured, too. And I'd have blown myself up rather than depressurizing my helmet. Because I already know what that looks like."

Vivian put her hand on Brock's arm. "Please, Terri. Stop. Don't."

"Oh, I'm fine," Terri said very calmly. "I'm just saying, is all."

A long silence.

"And on that uplifting note," Pope said, "I move we stop talking about this and get some shut-eye."

"Seconded, oh my God," said Vivian.


Seventeen hours later, once everyone had gotten some rest in two overlapping sleep shifts and done more EVA work to get stuff organized, Peter assembled his whole Night Corps contingent out on surface once more.

He took roll call, dealt with some housekeeping items related to Bricks One and Two, and then paused. "Okay, enough of that." He studied his clipboard. "Looking forward, we'll eventually need to do full forensics on everything that's left in there." He waved his hand toward the Door. *Everything in there* now included the suited corpses of all the enemy combatants, well separated from the American dead.

Aside from some stockpiles of enemy arms and armor, the outside surface was relatively orderly by now. "The good news is that it won't be us, or at least not most of us because that'll be a big job that we're not equipped for. Everything in there will keep. Unless it rains, of course."

More bobbing from the suits around him.

"We'll be leaving a detail here under Rodriguez and Pope, to keep the area secured. Most everyone else will be withdrawing to Kepler or Vaporum. We'll be setting up ground transport: the Air Force MOLAB, the bikes, all that. We have the two rovers from Copernicus already on-site, which can take three people apiece, and the two USAF rovers at Kepler are already on their way, with trailers, so's they can take six each. Once we've pulled back, some of you will stay on-surface while others return to Orbital. We're in the process of making those assignments. Rod and Pope will be heading up the forensics here once the next team arrives, so they'll be really sick of Marius by the time they leave." He glanced at Vivian. "No offense."

"Oh, none taken."

Sandoval waved at the other MOLAB, Vivian's NASA truck. "So, Carter, d'you want the honors? Want to drive your rocks back to US-Copernicus?"

"A last road-trip, for old time's sake?" Copernicus was five hundred seventy miles from here. Five days, if they stopped for the nights and didn't drive around the clock. Kepler, if they stopped there first, was less than half that. The terrain would be new to her, at least from ground level. Then again, most of it would be Procellarum, which was just one big boring mare.

So nothing particularly thrilling, but Vivian might have been tempted. One last relaxing ride across the Moon? Might even be therapeutic, after what they'd all just been through.

Except that she didn't have time. She was already long overdue to go work her ass off on Apollo Venus Astarte. Her NASA crew and ground support people were probably cursing her name every night and morning, and some afternoons too, for not being at L5 yet. She needed to get off-surface as quickly as possible, get her head in the new game, start really building her crew into a solid team, making decisions, retiring risk, running integrated sims with Mission Control—all of that.

And besides, she'd made a promise a while ago not to keep all the cookies for herself, where possible.

So, she said: "I've done lunar road trips before, a lot of them, for weeks at a time. Plenty of others haven't and might welcome the opportunity. And for a trip that long it would be more comfortable for them than the open rover rides."

"You'd entrust your rocks to other people?" Sandoval said.

"No, sir. Not to just *anybody*. But your people? Absolutely."

Surprise and a deeper emotion briefly flashed in his eyes. "Good to know. So, ask 'em."

"Me? Okay. Sure. Night Corps, any volunteers who'd like the experience of crewing this fine truck on a five-day drive to Copernicus?"

She was already looking sideways at Brock, of course, who dutifully raised her hand. Good. They'd need someone with prior MOLAB experience.

Other hands started going up. Someone called out: "Is there any food aboard?"

"Some," Peter said. "Not enough. We'll transfer some MREs from the Night Corps MOLAB." He considered the volunteers. "You four, the next four hands, step forward. Jaffe. Townsend. O'Rourke. Powell. And Brock, commanding. Go check out your new bus."

He looked at Vivian again. "Next, we need Buchanan shipped back to Copernicus for debriefing, ASAP."

"Honor's mine," Vivian said immediately. "Us crazy NASA types need to stick together." Now that the smoke had cleared the NASA Administrator and management knew where she was, and there were plans under way to come get her, but she'd be easier to airlift out from Copernicus. "So, are we taking LM-3? Since Commander Jaffe is apparently taking the low road home?"

"LM-3, that's a roger."

"Fine with me."

"Good." Sandoval turned to look at the Pod. "Okay, Casey?"

"I'd be delighted."

"Great." Vivian gave him the thumbs-up through the Pod window. "Though, regret to inform: you'll have to sit outside for the flight in one of the gunner seats."

"What?"

"Kidding," she said. "At least, I think I am."

"Phew. You do know I've got a bad heart, right?"

"Actually, I didn't. Man, you're a mess."

"You know it."

She turned, whole-body, back to Sandoval so he'd know she was addressing him. "So, when?"

"Soon as y'all are ready."

"Roger that," she said.

Sandoval nodded to her, then turned away ... regretfully? ... to talk to his team.

Which all meant that Vivian *still* wouldn't get time to talk to Peter alone, *still* wouldn't be able to check that he was really okay. And who knew when they'd ever be in the same place again? She sighed. *Hopeless.*

But it also meant that Casey would need to suit up and get over to LM-3, and the doctor would likely stay with him for that transition. Just getting him out of the Pod would take a little while, and it would be useful to have him there for the platform alignment and takeoff prep.

She looked back at the Pod window. "Guess we have our marching orders. But take your time, Casey. I need to pay my respects to an old friend first anyway."


Just a twenty-minute dirt bike ride away along a route well-marked by the chevron pattern of rover tire-tracks, Vivian found her Apollo 32 Lunar Module descent stage. Athena's lower half, exactly as she'd left it on the day she and Ellis had launched back into orbit in the ascent stage, mated it with Dave Horn's Minerva, and—at very long last—gone back to Earth.

She studied the boot prints and other tracks in the dirt around the abandoned stage. She could easily tell her traces from Ellis's and could even mostly guess which footprints and rover tracks corresponded to which days and EVAs. It was all still burned into her memory.

She wandered around for a few minutes. Studied the ALSEP, the PLSSs they'd shoved out the hatch before taking off, all the other garbage they'd left lying there, at the end of a mission well done.

"Good times," she said.

She climbed up the ladder and sat on the descent stage, looking all around her at the Marius Hills. Living the memories again. Processing her thoughts.

But just for a few minutes. And after that, Vivian Carter was more than ready to leave all of this behind and move on.

# CHAPTER 32

## Zvezda-Copernicus: Vivian Carter
## March 28, 1983

CASEY was in a bad way. He was physically weak and a little broken down, sure. He'd been rescued, he was alive, but that somehow made it even worse for him. The crushing guilt of the information he'd provided to his captors, the guilt for living through it at all, weighed on him much more heavily than his physical ailments. He'd told Vivian that he wanted to die, and Vivian believed him. His deep remorse was heartbreaking to behold.

After all this time, after surviving this long, Casey wanted to do his duty: be debriefed by the CIA, give them full information on the beans he'd spilled, but after that? Once that was done? Vivian didn't know how long she expected Casey Buchanan to hold onto life.

She'd flown LM-3 back to Zvezda and had been looking forward to doing that with Casey as her LMP. She'd thought that might have been a kick for both of them, but … Casey couldn't do it. He helped with some of the switch-setting, and did that right, and he was solid on reading the PAD numbers into the guidance computer, which was, after all, simple repetition. But once Vivian pressed PRO and they lifted off, Buchanan didn't have the concentration and rapid reactions to pilot for her and read numbers and work the computer through the hop to Zvezda-Copernicus. So Vivian had done it all. Which was fine. She'd had a lot of practice with multitasking recently, and with soloing LM flights in general, and they made a safe landing close in to US-Copernicus.

She'd never seen a guy look so frail, and still be capable of speaking in whole sentences. Most of the time.

When Starman saw Casey Buchanan, he got about as close to losing his shit as Vivian had ever seen a US astronaut come on active duty. He shook Casey's hand mighty hard, that was for sure. Pummeled his shoulders, which was not exactly what you did to a guy with leukemia who was recovering from extended captivity and torture, but at least it wasn't the worst thing that had happened to Casey lately.

And once the joyful hellos were over, everyone had a lot to talk about.

"Well, hi, Svetlana. How's it going?"

Belyakova gave Vivian a smile and stood up from behind her desk to shake her hand. "And here you are again. Like … there is a phrase, from my English lessons. It is funny, about money, about a coin?"

"Like a bad penny?" Vivian said.

"That is it," said Svetlana Belyakova. "A bad penny."

"Better a bad penny than a fake good cop," Vivian couldn't help saying in reply. But at least she smiled as she said it.

Svetlana shook her head. "And still you are doing that? Stop."

"Okay. Fair enough."

"And you? Despite all your protests, I think that you were a member of Night Corps all along. No?"

"That's a big No, Svetlana. I just tagged along for the trips to Mare Vaporum and Marius. A brief reassignment. I was never any part of Night Corps before. Doubt I ever will be again."

"As you say. Anyway. Your mission was a success?" Blond Svet sounded glad. Then again, Belyakova was an excellent actress and must have been warned Vivian was coming. Once again, Vivian had been waved through Checkpoint Charlie without any holdup, which was still a privilege no other US astronauts enjoyed.

"A complete success," Vivian said. "Cryptonaut base destroyed. Threat removed."

"And Casey Buchanan?"

"Rescued."

"And he is all right?"

"Bashed up. Weak. But still the same Casey, when all's said and done." She hoped.

"That is a relief."

Vivian was watching Belyakova carefully, but the Soviet genuinely looked happy about it, and now Vivian recalled that Svetlana liked Casey. For having the balls to flirt with her.

Belyakova considered her next question. "You were able to take captives?"

"Afraid not. Seems like the cryptos had a suicide pact in place. Well, different values of 'suicide.' Sometimes, it was enforced."

Belyakova swore in Russian and helpfully translated it into English for Vivian's benefit. Then the Soviet gestured her toward a seat, which Vivian gratefully accepted. The banging around in LM-1, the yomping through the lava tube with Alpha Squad, and that last insane fight with the two cryptonauts had wrenched and overtaxed about every muscle in her arms, legs, and neck. She felt like she'd gone ten rounds with, well, Bigfoot.

"And thank you for that last-minute warning. You may well have saved American lives. Perhaps even mine. It really helped to know we were expected." Vivian paused. "So, you knew who they were, right?"

"Who? No. But I knew where from. I knew that they were Chinese."

Vivian studied her. "And tell me again exactly how you knew that?"

"I told you that we detected the message sent by the double agent in your US-Copernicus site. The return message came from Earth. We detected it in both directions."

"Where on Earth?"

"Their main launch site, in the Gobi Desert. Jiuquan."

"You saw this directly? I mean, yourself, on some console or other, with your own eyes? You swear it's true?"

Belyakova shook her head. "It was an Almaz in lunar orbit that detected the transmissions. Salyut-Lunik-B."

"Lunik-B." Vivian allowed herself a grin. "Cute."

So, it might be true, and it might not. And Belyakova herself might believe what she was saying, and she might not.

"As I said, I thought it better that you find out for yourself, not hear it from me. No? And besides, there was no time to answer questions."

Vivian grimaced. "Of which I still have a thousand. Questions, I mean."

"As do I. The Chinese base was *inside* the lava tube? I am intrigued to know more."

Vivian saw no reason not to tell her. Even if Belyakova didn't already know, the details hardly mattered. Vivian did, of course, gloss over any information about Night Corps capabilities or tactics. Svetlana herself occasionally noted this with an amused glance.

And once Vivian had satisfied some of Belyakova's curiosity, she launched in with some questions of her own. Her first was blunt. "So. Who is the traitor in the US camp?"

"I do not know. The message gave no identifying information. We will provide you with a transcript of the exchange, if it would be useful."

Vivian looked askance. "And why would you be so helpful?"

"It is not in Soviet interests for the People's Republic of China to be stealing US secrets, destroying US assets, and blaming it on us. I am sure this must be clear. We wish to cooperate in good faith."

"Uh. All right, but … what if this mystery guy is a Russian asset, and not a Chinese asset?"

"He is not."

"Major-General Belyakova … it must have crossed your mind that this could have been a Soviet effort, disguised as a Chinese endeavor. It might not be the first time your masters have fed you misinformation."

Svetlana looked puzzled. "The KGB says the US-Copernicus spy works for China. There is still no evidence for Soviet participation in the cryptonaut base, or their attacks. And it was they who instructed me to give you the warning that your attack was expected. My bosses have never fed me misinformation."

"Ha."

"They never have." Belyakova paused. "Sometimes they have failed to give me details that might have been useful, but never have I been lied to."

Was Belyakova staring at Vivian a little too intently while she said this? Perhaps.

Here in Zvezda Base, in her own office, it was likely that Svetlana Belyakova would always be "talking to the walls." It was too much to hope that the KGB were not monitoring the conversations in here. And with Vivian's mission clock ticking, she could hardly set up another candid chat in Copernicus Crater.

And none of this was Vivian's problem anymore. Except that somewhere in US-Copernicus there might still be a double agent capable of doing Casey Buchanan harm.

"In this, I am genuine. You will just have to trust me." Svetlana put her head on one side. "Somehow."

That blond, blue-eyed smile probably melted hearts all over the Soviet Union. Of people who didn't know her, anyway. Vivian breathed deep, and just nodded. "I suppose I will. Anyway, goodbye for now, Svetlana. And thank you. For hauling my ass out of Kopernik on the end of a rope. And then for later showing me what that crater was really like."

Belyakova bowed her head briefly. "You are very welcome."

Vivian thought for a moment, and then went for it. "Which reminds me. Orthopyroxene. What's that, again? Remind me how it differs from olivine?"

Belyakova studied her in silence. Finally, her lip twitched. "A test?"

"Just a question. Between fellow lunar geology buffs."

"You believe I was pretending my interest in lunar rocks, in order to improve a bond between us, when we were in Kopernik?"

"Of course not." Vivian held her eye. "But I was instructed to probe you for information. By my superiors. You know how it is. It would be nice to reassure them."

"You perhaps remember that I was the first woman to walk on the Moon? That the Moon has fascinated me my whole life? Do you doubt that?"

"No, I really don't. I believe you're completely sincere about that, at least."

Belyakova nodded briskly. "Very well. They are two of a group of silicate minerals. If I remember correctly, pyroxene is $MgSiO_3$, and olivine is $Mg_2SiO_4$."

"So, what's the *ortho*—part?"

"Something about its crystal arrangement, I think. But you had better check that. It has been a little while since I studied."

"I will. Thanks." Vivian grinned. "Moon rocks are cool, huh?"

"Yes, Vivian. Moon rocks are cool."

Vivian glanced up at the clock, which was over the door, where clocks always were in Zvezda. "Well, time to go, I suppose. Unfortunately."

"We will see each other again, you think?"

"I certainly wouldn't rule it out," Vivian said. "Stranger things have happened."

"Until we meet again, then."

"Until that happy day."

Vivian didn't hold out her hand but stepped forward. Belyakova looked at her thoughtfully, then stepped in—slowly, so that Vivian could retreat again if necessary.

Vivian did not, and Belyakova kissed her on her cheeks, Ukrainian-style, left-right-left.

*Okay,* Vivian thought. *Even if she's still trying to manipulate me; even if the Pod incident with Okhotina has given Blond Svet the idea that I might be into women, she was the first woman on the Moon; I'll allow a goodbye kiss. If I ever meet Alexei Leonov, I'll likely let him kiss me too.*

*Unless he's trying to kill me at the time, that is.*

"Thank you," Vivian said, and smiled warmly. *Who's manipulating who, now? Who even knows, anymore?*

Belyakova released her. "And so, what is next for you, Vivian Carter, once you are back to Earth?"

"Not going there." Vivian looked her in the eye. "Because, guess what, I have another mission. I'm moving to the L5 Project."

"Really?" Belyakova shook her head. "I did not think that would be for you. I really did not."

"We'll see." Vivian paused. "I half-wish you could come along. Despite everything. Better the devil you know, right?"

"Me? To L5?" Belyakova made a motion that was very much like a shudder. "I cannot imagine any place more boring."

*You know?* Vivian thought, *maybe Svetlana and I are more alike than I give us credit for, after all.*

Next up was a one-on-one with the commander of US-Copernicus. She poked her head around his door. "Hi. Got a moment?"

"Vivian! Sure thing, come in." Starman actually got to his feet and ushered her to a seat. He looked a little sheepish. "Hey, uh, look. Sorry about … all that, the last time we met. I had a lot going on and didn't know which way was up. I shouldn't have taken it out on you, though. Truce?"

"Yeah. You didn't catch me at my best, either, if I'm honest. Let's just declare peace and move on."

"Absolutely. So, how was Marius this time around?"

"Even more exciting than last time," she said, straight-faced.

"So I hear. What can you tell me about it?"

"All of it." Vivian had already checked with Peter Sandoval. Given Starman's rank, he was totally on the need-to-know list about everything that had gone down in the Marius battle.

"Splendid." He sat back. "In that case: you have the floor."

For the next twenty minutes Vivian told the tale, taking care to include any detail she thought he might need to know. At the end of it, she eyed him quizzically. "Okay, now it's your turn. So. Why did the cryptonauts take Casey? Really?"

Starman affected innocence. "Because he's a long-standing intel asset, and they knew that?"

"And?"

He looked wry. "I should have known you wouldn't be able to let that one go."

"Well, I do have some skin in the game."

"All right." Starman nodded. "Casey always wanted to be useful. Which he obviously was, just in terms of his experience and mentorship and all. But he wanted to have real work to do. A task that was all his, so that he could feel he was contributing to the mission. Said it helped keep him alive."

"Yeah, I get that. I aim to stay too busy to die, as well."

"So I put him in charge of looking into the thefts of US equipment and supplies at US-Copernicus. He was the one doing the deep dive, keeping the master list of what had disappeared and when. Looking for patterns that might help us safeguard our stuff and reduce losses in future.

"He became convinced that it was an inside job, that an American— one of us, inside US-Copernicus—was in on it. Doing some of the thefts, hiding stuff, maybe even making caches for the cryptonauts to pick up."

Vivian raised her eyebrows. "Meaning: a Chinese—or Soviet—spy in the US Copernicus crew? And Casey was onto that, long before Belyakova said anything to me about it?"

"I didn't buy it," Starman said. "I really didn't. A double agent in among my NASA astronauts? Every US astro here has the same Top Secret clearance you and I have. They've been through the highest of security checks, and you know how detailed *that* is. And with all that, the most useful thing they can do is steal odds and ends to pass on to the Soviets? To me, it made a lot more sense to assume that Zvezda was bugged, and the Reds were monitoring our radio transmissions besides, and they just figured it out for themselves."

"And does it still?"

"Sure, kinda."

"But if there was an agent, he'd certainly know what Casey was doing. Might even have been worried that Casey was getting close and that he was in danger of being revealed? And if so, Casey had to be taken out of the picture."

"Maybe. Vivian, *all* of this is 'maybe.' We can't prove anything."

"At least, not yet," she said. "Look, everything becomes easier if the Soviets have someone on the inside. Figuring out the right time and place to attack LGS-1 at the South Pole. Knowing where Casey and Gisemba and I were, the night they attacked us here. And, of course, sending on that intel about Night Corps' discovery of the cryptonaut lair out at Marius."

"They could have worked out everything they needed to know from publicly available information and from doggedly tracking the NAVSTARs to calculate their ephemerides. None of that was exactly rocket science."

"But it would be easier if they had someone just feeding them the information on a plate."

"It would," said Starman. "But I still think that's a huge stretch. Especially as Casey himself never really managed to pin down who it could be." And at the same time, he winked at her, except there was no twinkle in his eye.

About to say something else, Vivian stopped with her mouth open. And instead said, "Yeah. Well, okay. To tell the truth, I can't really imagine any of our colleagues doing this either. You're probably right," while at the same time scribbling a few words on the pad of paper in front of them and spinning the pad around so he could read it.

*Protect Casey. All the time. Like his life depends on it.*

Starman nodded. "Anyway, you can trust that we're *on the case* about getting you off surface and up into orbit, for whatever NASA has in store for you next. No doubt you're pretty sick of all the politicking that goes on around here by now."

And that *on the case* was all Vivian needed to know that Starman understood.

NASA Administrator James Beggs had said it to Vivian, straight out: *We've been concerned about listening devices and espionage activities at US-Copernicus for some time.* Not Zvezda. He'd explicitly said US-Copernicus.

And when Pope was talking about enemy action, he'd said: *One or the other, we can't rule anything out,* meaning a potential foreign agent at either Zvezda or Copernicus.

And now all the pieces were falling into place. Except for that one vital piece: the identity of the potential double agent. But that wouldn't be Vivian's job to solve.

"About that," she said, "can I get going today? Because it really needs to be yesterday. Places to go, people to see."

He grinned. "You fly out early tomorrow. So, say your goodbyes."

"Only one left I care about, and I'm looking at him." Vivian stood up, held out her hand. "Thanks for everything, Starman. Happy lunar trails. And I hope you get everything figured out, here, and get home soon."

"From your mouth to God's ear." Starman stood as well, shook her hand. "And thank you, too."

"For what? Making your life difficult?"

He grimaced. "Uh. Well, *that* went both ways. I was a jerk to you. I was seriously ticked off, going out of my mind. Worried about Casey, and then at the end of my rope about NASA keeping me out of the loop. And then fricking Night Corps, holy crapoli. But I shouldn't have taken it all out on you. That was just dumb of me."

"Well, now that you mention it ..." She grinned. "All behind us now. Just be super nice to me in future."

"Will do." Starman paused. "Does that mean that you'll be in touch, once we're both back Earthside?"

*Once we're back* ... Well, that would be a while. But that was the one thing she couldn't tell him.

"Oh yes," Vivian said. "Count on it."

# CHAPTER 33

## Cislunar space: Vivian Carter
## April 2, 1983

**WHAT** goes around, comes around.

Vivian Carter was back in an Apollo Command Module with Dave Horn in the seat beside her. It felt like coming home, even though she was leaving both of the homes she'd ever known far behind. Because the Moon was shrinking in their windows. The Earth, too.

It would be a long, long time before Vivian went back to Earth, and she'd likely never go back to the Moon. Although with Vivian's luck, perhaps it would be unwise to say *never*.

Safe to say that whatever Vivian's life in space had been like so far, the future would be completely different.

Vivian studied the instrument panels in front of her, eyes skimming all the switch and dial settings and readings from long experience. It was just the two of them, her and Dave—plus a bunch of vital equipment and supplies taking up much of the rest of the internal volume. She and Horn had two couches unfolded right now, for comfort and ease of conversation. After all, it was a long way to L5, and they had a lot to talk about.

"… So obviously, I'd known all along that they wanted you for this. I was really hard-pressed not to tell you when we were at Daedalus. That sucked."

Vivian nodded. "Must have done. For what it's worth, you're awesome at keeping secrets. Even from me. Everything you told me about L5 made it sound like the dullest place in the universe."

"Damn it." Horn shook his head. "I *always* overachieve."

"Yeah, man, it's your curse."

"Anyway. I couldn't tell you. We were waiting for you to be done with LGS-1 before we broached it with you. We didn't want to distract you. LGS-1 was important, the lunar circumnavigation and the exploration of the two poles. All the achievements of that trip were important. I could only drop very gentle hints, and those didn't work worth a damn."

"No, Dave, they didn't. So next time just trust me, and fricking *tell* me."

"If it had been up to me, I absolutely would have. And if I had, maybe you wouldn't have gone outside alone on a completely optional EVA and gotten yourself thrown in a crater." Horn's expression betrayed his former frustration. "All of a sudden, our MVP was down. Injured. That caused us some stress, I don't mind telling you."

"Well, at the time I didn't know I was supposed to be wrapping myself in cotton wool for yet another batshit mission."

"So there you were, still at US-Copernicus, damaged, and we didn't know what to do. We figured it would be better not to tell you that you might miss a Neil Armstrong-level historic opportunity because you had a few survivable but temporarily incapacitating injuries. That might have stung a bit."

True enough. If Vivian had gone back to Earth never knowing that she'd been in the running for Apollo Venus Astarte, she might have made a fair enough job of the readjustment. At that point, she'd even *wanted* to go home. But to be sent back to Earth for the rest of her life, knowing she'd missed out on Venus? That would have been hell. "You're right. Thanks for not telling me. Really. But hey, all's well that ends well, right?"

"Uh. Maybe? We still don't know yet if the whole cryptonaut thing has ended well. Where does *that* leave us?"

Vivian sighed. "It leaves us still not knowing whether the Chinese stole military and industrial secrets from the Soviet Union sufficient to engineer their own rockets, boosters, and lunar landing craft, or developed them independently on their own, basing some of the

411

look-and-feel on Soviet craft for convenience. After all, the Soviets based parts of their designs on NASA spacecraft designs, just by studying the information we made public.

"One step higher than that, we don't even know whether it was the Chinese or the Soviets in the driving seat. It would fit what we know if Soviet hard-liners cooked this up with enough skill that they could convincingly point the finger at the Chinese and be able to deny Soviet involvement."

"And finally, we don't know whether Belyakova was in on this all along, part of a larger Soviet plan, whether she was deliberately manipulated by her own people, and—or—whether she was actually being genuine all along."

He studied her face. "So, what do *you* think?"

Vivian took a deep breath. "Believe it or not, I'm in the Trust-Svetlana camp. I think she was being genuine. I mean, I agree with Peter and the others that the Soviets *must* have been neck-deep in this, either as the brains behind the cryptonauts from the beginning or helping the Chinese out behind the scenes. But I think Belyakova has no inkling. She's been told by her people that the Chinese were behind it, and she accepts that."

Horn looked skeptical. Vivian didn't miss that. "Look, I just don't think Blond Svet sides with us against Yashin, who is Andropov's hit man, and then three years later knowingly sides with Andropov himself against us. Why would she do that? Even lacking Nikolai Makarov's humanity to keep her in check? I also don't think she plays me that hard, that well, and that long without me picking up on it, even a little bit."

"Well. Okay. I'm just glad *I* won't ever need to trust Belyakova on anything."

"Whatever." Vivian sighed. "I guess it doesn't really matter. Anyway, if the cryptos were controlled by Moscow, then Moscow knew to cut their losses right away, once they found out a massive US strike on Marius was imminent. So, a great way to maintain their credibility was by having a Soviet warn us herself. And so that's what she did. Maybe the Soviet hard-liners masterminding this thing even arranged to put Belyakova in command of Zvezda as part of this thing deliberately, knowing that she was a good soldier who would be credible to us, though perhaps that's—"

"Hang on, incoming. Hold that thought." Horn touched his ear, the one with the headset covering it, while he listened. He then pushed-to-talk. "Houston, Apollo 59A." He listened. "Understood. Let me find out."

He flipped the comms off and looked over at her. "So, Commander. No big deal, but CAPCOM is telling me that Peter Sandoval would like a word. Secure line."

Vivian rocked back. "Shit."

"I could decline the call. At least stall. Operational reasons. Maybe you're asleep, or in the middle of a critical conversation on another line."

"No. It's all right. I guess I need to do this sooner or later."

Vivian chewed her lip, looked out of the window. Horn waited a while, then said: "Uh. None of my business, ever, and you know that, but are you okay?"

"I don't even know anymore. Lost all my frames of reference." She considered. "So, you and I are going to be in a tin can all the way to Venus and maybe even frigging Mars, for like two and a half years, right?"

"Sure looks like it, Commander."

"I'm not 'Commander,' right this second."

He looked at her, nodded. "Okay. Sure, Vivian."

"Better." She took a deep breath. "Peter and I had a relationship, back on Earth. It didn't go great, which is totally on me."

Horn nodded.

Vivian narrowed her eyes. "Because it would obviously be me that was the problem?"

"Did I say that?" Horn raised his hands in defense. "I'm just listening, here. No judgment."

"Ha." She shook her head. "Don't tell anyone, but I frankly suck at this whole thing. People. Relationships. Plus, during all this I was back on Earth, and I didn't want to be there, and that just helped me mess things up even worse."

Again, Horn just nodded and said nothing.

"Look, Peter is a great guy, and any sane woman, literally *any* sane woman, might have … well, handled it a little differently than I did. And now, here I am."

"Although, to be fair, most sane women don't get offered *two* planets."

"Sure. I guess."

"Meaning you're unique."

413

Vivian laughed. "Wow. Nice spin."

"It's just the truth."

"It's really not." Again, she looked out the window. "I'm just, like, a very ordinary person in a very weird situation. Handed something that most people don't get."

"Handed?" At her expression, he shrugged. "Yes, ma'am. So … Sandoval now, or Sandoval later?"

"Sandoval now. You have your headphones, right? Go listen to Elvis Presley or Glenn Miller or some shit. Turn it up loud."

"Glenn Miller? Seriously?"

"Fine, Aerosmith then." She gestured. "Tell them to patch in Sawbones on Secure. And then go full Dream On."

He grinned, pressed buttons, and swung the microphone on his headset up in front of his mouth. "Roger that. You willing to talk to him on visual?"

She tilted the small screen toward her. "Sure. I guess. In for a penny, in for a pound."

*In for a very bad penny*, she added to herself.


"Hi, Viv."

"Hi, Peter." She paused, looking behind him at the background, which was safely anonymous. "So, where are you, right now? Still at Marius?"

"Still here, for my sins."

"So, I've been thinking about that. You have a *lot* of hardware at Marius now. Accommodations for a large team, and quite a few vehicles. Some food and oxygen you might not want to pack out, right? Once Night Corps is all done with its forensic activity and cleanup, there's still a lot of terrific science to be done in the Marius Hills. What you already have on-site would make a great start to a permanent science base."

He grinned. "Same old Vivian. Don't ever change."

"So maybe talk to NASA about some kind of hand off?"

"I'll take that under advisement. Though it's not exactly why I called."

"I know." Vivian took a breath. "Peter, I have to tell you, you might not see me again for … a while. And apparently, for whatever reason, I'm *still* not allowed to tell you why. But soon I should be able to."

She could see him sag, just a little, though he managed to keep his expression neutral. "I used to say much the same thing to my ex-wife. Except in that case there was no 'soon enough.'"

She nodded. "I finally realized how hard it was for you to keep secrets from me. Sucks, doesn't it?"

"Yes, it does." He sighed. "Oh, well. Okay—I can wait."

"Once we're up and running I'll be able to call you, if you want."

"Of course I want."

"Then I will. But I still won't be home for quite the while."

"Okay." He looked away.

Vivian studied him. This screen was too damned small. "Peter, what is it?"

Peter inhaled, appeared to steady himself. "I need to tell you something."

Something bad, clearly. She steeled herself. "Go for it."

"During the battle, I lost it for a while. I didn't have command. I was out of pocket. Out on surface after the MOLAB rolled, I got into a firefight, killed my guy, but after that, I was down. Freaked out and ..." He swallowed.

"And what?"

"And I was panicking. Panic attack. Rod had to take over command for me."

"Shit." Vivian tried to imagine it. "Must have been ... not great."

Sandoval took in a shuddering breath. "It wasn't great."

"It all worked out, right?"

"But I wasn't in command. When it mattered, *I broke down*. I lost lock."

"Okay. And then your people took over and gave the orders. The people *you* trained. *Your* team. And it worked out."

"... I guess."

Vivian considered. "Was that the first time?"

"Second. The first was on a spacewalk in Earth orbit, just before I was posted to the Moon again this time."

"Was everything okay?"

He knew what she meant. "No damage, no one was put into harm's way. It was on an EVA after a training session with new recruits. I caught sight of the freaking Moon and ... boom. But I got myself under control, that time. This time was worse, and in a combat situation." He shook his head.

415

"You've told your bosses?"

"Yes, right away."

Of course he had. He was Peter Sandoval—always a straight arrow. Vivian wasn't sure she would have owned up quite as readily. "And?"

"And I might not fly again. Or I might. No one knows yet. I need to go back to Earth, get psych tests. And we all know how *that* goes."

"Okay, that really sucks. I'm sorry, Peter. Really sorry."

"Just had to tell you. Needed to be honest. Wanted you to know."

She took a deep breath. "Peter, I wish I could hold you right now and tell you it's okay. But I can't."

An extremely long pause ensued. Eventually, he gave her a half-grin. "Hold me, you say?"

"Yeah." She inhaled. "And I wish I'd held you more before and been …" God, this was impossible. "Well. Different, when we were on Earth. Because maybe sometimes there ought to be more to life than the mission."

She waited the long second and a half for him to hear this and for it to register. When it did, Sandoval put his head on one side and looked quizzical. "Sorry, who is this?"

"Oh, you know. Just crazy Vivian who doesn't know what the hell she's doing half the time."

"Me neither." He studied her. "So this thing, this new NASA mission you've signed up for. It's really worth it?"

"It really is, Peter. Notwithstanding what I just said … I honestly don't know who I'd be, if I turned *this* opportunity down."

"Okay."

"But once it's over, Peter, after this one, that'll be it."

"A likely story." He grinned, trying to keep it light, but had to add: "You're quite sure of that?"

She paused. Who the hell knew what was around the next corner? Not Vivian. That had been proven many times by now. "Mostly sure. Almost positive."

"Uh-huh."

He just looked at her, and she looked back at him, and hadn't a clue what to say next.

And then Sandoval said: "I love you, Vivian. You know that, right?"

Vivian clutched her temples, leaned forward. "Oh, God, don't say that."

"Vivian?"

"I ... Peter, I love you too. I do ... I love you too."

She could see and hear him breathing. It was the first time they'd ever said the words.

He didn't seem to know what to say, so she continued on. "Remember that. I mean it. I do. But like I said ... you'll have to wait a little longer. Or a lot longer. That's all I can say."

He found his words. "I'll wait as long as I need to."

Vivian clutched the console in front of her. Hell, she was about to lose it, could fall apart any second now. Beside her, Horn glanced over for a fraction of a second, and looked away again.

"Peter, I won't hold you to that. Just so you know."

"Oh, you can. Always."

Vivian blinked. Sat up. Got some control back. "Okay. Roger that. And, whatever happens next, I appreciate you saying it more than you could ever know. But I have to go now, really. Sorry."

She could see all the emotions he couldn't voice. "Understood."

"Look after yourself. Talk soon." She paused, her smile bittersweet. "Soon-ish."

"Good," he said, and she could tell he really meant it.

Vivian nodded and broke the connection.


Vivian pulled herself up to a window, looked out of it back at Earth, back at the Moon. Then she brought her gaze back inside, scanning the instrument consoles and checking readings and switch settings and angles. Everything was nominal, of course, because Dave Horn had been keeping his own eyes on the same consoles during her conversation. Now, seeing the call was over, he pressed a button, slid his headphones off and put his much smaller comms headset back on.

Eventually, she turned to him. "I'm quite sure you heard none of that."

"Not a single word," Horn said.

"Sure, man," she said. "Sure. What were you pretending to listen to, anyway?"

"Elvis ... Costello."

Her eyebrows shot up. "Well, well. There's hope for you yet."

"Hey, as you said a while back: times change."

Again, Vivian looked at the retreating Moon. "Don't they just?"

*Three days later ...*

The view from L5 was almost spooky.

Behind Vivian and to her left she could see the Moon, the same size as it appeared from Earth.

To her right, a hundred and twenty degrees away, she could see the Earth the same size as it appeared from the Moon.

The math was obvious. She was at L5, after all, the fifth gravitational Lagrangian point that formed an equilateral triangle with the Earth-Moon system. But it still somehow felt wrong.

Anyway. That was the view behind their Command and Service Module.

In front of them was L5 Prime Station. Which was not about L5 at all, but Venus, and maybe Mars too.

Although Vivian hadn't been inside yet, she knew the Skylab that formed the main part of the Apollo Venus Astarte stack was laid out similarly to the Columbia and Eagle Skylabs but tricked out with a lot more equipment. The crew sleeping space took up much of the whole bottom deck, with three times as much space per person than on the orbiting labs and two complete personal hygiene areas. Redundancy of key systems was a lot more important for a vessel about to take off on a voyage with a minimum length of several hundred days. Even if something went critically wrong on Venus Astarte, they couldn't just turn around and come back. Once on their way, they wouldn't have anywhere near enough fuel to arrest their forward momentum and reverse their trajectory. Just like the Apollos to the Moon, they'd have to carry on to their destination and loop around it to get back to Earth. Once Astarte left L5 it was going to Venus, and that was that. Even if the crew were all dead by the time it arrived.

*But we don't think like that.*

And there was no reason to think that might happen. Astarte had redundancy built on top of redundancy. By the time it set course for Venus, it would have three independent sets of rocket engines that could each do all the correction burns required. Most of those burns were already programmed, so even if Dave Horn fell sick—even if they *all* fell sick—their spacecraft should still bring them home.

This Skylab also had *windows*. Big thick chunky windows. A ship designed for planetary flybys needed a much more direct viewing capability than stations like Columbia and Eagle, with their single large porthole in the kitchen area. Vivian had always secretly thought that was just poor design, but apparently ten years ago when the first Skylabs were built, it was tough to design large windows safely for space. Now: not so much.

The Astarte Skylab already had one of the newer Command and Service Modules connected to its axial port. This was a spaceship, not a space station, and Astarte would have to do complex maneuvers. It would be easier to perform those in a cabin set up exactly like the ones they'd all been flying in for so long. Three of Vivian's crew were trained Command Module pilots, any one of whom could do the job in their sleep. And Vivian herself would also be competent in the role, once she'd completed a few more training runs and mission sims.

They even had a backup CSM; the second was docked in the Multiple Docking Adapter radial port, currently facing sideways. Both were fully plumbed into the Skylab electronics. Which also meant that if needed, the CSMs could separate from the Venus Astarte and serve as lifeboats for its crew.

No one was reinventing the wheel, here. This was all tried-and-true technology.

Meaning that it was basically 1970s technology. Which would be going all the way to Venus, and maybe beyond.

The combination of all these components wasn't pretty, and it certainly looked nothing like a classical "rocket ship," but it didn't need to be aerodynamic. At the distances they'd be passing by Venus and Mars there'd be very little atmospheric drag, and not for very long.

Now that Vivian had arrived at L5, she couldn't wait to get going. Even though she hadn't finished half the training she needed to do, or even a quarter of it. There would be plenty of time for that in the months ahead, here at L5 and beyond, on the road to Venus.

She'd have the best people with her all the way. She already had Dave Horn by her side, and even now Rawlings and Dardenas were aboard the Astarte, getting everything ready for the mission. And Vivian had full confidence in her other four crew members, even though she had yet to meet them in person: her doctor, her solar physicist, and her two planetary scientists. Plus the bonus of having Ellis Mayer as the stay-at-home ninth member of her crew. As her lead CAPCOM, Vivian would be hearing his voice and relying on his calm, competent strength almost daily. Just as he had been for LGS-1, Ellis would be her eyes and ears on Earth and the advocate for her crew back at Mission Control. And just maybe he'd save all their lives one day. That was his strength, after all.

Vivian had left the Moon behind, probably forever. And soon she'd be on her way again, heading farther from Earth than most people could comfortably imagine.

Who would she be when she came back?

She didn't know, and right now, she didn't even care.

Vivian Carter was in space. The only place she really wanted to be. With a great crew, and good friends. She had the whole universe in front of her: that radiant sky she had always loved, that had been above her, or before her, always. A sky that would surround her all the way to Venus, and beyond.

Dave Horn had been sitting back, waiting for Vivian to take it all in. Now he raised his eyebrows, his eyes glinting. "Everything look nominal to you on first inspection, Commander?"

"Sure. Better than nominal. Fantastic."

He nodded. "Good to know."

Vivian looked around again and took a deep breath. "So, let's get to work."

# ACKNOWLEDGEMENTS

For as long as I can remember, I've been in awe of the Mercury, Gemini, and Apollo astronauts and the hugely dedicated 400,000-strong NASA crew who stood behind them and enabled their activities in Earth orbit and beyond, all the way to the lunar surface. Above all else, I'd like to acknowledge their skills, dedication, courage, and sacrifice.

Meanwhile, for this second outing into my *Apollo Rising* universe, I'd like to give thanks and major props to:

Caitlin Blasdell, my awesome agent at Liza Dawson Associates in New York, and the others who work with her;

My CAEZIK family, who now spread across multiple continents in origin and current location, particularly: publisher Shahid Mahmud, editor Lezli Robyn, proofreader Debra Nichols, and artist Christina P. Myrvold;

The subject-matter experts who helped me along the way: Alex Shvartsman, for assistance with Russian translations, phrases, and cultural references; Tetyana Royzman, for additional guidance with the Russian and Ukrainian languages and cultures; and Brad Aiken, for answering my questions on medical issues and assisting me in devising realistic astronaut wounds and treatments. Any variances, gaffes, slip-ups, or howlers that may remain should be lain solely at my door;

And finally, my dedicated and insightful beta readers Kelly Dwyer, Karen Smale, and Stephen Blount, and more members of the writing and space science communities than I could possibly list here for their friendship, enthusiasm, and support over the years.

# DRAMATIS PERSONAE

*NASA LGS-1:*

Vivian Carter—Commander (also: Apollo 32 CDR)
Feye Gisemba—Deputy Commander (also: Apollo 29 CMP)
Bill Dobbs—Mission Specialist: Geologist (also: Apollo 26 CDR)
Christian Vasquez—Mission Specialist: Geologist (also: Apollo 26 LMP)
Katya Okhotina—Mission Engineer (also: Soyuz TS-5)
Andrei Lakontsev—Mission Engineer

*US-Copernicus*:

Ryan "Starman" Jones—Base Commander (also: Apollo 22 LMP)
Daniel Grant—Deputy Base Commander (also: Apollo 38 CDR)
Casey Buchanan—Associate Commander (also: Apollo 21 LMP)

*Other NASA Astronauts:*

Karl Johnston—Commander, Daedalus Base
Gerard O'Neill—L5 Project Scientist, Daedalus Base
Dave Horn—L5 Mission Lead, Daedalus Base (also: Apollo 32 CMP)
Doug Greenberg—Doctor, Daedalus Base
Ellis Mayer—CAPCOM, Mission Control (also: Apollo 32 LMP)

*Night Corps:*

Peter Sandoval—Commander
Terri Brock—Flight Engineer (also: Apollo 25 LMP)
Kevin Pope—Flight Engineer
Jose Rodriguez—Flight Engineer
Jacobson—Flight Engineer
"Major Alpha"—Lunar Squad Captain

Krantzen—Rookie
Newell—Rookie
Scheer—Rookie
Doyle—Pilot
Godfrey—Pilot
Jaffe—Pilot
"Steve"—Gunner
"Jeff"—Gunner

*Other Soviet Cosmonauts:*

Svetlana Belyakova—Commander, Zvezda Base (also: Soyuz TS-1)

# TECHNICAL AND POLITICAL BACKGROUND

Spoilers follow! If you just flicked back here without reading the book … you might want to do that first.

## The Apollo Applications Program

NASA certainly never wanted to terminate its Moon missions after Apollo 17, and fought vigorously to continue pushing the envelope in space using the Apollo technology they'd already developed, plus some new enhancements that were within their technical reach at the time. As early as 1966, NASA was developing the Apollo Applications Program (hereafter AAP). In our world, President Lyndon B. Johnson placed a higher priority on his Great Society domestic programs than on continued space adventuring, and I'm certainly not here to argue that was a bad thing. But, had we somehow found the money to continue with more of the ideas developed within the Apollo Applications Program, our timeline in space might have hewed relatively closely to the scenarios presented in *Radiant Sky*.

The Apollo Skylab missions were part of AAP, and several of those missions were flown. However, in addition, the AAP also encompassed modifications to the Apollo Lunar Module and Command and Service Module to expand Moon on-surface time to two hundred days. The three-person Apollo LM Taxi variant, also proposed as part of the AAP, has already made an appearance in *Hot Moon*, in use by some of the crews making up Hadley Base.

I won't go into further rapturous details here, but two reasonable online summaries can be found at:

- https://www.wired.com/2012/08/before-the-fire/
- https://en.wikipedia.org/wiki/Apollo_Applications_Program

## What about the Space Shuttle?

NASA operated the Space Shuttles from 1981 through 2011. The fleet of five orbiters (well, technically a flotilla, and they never all "sailed" at the same time anyway) achieved an impressive total of 135 missions and provided the major workhorse for the assembly of the International Space Station, along with many other scientific and technological milestones.

In our timeline, NASA retired the Saturn V launchers and moved to developing the Space Shuttle. This was supposed to save money, and in the long term, maybe it did. However, the Shuttle was limited to Earth-orbit operations. As a space truck allowing us to ferry ISS components into low Earth orbit it was excellent, or at least as good a deal as we might have expected. As a vehicle allowing NASA to build on the successes of Apollo with longer stays on the Moon or further exploration of deep space ... not so much.

It seems clear that if the Apollo missions had continued and the pace even accelerated, in the 1970s this would have—at bare minimum—delayed the implementation of the Shuttle. The timing of events in the *Apollo Rising* series provides a serious obstacle to the Shuttle development.

Here's our history: as early as September 1966, NASA and the USAF were concluding that a new, reusable space launcher would be required. George Mueller, the head of NASA's Office of Manned Space Flight, announced the plan to move to the Shuttle in August 1968. A Space Shuttle Task Group was created that December and reported out in July 1969, followed by considerable design efforts. Construction of the first shuttle, later to be named Enterprise, began in 1974, but it took until April 1981 before the Columbia STS-1 mission achieved orbit.

Clearly, in a history where the Soviet Union lands on the Moon in May of 1969 and NASA redoubles its Moon focus for the next decade, the Shuttle isn't going to be such a great contender. The Shuttle did well at bringing satellites and International Space Station components piecemeal into Earth orbit, but it could only lift a payload of 65,000 pounds. The Saturn V could heft 260,000 pounds to LEO in a single shot, and an ISS-like structure in orbit just isn't a priority if you're focusing on Earth surveillance and lunar exploration.

Don't get me wrong. I'm very grateful for the Shuttle program and was personally invested in it. I originally came to the United States in 1988 to work on STS-35, a space science Shuttle mission. I served as the Experiment Controller for an X-ray astronomy instrument—BBXRT, the Broad Band X-ray Telescope—that was part of the science payload for that mission, and (more importantly, career-wise) designed and implemented the data analysis software that helped the team maximize the science. In the universe we currently inhabit, NASA and its international partners gained valuable experience living and working in space using the Shuttle and the ISS. Friends of mine flew those missions, and they did great stuff.

However, in the *Apollo Rising* series, NASA and the US are all-in for Saturn, and for developing heavier lift versions in preference to developing the Shuttle. I'm not (yet) saying that you'll never see a Space Shuttle in the Vivian Carter universe, but if STS development work is going on in the background, it's at a low level and certainly hasn't born fruit by the time of *Radiant Sky*.

One of the big touted advantages of the Space Transportation System, of which the Orbiters were a part, was its reusability. And reusability leads to great savings in cost and time. So in a world like Vivian's, where the US needs uninterrupted access to space through the 1970s and 1980s, they try to build Saturn V rockets more cheaply, and make them more powerful. And, along the way, they'll likely put some effort into figuring out how to recover, refurbish, and reuse the S-IC Boeing first stage and S-II North American Aviation second stage, in addition to often using that S-IVB Douglas Aircraft empty third stage as a "wet workshop" for additional pressurized volume and working areas for US astronauts.

## Venus and Mars Flybys?

Yes, even this was a part of the Apollo Applications Program as originally formulated. A mission of that length would require a new and
expanded crew space, but it could have been constructed and flown
using 1960s technologies, propulsion systems, and computational capabilities. Bellcom, Inc. did an extensive study of the project, released
in 1967. Everything in it was feasible, although technically challenging. It's mind-blowing, but true: NASA could have flown humans to
Venus fifty years ago.

And you really can get two for the price of one. It turns out that
for various orbital-mechanics reasons, literally the "easiest" (!) way
to get to Mars is to slingshot your way there with a close approach
to Venus. It's also the quickest way, and the method with the slightly greater number of potential launch opportunities. It reduces fuel,
weight, and cost. Win-win-win. (Probably closer to fuve-plus wins,
but I won't belabor it.)

## Chinese Taikonauts/Yuhangyuan on the Moon by the Early 1980s?

Once again, this plot development is by no means as unlikely as it may
appear at first. The Chinese were originally on the road to developing
a human spaceflight program at a much earlier date than is frequently
supposed. It was the political will that was lacking, rather than any
technical issues.

In our timeline the first Chinese astronaut, Yang Liwei, orbited the
Earth for twenty-one hours in Shenzhou 5 in October 2003, making
China the third country to put humans into space. But the Chinese
space program has much deeper roots than that, dating from October
1956 with the founding of the so-called Fifth Academy, a classified
Government ministry to develop basic missile and rocketry technology.
Concepts for Earth satellites were already being explored in China in
1956, at the same time as in the US and USSR. Following the launch
of the Soviet Sputnik on October 4, 1957, Mao Zedong pronounced
publicly that China should be the equal of the other superpowers and
develop a satellite capability as well. A sounding rocket program followed, and on April 24, 1970, China launched its first satellite, Dong

Feng Hong ("The East Is Red"), into Earth orbit using the Long March 1 rocket, from the Jiuquan Satellite Launch Center in the Gobi Desert.

By this time, a crewed space program had already been initiated by Mao and Zhou Enlai. By March 1971 a first cadre of nineteen astronauts had been selected, with the plan of launching two of them into space in 1973 (note the extremely rapid turnaround time here).

And then, politics happened. Which, in the People's Republic of China, is generally a massive understatement.

The Cultural Revolution (1966-76) was extremely complicated, both historically and culturally, and I can't possibly do justice to all its complexities here. Suffice to say that Mao chose not to fully fund the human spaceflight program in favor of other priorities, and it was quickly canceled. China's space industry survived largely through the efforts of Zhou Enlai, who went to some risks to protect its scientists from the revolutionary fervor that might otherwise have destroyed their lives. The death of Mao in 1976 and the ascent of the Gang of Four caused even greater turbulence, but eventually the "rectification program" under Deng Xiaoping restored discipline in the space program. (Even through this period, however, launches continued, especially the Ji Shu Shyan Weixing series of four satellites likely devoted to electronic intelligence gathering.)

But that's just our timeline. If the Soviets had landed cosmonauts on the Moon in 1969, you can be very, very sure that Mao and other senior Chinese leaders would have paid attention. Mao might well have placed a much greater importance on matching the Soviet achievements, applied money where it was needed, and China's space program might have made great advances over the following decade. Even allowing for an extended hiatus during the rule of the Gang of Four, Deng Xiaoping's enthusiasms for technological development in general and space in particular could well have brought about a limited lunar capability in the early 1980s. China likely had sufficient skills among its own scientists, but it's also worth noting that they also pursued extremely diligent technical espionage efforts against the Soviet Union throughout the 1970s: see *https://en.wikipedia.org/wiki/Sino-Soviet_split* for the background, and the four-part Wilson Center article for the specifics, beginning with *https://www.wilsoncenter.org/blog-post/soviet-chinese-spy-wars-1970s-what-kgb-counterintelligence-knew-part-i* for extensive details.

## American and Soviet Politics of the 1980s

In the alternate universe of *Apollo Rising*, superpower politics is already very different by the early eighties.

On the American side, Nixon survived his second term and Ronald Reagan was sworn in as the 38th President of the United States in January 1977, after decisively beating Georgia upstart Jimmy Carter. This then results in George H. W. Bush also taking the presidency four years earlier than in our timeline, in 1985, and serving two terms instead of one. (Please don't make any assumptions about my own personal politics from these developments; I'm not saying I would have preferred such outcomes, merely that they make sense for world-building purposes.) Many things are different in the US as a result, although since the *Apollo Rising* series takes place entirely off-world you'll have to guess at most of them.

And in the USSR, Brezhnev is ousted by Andropov in February 1980 instead of serving as General Secretary until October 1982, substantially changing the Soviet political landscape in the early 80s. In our timeline we got Chernenko after Andropov, followed by Gorbachev. But it's surely clear that it's not even "butterflying" to conclude that there will be extensive differences by the mid-1980s propagating out from a Soviet lunar triumph in 1969.

However, one hard and unavoidable fact would remain: the Soviet Union could not possibly accommodate the continued major spending required to maintain an extensive human presence on the Moon, in addition to a massive arms buildup on Earth.

Reagan knew this in our timeline, and he likely knows it in the Vivian universe as well. The Soviet Union fell in our world because they were basically outspent by the US. The same thing will inevitably happen on the Earth of the *Apollo Rising* books, sooner or later. Even with the boosts to the economy due to the technical spin-offs, even with the benefits to the Soviet military-industrial complex that will inevitably come from the space program ... they're still in trouble. The other factors will still play in. The Soviets just can't afford to keep pace. And yet, they can't afford not to.

The Soviet Union is still going to collapse. But not just yet.

Rewinding back to the *Radiant Sky* years, the point is that by the early 1980s we have a Reagan-Andropov face-off, not the

Carter-Brezhnev discussions of our timeline. And this makes a big difference to how events will unfold going forward.

## Secret Space: Dyna-Soar

Cheesy name, but a much more solid project than space history gives it credit for. Dyna-Soar was canceled in our timeline in late 1963, but as formulated it was certainly feasible and might have worked really well. If the project had flaws they were in its limited imagination. It was a little ahead of its time in terms of controlled reentry, and suffered funding problems through not having specific goals that could be clearly articulated, and the lack of a booster (at the time) that could get the space plane where it needed to be. But by the time we get to the 1970s and 1980s in our Vivian-world of competing space superpowers, a two-seater fighter craft that can get into orbit has a clear role and a clear advantage.

And in a universe where the USAF can flex sufficient power to win Blue Gemini, wins MOL, and has revived a version of its proposed LUNEX base on the Moon in the form of Daedalus Base, it must surely be conceivable that they'd also resurrect the Dyna-Soar program. It'll be bigger and better, of course. Sandoval's Dyna-Soar is much more capable than the single-seater, single-orbit craft that was originally envisioned. A decade or more further on, Sandoval's Dyna-Soar is no dinosaur at all.

# BIBLIOGRAPHY

In addition to the books mentioned in the original *Hot Moon* bibliography, I found the following books and materials useful while writing *Radiant Sky*.

Chun, Clayton K.S. *Defending Space: US Anti-Satellite Warfare and Space Weaponry*. Osprey Publishing, 2006.

Davies, Peter E. *North American X-15*. Osprey Publishing, 2017.

Feldman, M.S. et al. *Manned Venus Flyby*. Bellcom Inc, on contract to NASA, 1967.
Downloadable from *https://ntrs.nasa.gov/citations/19790072165*
For additional takes on Venus Flyby, see:
*https://www.sealionpress.co.uk/post/*
    *apollo-goes-to-venus- the-manned-venus-flyby*
*https://arxiv.org/ftp/arxiv/papers/2006/2006.04900.pdf*
*https://www.space.com/mars-astronauts-venus-flyby-idea.html*

Gorbachev, Mikhail, and George Shriver. *On My Country and the World*. Columbia University Press, 2000.

Hall, Rex, David J. Shayler, and Bert Vis. *Russia's Cosmonauts: Inside the Yuri Gagarin Training Center*. Springer Praxis Books, 2005.

Harland, David M. *Moon: Owners' Workshop Manual*. Osprey Publishing, 2016.

Harvey, Brian. *China in Space: The Great Leap Forward*. 2nd edition. Springer Praxis, 2019.

Harvey, Brian. *China's Space Program: From Conception to Manned Spaceflight*. Springer Praxis, 2004.

Miles, Simon. *Engaging the Evil Empire: Washington, Moscow, and the Beginning of the Cold War*. Cornell University Press, 2020.

O'Neill, Gerard K. *The High Frontier: Human Colonies in Space*. William Morrow and Company, 1977; reprinted by Space Studies Institute Press, 2019.

Preston, Bob, et al. *Space Weapons, Earth Wars*. RAND Corporation, 2002. *https://www.rand.org/pubs/monograph_reports/MR1209.html*

Reichl, Eugen. *The Soviet Space Program: The Lunar Mission Years, 1959–1976*. Schiffer Military, 2019.

Remnick, David. *Lenin's Tomb: The Last Days of the Soviet Empire*. Vintage, 2014.

Schirra, Wally, and Richard N. Billings. *Schirra's Space*. Naval Institute Press, 1995.

Shayler, David J. *Apollo: The Lost and Forgotten Missions*. Springer, 2002.

Strattman, H.G. *Using Medicine in Science Fiction: The SF Writer's Guide to Human Biology*. Springer, 2015.

Thomas, Kenneth S., and Harold J. McMann. *U.S. Spacesuits*. Springer Praxis, 2007.

www.ingramcontent.com/pod-product-compliance
Lightning Source LLC
Jackson TN
JSHW081322130125
77033JS00012B/409

* 9 7 8 1 6 4 7 1 0 1 1 5 2 *